I0699047

The Bon Ton Vagabond

The Bon Ton Vagabond

Lisa Warren

THIRSTY QUILL

PRESS

This book is a work of fiction. All characters, organizations, and locales, and all incidents and dialogue, are drawn from the author's imagination and not to be construed as real.

The Bon Ton Vagabond Copyright © Lisa Warren 2024. Manufactured in the United States of America. All rights reserved. No part of this book may be reproduced in any form or by any electronic or mechanical means including information storage and retrieval systems without permission in writing from the publisher, except by a reviewer, who may quote brief passages in a review. Published by Thirsty Quill Press.

ISBN: 979-8-9886048-0-8

Interior design by Ray Rhamey
Cover Photography by [Leonardo Baldini] Archangel Images

Acknowledgments

Thanks to Donna Lenhart, Tammie Bradford, Kathryn Craft, Lorin Oberweger, FTHRW group, Ana Morgan, Zara West, WFWA, Kathy Dodson, Claudia Armann, Sydney Clark, Linnea Sinclair, Laura Lippman, Sterling Watson, Chris Morey, Veronica Lynch, M. Jayne LaDow, Ray Rhamey, and most of all—to you—the reader.

For my mom, Donna, and my sister, Tammie

Chapter 1

FAYE
Pennsylvania, 1933

The Main Line train shuddered beneath her feet. Air brakes squealed, and a loud hiss escaped as it slowed alongside the depot. Passengers swayed, steered by an unseen force.

Faye Harmon shifted her stance and braced for the inevitable jolt to come.

Bed. All she longed for was to get home and to collapse into an uninterrupted sleep. She'd stayed longer at the party than she should, but it'd been a real smasher.

She couldn't resist dancing to the bee's knees of all Philadelphia's bands. Miss out on the midnight toast to bid adieu to nineteen-thirty-two. Or pass indulging in another champagne glass or three. The bubbles had tickled her nose, tingled her tongue, and allowed her inhibitions to run free.

Ugh. But there was always a price to pay for having that much fun, and now she'd landed hard. Her head spun woozy, and the taste of those grapes in her mouth had turned bitter. Inside the train car, white curling tendrils of cigarette smoke stung her eyes and made her stomach churn.

If she didn't get some fresh air soon, she'd lose what little she'd managed to eat last night.

"Haverford Station," the ticket collector shouted. "Next stop, Radnor."

Faye pushed against Jane's gin-perfumed coat, urging her friend to move.

Jostled in a sea of arms and elbows, she managed to push her way onto the station platform. The icy wind slapped her sober.

Jane pouted and briskly rubbed her hands together for warmth. "Holy moly, it's cold."

"Because you're standing still. You'll be warmer if you sulk and walk at the same time." Desperate to get home before her father ventured downstairs, Faye tottered on her heels along the brick road. The glow of dawn streaked the horizon, the sun stretching its many legs. She winced. Bright light, booze, and no sleep made for a bad morning mix.

Jane blew out a breath cloud. "Just leave me here and send Rozario back for my frozen body." She pulled off a slouched hat and ruffled her blunt, auburn bangs. "Why have a chauffeur if you don't use him when he's most needed?"

"Must we go over this again? Because what Rozario knows, Daddy knows soon after."

"Always worried about your father—" Jane squealed and skidded. Flapping her arms like a flightless bird, she dropped without grace.

"Always a goose, never a swan." Faye shuffled over to help. "You're zozzled. I told you to eat something this morning."

"Says the grown girl sneaking home in time to have breakfast with her jailer. Until your next warden puts that manacle on your finger, you need to stay out, have fun with me, and shimmy-hop with no regard for tomorrow."

"Easy for you to say." She hefted Jane up. "Your parents don't give a fig what you do, you Bohemian."

Jane snapped her fingers and hummed, moving her hips like an Egyptian belly dancer. That was her friend: bold, free-spirited, and eager to entertain.

Home. At the top of the hill, Faye peered through the spaces in the wrought-iron fence that enclosed Willow Wood. The mansion's façade gleamed like a royal French chateau straight out of Madame Bovary's romantic daydreams.

"Think you can sneak out again tomorrow night?" Jane pulled a pack of Luckies from her pocket, tapped one out, and cupped the cigarette to light.

"I'll try."

"Toodle-oo, Pipperoo."

ॐ

Faye slipped in the servant's door next to the kitchen. The scent of fried sausage assaulted her nostrils. She leaned against the wall and swallowed several times in a silent battle with her stomach.

Never again. But she recalled giving herself the same warning about drinking too much just last week.

A voice called out from the next room.

"Rats and cats," Faye mumbled and shed her coat, wiped off her lipstick, and mussed her hair. "Just me," she sang out and entered the kitchen from the hallway.

Their cook sat reading a newspaper at the table, her gray hair wrapped in the usual tight bun. "What's the occasion, Pip? Nowhere near close to noon," Abigail said with her Irish lilt. Peeking out from behind her paper, she squinted one eye. "You just getting in?"

Faye heaved a sigh of relief that her father wasn't present and poured herself a glass of milk. "Penn Kinsey had a party. I tried to come home, but Penn insisted I stay until morning." She didn't have to add not to tell the other servants or her father. Abigail could always be relied upon to keep her secrets.

"Oven biscuits are almost ready."

"I'm not hungry." She sat and stared down at her glass.

"Keep this up and Charles Carlton'll be marrying a pretty dress o' bones."

"If it were up to you and Betty Crocker's radio recipes, Lord only knows how often I'd need to let out my mother's wedding gown."

"Crocker's Home Legion's Creed says you shouldn't starve yourself for any man. The dress looks grand. I'm proud you insisted on wearing it, as would be your ma." Abigail made the sign of the cross and glanced upward.

"Yet looking good appears to be my only role. After all, I am but the bride."

"Ah. Is Charles's mother at it again?"

"Her usual self. Think alike, be alike, smile pretty." Faye shook her head. "But my worry is the gossip I overheard last night. Someone at the party said the *Philadelphia Brief* claimed father's banks are in trouble. Any word in the *Daily*?"

Abigail passed the newspaper over the wooden surface. A bold headline of the past Friday's edition caught Faye's attention:

KINSEY HARMON BANK AND TRUST IN LOCKDOWN

> Yesterday morning, bank officials fended off a frantic surge of panicked clients. To prevent a bank run, all locations closed. On Chestnut Street, furious customers demanded, 'We want our money!' Police escorted President Marshall Harmon from the building. The men in blue had to hold back the disorderly crush before a riot ensued.

Faye worried her lower lip. The *Daily* was a reputable paper and known for printing the truth.

Abigail sighed. "Reporters earn their pay making much ado about nothing."

"Has Daddy seen this?"

"He's not come down yet. He came in late last night." She looked as if she'd say something more but pressed her lips together instead.

Faye raised an eyebrow, cueing her to spill the details. "Dish it."

"I mind me own, you know, but he wasn't himself. He'd been on a binge and so wrecked he could barely stand upright." She fluttered her fingers over her aproned chest. "Mercy, Mary, and Joseph—he made one heck of a ruckus—thumping walls, breaking glass, and cursing words I never heard a gentleman use. Put me heart crossways. Wanted to look in on him, but I was too frightened to move."

Words caught in Faye's throat. This was so uncharacteristic of her father, who typically demonstrated the highest level of respectability and dignity.

"Don't you fret," Abigail said. "It will all sort out. Thought I'd let him sleep off the fumes, but the morning's getting on. He'll be wanting something solid in his belly."

Faye downed her milk. "I'm heading up. I'll check on him." But then she remembered what was on the upcoming agenda and lightly slapped her cheek. "Oh, crackers, I almost forgot to tell you—the ladies from League are coming here tomorrow for lunch. Missus Carlton cannot host them. She let go of her kitchen staff again."

"That woman goes through help like I go through Oxydol in me laundering. Fine. But I'm not serving and plan to hide if I see her coming."

Faye choked back a laugh. She solved the problem by motioning toward the buffet cabinet. "Just set up the sideboard with cold meats, cheese, and croissants."

"Hmm. The women won't like that."

"Trust me. All they'll care about is the wine."

Faye went to the kitchen faucet, filled a cup, and then entered the foyer. After watering the potted poinsettias on the floor, she adjusted her mother's photograph in the middle of an elegant centerpiece amongst Christmas greens, pinecones, and red roses.

"I made this for you, Momma."

The pain of her mother's absence was particularly noticeable during the festive seasons. But with this new storm cloud hanging above their heads, her loss cast an even darker, emptier shadow.

Faye detoured to her bedroom and changed into a night dress. She eyed her bed with longing, eager to displace its smooth bedspread. But first, duty called.

At her father's room, she lightly tapped his door. "Daddy?" No reply, she inched it open. "Up and at them, sleepy head."

His bed remained pristinely made. Where the heck could he be? Passed out on the floor? She checked his bathroom. Towels neatly hung and folded indicated he hadn't used this room for some time. He must have fallen asleep at his desk again, which was his habit of late. Annoyed, she marched down the stairs and headed toward his study.

What would he do without her once she married? Being the woman of the house came with great responsibility. He'd soon discover how hard she worked to make his life easier, half the time more a parent to him than he to her. But his recognition would come too late. She'd soon have a new home and a husband to tend.

Her father might just have to remarry. Lord knew he needed a woman in his life. Not the current one, though. Please, not Helen. That habitual pleasure seeker didn't have a clue about how to run a proper house and entertain serious men of business. Or how to keep her father on the right path, which she planned to do just now—smack him sober with the truth of the financial and societal impacts of the news and figure out how to deal with this dilemma.

After a quick knock, she swung open the study door.

His body hung suspended from a beam on the ceiling.

Her head jerked back as if struck.

A shaft of light from the window shone on the new shoes she'd helped pick out, now dangling several inches off the floor. Her vision tunneled on the taut rope stretched down to his twisted neck. His face was contorted into a ghastly expression, barely recognizable and a horrid shade of purple. Milk-cloudy, blood-splotched, soulless eyes looked down at her, unseeing.

Something primal wormed up her throat, followed by a long wail.

Footsteps clattered down the hallway, and then an operatic scream filled the room. Abigail made the sign of the cross over her chest. "Oh sweet, sweet Jesus," she cried out. "Lord have mercy."

Braced against the doorframe, Faye gulped for breath, resisting a swirling abyss that threatened to pull her down its depths. Shadow and light shattered into spots, bouncing in her blurred vision. Darkness won.

Chapter 2

JAKE
rural Southwest Kansas

He was pretty sure his marriage was over. Jake Boyd ducked as another glass flew over his head and shattered into shards against the wall. The second projectile toppled the decorated twig that served as their Christmas tree, spilling its ornaments across the sitting room floor. He shifted his gaze to his eight-year-old son, who was watching from the safety of the kitchen. He needed to defuse the situation for the boy's sake.

"Sarah, honey, if you'll just settle down. I forgive you." He realized he'd said the wrong thing as soon as the words left his mouth. Most times, a woman's thoughts and feelings were beyond his understanding. But not now.

"Forgive *me*?" She picked up another object and held it high.

Gripped in her hand was the gift their son had spent hours making. If she smashed it, that would surely break the boy's heart.

"Not that one," Jake pleaded, readying himself to save it.

Recognition entered her face. She gently placed the popsicle stick creation down. The tiny crease between her eyebrows deepened. "Don't you dare make this my fault. If anyone needs forgiveness, it's you. I've wasted almost ten years on your empty promises." She stomped to her travel case, hefted it, then stormed out the door.

Dammit. That didn't go as well as hoped. His son stared his way, all puppy eyes and trembling bottom lip, silently pleading for him to do something.

Jake cursed under his breath. "I'll try," he promised and went after his cheating wife.

"Sarah, hold on." He caught up with her as she stomped toward an automobile parked on the road. Leaning against it waited the man who'd take her away from him. Jake's knuckles itched to hit the coward one last time.

Sarah jerked away from his grasp. "Papa warned me not to marry you. Said you had no ambition. Wouldn't take care of me as you should."

That Alfred Hahn had such a low opinion of him came as a surprise. He'd always assumed he had good relations with his in-laws. But maybe Sarah was just getting in a final dig. It wouldn't be the first lie to drip from her pretty lips—hell, or the hundredth and one. He glanced at the fancy Roadster running idle. Garron Schmidt didn't even have the guts to face him like a man. "If you don't care about me anymore, think of Elsa. Your sister loves him. He's her intended."

"I can't help it if he loves me more."

He pressed his fingers hard into his palms. "Then think of our son, dammit."

Sarah turned and stared toward the farmhouse. Jake knew what she saw— a ramshackle of a home that probably hadn't looked good even in its heyday. He experienced shame as a provider for the first time since their marriage began.

"We'll send for him once we're settled," she said.

His blood began to boil. "Over my dead body."

"See? That's exactly what I'm talking about. You say you want what's best for Rudy and me, and then you're completely unreasonable."

"You're not taking my boy from me."

She planted her fists onto her hips. "*Our* boy. I don't remember you pushing him out after hours of agony."

This was going south fast. He worked to contain his temper. "Don't go. Please. Let's go back inside and work this out."

"The time for talking is over."

Though his size and strength showed strong, she thought he was weak.

Maybe I am.

He slumped his shoulders in defeat as Sarah hurried away, threw her bags onto the backseat, and embraced her lover. Allowing the pain in his heart free rein, he watched the Roadster's cloud of dust until it disappeared out of sight.

A tug on his flannel shirt pulled his attention back home. The hurt and disappointment on his son's face hit him with another gut punch.

"She gone?"

Jake knelt at eye level and nodded. "'Fraid so."

Rudy wiped his tears. Jake could tell he and his son were doing the same thing, closing off one emotion after the other, banishing them to be dealt with another time, if at all. They had each other and the farm to tend, and that's all that really mattered.

Chapter 3

Charles had been her pillar of strength. Faye couldn't fathom what she would do without him. When her voice faltered, he took over with the line of people paying their respects. He whispered into her ear. "Take a break."

Her face still tight from false pleasantries, she excused herself and made her way to a seat in Willow Wood's ballroom. There, friends and associates mingled, speaking in hushed voices. She contemplated the almost clinical reserve of it all. Even at a time like this, showing emotion was highly frowned upon and regarded as unbecoming. Even so, they seemed overly composed and indifferent, as if they were going through the motions and didn't miss her father at all. Irritation simmered inside.

Her future mother-in-law approached her in a black mourning dress. An ostrich plume topped her black netted hat, adding color to the outfit's somber design. "Mind if I join you?"

Faye forced her lips into another false smile and shook her head, wary that her voice might divulge weakness.

Mrs. Carlton eyed her. "How are you holding up?"

"It all seems as if it's happening to someone else." Her voice quivered despite her resolve. "Right is left, up is down...I truly don't know how I'd keep my sanity without the help of your family and Charles. He's been so wonderful."

"He admired your father. You're helping him through this by allowing him to care for you. Men want to feel needed, especially in times of tragedy."

Relieved to hear the older woman's viewpoint, she let her grief settle in further.

A man strode over from the receiving line. He bowed then handed her a card. "I'm sorry to interrupt, but I have somewhere to be.

I just wanted to tell you how sorry I am for your loss. If you need anything, please do not hesitate to call."

Faye read the card aloud. "Graham Business and Investment Counsel."

Mrs. Carlton snatched it from her fingers. "Thank you, Mister Graham, but our family has our own trusted experts." She gave him a steely look. "Hurry on now. Don't you have somewhere to be?"

Mr. Graham made a long face and bowed his head.

After he walked away, Mrs. Carlton tore up the card and tucked the pieces into her handbag. "The nerve. My sweet, opportunists will be coming out of the woodwork to try to get their piece of your fortune. Allow Charles to deal with them. No reason to upset yourself about it."

Faye assumed Charles would manage her inheritance once they were married, but she wanted an equal say in how it was spent. His mother would disapprove, so she simply said, "Thank you, Missus Carlton."

A gloved hand caressed the top of her own. "Call me Mother."

The sign for THE TEA ROOM glowed with a hundred white and red lights in honor of Valentine's Day. Charles had reserved a cozy candle-lit corner table in the back of the restaurant. A large fern offered added privacy.

After perusing the menu, he placed their order. "We'll start with the tomato bisque. The lady will have the brook trout, and I'll have a medium-rare steak along with your finest Red."

"I'm sorry, sir. Unfortunately, we are not permitted to sell wine."

"Unbelievable," Charles muttered. "I'm used to having it with my meal at the club." He turned on his charm. "I suppose pilfering a claret from the church next door is out of the question?"

The man chuckled as though under the assumption Charles was joking. He wasn't.

Without acknowledging her presence, the waiter snatched Faye's menu away.

She wanted comfort food, the cream-sauced chicken with noodles for dinner, but Charles always decided. "Excuse me," she called back the server. "I'll have the pasta special."

Charles frowned. "I thought you wanted to lose weight for the wedding."

She had lost ten pounds. How thin did he want her? She nodded.

"The fish, please," he said to the waiter, who seemed put out for the time wasted. Charles reached across the table and clasped her hands. "I'm sorry about the picture show. I hope it didn't upset you."

She could have told him there was a man hanged in the film *Wild Girl* if he'd asked. She'd seen the play and read the book years ago. But she didn't want him to feel bad on their special night, so she pretended not to be bothered. "I'm fine."

Charles exhaled his relief. "I only chose it because you remind me of her."

"Salomy Jane?"

"No, the actress...what's her name?"

"Oh, Joan Bennett." Several people claimed she looked like the brunette version of the actress, but she didn't see the resemblance.

Charles let go of her hands and lit a cigarette. "Isn't this place great?"

She didn't like the sterile look of the black and white tiled floor and found the red wallpaper overly stark. "Very nice." Starving, she chose a salted nut from a small bowl and popped it into her mouth.

"A few years ago, Douglas Fairbanks and Mary Pickford ate here. They were passing through after attending Rudolph Valentino's funeral."

He thought celebrity, she heard death. Why did people around the world celebrate people dying? All Hallows' Eve, Easter, and even Valentine's Day. It all seemed so morbid.

She leaned back and placed her hands on her lap. "I've been thinking about making a few changes to Willow Wood. Make it more our own."

He shook his head. "The estate looks fine as it is."

"Nothing big at first. Renovate a room or two, add a fresh coat of paint to the front veranda, maybe extend the rose garden."

"My father suggested we invest with his man." He leaned away and crossed his arms. "Claims he's a financial genius."

That didn't sit well. She tensed. *"All* of it?"

"No," he said with a chuckle. "Of course not. What has gotten into you?"

With me? What's with you? Ever since her father died, Charles's fun-loving, devil-may-care attitude had changed into a controlling, patriarchal frame of mind. She didn't like it when he got like this. And to have a say in her own trust fund and future seemed perfectly rational. "I also think the servants should have a raise in pay. I know Abby is stretched thin helping her sister, and Rozario is saving for a new overcoat."

Charles clicked his teeth. "They're each paid more now than my mother's top staff. Leave the household worries to me."

But that was her job. What did he expect her to do? She took a deep breath to calm herself. Perhaps he didn't understand what their roles were yet. "Daddy always relied on me to oversee domestic tasks."

"Well, you don't have to worry about those things with me as your husband. I don't believe in women working."

Her dress shop. She clenched her jaw. Once married, would he insist she give up her business? Surely not. She loved him, but his arrogance of late grated on her nerves. "I don't worry. I enjoy the work, and I'm good at it."

Charles tamped out his cigarette in the peanut dish just as she intended to reach for another.

Filthy habit.

He withdrew a beribboned jewelry box from his pocket. "I was going to wait until after dessert, but maybe this will perk you up."

The Tiffany engraved box alluded to something expensive. Charles smoothed his blond hair and smiled as she lifted the lid. Enclosed was a delicate wristwatch of pink-rose gold and sparkly diamonds. A tiny red heart took the place of the number three on the dial.

A distraction. A way to change the topic of conversation. She'd let it go for now, but this discussion was far from over. "Thank you. It's lovely."

Charles took it out and latched it around her wrist. "Only the best for my gal." He kissed the back of her hand.

His girl. Soon to be his wife. Someday, the mother of his children. This was what they meant by the holy bonds of matrimony. She would then belong to him.

Chapter 4

Jake strode to the Thompson family's doorstep with his son trailing at his heels. He rubbed a hand over his shirt, his stomach coiled tight as a hitch knot.

Bern Schmidt wanted the Thompson's farm and was there to take it. But there was something the banker didn't know. The farmers of the county had had enough, and they were there to stop him.

Jake lingered a moment before knocking, summoning hope that they would win the day. The Thompson family's kid didn't seem so sure. He leaned against the porch wall with his head and shoulders bent as if drained of the innocence and joy of childhood, now flooded and weighed down with mature worry.

Rudy patted his friend's back. "Hey, Wyatt."

The boy maintained a vacant stare toward his shoes. He had grown half a foot since he'd quit school to help his father on their farm.

Rudy said, "Don't worry. That no-good-for-nothin' Schmidt ain't gonna take yer home." He puffed out his small chest. "Us farmers will see to that."

To be that young again and sure. Jake summoned his inner child.

"Honest to Pete?" Wyatt's voice cracked.

Rudy nodded and gave a three-fingered salute. "Scouts honor."

Heartened, Jake used the knocker.

Ian Thompson opened the screen door for his wife and daughter, letting it slam behind him. The man looked like he'd been punched in the gut.

Jake shook his hand, thick with corned calluses and gritty as sandpaper. "Everyone's in place. If things go well, this should buy you time until harvest." He turned his friend to see the crowd gathered around the auctioneer's wagon below.

Ian's Adam's apple bobbed. "This day will be the death of me."

"Have faith. Schmidt won't win this one."

"I rue the day I borrowed money from that man." Ian's lips twisted as if he'd tasted sour milk. "I've tried everything—butchered and sold my stock and all of our furniture. We've slept on the hard floor for weeks." He rubbed his lower back. "Schmidt refused the money I offered. Told me to pay in full or take my family back east and pick a new profession." He made a tight fist and punched a clapboard on his house. Blood welled on his knuckles.

His wife gasped. She placed their toddler on the porch floor and tried to tend to her husband's injury.

"*No*," Ian yelled and jerked his arm away from her. "If Schmidt's gonna take everything we've toiled so hard to build, I'll stain it with my blood to remind him what he's done. By God, may he *burn* in Hell for it!" He turned his flushed face away from her.

Poor man. Jake couldn't imagine what he was going through. He gently guided Ian's hurt hand so Mrs. Thompson could wrap it with a cloth that had swaddled their little girl's doll. He tried to lighten the mood. "Well said, but I doubt even the devil wants a banker in his midst."

Ian let out a short laugh that ended in a sob. "I was two years from getting back my deed. I told that to the county commissioner last week when I begged for his help. All the good that did."

"He and Schmidt are two peas in a pod. You mustn't blame yourself. We had boom crops when you and others put up your homes to expand your fields and purchase machinery. Nobody foresaw a drought bad as this."

"You told me not to trust him, Jake. I should have listened to you back then. I'm a damn fool."

The auctioneer climbed the wagon and announced the start of the bidding. Jake patted Ian's back and then headed to join a group of fellow farmers at the front of the auction wagon.

The auctioneer held up the first item, a grain shovel, and began his rhythmic chant. "Who'll gimme a penny, penny, penny?" He pointed at someone in the crowd. "Who'll gimme a dime, dime, dime, DIME, dime, dime?"

Jake and other farmers weaved through the crowd, stopping bidders with mean looks or, when needed, forcibly lowering men's arms as they attempted an offer.

The auctioneer began to fidget and ran a finger under his collar. His rapid speech became hesitant and off-beat as item after item went for pennies or without a bid. "Next up is a sickle-bar mower. Practically new and fits any sized horse. Easy as pie for young'uns to use. Who'll gimme ten, ten, ten..."

Jake blocked an arm mid-rise.

Alfred Hahn's eyes widened.

Dammit. Jake's jaw ticked.

Rudy waved hello to his grandfather.

The desperate, flustered auctioneer pointed at Rudy. "Sold!"

Jake scraped his hand over his face, his father-in-law being an unwelcome sight.

Alfred ruffled Rudy's hair. "Thanks, my boy. You bid for me a good price." He raised a brow. "Jake, I'm surprised you'd involve yourself in this. Not your fight."

How could Hahn not see what happened to one could happen to all? If they didn't stop the banker, he'd own damn near every property in town and beyond.

The man in question climbed the wagon and stood next to the auctioneer. Red-faced, Bern Schmidt hollered, "This eviction sale is over. I don't know what you hoped to gain by this display, but you only postponed the inevitable. Next time, I'll bring my own strongmen and the law. I know your faces. Many of you are in debt to my bank."

The crowd grumbled, and angry voices grew louder. Two men squabbling near Rudy knocked him off his feet. Jake led him to safety. More fights broke out, but the farmers outnumbered the bidders three to one.

The brawling men abruptly halted and made way for Alfred's daughter. She looked pretty in her blue-and-white striped dress, her blonde hair braided with a blue ribbon.

Seemingly unaware of her power to create peace, Elsa flashed a smile at his son.

"Hey there, Bug." She hugged Rudy. "Been a while since I've seen this handsome face. Let me get a good look." Cupping his jaw, she kissed up one cheek and down the other.

Rudy giggled and squirmed.

She laughed. "Think your pa would let me borrow you? Maybe do some fishing?"

Elsa gazed his way in question. She looked so much like Sarah; looking at her always stung a bit. But Jake knew his sister-in-law was nothing like his ex-wife. Elsa would never leave her family for another man. Still, he found it best to stay clear of her.

Rudy hopped in place, his palms pressed together in plea. Jake could feel Alfred's steady stare trying to intimidate him, which was unfair. He'd never intended to keep Rudy away from Sarah's family, but he didn't like being pressured or bullied into it.

"You should come too, son," Alfred said to him. "Might do you some good."

What was Hahn up to? Trying to push another one of his daughters onto him? Sorry, old man. Not a chance. "Another time. Got work to do."

Hahn grunted his disapproval. Rudy sulked and looked down at his shoes.

"Don't worry, kiddo." Elsa comforted him. "Those fish'll still be there."

Great. Now he felt like a real heel. "Er, I meant just me. The boy can go."

Rudy whooped and hopped over to his grandfather. "Can I ride up front and steer?"

Elsa mouthed a thank you.

Jake nodded. He quickly strode away before he said something he'd regret or cracked the protection surrounding his heart.

Chapter 5

Two months had passed since the funeral, yet Faye still couldn't think straight, her brain in a perpetual fog. Today, her mind wasn't the only thing in disarray. The grand parlor was also in disorder, cluttered as a clerk's office. Stacks of papers covered every table and lay scattered over the floor. Her father's attorney, Mr. Simmons, readied documents for her signature. Across from her on the settee sat Jane. Faye needed her friend's support now more than ever, but at the same time, she wished she didn't need it. Soon, everyone would know what Marshall Harmon had left his daughter: a monumental scandal.

Mr. Simmons handed her a selection of summaries detailing her father's failed business. Her pulse sped up on the third page as she studied the wording more closely.

"I don't understand. The bank owns Willow Wood?"

The lawyer sighed. "Marshall mortgaged the property and used it for investments after his stocks went under." He paused and added, "He chose poorly and then struggled to come up with the payments and estate taxes. At the time, combining his business and personal assets was his only choice."

Jane reached over and squeezed her hand. "I can't believe this is happening."

Faye barely felt the touch, her body growing numb.

Wake up, she ordered herself. *Wake up.* How could he?

Daddy had no right to take such reckless chances with their family's estate. He'd been the caretaker of it, never the sole owner.

"Why didn't he tell me? He never let on, not once, that we were in financial straits."

Mr. Simmons took a chair beside her and patted the back of her hand. His craggy face, which had intimidated her as a child, softened. "You are scarcely out of your adolescence. Barely a woman."

That stung.

"And he wouldn't worry you with his problems. Marshall was a proud man." He hunched his shoulders. "But he has left you in an unfortunate situation that calls for complicated choices. I will guide you to the best of my ability, but you won't like what I have to say."

She blinked away frustrated tears. The world had spun out of control and would not let her catch her breath. "There's *more*?"

"Holy moly. Now what?" Jane asked.

Mr. Simmons cleared his throat and gave Jane a look that clearly questioned her need to be present, then he turned back to Faye. "I took the liberty of wiring your father's sister in Colorado. She is willing to take you in." He raised a finger as she shook her head in protest. "My dear, it's for your own protection."

"Protection from what?" She stood, wrapped her arms around herself, and walked the room. "My friends are here. Everyone I love is here. I have a business to attend to. For goodness' sake—I'm to be married in two months. What a ludicrous suggestion."

Jane scrunched her face. "Pip's not going anywhere."

Mr. Simmons reached into his pocket and fished out a handkerchief. "You're not thinking clearly. If Charles marries you with this scandal over your head, Virginia will not accept you into her family, and she will cut her son off without so much as a Lincoln cent."

His words had some truth to them. Mrs. Carlton would prioritize her family's reputation over her son's happiness. "Charles loves me." She declined the linen square he held out to her. "We don't need her money."

"I do not doubt that the young man cares deeply. But what do you believe he can do to support you? Chore labor? Everything the boy wants has been handed to him, including a high-salaried, cushy career of choice in a few years. Be sensible, my girl. You and I both know he won't find proper employment without family connections."

She reached up to the marble fireplace and gently lifted a Baccarat crystal vase. As she turned it in her hands, she considered selling some of her possessions if needed. "Charles and I will postpone our wedding until he's graduated from the university. In the meantime, my dress shop will provide for me."

"And you may stay with us," Jane chimed in. "My family will insist."

Faye conveyed her gratitude but didn't think it would come to that. She'd fight with all her might and determination to save Willow Wood.

Mr. Simmons raked his hand through his white hair, stood, and paced the room. "Your father financed your business, which is in his name."

What was the man going on about now?

"I'm sorry to say that Buttons and Bows is no more."

"That's impossible." Tightness constricted her chest. Why had her father picked such an incompetent lawyer? Hadn't he been hired to fix these problems?

"Your shop and all its contents are to be auctioned off."

No. That wasn't going to happen. But there was no sense in arguing with the man. Come tomorrow; she'd seek new representation.

"So, do you see? Your choices are somewhat limited."

She lifted her chin. "Then I will find other employment."

"Put aside the economic recession wracking the country." He pinched the bridge of his nose. "Put aside the flood of family men who are unable to find work and cannot provide for their children except through charity and breadlines. In truth, the inferior community will not welcome you, nor will they be sympathetic. As your adviser, I would be remiss in my duty not to stress the urgency of my counsel."

Exasperated, Faye used her father's favorite expression. "What in the Sam Hill does that have to do with me? It's not like somebody will hire a man for a job I'm capable of. A family man should get a loan from the bank until he is back on his feet again."

"That is not an option for most. Borrowers' inability to pay loans is partially why your family's bank will go under. The Reserve and larger banks are refusing assistance. The Department of Banking of the Commonwealth has taken possession and is currently inspecting the books. Board members and shareholders are crying foul, turning on each other, and insisting on compensation before all others. With your father not here to defend himself, people from high to low will be itching for someone to blame. God forbid the anarchists join in."

Her hand twitched. She returned the vase to the mantle, suddenly fearing for its safety. "That is why I must stay here. Someone needs to stand up to them. My father may have made wretched choices with our personal lives, but he would never jeopardize other people's savings or his bank's integrity. Of this, I know."

Mr. Simmons lit his pipe and took a few short puffs. The sharp, pungent scent of tobacco spread across the room. "I admire your loyalty, but you cannot sway agitated minds. Before all is done, they will drag you down along with Marshall's reputation. You need to leave the city—the *state*—before the bank's depositors realize that most of their money is gone."

Where did the people's money go? It couldn't have just disappeared. She added that to her ever-growing list of things to discover.

Mr. Simmons kept on. "There is nothing left for you here but grief and heartache. Go to Colorado until all this blows over. Or get a fresh start someplace—London, perhaps." He tapped his pipe on the ashtray. "That would greatly please your grandmother and may be for the best."

That was it. She'd had enough of the lawyer's ledgers and dire proclamations and oh-so-thoughtful advice. If he was working with her grandmother to manipulate her choices, she couldn't trust him. If he wasn't for her, he was against her.

She pressed her hand over her forehead. "I think I've had enough for today. I have a terrible headache and need to rest." If he considered her a flower wilting on the vine, she'd play the part to her advantage. Come tomorrow, pursue better advice.

Jane hugged her. "We'll figure something out. Call me when you feel up to it."

Faye regretted her excuse. She only wanted Mr. Simmons to go.

He sandwiched her hand between his own. "Please consider everything I've said. Marshall would have wanted you to. I made a promise long ago to watch over you if anything ever happened to him."

Faye gave him a curt nod, eager for her hand back. She saw him out as far as the door, pulled a window drape to the side, and watched him go.

Pain pulsed inside her head somewhere around her eyes.

"Daddy." She could envision him lounging in his leather upholstered chair. "I can't lose Willow Wood and my shop." There must be a way out of this. "I won't lose them." *And Charles?* "No, I will not lose anyone or anything more." What did Mr. Simmons know about true love? Did a lawyer even have a heart? She sighed. "Don't worry about me. I'll find a way." Her father faded.

Simmons's automobile parted the flock of reporters and high-neck gawkers gathered beyond the front gate. When they got wind of this, the newsmen would surely blow it all out of proportion.

She retreated to the parlor and snatched a decorative pillow from the settee. Burying her face in its padding, she let out a muffled scream.

There had to be more to this story. This couldn't be the whole truth. Someone else had to know what the hell was going on and why this was happening.

She picked up the telephone's handset and dialed her father's partner at the bank, Penn Kinsey. The line kept ringing. No answer.

Mr. Carlton Senior sat on the bank's board of directors. Maybe he had told Charles something. Rotating the dial of the telephone again, she shouldered the receiver and twirled a lock of hair.

The butler answered the line. "Carlton residence."

"Hi, Stokes. Pip here. Is Charles around?"

Silence. She thought they were disconnected, but then she heard him say, "Master Carlton is unavailable."

He sounded strange. Impersonal. *Clunk.*

She held the phone's receiver out and stared at it. Did he hang up on her? Surely not. Stokes had never been anything but polite. She rolled her eyes at her paranoia. "Get a grip, Pip."

Throughout that day, she watched the unmerciful clock. When it grew dark enough to sneak past the reporters, she slipped out the side gate and broke into a steady jog. She needed Charles. For him to hold her and tell her everything would be all right, for his family to help her decide the best path forward.

A scatter of lights remained lit at the Carlton's white-bricked Colonial Revival mansion; its overwhelming size meant to proclaim their wealth and intimidate all who entered. The bright lamps of the driveway made her feel exposed rather than safe. An odd reaction, considering this was soon to be her new home if they couldn't save Willow Wood. But as she climbed the stairs on the front porch and shook the rain off her coat, she couldn't shake the sense that something was wrong. Chastising herself for being overdramatic, she quashed all negative thoughts, stood straighter, and pushed the bell.

An overhead light came on when Stokes opened the front door. He cleared his throat in greeting.

Faye cringed at his stony expression. "I am so sorry. I know it's late, but I must speak with Charles."

"Very well." Stokes warded off her entry with his hand. "Wait here, please."

She paced the veranda, her paranoia back again. Why didn't Stokes invite her inside? What was the man's problem today?

A few minutes later, the door opened again. Virginia Carlton emerged with her customary composure and regal bearing. Dressed in velvet and pearls, she held her head high, her blonde chignon wrapped smoothly without a hair out of place. Always perfect.

Faye managed a smile. "Oh. Good evening, Mother. Stokes must have misheard me. I'm here to speak with your son."

Virginia tightened a fur stole around her shoulders and settled on a porch chair with her back straight and ankles crossed. "Join me." She patted the arm of the seat next to her.

Faye sat and matched the older woman's comportment. She couldn't help but feel something was wrong.

Where is Charles?

She steeled herself for unpleasantness and waited for Mrs. Carlton to speak.

"I want to tell you what I wish my mother had told me at your age. Something all young women should know before choosing the right man." Virginia waved dismissively. "Women your age will change so much in the next few years. Your wants. Your needs. Your desires. What seems a certainty today may be all wrong five years from now, when you're married, most likely with at least one child, catering to their wants and needs instead of your own. Understand?"

Faye nodded, though she had no idea where this conversation was going. Charles was the ideal match for her. Why would Mrs. Carlton question whether she knew her own mind? Why now when their wedding was so close at hand?

"Without us, men would have no ambition, no reason to achieve great success." A hard edge crept into Virginia's voice. "We stand behind them while they play the game, but we have the real power. We control their fate. Therefore, we must nurture and mold them into the men we wish them to be." Her eyes locked on Faye's with a long, unsettling stare.

Faye surmised this was her cue to reply and said softly, "I know my duties."

"We are alike, you and I." Virginia soothed her tone. "I would have enjoyed having you as my daughter, taking you under my wing, and teaching you all I know. But I think you realize that is not possible now. You must set a new path. Go to London and make a fresh start. Your grandmother will help you marry a man from the noble class. A man with good judgment. A man who is not my son."

The last words spoken replayed in her mind.

It felt like she'd been pushed into a river that changed direction midstream, and now the current was taking her to an unknown, treacherous destination. She gazed out beyond Virginia's shoulder at the mixed sleet coming down. They were nothing alike. She knew Charles in ways his mother did not—the most important part of him—his heart.

They'd elope. Move far away. Go to New York or Boston or a bustling city out west. It would serve his mother right.

Mrs. Carlton stated firmly, "Charles asked me to speak with you. He said he could not manage to see you cry."

Faye swallowed against the lump in her throat. The empty pit in her stomach expanded into her heart. He'd sent his mother to deal with her. After five years of being together, this was how he chose to end it, hiding behind his mother's skirt. *Coward.*

Mrs. Carlton stared at her steadily as if searching for something. She raised a brow. "Good girl. Anger. Hold onto that in the months to come. It will motivate you and give you strength."

On the walk back home, their conversation swirled over and again in her mind. She picked up a rock and threw it with all her might. She didn't need them. Didn't need anybody. Come morning, she would fix everything herself.

Music filled the room. Arms embracing air, Faye moved with her phantom partner across her bedroom floor. Ruth Etting wailed "All of Me" through the flaring horn on the phonograph as the record skipped a well-worn groove.

"Why not take all of me?" She sang along with the chorus, then collapsed onto her bed, buried her face into her lavender-scented pillow, and groaned in frustration.

The meeting with the new lawyer hadn't gone well. Neither had the appointment with her father's accountant. And Charles had all day to act with integrity and tell her that he no longer wanted her in his life. No longer loved her.

Nothing she did seemed to matter. She sat up, brushed away her tears, and checked the phone line. Judging by the dial tone's steady warbling "E," it worked fine. The clock above the fireplace struck eight o'clock. Inundated with self-pity and restlessness, she slid off the bed.

Maybe things weren't as bad as they seemed? Perhaps Charles intended to come in person, was figuring out the right words to say or planning how they'd run away together.

She took a swig from the nearly empty bottle of wine and walked the hallway. Her slippers slapped as she descended the stairs. The wind whistled from the direction of the great hall. She entered and flipped on the chandelier, causing a glow under the stained-glass domed ceiling and over the wall's trompe l'oeil depiction of cherubs. Water puddled on the wooden floor near a set of open French doors. She crossed the Persian rug and stuck her head outside. Cold rain splattered. Not seeing anything amiss, she ducked back under cover, wiped her face with her sleeve, latched the doors, and gave them an extra tug to ensure they were locked.

She needed to scold Rozario for his carelessness in locking up. She couldn't afford to pay him anymore, but he still lived there, which meant he had some responsibilities for the roof over his head.

"Hic." Good grief. Her hiccups were back. Holding her breath, she switched off the light.

A rattling bang pounded outside the French doors.

Startled, she flicked the light back on and stared hard in their direction. Her vision obstructed by the chandelier's glare, she moved toward the doors with hesitant steps, butted her nose to the glass, and turned on the patio light. A tree the gardener had planted last spring bent from the wind, its branches thumping the gardener's shed. She scolded herself for being so skittish.

Her chest spasmed another "Hic." She headed to the kitchen for a glass of water. In a hallway mirror, the glimpse of a man with a hat went by.

"Rozario, you forgot to lock all the doors." She moved toward the end of the hall. "Rozario?"

Clang, clang, clang. She hopped. The noise came from the kitchen. Her heart thumped in her chest. "Not funny, Rozario," she said, though even to her own ears, her voice sounded unsure. She entered the kitchen through the service doors and turned on the light.

A soup pot, skillet, and utensils lay strewn about the floor. A drafty breeze came from the back of the kitchen. Faye rushed to the open door just as Rozario entered.

She smacked his chest. "Why didn't you answer me? You scared me half to death."

He scrunched his brows. "What are you talking about?"

"I saw you in the hallway just a moment ago, and you completely ignored me."

"I'm just getting in. I came thisa way because I noticed the door was wide open."

Faye rubbed the base of her neck. Her stomach signaled something was wrong. "Hurry. We need to check on Abby." She pulled at his arm.

"I dropped Abigail off at her sister's place. Stay *calma*." He led her to the kitchen table and helped her to a chair. "Your face is white as a full luna. Breathe." He took a deep one with her. "Good. Now, tell me what you saw."

Her mind raced. She grabbed his sleeve. "A man. A strange man was in the house." She told him what had happened.

He telephoned the police.

After a thorough search of the house and grounds, the police found nothing. They didn't believe her, but Faye couldn't blame them. She inwardly questioned herself if she'd seen the man at all.

Chapter 6

Faye smoothed out her town suit and adjusted her hat. "I'm interview-
ing for a job in the city, which means a long commute, but I believe
it's worth it to work somewhere you enjoy." She asked the man seated
beside her on the train, "Don't you agree?"

He didn't answer. Rude.

There was something menacing about him, like some gangster
from the movies—James Cagney, maybe—full of rough edges in his
criminal persona. But Mr. Fedora Hat wasn't acting. The hard glint
in his stare cut through her, judging her: she was a woman, he was a
man, and he deemed it his right to intimidate her.

Penal bound palooka.

The locomotive barreled around a bend and tossed her against
the man. He reeked of cigarette smoke and vinegary sweat. Underneath his hat's snapped-down brim, his colorless mouth tightened.

"Pardon me." She righted herself and stared at the raised scar that
striped his face, cheek to chin.

Scowling, he snapped open the March 20th, 1933, edition of *The
Philadelphia Brief,* sending his sharp elbow into her side. No beg-pardon
utterance followed or even a twinge of self-reproach. Finding it best
not to provoke him, she sat quietly and skimmed over the ridiculous
headlines. He readjusted the paper.

At the top of the new page was a printed picture of her and her
father. She squinted as she read the caption but could only make out
a few lines from the accompanying story.

MARSHALL RAY HARMON AND HIS DAUGHTER, PHILIPPA FAYE.
A fortune has disappeared under questionable circumstances. Is the banker responsible for this theft
and the ruin of his trusting clients? Why is his family

hiding and refusing to provide answers to this reporter's hard questions?

Faye's stomach sank.

The man flapped and readjusted the paper before she could read more.

How could they publish such a blatantly false report without consequence? What audacity. She resolved to compose a scathing letter to the editor and hand-deliver it first thing tomorrow morning. Ask *them* the hard questions.

After the train reached Broad Street Station, she secured her handbag and joined the mass exodus of passengers. Someone shoved her from behind. She turned and glanced up at his expressionless face.

Mr. Fedora Hat Man.

She'd had enough of him. "Lucky for you, bad manners aren't a crime, so feel free to crawl back to the cave you've come from."

He acknowledged her with a stone-cold glare that gave her the willies.

Faye quickly left the station and managed to flag down a checkered taxicab. As the cityscape rolled by, she couldn't help but worry about the recent news story.

Would this tarnish her chances of finding a job? The press had run rampant with false accusations, smearing her family's name with a tissue box of lies and leaving it up to her to prove her father's innocence. To do their job for them. Unbelievable.

Arriving at Ninth and Market, she buttoned her mink coat and dug into her handbag money for the fare. She weaved through the crowd and entered Gimbels. Familiar with every corner of the largest retail building in Philadelphia, she took in the sparkling displays and breathed in the aromas of perfumes. She could easily envision herself as a shop assistant or working behind the scenes in fashion.

But it was best not to seem too eager. After all, there was her salary to negotiate and terms of employment. She glanced at their slogan on the wall—SELECT, DON'T SETTLE—and agreed with it.

She had specifically chosen this company for her new career and felt confident she would find her place here soon enough. Possessed the necessary skills to make the company even better.

But her confidence waivered after the elevator reached the top floor and the uniformed operator slid open the gated doors. A long row of women waited outside the chief of staff's office.

She positioned herself at the end and asked the young woman ahead of her, "Excuse me, is this the line for employment?"

The woman nodded. Draped over her arm was a pattern-pinned dress. On the floor, a man's briefcase. Every woman ahead had the same.

Faye observed their unhappy faces as one after the other exited the chief's office. Uncertainty crept into her mind. When it was her turn, she strained a false smile and entered the room. A short, slim man with a square mustache greeted her by name. The plaque on his desk identified him as MR. BILLINGS.

He frowned. Not a good start. "Resume of previous experiences and references?"

Her anxiety spiked. "I wasn't aware I needed those." She strained to stop the quiver from her voice. "I filled out an application, though."

He narrowed his eyes at her. "For this interview. For seamstress. No sewing samples of your work?"

This was a disaster. Panic flooded through her veins. She fought back the tears threatening to spill and sputtered, "N-no, sir, b-but I can quickly go get them."

Mr. Billings tilted his head. "Where did you think you were coming today, Miss Harmon? A tea party? A women's lunch?"

Snarky.

She needed him to understand her situation. The trembling moved down to her hands. "No, of course not, but this is my first employment inquiry. I own—owned my own business. Please, Mister Billings, give me a chance."

He tossed her application into the trash bin. "We pride ourselves on being the best. The finest merchandise, a wide selection of quality goods, and ambitious workers who take pride in bettering themselves. We don't *settle*, no matter how low the position."

"I thought I was applying for shopgirl, but I don't mind starting at the bottom," she said with a breathy voice. "I'll be a hard worker and do any job. Please, sir."

"With your current problems, we couldn't very well have you interacting with the public." His pinched expression relaxed. "Miss Harmon, you seem like a nice girl. This is by no means personal. It's business. Your family has created quite a stir, so I regret that we cannot offer you employment at this time. I do wish you the best of luck in your future endeavors. Good day."

This certainly felt personal. Pride stopped her from groveling at the man's feet. She left the room as the next fresh face entered to have her hopes and dreams dashed.

If Mr. Billings knew her troubles, why offer an interview in the first place? Curiosity? To put her in her place? Him with his stupid smug face and condescending, patronizing tone. Who the hell did he think he was? The morality police?

Shopping always made her feel better, though she now loathed to give them her patronage. After stocking up on personal care items on the fourth floor, she made her way down one level to apparel. She had depleted her bank account with a withdrawal of nine hundred dollars, all that remained in her name. Budgeting called for choices. Which one? A tea-length polka-dot skirt or a pleated plaid?

"Pip? Is that you?" Her father's best friend, George Dixon, sat by the changing rooms. "I thought so," he said, forming his lips into a pretend frown. "Miserable business, this, wasting hours while Marje and our daughters try on half of the store. It doesn't get easier with age. I'd rather be at the barber's getting a tight shave from a rusty blade." His hand smoothed his bearded chin. "How are you, dear girl?"

His concern seemed superficial, at best. "Getting by."

He averted his gaze and gave a slight nod. "I'm sorry I haven't been around. I just—well, Marje is angry. She believes Marshall deceived us, that he knew and should have informed us about the bank's problems so we could have pulled our money out in time." He shook his head. "Hell, I don't know what to think. Hard to tell what a man will do when his back is against the wall."

His betrayal of her father hurt beyond words. She was about to rebuke him when a flash of light blinded her periphery and distracted her from what she'd meant to say.

Two men approached. One held a camera. The other clutched a pad of paper. He retrieved a pencil from behind his ear, licked the tip, and waved it. "You're her, right? Miss Harmon? Care to make a statement about how you spend the people's money?" He directed everyone's attention to her shopping bag. "Purchasing fine clothes and such while your father's victims go hungry." He glided a finger down her mink. "Bet that set you back a pretty penny."

Flash. The photographer got off another shot.

"Stop that." She slapped the reporter's hand away and glared at the man with the camera. "My father was not a thief. And I am not buying frivolous things—not that it is your business." She opened her bag and showed him cards of hairpins, lipstick, and a fifteen-dollar bottle of Bellodgia Caron Parfum from Paris. "Don't write scurrilous accusations without knowing the truth."

The reporter gave her an incredulous look and pointed at the perfume. "It would take more than a week's wages to buy my wife that."

Remorse for the extravagance followed shame.

Flash. The man with the camera shot again.

The reporter grabbed her arm.

Shame evaporated into anger. "Let me *go*," she said, fuming.

Dixon moved forward to intervene. "Hey, now. Better release the lady if you know what's good for you," he warned.

The reporter lightened his grip. Faye jerked loose. Dixon and the reporter exchanged harsh words. Marjorie came out of the dressing room and shouted her husband's name.

Embarrassed by the scene and with no fight left, Faye hurried out of the building and blended in, keeping pace with other pedestrians. Her mind replayed the unfair accusations from Dixon and the press. Most readers would agree with their opinions once the reporter's article was released and circulated. Gossip was insidious: once repeated, it seemed more authentic, causing more people to believe it. By tomorrow, the switchboards would light up like the World's Fair and buzz like the droning of a thousand angry bees.

∾

Along Faye's way to her dress shop, the crowd thickened and bounced against her. She climbed a step at a pharmacy to get her bearings. The front of her father's bank loomed across the street. People—hundreds, it seemed—filled the area. Some carried signs, and others shouted for justice. Communists and Socialists bellowed their economic and political theories while signing up followers. A party of supporters paraded past with a large banner, ANARCHIST WORKERS GROUP, determined not to be outvoiced or outdone.

Remembering what the lawyer had said about unruly anarchists and afraid of being noticed, Faye slipped into the pharmacy. She stared out the front window as the demonstrators clashed with a regiment of arriving police. Protesters threw rocks and debris at the uniformed men. The officers retaliated with clubs and bare fists. A gunshot rang out.

Customers inside the pharmacy crowded around her, murmuring with excitement. Outside, a policeman slammed a bloodied man against the glass pane. Faye flinched and drew back as a woman next to her screamed. An elderly pharmacist locked the front door and herded everyone toward the back of the store.

Bumped and elbowed in the panic to escape, Faye got pushed out first. She stepped around waist-high shelters erected from scrapped materials where homeless men shared a dirty liquor bottle. A vagrant dug in the pharmacy's trashcan and took a bite from its contents. She recoiled from the man and backed into another. He held out the bottle and, with a toothless grin, offered her a drink.

Her purse gripped tight; she hurried down the alley to a much quieter side street. Did people really live like that? Didn't they have a family to help them? Pharmacy patrons moved past, and the women looked equally upset.

She'd had enough excitement for the day and resumed toward her dress shop to call a taxicab. Along the way, almost every store had a CLOSED, OUT OF BUSINESS, or a BUY ONE GET ONE FREE sign. A small number of people hurried along the sidewalks with their heads down.

An uneasy feeling prickled the back of her neck. She stopped and looked behind her. A man stood at a distant alley entrance, his face hidden under a felt brim pulled low and the upended collar of his dark coat. Something seemed oddly familiar about him. He tipped his hat at her.

"Who goes there?" she called out.

Not answering, he stood still as stone.

Was the press following already? Hadn't she been abused enough today? Hurriedly rounding a corner, she bumped into a dilapidated cart. Apples toppled over the side. She tried to keep them from rolling into the street and apologized to the seller.

"It's all right." A girl touched her shoulder and repeated, "It's all right, please. Don't mess your fine clothes."

Cheeks streaked with dirt, the girl had a yellowish-brown bruised eye, and the sweater she wore seemed to have more holes than material. Faye clutched an apple, unable to speak, unable to look away.

The girl glanced behind and whispered, "Ain't no harm done. You want that one?"

Faye remembered her manners and came back to herself. The sign on the cart read APPLES FIVE CENTS EACH OR THREE FOR A DIME. "How many fell on the ground?" she asked.

The girl counted and set them aside. "They ain't bruised too badly. Got some nicer ones here unless you're baking a pie."

"Sure, that would be lovely." Faye figured Abigail would find some use for them and dug into her handbag for loose change.

Still, for a moment, while pressing the coins into the girl's hand, she was hesitant to break away. Could this have been her if fate were less kind? Another life? What was it about the girl that discomposed her so? But then, awareness finally dawned: beneath the grime, mussed hair, and thread-bare hat, the girl's face bore an uncanny resemblance to her own.

❧

Faye unlocked the front door underneath the BUTTONS AND BOWS WEDDING PROMENADE AND EVENING GOWNS sign.

She stopped at the showcase window, which featured a Carole Lombard look-alike mannequin dressed in a floor-length ivory satin wedding dress.

"I didn't get the job, Carole." She draped a lace-embroidered veil over its arm. "But will anyone hire the daughter of the most hated man in the city?"

With frustration, she flung her purse, bags, and keys onto the counter next to the empty cash register. It had taken months to purchase and arrange the décor, mirrors, and lighting to her satisfaction. To find the Hollywood glam portraits that lined the walls with images of Greta Garbo, Jean Harlow, and Faye Wray wearing the latest fashions. The images invoked the romance of the picture shows, portraying the chic styles that so many women were eager to imitate.

Her father had expressed his concerns about competing against larger retailers who could offer lower prices. Ironically, he'd mentioned Gimbels by name. She had pointed out that their merchandise was of lesser quality, produced in duplicate, and squished together on racks that customers had to sift through.

She'd been meticulous with her displays with pristinely folded silk scarves, elegant satin gloves paired at just the right angle, and hats of the latest designs placed strategically next to the gowns they went with best.

She sighed. If only Mr. Billings could see what she'd accomplished. *This* was her resume.

She caressed the chiffon material of a bridesmaid dress. In less than a week, the bank would take possession. All of this would be gone, empty as the hole in her heart. The space would probably be an accountant's office or a hardware and appliance store.

After today, she wasn't coming back. It would be too painful to witness the dismantling of her vision and heart's work. Perhaps someday she'd try again. Maybe with more affordable wear, dresses for the average woman with a modern flair. Maybe her dream wasn't over, just delayed.

She picked up the telephone's receiver and dialed for a taxicab.

Crash! The front window shattered, and angry voices followed the jarring noise.

With a gasp, Faye ducked beneath the counter. Rooted to the spot, she gripped the receiver as a voice tinned through the earpiece.

"City Taxi."

She peeked over the counter at the furious crowd on the street and took cover after more objects pummeled the front of the building. Hand trembling, she informed the dispatcher of the shop's address and begged the taxi company to hurry.

"What's that noise?"

Afraid he wouldn't send a car if she told the truth, she fibbed. "Oh, um, well—they are having some sort of celebration on the street. Better have the driver pick me up in front of the butcher's shop on Third."

"Will do, ma'am."

She reached to hang up the receiver as tomatoes splattered the front of Carole Lombard's beautiful wedding dress. *Animals!*

"We know you're in there," a man outside shouted. "Come out."

"I've telephoned the police!" she yelled back. "This is private property."

The scrimmage had grown larger and louder, their voices insistent. Her once peaceful shop turned chaotic as the crowd barged into the store. They ripped clothes off hangers, shoved anything in reach into pockets, and destroyed her beautiful displays.

One man even decapitated her mannequin. Its head careened toward her and clattered along the tiled floor. *Carole!*

Her heart raced as he strode her way, his next target.

"Stop!" She blocked him with her hands in a feeble attempt to create a barrier.

More people filled the shop, bringing more of their caterwaul. The man ruthlessly grabbed her arm and tore off her coat.

The cacophony of noise thrashed her ears.

"You have no right!" she cried. Her head throbbed from the sound of angry voices as stranger's faces swam her vision. Someone lifted off her hat.

Nearby, a bleached blonde woman snagged her keys from the counter and reached for her handbag.

My money!

Faye fought through the crowd and managed to latch onto a corner of her purse. After a seesaw tug of war, she yanked it from the woman's grasp. Using the crowd to escape, she dropped to the floor and scrambled on all fours past a sea of legs until she reached the dressing rooms and burst out the exit doors.

The checkered vehicle sat parked a distance away. She hurried toward it when the toe of her shoe collided with something and toppled her to the ground. Barely registering the gravel road's bite, the smarting of her palms, and warm blood running underneath her stockings, she stumbled into a staggered run. The mob followed, chasing ever closer to her heels.

"Drive!" she screeched, throwing herself onto the back seat.

With a look of confusion, the driver locked the doors. "Lady, what the hell is going on?"

The people pounded on the windows, their shouted obscenities ringing in her ears.

"Please, sir." She sobbed. "I need to get home. Please take me home."

Hot tears ran down her face as the cab bullied its way through the crowd. She released a relieved sigh when they were clear.

That was it. Enough was enough. *I'm leaving.*

Chapter 7

Lamp posts illuminated the parking lot of the Brookline Cricket Club. The familiar heavy scent of spruce and pine curdled Faye's fluttery stomach.

Jane's father opened the passenger door and offered his wife the aid of his arm. "Escort to three beautiful women. I'll be the envy of every man here."

"You speak sweetly now," Jane's mother said, "until a card game catches your eye. Mind you, I want to dance tonight, not sit on the side like some awkward wallflower."

Faye stiffened her spine as they stepped inside. In the weeks since the press accused her father of numerous crimes, she hadn't left the house. Hesitant, she stood away from people entering, wishing the floor would open and swallow her whole. But she needed to see Charles. To know once and for all that they were truly over.

"Pip, this way." Jane waved her forward.

Faye took her time handing her wrap to the coat-check girl.

Jane's eyes swept down and widened. "Holy moly. Where did you get that dress?"

Faye's cheeks warmed. She wanted to ask for her fur stole back. "I altered it."

In a different frame of mind when she'd designed the burgundy taffeta gown, she had wanted to remind Charles what he'd lost. It now seemed a terrible idea. The off-the-shoulder, low-cut bodice felt as tight as a corset. Practically indecent, it pushed her breasts high in front and scooped low in the back to a fitted waistline, exaggerating her curves. To complete the 'I couldn't care less what you think' look, she'd left her brown hair down in daring pin-curl waves instead of a traditional upsweep.

Now ill at ease with her audacious choices, she pulled her hair to the front and tugged up her long gloves. She glanced at Jane's parents, who were speaking with the club's manager. "Do you think your father would mind taking me home? I'm not feeling well."

Jane took her gloved hand and squeezed. "You look ravishing." She encouraged Faye into the ballroom.

The vast room buzzed with laughter and conversations from those her grandmother referred to as 'the Upper Crust.' Flutes of champagne clinked and silverware clattered.

A balloon bounced up a crystal chandelier and joined the cigar-smoke cloud drifting along the high ceiling. Her gaze followed the balloon's attempted escape.

Why had she let Jane talk her into this?

A male server moved through the crowd with finesse and offered her a shy smile and a glass of wine. She took a healthy sip, acutely aware of looks and snubs already directed her way. Pretending not to notice, she listened to the big band music and watched the dancers on the packed floor.

Charles glided into view. Tall, handsome, and dressed to the nines, he was in his element. His dance partner, Catherine Ellen Kerr, followed his smooth dance moves with cloddish steps. He smiled and said something in Catherine's ear. Kit-Cat, the ridiculous nickname Catherine bestowed upon herself, threw back her brassy blonde hair with a laugh.

Faye's throat constricted. She dug her fingernails into the sides of her beaded handbag and steered Jane to seats along a wall.

Jane gave her a look of concern. "Are you truly unwell?"

"I just need a moment." More than ever regretting her decision to come tonight, she composed herself and exhaled her next words. "Charles and Catherine?"

Jane's mouth thinned. "She's such a halfwit, always trying to tempt him with her vulgar dress and witless flirtation. Beyond gauche. But her father is new money, and she knows they'll never be accepted unless she's properly matched. Charles probably just took pity on her."

Faye knew how Catherine would benefit from pursuing Charles. She wasn't angry with the girl but was incensed with Charles for flaunting his newly acquired freedom.

Jane sighed. "I shouldn't have pressed you into coming tonight. I just figured this would be your last chance to say goodbye. Who knows how long you'll be away?"

"I'll be better once I get some fresh air. It's stuffy in here." Faye forced a smile, stood, and smoothed her gown.

"Want me to come with?"

"No need. I don't wish to lessen your night." She made her way through the crowd toward a set of balcony doors. A group of people blocked her path. She waited for an opening.

"Good grief," a man complained, "if I must hear again how much he lost in the crash and his false pleas of poverty, I'll positively scream. He's not fooling me. No siree. I know he's hoarding his money."

A man beside him took a sip of champagne and replied, "I prefer those who light-heartedly brag of loss over the embittered."

"Or like the Mitchells," said a woman with a haughty manner. "Putting on aggrandizing airs. I heard from a reliable source that they now reside in the chauffeur's quarters above their garage."

Mrs. Gibbons, the worst gossip in the room, tittered and then locked eyes with Faye. The rumormongers looked about to burst as she finally made her way around them.

"That's Harmon's daughter—"

"—that crooked banker."

"She has some nerve showing her face here."

Faye slipped onto the balcony and gripped the railing. She wouldn't miss people like them—the judgmental 'who's better than whom' narrow-minded, shallow sycophants who had nothing better to do to pass the time. Good riddance.

The orchestra broke into an upbeat modern tune. She imagined all the gray-haired looks of disapproval being cast the band director's way.

"I requested it for you," Charles said behind her.

She swallowed the bitterness lining her throat. "Go away, Charles. I will not ease your conscience."

"Please, Pip. For once, be reasonable."

She spun to face him. "I'm sick to death of people telling me how to be or feel."

"What would you have me do?" His expression puckered as though he had tasted something spoiled. "Forgo my future? Disappoint my parents and deprive them of the success of their only son? I have responsibilities, damn it." He glanced over her dress and blinked. "I—I love you. You know I do, but I cannot do a blasted thing about us right now. Give it time. Perhaps your difficulties will soon be over and we can be together again."

"My difficulties?" Faye assessed him with new eyes for the first time. "Is that what we're calling it now? My father stole from people who trusted him and then killed himself, providing me with a gruesome image that will be forever seared into my memory. I'm about to lose Willow Wood, the only home I've ever loved. My fiancé"—she tipped her chin up at him—"who promised a life of devotion through good and bad, had his *mother* cancel our wedding. I'm sorry my difficulties disturb you so."

"That's not fair. My mother wanted to ease the burden from—"

"I'm a burden now?"

"You know what I mean. Don't put words in my mouth."

"All of you act as though I have a scarlet letter branded on my forehead."

"No one blames you for what your father has done."

"Don't they?" She gestured toward a group around a table. "Our friends haven't spared me a word for weeks or even looked in my direction tonight. I thought these were my people, that they would understand, but they obviously do not." The realization stung. She'd never dreamed her peers would behave this way. That Charles would ever look at her with such an expression on his face. Why was he staring at her like that? Was it pity? His eyes all soft cornflower blue with—regret?

Out of habit, she reached to brush back the blond hair that curled sweetly around his ears. He once made her feel like the most cherished woman alive. But now...she halted her arm halfway and brought it down to her side. "I leave for Colorado in three days."

"I figured you'd have the sense to go to London. Lady Fitton has often written to my mother, upset that you refused to answer her invitations. Your family is concerned about you, as am I."

I don't have a family. "My grandmother gave up that right when she excused herself from attending my mother's funeral."

Across the room, a determined-looking Catherine strode their way, her mouth twisted into a sneer.

Faye sighed. The last thing she needed was an altercation with the girl. "Your date is coming to save you."

"We didn't come here together." He reached for her, but she side-stepped his effort.

"Goodbye, Charles." She hurried down the steps to the gardens.

"Pip..." he called but did not come after her.

Faye walked under a trellis, followed a brick path, and collapsed onto a bench. Tears stung her eyes. Rubbing the chill from her arms, she asked the moon, "How could you, Daddy?"

Laughter disrupted the night. Thistle Kinsey, the sixteen-year-old sister of her father's former partner, stumbled from the shadows. She held a bottle in one hand and steadied herself with the other. "How could you, Daddy?" she mimicked in falsetto.

It was no wonder the girl had few friends. Faye stood to leave. She wouldn't be Thistle's entertainment.

A larger form emerged from the woods. "Bring it back and quiet down," Marvin Stanton ordered. Charles's college roommate reached for the bottle but lost his footing.

Thistle giggled.

For a moment, Faye thought about leaving them to it. Thistle was not overly fond of her, and she did not look in any condition to listen. But her reputation would suffer, and Thistle's brother was a close friend and would want her to intervene. Faye wiped her eyes and moved into the moonlight, taking a firm stance. "You should be ashamed of yourself, Marvin Stanton."

"Who's there?" he slurred and attempted to stand, achieving it on his third try. He seemed to focus on her and gave a relieved smile. "H'roo, Pip. Shame is not what I'm feeling. Like to join? You look in need." He backed her against a tree and his face leered down. "Be a peach and give me a kiss." He puckered his lips.

She scrunched her nose and pushed at his chest. "You are crushing me. Get off, you lout."

"Don't be common and call a lawman," he slurred, narrowing his eyes. "Still think you're the belle of the ball? A debut deb with a great destination? Hate to tell you, Wurp—nobody cares. Better get used to knowing your place real soon." He pushed off the tree, freeing her.

This was a mistake, but like her father had always said, 'No good deed goes unpunished.'

"Go dry up." Thistle gave a look that radiated superiority. "Go back to the workhouse, Orphan Twist, and mind your own beeswax. Perhaps my brother can spare you a dime for the bus to Hooverville."

"Thistle, that's *enough*." Penn Kinsey stepped out of the shadows. The fury on Thistle's older brother's face did not bode well.

Faye's heart skipped a beat. She didn't expect to see him tonight. 'Too stuffy for my taste,' he'd once said of the Cricket Club.

Thistle put on a charming smile with her perfect teeth and tried to repair the damage. "We were just playing around. Right, Pip?" She shot a quick glare at Faye.

Good grief. Could this night get any worse? She just wanted to go home. Not that it belonged to her anymore. Maybe Penn would drive her.

"You were playing at her expense. Go clean yourself up and wait out front." Penn turned and scowled at Marvin.

Thistle cast a pinched frown Marvin's way as if daring him to stand up to her brother.

Penn looked back at his sister. "Now."

Marvin started to speak.

Penn punched him center face without warning.

Marvin's nose crunched, and blood dripped down the front of his white tuxedo shirt. "Aa!" he cried out, cupped his hands around his nose, and stumbled away.

Thistle glanced over her shoulder and then hurried out of the garden.

"I don't need you to fight my battles," Faye said, retreating two steps away from Penn's bloodied knuckles.

"I've always wanted to take a good sock at him," he admitted, cleaning his hand with a handkerchief. "Thistle, well, you know how she gets. If I apologized to everyone for her rude behavior, I would scarcely have time for anything else. I'll feel relieved when she goes back to New York. I've got enough on my plate right now."

She'd heard Penn was assisting the investigation and fiddled with her glove, ashamed that her father had abandoned him to deal with all this. "Have they found anything new?" she asked.

His forehead furrowed. "It's been a slow-moving fiasco. Protesters smashed the lower windows, painted obscenities on the doors, and threw garbage on the front steps. Half the time, it feels like I'm working in a war zone."

"I'm so sorry you have to go through this."

His voice grew hoarse. "When my father resigned and I took over his duties at our bank, it was one of the few times he showed confidence in me and—seemed to be proud of me." He gave a short, bitter laugh. "All that power he holds at the Federal Reserve, yet he refuses to help, even though he could fix everything with one swipe from a pen. Says it wouldn't look right. That weeding out weak banks is a necessary task. But it comes down to the fact that he always considered himself the better businessman and treated your father and me more like employees than partners. Now he's gloating. He knows damn well I can't save it without him."

Guilt by association for his troubles weighed on her. She nearly missed the quick cursory glance he gave her gown before his gaze rested on her face. He reached out and gently moved her hair off her shoulder, then glided his finger down her arm, leaving pleasant tingles in its wake. He'd never been this bold with her. Distracted, she'd missed what he was talking about.

"—and don't lose faith in your father. Let the investigation work through. I'm following a paper trail that I hope will prove his innocence." He paused in thought. "Did he, by chance, ever mention anything to you about moving money? Or did you find any keys that did not match a lock?"

She had missed something important but would look like a complete nitwit asking him to repeat what he'd said. "No, not that I recall. I went through everything that sold at the auction but haven't searched through what stays at Willow Wood for the new owners."

Penn nodded. "Just as well, best you aren't involved. I envy you leaving for greener pastures. When I'm through here, I plan to do the same." He brought her in for a hug, his touch comforting.

She breathed in the pleasant, spicy scent of his cologne. They had coyly flirted for years, knowing nothing would come of it. But things were different now. He no longer worked with her father, and she and Charles were finished. To be honest, she'd had a crush on him since her schoolgirl days. Nine years older, he always had the most attractive woman in the room on his arm. She never dreamed she had a chance with him.

But now, instinct told her that if she gazed up at his handsome face and tilted her head just a bit, he would kiss her.

Savoring the moment, she grazed her cheek over his neck, thrilled by the rough scratch from shaved whiskers. A pleasant sensation fluttered inside her stomach, changing to a heated zap as their eyes met.

He wanted her. His smoldering look said as much.

She parted her lips with an invitation. A breath caught in her throat as his hands squeezed her hips and brought her closer and closer until his warm breath wisped her face as their lips were about to meet.

"Are we leaving or not?" Thistle whined somewhere close by.

Penn blinked hard, stiffened, and pulled away. After an apologetic smile, he landed a quick, closed-mouth kiss on Faye's forehead instead.

Well, fudge. Why couldn't he be an only child?

Chapter 8

Snip. Snip. Snip.

Faye scrutinized herself in the bathroom mirror, trimming off her damp hair until it brushed the top of her shoulders. With each clump that dropped to the floor, she sensed a change within herself. Liberating. Renewing.

She ran her fingers through her cut layers, lightly ruffled her bangs, and tilted her head from side to side. The shorter style made her neck look longer, her dark eyes more prominent, mirroring those of a long, lost waif.

Which she now was. A homeless fledgling cast from the nest and expected to fly.

Tonight was the last night in her childhood home. Forever.

Most of the servants were staying on after the new family moved in. For that, she was thankful. Before they took possession of Willow Wood, Abigail took the time to visit her sister. It was the hardest goodbye, but Faye hoped another little girl would benefit from Abby's mothering, climb the towering elms and colorful maples, and come to love the Victorian gardens—rosebushes that, for her, would never again bloom.

Thickness invaded her throat as she entered her dimly lit bedroom, moving with dulled awareness of the furniture edgings.

A sudden invasion of melancholy made her sink into the nearest chair. Hands folded on her lap, she sat in repose, staring out her window at the moonlit rotunda where she'd celebrated her twentieth birthday the previous summer and had accepted Charles's romantic proposal last fall.

Despite being dressed in formal attire, he'd knelt and said, "I may not be the wealthiest or most successful man yet. Occasionally, I'm a gloomy Gus and get jealous of how other men look at you. But please know I become like that because I love you so much. Can't imagine my life without you beside me."

Liar. Turns out his mother's overbearing opinions weighed heavier than his overwhelming love.

The clock chimed the midnight hour. She stirred from her reverie, changed into nightclothes, and gathered and folded the items her trip required.

In need of her father's travel bag, she paused outside his bedroom door. As she opened it, a waft of his cologne greeted her, bringing memories that hurt her heart. The family who purchased Willow Wood wanted the furniture and everything not sold at the bank auction. Even so, the room seemed empty, the air stale. She turned on his radio for company.

After unfastening the armoire, she smoothed over his clothes, which she couldn't bring herself to sell or discard. Better used to improve someone's life. Rozario had vocalized interest. She leaned in and inhaled the scent of her father's shirt. Woodsy with a hint of peppermint—candy he'd chewed to stop smoking.

At the bottom of the armoire, his tweed and leather Zephyr case looked manageable for her trip. She traced the latch where his initials were engraved and over the angled stickers from the fine hotels he had visited: Bellevue Stratford, Waldorf-Astoria, the Ritz-Carlton, and the Fairmont Copley. For him, only the best. He'd upended her life and ruined her chances in society, yet she still missed him. Needed him. Loved him.

A radio announcer startled her with his loud, fast-talking enthusiasm, *"Welcome to the Ziegfeld Follies of the Air. Glorifying the American girl. Tonight, we bring you a special broadcast to pay tribute to the late great Florenz Ziegfeld, creator of Broadway's biggest show!"*

The song 'A Pretty Girl is Like a Melody' played. She detested the lyrics, offended by the song's portrayal of women, valuing their looks above all else. She lowered the radio's volume.

Her hearing perked to a sound downstairs. She moved to the end of the dark hallway with hesitant steps. A beam of light shone through the beveled glass of the front door. Muffled voices spoke beyond.

Faye stood still as stone.

The lock clicked, and the door cracked open. Someone with a key? Maybe Abigail coming home early?

Four shadowy figures entered.

She snapped out of her paralysis and hurried to her father's room. Quickly turning off the lamps and radio, she pushed the case underneath the bed and wiggled in behind it.

Not long after, footsteps sounded down the hall.

"Ouch! Watch where you're going, you big lug," a female voice shrilled.

"Sorry, Deloris," a deep male voice said. "I can't see with this thing."

"Switch your flasher off, Cappy. It needs to rest to work better."

Steps shuffled closer.

"Shut your yaps and start searching," another voice ordered. "We don't got all night."

Faye viewed their shoes as they entered. Spots of lights beamed on the floor. She tucked her legs in tighter as a pair of brown two-toned brogues walked by the bed. The sound of a dresser being opened and searched was followed by, "Hey, get a gander at this."

A pair of black and white oxfords speckled with something red on the tip came over. "Mitts off, Fingers. Don't take anything but what we've come for."

Why are they here? Faye repositioned to hear better.

Across the room, a pair of blue peep-toe high-heels turned and stamped the floor. "Aw, Micky. Why can't we keep a souvenir? You said yourself you followed her to the station. She ain't coming back for none of this."

Earlier, she had supervised the delivery of her Louis Vuitton trunks to the train station and had them stored. These people had been following her. This wasn't just a random robbery.

"The boss said so."

"Then hurry it up. This mausoleum gives me the heebie-jeebies," the woman whined.

Oxford moved closer to the bed. "If these numbskulls did the job like they were told, we wouldn't be here at all."

What job? The mattress springs dipped and trapped Faye's hip to the floor. A pair of overly broad loafers pointed away. She tried to release herself by moving onto her stomach but remained stuck. Her movement stirred up dust beneath the bed. A sneeze began to build. Panic-stricken, she pinched her nose with one hand and covered her mouth with the other.

"Now look what you did," Two-toned said. "You hurt his feelings. Cappy just got carried away. We tried to scare the information outta the banker, but the guy was so hammered he could barely talk."

Scare Daddy? Why?

A flashlight dropped to the floor. Oxford reached down. On his middle finger he wore a silver ring engraved with PEA. After fixing the laces of his shoe, he picked up his light. "Muzzle your excuses. We don't got time to go down memory lane. Split up. Cappy and I will search downstairs. You two keep looking up here."

The bed rose from her hip, but it was a short reprieve. Moments after the two men left, another backed the woman up to the bed and bounced her upon it.

"Ick! Dead man's bed! Dead man's bed!" the woman squealed and scrambled off.

"He wasn't snuffed in here. We strung him up downstairs."

Faye's breath hitched. A whimper escaped her hand. Her father didn't kill himself. No, these hooligans had been responsible for his death. A sob formed in her throat, but she choked it down. They'd likely kill her if they knew she was there. She took shallow breaths and made herself still by pressing her fists on the floor.

"His ghost is here," the woman said adamantly. "I feel his presence. The other dancers at the club say that I'm in tune with the spirit world. Remember when Lorraine's gran died, and she was all a fret searching for the old broad's jewelry before her sister nabbed any? I helped her find it—for a fee, of course. Let's go see if Miss Blue Nose left anything worth taking."

Faye watched their shoes depart, too scared to move. Would they be back? Should she stay put or try her luck and run for it? Neither option appealed. If they found her under here, she'd have nowhere to go, and no one would hear her cries for help.

Taking a deep breath and summoning courage she didn't feel, she rolled out and scanned the room for a better hiding spot. Her vision focused on the armoire—no, they might look there again. The long draperies—too flimsy. And the windows—too high a jump to the outside grounds. On shaky legs, she crept to the door. Glancing down at her violet dressing gown and bare feet, she bit her bottom lip and silently berated herself. But this was no time for modesty. She needed to find someplace safe. The kitchen pantry? Why would they look there unless they were hungry?

In her suite of rooms next door, it sounded as if they were rummaging through her things. She didn't care what they took if that hurried them to leave.

"You should've seen Cappy in action," the man told the woman. "He jabbed. He jabbed again. A bob and weave, then—Pow! It was like he was back in the ring again. Even if the boss hadn't ordered us to take Jim on a ride, sooner or later, I would've taken care of him myself for carrying a torch for my girl."

"Yeah, yeah. I've heard it all before. You think every man that looks twice is stuck on me. Jimmy only ogled me a bit. Ain't no harm in that."

"The boss paid him to deliver booze, not gawk at you so long he could paint your friggin' portrait."

With her back against the wall, Faye inched down the hallway and braved a peek into her room.

The woman stood near the closet, yanking clothes off hangers and tossing them onto the floor. "Will we ever live in a house like this?" She paused on a favorite gown.

Not that one.

The man sat on the vanity chair and patted his lap. "You bet, Doll. When done with this score, I'll buy whatever you want."

Clutching the dress to her bosom the woman straddled him. "Sassy and classy. I hail from Tallahassee."

As they kissed, Faye mustered her courage, crouched low, and hurried down the hallway. With the aid of the railing, she padded down the stairs. Her heart pounded against her chest as if it, too, were trying to escape. Inch by inch, she tiptoed toward the kitchen.

A blinding light shone on her. A man shouted. She yelped and sped toward the front door. His steps grew louder and closer as she fumbled with the knob. Finally yanking it open, she sprinted across the lawn. Sensing someone following, she dared not look back.

A loud bang thundered. Then, *Zing.* Something whizzed by, narrowly missing her head.

She squeaked a cry. Fueled with fresh fright, she pushed herself to go faster, breathing deeply from her diaphragm like she used to when running the school track. Another gunshot rang out.

Holy bologna!

She veered into the forest of trees and barely slowed despite the pain of being barefoot over rocks and sticks on the cold ground.

Chapter 9

Faye clenched the blanket Penn had wrapped around her. He was her first call when the police brought her home after giving the all-clear.

The detective, Edgar Elmsworth, paced her parlor floor and concluded his take on the burglary investigation. "So, they left without stealing anything and locked the front door behind them. Very courteous. Wouldn't want thieves to get in." The detective chuckled, joined by snickers from some of his men.

"My father was murdered." Faye enunciated each word, feeling an inner jolt at saying the word murder for the first time. "And the animals who killed him are out there scot-free while you interrogate me."

Penn put his arm around her and glared at the detective.

Elmsworth cleared his throat. He changed his tone to sound sympathetic. "It is plain to see you had a fright tonight, but is it possible you had a bad dream?"

Somehow, the detective managed to placate Penn and dismiss her concerns at the same time. Her hand ached to slap him. She gripped the blanket tighter. "I did not imagine it. I'm not someone who makes up stories or needs attention. I gave you their names and descriptions."

"Nicknames and types of shoes. I wear oxfords. Case closed." He and his men chuckled again.

"What good are you?" she asked. "*Detect*, for God's sake."

Elmsworth frowned. "One of my officers found an open bottle of whiskey, freshly poured. How much have you had to drink tonight, Miss Harmon?"

She rolled her eyes. "Oh, please. Here we go again. I haven't had a drop tonight."

Penn patted her shoulder. "Detective, you know that silly law has never applied to us."

Elmsworth shook his head. "Hard liquor is still illegal for every-one, Mister Kinsey, though I'm willing to look the other way as long as my department does not come across poorly in the papers."

"You don't believe me." Her eyes stung as she fought back frustrated tears. She would not cry in front of these horrible men. She tried to regain calm and looked toward her only ally in the room. "You believe me, don't you?"

"Of course I do." Penn maintained a fixed stare toward the detective. "The police will recheck the grounds and ask the neighbors what they heard or witnessed. If a gun was fired, bullet casings were most likely left behind."

"You dare tell me how to do my job?" Elmsworth scowled.

Penn tilted his head and raised his brows. "Not at all. I will leave that to the chief when we share an illegal drink at the next police fundraiser. What I tell him is entirely up to you. Will it be your callous disregard of the needs of a young woman in distress, or will I be able to say that out of deep concern for her welfare, you insisted on posting two men outside her home tonight?" Penn looked her way. "I will stay over and get you on that train tomorrow. You'll see—once you get away from here, you will start feeling like your old self."

There was no sense in discussing this further. They would only continue to treat her like a child. Beyond frustrated and tired, she let Penn walk her to her room. She knew it was inappropriate but was beyond caring about social mores. She moved her father's case from her bed.

"Marshall's?" Penn asked.

She nodded.

"I'm going to miss our travels." His hands opened and closed with a crack from his knuckles. "My *god*—if I could get my hands on the men who did this." His eyes sparked with anger. "You have my word that I will stay on the police until his killers are caught and justice is served." He helped her to bed and tucked the blanket.

"I know you will. I only wish I could stay and help. I'm the only one who heard their voices."

Penn sighed. "If you stayed, you'd fill me with worry every minute of every day. I need to know you are somewhere safe."

"I'm sorry to be such a burden. I didn't know who else to call."

He leaned down, kissed her forehead, and sat on the edge of her bed. A wavy strand of dark hair fell over his forehead. His amber-brown eyes lingered on her face. "No matter how far, I will always come when you need me." His finger traced her bottom lip.

The simple act made her breath stop and her toes curl. She was afraid to say anything and break the spell. After such a terrifying evening, she wanted to be held, needed to be kissed, and desperately longed for his touch to make her feel something other than misery. She parted her lips and held his stare.

His gaze moved from her eyes toward her mouth, then back again, his look questioning. Slowly, he lowered his mouth to hers. Soft as a whisper, he kissed her lips, then his mouth glided across her cheek to the sensitive spot behind her ear. It tickled, and his warm breath sent delightful shivers down her spine. His lips returned to hers, and he deepened the kiss.

Unlike Charles, his mouth moved with skill. He was a man, not a boy. Like a dance, she followed his lead, hoping she was doing it right. Feeling bolder, she pressed closer.

He groaned and drew back, holding her at arm's length. "I need to ask you something personal." His hands rubbed over her skin, freckling goosebumps down her arms.

She squeezed her eyes shut and reveled in his touch. The friction from his palms and roaming fingers on her skin sent flutters from her stomach to her breasts. Why did he want to talk when he should be kissing her? She pouted and peered up at him.

His intense stare moved down her cleavage, then back to her face. "Did you and Charles ever make love?"

Her face heated. Why was he ruining the moment? What did her relationship with Charles have to do with him? With now? "No, of course not. We were waiting until marriage."

He nodded to himself like he'd known what her answer would be. He stood and took a few steps away, his back toward her.

She covered herself with her robe and brought up her knees. Her thoughts scrambled to understand. "Why does it matter—I mean, to you? What difference does it make whether I gave myself to Charles or Gary Cooper or one of the Marx Brothers?" Why did everyone think they knew what was best for her? Instead of helping her feel better, he'd made her feel worse.

Penn turned and gave her a pained look. "I'm sorry. I want to be with you, but I don't bed virgins. You'll understand when you are older. When you meet a marrying man."

She widened her eyes and then quickly looked away. It didn't occur to her that he would want to do *that*. She would look like an unsophisticated fool if she admitted to being so naïve. Instead, she nonchalantly shrugged and attempted to sound flippant. "A marrying man like Charles? That worked out well."

"No. Not like that prim-line dandy. I'm glad you didn't marry that foolish boy." He leaned down and kissed her forehead with a light peck. "Goodnight, sweet temptress."

The door closed softly behind him.

Faye stared up at the moonlit ceiling and hugged her pillow. She had never felt this way after kissing Charles. Her mind replayed the moment and raced with questions of what it all meant, and she realized she experienced something she had not felt before. Need.

Would anyone love her again? Or would time run out and label her an old maid?

She didn't have those answers, but there was one thing she knew absolutely and without a doubt. After a few days' visit with her aunt to appease everyone, she was coming right back. She'd sneak into the city, and together with Jane's help, they'd seek out her father's killers.

Chapter 10

The train chugged West.

When Faye thought of Kansas, she had envisioned vast stretches of verdant farmland giving way to wind-blown wheat. But this landscape seemed to have been, well, erased. Instead of a heartland of dancing golden kernels, the scenery was a dull palette of browns, sparse trees, and half-buried fences tangled with tumbleweed. It was beyond boring—it was frightening—a land without hope.

She voiced her thoughts to her fellow travelers seated across. "Who would willingly choose to live here?"

The passenger train's whistle drowned out their replies, and a sudden jerk nearly toppled them from their seats. The locomotive slowed alongside a depot. A billowing cloud of steam dissipated.

Country folk wearing worn overalls and plain cotton dresses disembarked as new arrivals clambered in.

Poor dears. She hoped these clothes weren't their Sunday best. Servants back home wouldn't deem them worthy of the rag bin. But there was a hint of sadness in their expressions she connected with.

"Is it time yet?" Millie asked for what felt like the hundredth time.

Faye shifted her focus back to the two elderly women.

Millie and Winnifred sat dressed for the evening meal. The ladies had shared her sleeping compartment since she'd boarded in Philadelphia.

The sisters' appearances and personalities were of a contrary nature.

Winnifred was serious, frugal, and plain. Her straight-backed posture would put a schoolmistress to shame. The only adornment she displayed was a thin gold chain attached to her round nose-pinch spectacles. She positioned them in place to look at her pocket watch. "Almost," she answered with patience. "I will tell you when."

Draped in gaudy costume jewelry, Millie pinched her lips and fidgeted in her vibrant Edwardian frock. Above her wavy white hair perched a flamboyant red hat. She splashed perfume on her neck and wrists, the floral scent overwhelming the enclosed space.

"Will you be joining us in the dining car, Faye?" Winnifred glanced up from her embroidery, not missing a stitch in her task.

Faye had kept to herself throughout the trip to avoid answering personal questions. It felt freeing that no one knew of her family or her circumstances. "Thank you, but I had a large lunch." She stifled a yawn and reclined on the seat bunk. Her betraying mind ventured back to Penn's kiss and remembrance of home.

Cigarette smoke filled the lounge car, making it impossible to enjoy her evening tea. Faye decided to head back to her compartment.

The lights in the corridor buzzed and flickered. As she turned a corner in the hallway, a large figure departed her room.

A bedding attendant, she figured, until the sporadic flashes of light illuminated something grasped in the person's hand. Her travel case.

"You, there. Stop!"

The lights went out completely.

She grabbed the handrail for support. Why would someone steal from her on a train? Where would they go?

The lights popped back on as the man entered an enclosed walkway between the train cars. The door slammed shut behind him.

Faye strode forward, though the train's motion slowed her efforts, rocking her from side to side. She pressed on, reached the door, and swung it open.

A hand forcefully clamped over her mouth as another brutally twisted her arm behind her back. The unnatural position made her head dizzy and her legs weak. She let out a muffled scream.

Her assailant tightened his grip.

A sharp pain burrowed into her shoulder as panic coursed through her veins. Gathering all her strength, she struggled but only managed a half-turn of freedom.

He gripped her neck and lifted her to the toe points of her high-heeled shoes.

She frantically tried to pry away his fingers that squeezed the sides of her throat.

The door light cast a weak red glow on his face. Steely eyes locked on her own. In an instant, she recognized his menacing features under the black rim. A face bearing a jagged scar that stretched from cheek to chin. The fedora hat man.

She twisted and tore at his hand.

Air. She needed air.

In desperation, she felt for something she could use as a weapon. Her fingers brushed over a handle behind her, and she yanked up the lever with all her might. The outer door slid open and stuck part way, rushing wind through, fanning her hair forward over her face. Mindlessly, she clawed in his direction. Her fingers hit the mark and jabbed something soft.

He growled, "*Sonofabitch.*"

When he released his grip, she dropped to the floor and gulped as much sweet oxygen as her lungs would allow. Her vision focused on his shoes. Black and white oxfords speckled red on the tip. He found her. Her heart thrummed in her chest, but she forced herself to peer up at him.

The man cupped his hand over his eye, the fury on his face palpable. He snarled and moved slowly toward her.

Faye scooted back. The wind whipped her blouse when she neared the edge. The blur of train tracks whizzed by below. She managed to stand but inched back a bit too far. Flailing her arms to regain her balance, she shouted, "Help me!"

The man's grin reflected satisfaction and desire for revenge at the sight of easy prey. He lifted his arm to use her own travel case against her.

Oh, dear God! I'm going to die! "Please. No!"

She made a desperate lunge for her case to steady herself. As she grasped the handle, the man lost his grip.

She stumbled back.

There was no longer a floor beneath her feet. The wind caught her body in free fall.

Chapter 11

RUDY
Southwest Kansas

The train clanked by on the rails. Rudy guided the hobo kids to where it slowed when it rounded a bend. Chaska jumped and wrapped his arm around a rung on the ladder between the railcars. Rudy ran alongside Chaska's sister, carrying the kids' bindle over his arm. If his new friends missed this train, it might be days until another came through. He wanted to help them get on their way, but there was only so much he could do.

Two men and a woman seated on top of the tail end of the train hollered encouragement. Just as Rudy readied himself to help the little girl up, one of the men on the roof swung a baseball bat down, barely missing Chaska's head.

Chaska yelled, "What'd you do that for?"

"Relax, kid." The man grinned. "Just practicing my swing."

"Well, knock it off."

The man laughed. "I'm trying to." He swung down again.

Chaska ducked and lost his footing. He cursed as he struggled to connect his worn boot with the ladder. His dog barked frantically, half leaping toward the train, half running alongside. The man looked ready to swing again. Chaska leaped off, hit the ground hard, and rolled.

Rudy came to a halt and dropped their bundled possessions. "You okay?" He clasped his newsboy cap as a strong gust of wind whipped around the back of the train.

The group on the roof laughed and waved.

Chaska stood and dusted off his overalls. "What a louse. Coulda killed me. That's how Ol' Shoestring Sam met his end—bounced off the bumper, hit the grit, and got made part of the tracks."

"Golly." Rudy glared at the train as it sped away.

Chaska spat away from the wind. "Wasn't goin' to work, anyway. There wasn't anywhere for S'unka to jump onto."

The boy's pet looked more like a wild wolf than a domesticated dog.

Chaska patted its head. "We need to flip a cargo rattler. Somethin' slower with wide doors. How often they come through?"

Rudy wasn't sure when the freight trains came along. "They're not set on time like the people ones."

The little girl, Niya, broke into a coughing fit. She didn't look good either. Dark circles outlined her eyes, an irritated nose had a crusted tip, and her black hair lay matted in a tangled mess at the back of her head. The paleness of her lean face differed from her brother's golden skin.

Rudy figured her a couple of years younger than himself, five or six, but it was hard to tell. Girls were usually weaker and smaller than him and his friends. Except for Gabby Holderman—who looked like a boy, dressed like a boy, and could run like the wind. She'd wanted to kiss him once. He shuddered at the memory.

Chaska appeared to be about the same age as Rudy, but his chopped hair stood up on top and gave him the added edge of an extra inch or two.

Chaska kicked at the dirt. The dry Kansas wind blew it back on him. "You know anywhere we can bed down for the night?"

The dusk sky was tainted red, the wind gusting strong. Rudy considered taking them home with him, breaking his pa's biggest rule—no strays.

His dad kept to himself and expected the courtesy of others to do the same. But Rudy wasn't like his pa. He longed for the company of other people as much as his dad strove to avoid them. It got to be lonely on the farm, mostly since the schoolhouse closed. He thought about taking them there, but it was locked tight until a new teacher could be found. Miss Middleton got married and said she couldn't be their teacher no more. He didn't understand why she couldn't do both. Grownups didn't make much sense most of the time.

"I'll sneak you into our barn, but you got to keep quiet. My pa will be madder than a wet hornet if he finds you there."

The mile walk back to the farm was filled with Rudy's questions about their life on the road. Night descended and tilted the wind. No lamps shown in the windows of the farmhouse. Once inside the barn, Rudy helped the boy to fluff up a bed of hay.

"That'll do," Chaska said, brushing straw off the front of his overalls.

His dog stared steadily at Rudy, displayed its teeth, wrinkled its muzzle, and rumbled a low growl.

Rudy eyed it back, retreating a few steps for good measure. "He won't bark, will he?"

Niya ruffled its thick gray and white fur. The dog immediately calmed and snuggled by her side.

Chaska rested on his back with his hands behind his neck. "Don't worry. We'll be long gone by the peep of dawn. No one'll ever know we were here."

Two of the draft mules poked their heads from the stalls. Bruno's eyes were tired-looking liquid pools. His lips and ears twitched. Next to him, the younger Fergus wheezed then brayed, ending with a loud *ee*-ah-aw and a grunt. Rudy scooped feed and offered it with the flat of his hand. He petted the mule's thin mane to calm it.

"Ol' hardtail got a good set of lungs," Chaska said.

Rudy switched to Bruno and knuckle massaged the white patch between its eyes. "Mules don't like dogs. That's why I ain't allowed one."

Chaska alerted the dog with hand signals and commanded, "S'unka, *tokhel iyaya*."

The animal took its time to slink out the open barn door into the night.

Chaska smiled. "He's a good mutt. We met him a while back on the Okie prairie. We'd made it to the front stoop of an abandoned place when S'unka greeted us. A real bone crusher, by the look of him, showin' all teeth and drooling buckets. I thought we were done for. Near stopped my heart when Niya went up and petted him like a newly weaned pup. He's been with us ever since and gotten us out of trouble more than a time or two."

"Is that where yer tribe is? Oklahoma?"

"Naw, we lived way up in the Dakotas. A miserable place. Summer fleeted by quick as a firefly's twinkle and winter lasted forever. The land up there is barely fit for animals, let alone people."

Rudy shivered. "I don't like being outside when it's cold. Did you live in a tipi? I read about 'em in my Buffalo Bill books."

Chaska shook his head. "It was a small shack built near land given by men who had no right to give it. Mother Earth has no master." The boy's gaze flicked upward. "Any more than the *Wakan Tanka* can be kept from any creature or livin' thing." He spread his arms out and then brought them together over his chest. "The Great Spirit brings us together and flows through all things—the critters on the Great Plains, fishy things under water's flow, the wise trees that friend the birds. We are all one." Chaska nodded toward Rudy. "Just like you are my brother as she is my sister. We are all responsible for one another."

Rudy scratched his temple. The boy talked a bit strange, but what he said made sense. And he had always wanted a brother.

Niya sat curled in a deep coughing fit, pressing her chest. Her small hand moved down her stomach as her watery gaze drifted over Rudy.

"Haven't had much luck with my snares," Chaska said. "For two days, we've eaten nothin' but the dirt the wind feeds us."

Rudy buttoned up his coat and put on his newsboy cap. He'd purchased the hat with his egg money to remind his dad of his promise to allow him his first paper route. He needed a bicycle to make deliveries, but his dad said money was tight. Rudy felt bad for even asking. His new friends went without what he took for granted every day. "We've got lots of food. I'll be right back."

He stepped into the darkness and struggled to push forward against the pummel of grit. The wind shrieked in his ears, and far above, the windmill's blades whirled and clattered in the blowing tempest.

Rudy unlatched the icebox on the back porch and withdrew a hunk of cheese and a gallon tin of milk. A stronger gust of wind blew as he opened the kitchen door, banging it against the frame. He closed it and stood stock still in the dark, listening. When nothing stirred, he skirted the kitchen table, patted the counter, and placed his goods so he could light a kerosene lamp. Before he could strike a match, a faint glow illuminated behind him.

"What are you doing, boy?"

Rudy flinched and turned. His dad stood over him with reddened eyes, an unshaven face, and tousled dark hair. He looked half asleep.

"I'm hungry, Pa. You want some?"

His dad lifted a brow and stared long. "A bear could last the winter with what you ate all day." He slapped the back of his hand on Rudy's forehead and felt both his cheeks. "What's wrong? Your face is red."

Rudy ducked away. "I feel fine." He took a large bite of cheese for show.

"I should've named you Esau. You'd give up your birthright in a heartbeat for a bowl of stew."

"If I had a little brother, he could have whatever he wants."

Pa cleared his throat. "Don't be holding your breath on that wish. Get to bed. No dawdling with your chores come morn." His dad climbed the stairs.

Rudy lit a lamp. He poured the milk into a cup, sliced some bread, and wrapped the rest of the food inside a quilt from the sitting room. He quietly headed back to the barn. "Sorry. My pa woke." He handed the cup and the bundle to Chaska. "Hide everything under the hay before you leave."

"I will." After one quick gulp, Chaska offered Niya the milk.

Rudy thought he saw tears in the boy's eyes. "Welcome. I better git. Guess this'll be goodbye if you catch that next train."

"We don't say goodbye." Chaska said something in his language as he chewed his sandwich. "It means I'll see you again someday."

"Toke shaw awkay..." Rudy sounded out.

The small church in town was crammed tight. With no seats to be had, Rudy stood by his dad behind the back pews with several other men.

"Elijah the Tishbite," the preacher at the pulpit shouted, "said unto Ahab, as the Lord God of Israel lives, before whom I stand, there shall not be dew nor rain these years, but according to my word. Rain through prayer instead of pay. Not wasting your hard-earned money on the charlatans invading our town with deceit and charms, claiming only they can bring the rain."

Bored with the preacher's sermon, Rudy yawned. His gaze wandered.

A bench on the left held the entire Pritchard family; the youngest twins held on their parent's laps. The girls, all six of them, matched in flour-sack dresses. In other rows, he noticed a few women sneaking glances behind. He followed their line of vision up to his dad.

Goo-goo eyes. *Yuck*. His dad didn't seem to notice.

On a front pew sat Rudy's best friend, Matthew Martin, and Matt's mother. They were hard to miss with their orange-red hair and splatters of freckles. He wished his dad would marry Matt's widowed mother so he and Matt could be brothers, but his father soon ended that notion. Pa said about women, "They are cunning, deceptive, useless creatures created by God to torment man." After that, Rudy knew he would always be an only child.

When the service ended, his dad shepherded him out the door. Disappointed not to spend time with Matt, Rudy glanced behind and understood the reason for his father's rushed exit.

Mrs. Johnson and her daughter were following. "*Yoo-hoo*, Mister Boyd. *Yoo-hoo*."

"Get on up," Pa ordered through his teeth and hurried to untie the mules.

Rudy climbed up the box wagon just as the women arrived. He was amazed Mrs. Johnson could move so fast at her age. He figured she had to be over forty.

"Mister Boyd," Mrs. Johnson said as she gasped for breath and attempted a pleasant smile. "You remember my daughter, Johanna, do you not?"

Johanna smiled, displaying a large gap in her front teeth. A light breeze blew at thin blonde hair clamped with fancy barrettes.

"Yes, ma'am." Pa removed his hat and held it to his chest.

Mrs. Johnson nudged her daughter forward. "Johanna would like you and your son to join us for our Sunday meal. She is an excellent cook, among her many talents. We are having baked ham and shucky beans with pie for dessert." She turned toward Rudy. "Does that appeal to your liking, young man?"

"That sounds swell. I love pie." Rudy pasted a big smile on his face, pie being his favorite food.

His dad stink-eyed him.

Rudy responded with a playful smirk.

"We thank you, but we—have much to do." Pa pulled himself up on the bench and plopped his hat back on.

"On the Sabbath?" Mrs. Johnson fanned her face as though she'd faint.

"No rest for farmers." His dad tipped his hat. "Enjoy your day."

Automobiles and wagons kicked up dust on Main Street while they rode through town. Halfway through, a crowd surrounded a traveling showman's yellow Model A truck.

Pa yelled, "Whoa!" to the mules, and the wagon abruptly stopped.

A group of girls waved the dust from their faces as they cut in front. Rudy perked up at the merry tune coming from the Victrola.

A top-hatted salesman stood on a crate. The sign next to him proclaimed cures for many ills: ASTHMA CIGARETTES, HURT TOOTH DROPS, HAIR TONICS FOR BALDNESS, AND THE FAMOUS PHARMACY BOB COUGH ELIXIR.

"For a small price, I will *blast* rain from the sky," the salesman hollered as he held up a block in one hand and a stick of dynamite in the other. "Salt the clouds for your crops, so they wither no more."

"Pa?" Rudy poked his dad's arm. "How does blowing up a salt lick make it rain?"

His dad clicked his tongue, and they were on their way again. "Don't know, but folks are willing to try just about anything now." He looked up at the sky. "We need the rain—yesterday."

Rudy bowed his head and folded his hands in prayer like the preacher said to do. These dry years were taking their toll on farms, his dad, and his favorite fishing hole.

Chapter 12

Faye cracked an eye, assaulted by the light. A sudden pain caused her to suck in a hard breath. Patches on her skin itched with sharp, heat-filled stings. A noise turned her head, earning her a cramp in her neck. She clenched her jaw and squeezed her eyes shut until it eased.

The train. That man. The memory and a rough breeze chilled her to the bone. He'd wanted to kill her. Why? What was he after that was so important for him that he'd follow her partway across the country?

The hem of her travel garment moved near her knee. She opened her eyes and focused on the direction. A creature with an ugly feather-less red head tugged at her skirt with its pale, hooked beak.

Faye uttered a guttural sound that built into a full-blown scream. She side-swooped her leg at the bird. "Get away! Shoo! Wretched thing."

The bird stared at her with dark, beady eyes, hopped backward, and flapped its broad wings. It took flight with a raspy hiss and stirred up a dust cloud. Faye covered her face and chest-coughed into a sitting position.

When the dirt settled, she took stock of the sources of her pain. A nasty gash on her forearm still bled. Bruises were everywhere like she'd gone three rounds with Jack Dempsey. Even her hair hurt. A tingling sensation underneath her skirt demanded attention. She pulled up the fabric and found ants scurrying down her legs. Letting out another cry, she slapped her skin and then scratched through her hair. "Oo—get off, get off, get off."

Running her hands over her thighs, she searched for stragglers. Tiny red dots on her skin itched where they had bitten her.

The 'Ant and the Grasshopper' fable came to mind.

"He should've eaten you," she muttered.

Shivering, she took a deep breath and smelled something rank. First sniffing at her blouse, she then glanced at where the bird had been. Fur-encrusted entrails and a decapitated head of something long dead lay by her leg. She gagged and scooted backward, managing to stand partway, sending white-hot pain up her left leg.

"Hell's bells in church!" She shifted all her weight to her other leg and looked down.

Her travel clothes hadn't fared any better than her body. The puffed sleeves of her blouse were deflated and torn, a tear in her skirt went from ankle to thigh, and she couldn't begin to guess where her shoes had gone.

She hopped on one leg up a mound to the railroad tracks. Her arms held out for balance, she circled. For as far as her vision could reach, a sea of yellow-brown and orange-tipped grass bent and flowed with the rushing wind. The prairie seemed to go on forever.

Her pulse raced. "Hello?"

Nothing answered but the rustling grass, chirping bugs, and the trill of birds in the distance.

"Hello," she called out with a shrill tone. "Is anybody there?" Where were all the houses? People? "Help!" she shouted at the top of her lungs and then stopped.

Crickets.

"No, no, no. This isn't happening." Her breaths burst in and out, making her lightheaded and woozy.

What a stupid, ridiculous predicament. Surely, a town was just around the bend.

"Get a grip. Another train will come. They have schedules. Predictability. Order." Even in the wilderness.

The upside-down suitcase lay a few yards away. Teeth clenched, she tottered to it, turned it upright, and flicked the latch. She pulled out her coat and slipped it on, its warmth a consoling hug. Adjusting the fur collar, she squinted up at the light blue sky and wispy clouds. Large birds circled overhead. A shiver traveled her spine. She'd hated big birds ever since a gaggle of geese had attacked her once when she'd visited a friend's equestrian farm. She'd never forget. Never forgive.

No roads in sight, it seemed best to stay close to the tracks until help arrived or she reached civilization.

She spotted her shoe and rescued it from a clump of dry grass. The heel had broken off. The toe of her other shoe lay buried in loose dirt. After sliding them on, she grabbed the case, hobbled the mound again, and limped westward.

Faye itched all over and felt like she'd run a one-legged marathon. *Just a little farther.*

"Humanity! Humanity!"

Crickets.

High in the sky, the golden blob bathed a meadow in sunlight. How was it possible to have walked this far without passing a single house or person?

She hated Kansas. Or Colorado. She hated both states, just to be sure. "Does *anyone* live in this godforsaken place?"

Crickets.

She left the tracks, climbed a big rock, and took a jar of lotion from her case. After pulling off her shoe, she grimaced as she gently touched bubbled blisters where it had rubbed her skin. Her legs itched something fierce. She scratched them and then slathered each limb with lubricant. A gurgling in her stomach switched to a growl.

She'd missed her morning tea and eggs. Oh, what she would give to smell Abigail's homemade bread or oatmeal cookies baking. To gulp down a simple glass of cool water. She envisioned an oasis of a clear blue pond and smacked her cracked lips, her mouth dry as cotton.

What was Jane was doing right now? Penn? Probably having lunch. She was glad nobody back home could see her now—filthy and dressed in raggedy clothes.

A rustle of grass sounded nearby. A large brown dog with pointy ears moved swiftly into the clearing. It caught and attacked a small creature that squeaked a horrible, high-pitched death cry. Other skinny, tan-colored dogs joined it, making strange yipping noises.

They look mean and scrappy, unlike a man's best friend or a woman's. She quietly moved to the flat top of the boulder.

The large alpha male raised its head and stared her way. The dog moved furtively toward the rock with the rodent still in its mouth.

"Good, doggy." Faye held up her hand. "Stay where you are."

It kept coming with a menacing glare and growl.

Her skin grew clammy and broke into a cold sweat. Jane had told her once that dogs could smell fear, but these weren't like her friend's Pomeranians. Their fur was matted, and the big one seemed to have acquired some sort of skin disease.

She made her voice sound calm yet assertive and moved her hand in short motions. "Go home now—shoo."

The dog made it to the boulder's base and stepped up.

Her muscles tensed. She would never be able to outrun it, not like this. She gripped the long stick she'd been using as a cane and stabbed in its direction. "I'm warning you. Not a step more."

The odds of fighting against all of them with such a primitive weapon were not good.

Out of the corner of her eye, she noticed an even bigger animal steal through the grass.

Could things get any worse? This one looked like a wolf.

Ears flat, it lunged at Alpha. They wrestled on the ground with fierce growls and snapping jaws, grabbing each other's fur. The gray and white thick-furred animal quickly won the fight, dominating with its massive muscular build and swiftness. The brown alpha yelped a surrendering howl while pinned. The wolf-like animal bit its neck. Low to the ground, the other dogs slunk away with their tails between their legs. Bloodied and wounded, the alpha broke loose and followed its pack.

Faye froze in place and held her breath as the gray and white wolf moved toward the boulder. Beautiful but deadly, it stared up at her with amber-colored eyes.

She crouched low to make herself as small as possible and lowered her head submissively.

It barked, not angry, but more like it was trying to tell her something.

She peeked over at it. "I don't speak canine. Please don't hurt me."

It barked again, swished its tail, and snatched up the furry rodent. After a final look back, it turned and trotted away.

Her legs rubbery; she plopped down on the boulder, wrapped her arms around them, and rocked in place. Too dehydrated for tears, a dry sob escaped from somewhere deep.

Faye stumbled from railroad tie to railroad tie, aided by her long stick.

At first, all she saw were endless mounds of dirt laden with sagebrush. But then, through the orange haze created by the setting sun, she spotted something block-shaped off to her right. Was it just another mirage? More false hope? She had been fooled before, had gone to what she thought was there, only to discover it was a trick of the eye.

This time, it didn't blink away.

Leaving the tracks, determination pressed her forward, and she struggled toward what grew into a small house. Next to it, she noticed a tiny grave marked only by a pitiful cross made from sticks twined with knotted yarn. A beloved family pet, most likely. Hopefully better behaved than the dogs in the meadow.

Seeing the house up close, she cursed under her breath.

The shack's roof had partially caved, and the entrance was missing its door. A loose board slapped against the porch with a constant bang.

Her heart sank. No help here. It had been abandoned long ago.

She cautiously climbed the rickety steps and entered. A stiff breeze stirred up clouds of dust inside, and shreds of faded curtains flapped in the missing windows. Dish shards and piles of sandy soot covered the rotted table. A scratching noise came from a potbelly stove. Something was nesting; mice came to mind. She shivered, eyes fixed on the shadows creeping up the walls. It would be dark soon.

Exhausted, her hand dropped the case. She would spend a night alone for the first time in her life. No one was coming to the rescue.

No one would offer a clean, warm place to lay her head. The banging on the porch grew more insistent. Whispers filtered in from the cracks in the walls.

The wind carried a howl from something in the distance. Panic gripped her and plunged her into despair. Was it safe here? Anywhere?

She searched for a weapon and something to sleep on. An abandoned wash basket appeared to contain baby items. She carefully lifted out a knit baby bonnet with embroidered pink flowers and green leaves. Though dulled by the elements or age, the detail was exquisite, made with loving hands. A mouse-chewed knit gown and tiny booties had the same design. Scattered at the basket's bottom lay corroded diaper pins, a tiny rusted spoon, the remnants of a patched bib, and a crude attempt at first shoes.

She worked the edges of a sealed metal container, pried it apart, and unfolded a beautiful, cross-stitched cloth that read: MY DAUGHTER PETAL BLOOMED MY WORLD.

Why would they leave such treasures behind?

Dread filled her empty stomach.

The grave. A baby. Dear God.

Losing her parents was painful. She couldn't imagine the overwhelming grief that would follow losing one's child. The tomb her own parents were buried in was practically a shrine. But this little one would have no etched name, loving family remembrance, or farewell quote to adorn her grave. She'd remain forever alone in this godforsaken, barren place.

It was too terrible to ponder. Briskly rubbing her arms to calm herself, she tried to stop shaking.

The shadows on the wall shifted and transformed into a silhouetted youth with curly hair. A carefree titter of laughter followed. Images of the girl Petal might have been appeared: helping her mother in the kitchen, playing with her favorite doll, and being held on her father's lap while he read to her. Memories stolen. The promise of a happy life and the warmth of love replaced by the reality of cold, dark emptiness. Faye shuddered.

Outside, the wind grew stronger. The roof creaked, and the walls groaned in protest.

It sounded like it could collapse at any moment. She couldn't stay here. It wasn't safe.

She folded the cloth with care and slipped it into her coat pocket. "I must go, Petal. I'm so sorry. I truly am." She couldn't fathom how the baby's parents must have felt about leaving her behind. If she lived through this and were permitted to have a girl someday, she would name her Rose Petal and lavish her with love. "You and my mother will be honored and remembered," she whispered.

A tear trickled down her cheek as she lifted her suitcase and walking stick.

She left the shack with a sense she would somehow be missed.

A rhythmic sound broke the silence and grew louder.

Her breath caught in her throat as she circled, trying to figure out what it was and where it was coming from.

An extended hoot hoot sounded in the distance.

A train!

Ignoring the pain it caused, she took off running. Each step punctuated her hurt leg with intense agony, but hope blossomed. She could see the train now; its bright headlamp a beacon, an emerging sun cutting through the encroaching night's gloom as it raced closer.

She jammed the stick into the ground like a third leg, grinding her teeth from the excruciating torture.

The train's whistle blared, and the clatter of metal against metal rumbled with each beat of her heart.

It was moving so fast. Too far away. She threw the stick and attempted a sprint, full pressure on both legs. If she could just get someone's attention.

But blinding pain shot through her hip, and a crushing cramp made her leg give out. She lost her grip on the suitcase and cried out as she toppled toward the ground.

"Please, no," she begged.

She bit her lip and rolled over, staring up at the dark array of nothingness. The train passed and sped away. Hopelessness overwhelmed her.

This is how I die.

Alone in the wilderness, picked apart by scavenging birds, without even a stick to mark her grave. No one would know what became of her. At some point, no one would care.

Chapter 13

Something panted warm breath on Faye's neck. She twitched her eyes right and left, the view black as pitch. Whatever it was loomed above, breathing hard, and then a furry weight pressed against her chest.

Holding her breath, she concentrated on repositioning her leg, foot, or even a single toe but remained stuck in place, paralyzed both in body and fear. The heavy breathing under her chin changed to whispers, then voices. Lighter figures gradually took form in the darkness. Walls rose. The scent of tea and scones with berried jam teased her nose. She was back in her grandmother's dining room those many years before.

"Pip, go play with your cousins and let the grown-ups talk," Momma's voice urged.

"But Mom, they're so much younger than me. Please, Grandmama. I'll be quiet."

Her grandmother took shape at the head of the long table. The dining room brightened.

Daddy stood and paced the room while sipping amber liquid from a glass. He seemed upset.

"Rose, let her be," Grandmama ordered, "and pay attention to the business at hand. Your father's will could not be clearer if written on glass. Your brother George will manage the mines and tenant farmers in Scotland, Edward will continue managing the stores here in London, and your husband will resume your father's position on the board. Over by the Holland House, they are building lovely new homes. We will have a view tomorrow on our way back from tea at Gwyneth's Gardens."

Momma gripped the edge of the table. "I have a lovely home. In Haverford."

"Your father's only stipulation states that you move your family to London. If not, you and your husband receive nothing."

Daddy stopped pacing, his stance firm. "Her husband is standing right here, Lady Fitton. Address me directly, please."

Grandmama narrowed her eyes and thinly smiled. "Very well, Marshall. Share with us how America is faring. Was it forty-five or forty-six who jumped to their deaths after the market plummeted? How much do you owe your creditors? Word is your business partner, Edmond Kinsey, left your sinking Titanic for greater seas. You see, I have little birds in Philadelphia who peep the goings-on, even throughout the Main Line."

"Stop." Momma worried her hands. "Please, don't argue."

Daddy downed the rest of his drink and slid the empty glass on the table. "I'm more than capable of providing for my family. I came here out of respect for my wife, but we are leaving tomorrow morning. If I must spend one more day here, better guard the roof, Lady Fitton. It may be forty-seven who jump."

Faye cracked an eye. Morning sunlight filtered in as something wet and coarse brushed up her cheek.

A wolf loomed over.

A slight noise escaped her throat as her pulse sped up. Dark spots bounced in her vision.

Its coarse tongue licked up her cheek again.

The tendons on her neck tightened, making it difficult to swallow. This was the same wolf who'd attacked the alpha yesterday. An image of its sharp teeth locking around her throat and crushing her air pipe took form. Too scared to scream, she balled her fist and readied herself for the attack to come. No human being deserves to die this way.

Its foul-smelling drool splattered her cheek.

Without thinking, she reached to wipe it off.

The wolf stuck its nose under her wrist and licked her hand.

Friendly? With caution, she petted over its head.

Movement caught her eye.

A few feet away, a little girl sat on the ground, legs crisscrossed. She wore dirt-stained trousers and a parka that looked three sizes too big.

Her black hair badly needed brushing. Big ebony eyes blinked against the sun. A serious mouth gave no hint of her thoughts or intentions.

Beyond the girl, an older boy dressed in a ragged coat and worn overalls rummaged through her suitcase. He held up one of her undergarments and gave it a quizzical look.

She eased up on an elbow, wiped her cheek, and then rolled her head from side to side. Just seeing people, even small ones, lightened her heart. But why was he going through her things instead of offering help? An indignant gasp escaped as understanding found her. She was being robbed—again.

"Hey, you." Her voice came out as a froggy croak. The boy did not respond, so she tried harder. "Hey, *you* there."

He jerked up and squinted her way.

Faye coughed from her efforts. Her mouth was dry as dust, her throat scratchy as a cactus. "There's nothing in there worth stealing."

The boy frowned. "We thought you were dead. Can't steal from a stiff 'cause a stiff don't need nothin'."

She patted the wolfdog's head. "Well, this beast figured out I wasn't dead. Guess that makes it more observant than you."

The boy's lips drew into a smirk. "Maybe he is, maybe he ain't. But one thing I'm sure of"—he chuckled—"S'unka never fell off a movin' train."

Struggling to stand, she tested her left leg. Nope. Still hurt. She steadied herself on her right and found balance. "How did you know I came from a train?"

The boy's gaze gave her another perusal. "Anyone smarter than a farm-raised tom turkey could figure that out. I seen mangy, disease-ridden foxes in better shape than you."

Rude. Self-conscious, Faye reached up to her hair. If she looked as bad as she felt, she must be a fright, but it was so unchivalrous for him to point that out. She wanted to school him on his behavior, but words hurt her throat. She ran her tongue over her dry, cracked lips. "Do you, by chance, have any water to share?"

The boy dropped a bundled blanket slung on his shoulder to the ground and dug through his belongings, pulling out an old canteen. He hesitated before handing it to her.

Despite the water's notes of rust and grit, the effect was heavenly. She held the second sip in her mouth so her gums could absorb it and restrained herself from gulping the rest. She mourned the loss of the canteen as she passed it back.

The boy squatted beside the little girl, and they both stared up at her as if she were a freak circus attraction.

"Where are we?" She swept her arm and immediately regretted the broad movement.

"Kansas."

Pressing her fingers to her temple, she rubbed small circles. Was she ever to be rid of this hellish state? "How close am I to a town?"

The boy pointed in a direction. "Union Junction," he said. "About a day's walk from here."

She groaned. Walking had become her least favorite thing. "Hmm. Would your parents be so kind as to let me use their telephone? I need to report a crime and have someone come get me."

The boy and little girl exchanged a look.

Faye noticed the interaction. "No phone?"

"What's a phone?" the boy asked.

"Oh my." She carved her hand through her hair and held it back. "Could you take me to where you live then?"

"You're lookin' at it. Here." He pointed in one direction and then another. "There. Everywhere."

Her breath caught in her throat. She had barely made it through the night. She could not imagine anyone, let alone children, living out here alone. Where did they sleep? What did they eat? How did they keep dry in a storm or warm on a cold night? They needed to be in school. "You should have an adult with you. What do you say we go to Union Junction together?"

"Who's the adult?"

"Me, of course."

The boy studied her. "You got a man? Kids?"

"No."

"You work? Clean? Cook?"

She crossed her arms. "Not anymore, no, and not very well. What does that have to do with anything?"

He shrugged. "Don't look or sound like a grownup to me."

She tried a different tactic. "Listen, if you have nowhere particular to be, would you be so kind as to take me to Union?"

The boy's eyes brightened. "We'll take you all the way to Garden City if you want. Depends on what you have to offer for our services." He dug into her case and lifted a tea rose silk brassiere made in France.

Faye raised her eyebrows. "Why on earth do you want that?"

"Rabbit trap." The boy fingered the material.

She lifted her chin and opened her mouth, but words eluded her momentarily. How on earth could her bra catch rabbits? The very thought was ludicrous. "Absolutely not. Put that back."

"This?" He picked up her girdle, eyed the strap, and pulled to test its give.

"No! It is improper for you to touch a lady's undergarments. A young man should want to help without anything in return. A good deed."

The boy made a funny face. The little girl giggled.

"Why would I do that?" he asked.

"To make you feel good about yourself by helping a woman in need."

He picked up his belongings. "Tell it to Sweeney, lady. We all got our troubles. The sheriff in Union told me the next time our paths crossed, he'd lock me up and throw away the key. Him and me had a misunderstandin'. You'll need to throw in some cabbage and bits to make it worth my while."

She chewed on his words, but then it dawned on her. "Oh, you mean money. But I left my handbag and coin purse on the train."

"Have it your way," he said, turning to the little girl. "C'mon."

Faye glanced at her surroundings as they walked away. The thought of being alone out here another day and possibly night was unimaginable.

The wolfdog barked at her and tilted its head.

"I'm thinking," she said to it.

It rolled over and played dead.

"Good point." She took the bra out and snapped the case closed. "Wait. *Please.* We can work something out." She limped after the kids to catch up.

Chapter 14

Panting more than the dog, Faye dropped her case and plopped down on top of it. Behind her, a leafless tree offered no shade but served as a good backrest. She removed the shoe with the heel and rubbed her foot.

Chaska stopped his sister, and they returned to join her.

"I could take care of that stilt for you. Make it match the other," he offered.

She narrowed her eyes. "What's that going to cost me?"

He chuckled. "Nothin.' I'm wantin' this good feeling you promised. At this pace, it'll be harvest by the time we get there."

"Sorry. I just need a quick rest." She handed him her shoe. "How close are we now?"

"About halfway. We won't make it by night." He hit the shoe's heel to the side of the trunk, popped it off, and stared at the tree.

Faye looked up at the area but saw only bark. "What are you looking at so intently?"

"Here." He pointed with the toe of her shoe and traced over an image. "We roamers carve marks in trees to help each other. Shows if a place is safe, worn out of charity, and where goods may be."

Roamers meant beggars. She mentally filed the word into her new vocabulary. Stretching, she stood to get a closer look. "You get all that from a tree? All I see is some squiggles and an X."

Chaska nodded. "It means we're in luck." He traced the squiggles with his finger. "Shows there's a creek. Water's scarce as hen's teeth out here, and we're almost out." His expression indicated they were low on reserves because of her. "The X in the middle of these two circles means a camp. If they share, we eat tonight." He tossed back her shoe.

Faye would never take the simple convenience of food and drinking water for granted again. She hefted up her suitcase and followed.

A while later, they looked disappointedly at muddy puddles in a drying creek bed. The wolfdog went down, stuck its dirty paws in the water, and lapped its fill.

"Should be okay if we boil it," Chaska said.

Faye glanced at his face, worried by his less-than-reassuring tone.

He pulled a small pot from his blanketed essentials, and she helped him gather sticks. Niya curled up on the blanket. It wasn't long until the little girl was fast asleep. The wolfdog rested its head on her side but kept its eyes open.

Faye leaned against a dead tree and studied the practiced movements of the boy. She'd never seen the like. He assembled what looked like a bird's nest of dried grass and twigs, then scraped and beat an oddly shaped rock and rusted pocketknife together until they caused a spark. He gently blew on the smoke, adding sticks to build a fire.

Amazing. "Wowzer. Did your dad teach you that?"

"Never knew him. He left before I was born. I don't remember not being able to make fire. Did yours teach you?"

She couldn't recall her family ever doing anything outdoorsy together. How she wished they had. Her father had flaws, but he'd been a good provider and had spent time with her when he could. She didn't think Chaska would want her sympathy, so she said instead, "I never needed that skill."

"Spring winds blow pretty cold at night. Even in April. You should learn." Chaska put the filled pot on hot embers on the side of the fire. He pointed at the remaining water in the creek. "We can wash up with that. Just don't get any in your mouth."

Wouldn't dream of it. She limped behind him along the smooth creek bed floor.

Chaska unhooked a shoulder strap on his overalls, then went still and secured it again. He crouched and splashed the muddy water over his face and head.

Faye tested the water. "I can tell you're a girl, you know."

Seeming ill at ease, Chaska denied it and looked away. "Don't know why you'd think that."

Was the boy a bit effeminate? "Sorry. I sometimes say things without thinking first."

Chaska bit his lip, then continued in a higher, softer voice. "It's easier and safer this way. Sometimes, I forget and need to watch myself." She rubbed her hands over her spiked stalks of hair. "Mine used to be longer than yours but straight."

"It must have been beautiful."

Chaska shrugged. "No tangles this way." She tipped her chin toward her sister. "Niya won't let me cut hers or even brush it out. Guess she's afraid I'll chop it off. Wish I could. It's dangerous to be a girl in this world."

She was beginning to see that. "Does Niya talk?"

"Some. When she knows you better and has somethin' to say."

Faye unbuttoned her torn blouse and tossed it on the bank's edge. Filthy as the water was, at least it would cool her off.

Chaska watched her with a curious face. "Why you wear that thing under your shirt?"

She couldn't hold back a smile. "It's called a brassiere. It holds everything in place."

"Hmph. Looks irksome." The girl pulled out the top of her collar and peeked in. "Will mine grow that big?"

"Hard to say. We all come in different sizes."

"I won't wear one of those things. My people ain't like yours."

Faye scooped water and let it trickle down her neck. "Where are they now? Your people? It seems you are both barely surviving."

"We get by. There are worse places to be than free."

"Surely there was someplace that would take you in."

"We lived off the reservation, in-between where the ranchers grazed their cattle and sheep, and the tribe grew oats and corn to last their long winters. I traded some, but when I hunted, they claimed I was trespassing. On the rancher's side, deadly accidents happened to those like me who strayed too far. And the tribe had problems enough lookin' after their own. I never felt like we belonged."

Her teachers in school had barely touched on the Native's way of life. "Is that why you left?"

Chaska shook her head, spraying tiny droplets from her hair. "Sickness spread. Our mother died and left us with Niya's sire—a mean ol' cuss. He was a white trapper who was angry all the time 'bout nothin. I took what his fists had to offer and reckoned sooner or later he'd kill me. He made it clear he didn't want Niya or me but for our rations he could trade for smokes and shine. Niya was too young for the road, so I waited long as I could."

She pursed her lips; couldn't imagine living in fear like that. Depending on a brute of a man who abused children. "Niya's lucky to have you."

"Maybe she is, maybe she ain't. Sometimes I wonder." Chaska's gaze softened as she looked at her sister again. It took a moment for her to speak. "No goin' back, no how."

Faye dipped in the water and returned to washing but couldn't let it go. "What about the police? Surely, they would have done something to protect you."

The girl shrugged. "In their opinion, I wasn't his kin, so I was lucky he allowed me to stay."

"How awful. We can fill out a report in Union. I'll help you. Perhaps it's not too late."

"N-no." Chaska's eyes widened. She shook her head hard. "You can't tell anyone. Especially the law."

"Why not? What if he hurts another child? Surely you don't want that on your conscience?"

The girl looked away. "He won't." Her voice rasped, "I was out checkin' my traps one day. The ol' cuss had been drinkin' long into the night, so I figured it was safe to go hunt—thought he'd sleep the day. But he woke right before I made it back and ordered Niya to cook for him. She could barely reach inside the kettle pot, so small. Burned his food. He was beatin' her when I walked in. It happened so fast—I held a dead squirrel in one hand and my knife in the other. Niya was screamin' her head off. He came at me. Then there was this strange look on his face and blood spreadin' across his chest. Lots of blood." She lowered her hands, which replayed the attack. "We took everything we could carry, followed the tracks, and then hopped on a slow-movin' drag. I cut my hair, stole us new clothes, and thought up our new names. I don't feel bad for what I done, but Johnny Law may think different. We give them a wide berth."

Faye listened in stunned silence. It took her a moment to find her voice. "My God. I can't imagine—"

"Your god had nothin' to do with it." Chaska blew a puff of breath. "It was him or us. And I'd do it again if it comes down to us livin' or a man like him."

"You are so brave."

"I'm not. Far from it. I'm afraid every single day. There are just things we do when we have no other choice." She climbed out. "C'mon. We're losin' the light and the wind is pickin' up."

They had to backtrack to find the camp. Close to nightfall, Chaska went in first to scout things out. While she was gone, the sky darkened and the wind blew strong, whirling grains of dirt and sand. It got to the point where Faye found it challenging to keep her eyes open. She huddled with Niya under the blanket. The little girl traced over her face with a finger.

"Are you afraid of the dark?" She didn't think Niya would answer.

After a moment, she heard a quiet "No." The girl pushed up on the side of Faye's mouth. "*Heen akeeya.*" Then she reached to touch her hair.

"Want me to brush your hair? Get out those tangles?"

Niya scooted away. A gust of wind pulled the corner of the blanket from Faye's grip. She grasped it tighter over their heads and was about to try a different approach when Chaska lifted part of the blanket and slipped in.

"Small camp. Twenty people or so. We'll hide our stuff here, except the blanket. A woman I know is willin' to take us in for the night. You must be quiet. Keep your head down and don't talk to anyone."

They sneaked into the camp and then stopped at a rough shelter built from pieces of wood, cardboard, and draped wool blankets.

Faye raised her eyebrows at first sight of the humble structure. "This is where we're staying?" It looked like it could collapse in a soft summer breeze.

"Shh." Chaska pulled aside a crude door.

A single candle illuminated a tiny dark-haired woman and a little boy huddled on a colorful blanket. The woman said something to Chaska in a lyrical language. It sounded vaguely familiar, like what the Carlton's Spanish maid used to speak. Chaska replied in kind, taking a handful of something from the woman and the cup she offered.

"This is Maria and her son, Felipe. She says she is sorry, but this is all she has. We are welcome to it." Chaska held out a piece of dried meat to her.

Faye shook her head. "Oh, no. Thank you."

Chaska insisted. "It's okay. I'll hunt tomorrow and bring them somethin' better. I've fed them before. It'll hurt her feelings if you turn down her offer. They have a workin' well here, so the water is safe."

Faye took the drink and kept the water in her mouth long before swallowing. She studied the piece of jerked meat and reluctantly popped it into her mouth. It was unlike anything she'd tasted before. Possum, maybe? Squirrel? She struggled to swallow it.

The woman smiled and said something.

Chaska translated. "She says you're pretty. That you be careful around camp. She's not sure it is safe for you."

Faye's face warmed at the compliment. She sure didn't feel attractive. "Will you tell her I think she's pretty, too?"

Chaska's look made it clear the girl thought she was thickheaded. "She's tellin' you it is dangerous here, not flatterin' your looks." The girl padded the ground for them with the blanket and mumbled something that ended with "crazed white woman."

Maria blew out the candle and plunged them into darkness.

Faye sighed and pulled her coat up to rest her head. One more night of Hell in the sticks. By this time tomorrow, she would have real food and a soft bed in civilization. She hugged herself and tried to find a tolerable position.

Chapter 15

Faye opened her eyes to darkness. The morning chill seeped into her bones, her body angry at the slightest movement. To top off her discomfort, the need to relieve herself beckoned. She got up in a hunch and slipped out the cardboard door.

Her lower back twinged a warning, then stabbed a sharp pain as she tried to straighten upright. Stuck in the curved position, she limped through the camp. A soundless giggle flexed her throat. All she needed was a gargoyle, a bell to ring, and a cathedral to hide in. At the very least, she still had her sense of humor.

The stench of foul waste assaulted her before her eyes could adjust to the camp's squalor.

What the hell is that? She covered her nose, but it didn't help.

More clearly seen in the gray early-morning light, the camp looked almost as bad as it smelled. Strewn bottles, cans, broken glass, and maggot-covered food remnants littered the ground around a large metal can.

S'unka gnawed at a bone, not acknowledging her presence.

"Some guard dog you are," she muttered, taking in the dingy tent-like structures, dilapidated carts without wheels, and the skeletal remains of an old Model T motorcar.

She shivered, pulled her coat tight, turned in a circle, and scanned for what they would use as a bathroom. Not comfortable exploring, she favored her good leg and limped away from the camp, preferring an outer tree.

When she returned from gathering fresh clothes and toiletries from her case, a few camp people milled about in a lazy daze.

She stopped at the well and felt around the contraption for a faucet handle. Perplexed, she studied its design. Her fellow campers offered no assistance. After an impatient huff, she noticed a large man seated nearby in thick denim overalls and a dirty work shirt. He was busy carving a wooden figurine.

She hobbled over his way and called out first to not startle him. "Excuse me."

He didn't seem to hear, turning in his seat so his back was to her. She tapped his shoulder. He exhaled a groan.

"Excuse me, mister. Could you assist me for a moment? I can't figure out how to turn on the water."

Mumbling something unintelligible, he marched toward the well, his enormous work boots clunking against the ground. He grabbed a metal pail, placed it under the spigot, and rapidly pumped the long handle until the bucket filled to the brim. Without a glance, bow, or how-do-you-do, he returned to whittling as he strode away.

Hmph. His bad manners didn't deter her. "Thank you," she called out loud enough to ensure he heard this time. Without proper manners, there would be only anarchy.

She searched for a place to clean herself and safely dress. A woman tending a fire outside a blanketed tent looked to be her best bet.

Faye cleared her throat as she neared and said, "Pardon me."

The old woman raised her head, squished her eyebrows together, and tugged on her earlobe. "You talking to me, girl? Speak up."

Was everyone here hard of hearing? "I was just wondering if you could tell me where I may perform my morning cleanse—wash and change—with privacy," she emphasized.

The woman's eyes lingered on items cradled in Faye's arms. "Good deed deserves a reward. Not many teeth left, but my mouth could do with some refreshing. Name's Pearl. My husband is out checking our traps. For a bit of that tooth cleaner, I'll make sure you ain't bothered."

Pearl motioned toward their dwelling. Faye followed her in, the tent crammed with stacked boxes. A foul scent wafted from a soiled, bare mattress.

Eyes tearing from the odor of unwashed bodies, it took every bit of her willpower not to cover her nostrils. She wondered how long she could hold her breath before passing out.

Pearl pulled out a large bowl from a box. "Little cramped, but thieves, you know. That bucket is for hauling only. We have rules. Pour your washing water in here."

Faye emptied the water into the bowl and handed the pail to her. Pearl held out a finger and looked at her expectantly.

"Oh, right." She squeezed some of her toothpaste on the woman's finger.

Before putting it in her mouth, Pearl asked, "What you planning to do with those soiled clothes? Awful ripped up. I could take them off your hands."

"Okay. Sure," Faye agreed, eager for the lady to go. Once Pearl was gone, she took a long breath from her mouth and held it, tasting whatever made the tent smell so bad. She dressed in record speed and managed a half-decent job. It was amazing how fresh clothes could make one feel better.

Chaska was waiting outside the tent when she emerged. Faye handed Pearl the tattered clothes as promised and then adjusted her blue slacks and polka-dot sweater under her coat. Pearl thanked her, then gave Chaska a crooked smile.

"Morning," Faye chirped.

"What're you doin'?" Chaska asked with a hiss, grabbed her arm, and yanked her away. "I told you not to talk to anyone. Didn't think I needed to tell you not to give things of value away." The girl led her out of the camp.

"What are you so upset over? She's a harmless old woman, and those clothes were not fit to wear again. No harm done."

Chaska jerked her to a stop and stared fiercely into her eyes. "You don't get it. You're in my world now. Waste not, want not. Gonna get us in a heap of trouble if you don't start listening. Any tradin' done is done by me. Any talkin' is done by me too, not you."

She arched her eyebrows. "Fine. Sorry. I will ask your permission next time I wash my face." She tickled Chaska's cheek with her towel.

The girl said something, most likely unpleasant, in her Native language. She crossed her arms and blew out a puff of air. "I'm not lettin' you out of my sight. C'mon."

They went back to their stash to drop off Faye's toiletries and then headed out to the thickets. The last trap they checked was the one made from her dismantled bra. A jackrabbit lay trapped in its expensive silk lining.

Chaska whooped. "I knew it would work." The rabbit blinked. The girl picked up a large rock.

"Oh, it's still alive. Whuh-what are you doing?" She reached out and blocked the girl from dropping the primitive weapon. "*Aww*, don't kill it."

Chaska rolled her eyes. "You ever eat chicken, bacon, beef?"

"Well, sure, but—"

"And where do you think that meat comes from?"

She didn't like where this conversation was going. "From a butcher, wrapped in paper and twine. Not a cute little bunny. Please, don't. When we get to town, I can sell something and buy us a proper dinner."

"This isn't just for us. I promised Maria and Felipe that I'd hunt for them." Chaska twirled a finger. "Turn around. Don't want you to faint. Money or no money, I'll leave you here."

Defeated, she turned and watched the birds circling the sky in the distance. One landed on a lonely, gnarled, white-barked tree by a road in the distance.

If only her charm schoolteacher could see her now.

What would Miss Ross say? "Cleanliness is the most important part of your daily beauty regimen." *Check.* "Good posture must be maintained, whether standing, sitting, or sleeping. It shows others you are confident and self-assured." She pulled her shoulders back. *Check.* "No matter your size or shape, it is imperative that the fabric of your dress drapes to a straight hem." *Demerit.* To wear leisure slacks outside the home for anything other than playing sports was highly frowned upon. But, then again, hunting was a sport, so—*check.*

She'd learned how to walk while balancing a book on her head and what cutlery went with what, but nothing about plucking fur from a rabbit, cooking over an open campfire, or how to murder a late brunch in the wooded brush. Of that, she was certain.

Did they pluck fur? Faye almost turned to ask Chaska but changed her mind. She did not want to know. "I'm not eating that," she declared.

"Up to you, but we have a long walk today. We're not stoppin' to find you somethin' else." The girl started away with the skinned rabbit slumped over her shoulder.

"I'll find some berries. Maybe some greens to make a nice salad." Chaska scoffed. "Good luck with that."

Faye watched the ground for something to forage as she followed.

When they returned to camp, more people were outside their shelters. Pearl was wearing the torn clothes and sauntered with her head high, surrounded by women speaking animatedly with their hands. She stopped, pointed at Faye, and shooed them away.

"Here we go," Chaska muttered.

A group of women advanced on them, prattling with excitement and holding out their worthless, meager possessions.

"Pearl said you have things to trade," said a woman in a dirty yellow dress missing most of its buttons. A little girl clung to the woman's leg, wearing what looked to be an upside-down burlap sack with holes for her arms and head. All the women talked at once, asking for clothes, shampoo, and soap.

One cried, "Are you wearing lipstick?" Dressed in mannish trousers and a grimy shirt, the woman touched her own lips with longing.

A rough-looking man stopped drinking from a bottle, the giant man paused from carving wood, and young children halted play. They all stared in Faye's way.

Chaska put her arm up. "We don't got nothin' to trade, but you'll be welcome to some stew once cooked. Free of charge."

"You callin' Pearl a liar?" A harsh-looking woman indecently dressed without garments under her overalls pushed to the front of the group and took a sip from a mason jar.

"Now, Nancy, no cause for trouble," said Yellow Dress. "We were just hoping for fair trade. They don't want to. Let's leave them be."

Nancy set down the jar and pushed her stringy hair behind her ears. She pulled a knife from her pocket, flicked it open, and cleaned underneath her nails with the tip of the blade. "Our stuff not good enough for you?" she jeered. "Who's to keep me from goin' in there and just taking what I want?" Her pointy chin motioned toward the lean-to.

Chaska set her things on the ground. In a calming voice, she said, "I'm sure we can come to some kinda understandin'."

"Ain't talking to you, boy. I askin' Princess here."

Faye stiffened as the woman moved closer. She glanced at Chaska for guidance, who slightly shook her head. Unsure what that meant, she turned back to Nancy and forced a smile. "I regret any misunderstanding on my part. I'm sure you have lovely things, but I'm not in need of anything at present."

Nancy gave her a flat look. "You talk stupid."

"Pardon?"

"Did I stutter? You. Talk. Stew-pid."

Tension built in Faye's neck and shoulders. Why was the woman insulting her when her apology clearly stated she'd taken responsibility for any wrong? Would no words suffice? The irrationality of it all was beyond comprehension. "I'm sorry if I said something to offend. Certainly, that was not my intention."

Nancy's skin turned mottled. Spittle flew from her mouth, saying, "Who you think you are?" Her voice climbed in volume. "Coming in here actin' all highfalutin, starin' down your nose at us."

Chaska took a step. "Okay, hunger got our tempers up. Who wants to help me fix this rabbit?"

Nancy bared her mustard-colored teeth and locked her hand around the knife. "I'll tell yuh what I'm fixin' to do." She barreled forward.

After a slight stumble, Faye managed to keep upright. "Hey..." Her voice stuck in her throat as Nancy's arm swung out. The glint of the knife gave warning.

Chapter 16

Faye swerved.

Nancy stood in a crouch, shifting her weight, ready to attack in either direction. A man sprung forward and received a healthy gash on his arm for his good deed, putting to rest any hope the woman was bluffing.

She's insane. Faye took a few shaky steps back and bumped into Maria's shelter. Her pulse quickened with the decision to risk it. She bolted to the left.

Nancy leaped.

Head jerked back, pain radiated through Faye's scalp, her hair caught in the woman's grasp. A hard punch to her side knocked the wind from her lungs.

S'unka growled. Fur bristled, the dog pounced on Nancy and clamped its jaw over her hand. The woman dropped the bloodied knife and shrieked like a banshee, pounding her other fist on the wolf-dog. The camp erupted into chaos. Men shouted, women screamed, and children wailed as their mothers hurried them away.

Faye looked down in stunned disbelief as blood seeped through her sweater top. A metallic taste flooded her mouth while nauseous heat spread up her face.

"S'unka!" Chaska pulled her dog off Nancy.

The crazed woman cradled her hand to her chest. Wide-eyed with pupils dilated, beads of sweat glistened on her upper lip and brow. She spat on the ground, kicked at the men circling, and bared her mustard-colored teeth like a cornered animal. A low, guttural gurgle rose from her throat and grew into a roar of pure rage. Men from the camp attempted to grab hold and restrain her. She fiercely scratched a man's face with a clawed swipe and ran past him.

S'unka tore loose and chased her through the scrub.

The throbbing on Faye's side became a sharp pain and robbed her of breath. Her knees buckled. Strong arms seized her, and the giant man who'd been whittling lowered her to the ground.

The sky spun as though she lay on a children's carousel. Round and round went the cloud shapes. A heart. A giant mushroom. A crab dragging its shell. She swallowed hard and clenched tufts of grassy weeds to slow the motion. Cool air brushed over her skin as the bottom part of her sweater lifted away.

Chaska's face appeared above. "Dammit." The girl pressed something against Faye's side and shouted orders, instructing the camp people to search for items needed. She looked back down with a puckered forehead. "You sure know how to find trouble."

Faye opened her mouth and then snapped it shut. How was this her fault? She glanced up at the whittling man with the silent question. He looked concerned. Was she dying? It sure as hell felt like it.

I'm cold. Is that part of it? The heat drains out, then—poof—*you're gone?*

She wanted to see how bad the damage was, but the whittling man pressed her shoulders to the ground.

The woman in yellow came back with a needle and thread. Another gave over a handful of rags.

Chaska grabbed the mason jar and sniffed. "Wuh." She wrinkled her nose, took a healthy swig, and wiped the side of her mouth with her sleeve. "Brace yourself. This might sting a bit." She dunked the needle into the jar and then poured the liquid on the cut.

"Hell's bells!" Faye bolted to sit up. Her side burned like a bubbling boil. "Shoot, shoot, shoot!"

"Don't get dirt in it. Hold her still," Chaska ordered the men and knelt with the threaded needle.

"Let me up." Bile rose in Faye's throat.

The whittling man said, "Not gonna lie. This'll hurt like the devil darning socks, but it got to be done."

Her mouth filled with waterbrash. She said between swallows, "I'm going to be sick."

He let go. She leaned on her good side and threw up on the ground. Tears ran down her cheeks as she spat to rid herself of the bitter taste. A tinny ringing overcame voices in her head, and she collapsed on her back. Colors faded to shades of gray. Her vision swam, so she squeezed her eyes shut, but the movement still turned. Something sharp bit into her wound. It hurt worse than the alcohol.

She sprung her eyes open and glared at Chaska.

The girl jerked up a bloodied needle and thread. The pain from the next puncture hurt just as bad as the first.

The world spun faster. A scream surrounded Faye and suffused her. Then something dark tugged at her consciousness and she succumbed to the silent sanctuary within.

Faye came to inside of Maria's shelter. The pain greeted her first.

"How're you feelin'?" Chaska asked and took a sip from a can.

"Like I just went five rounds with Jack Dempsey."

"I don't know who that is. Lucky for you, you were mostly outta your head when I sewed you up. You got some lungs on you."

Faye leaned on her elbow and turned to see the stitched wound. It looked an ugly red, its edges swollen. She lightly touched the stitches, surprised by their heat and tenderness. "I don't understand why she attacked me. What did I do?"

Chaska gulped from the can and then wiped her mouth. "Nothin' you could help. She's long gone now. I tracked her trail to be sure, but she won't come back. Places like this have their own kind of justice." She held out a piece of dried meat. "Think you can keep anything down?"

Faye's stomach churned. A sharp pain shot out along her side as she moved to sit up. She sucked in a quick breath and then shook her head. "I keep seeing the look she gave me. How can a person hate another that much without knowing them? Without cause or reason?"

Chaska poured a cup of water and handed it to her. "Those who are at the end of their rope. We've come to know the signs and stay clear of them. It's the blank look on their face and the dead in their eyes. Nothin' resembling a human in the head anymore, and nobody left to care about. When they see someone better off—not sufferin' as much—it stirs up something animal. They need to hurt that person as much as they hurt."

Chaska lowered her head. "If I didn't have Niya to care about, I'd fear becoming that—like a feral barn cat survivin' minute by minute, hour by hour, day after day. Angry at the world and hatin' everything. Especially myself."

"I don't see you ever becoming like that."

The girl sighed. "Careful puttin' too much faith in someone. People always fail each other eventually, whether they mean to or not."

Faye handed back the cup. "I think I owe you my life."

The corner of Chaska's mouth quirked. "Yeah, well, I'll add that to my fee," she said with a grin in her voice.

Faye laid on her good side. Sleep beckoned until summer.

A cat disappeared into a heavy fog. Faye stretched upright and circled. Her skin prickled as mist seeped into her pores. It coated her tongue with what she imagined bitter moss on an old tree would taste like. Cool marble pressed against her bare feet. She looked down, and the cat was there again, one-eyed and flea-laden, flitting between her ankles. It arched its back and hissed.

The mistiness dissipated.

She traipsed curiously behind the cat as Bix Beiderbecke played the introduction to the song 'In a Mist' on his piano. He turned her way with an eerie smile.

Men dressed in top hats and suits with tails and women wrapped in gem-colored satin and taffeta ballgowns made way for her. Confused, Faye smoothed her burlap sack dress with one hand and clenched a gleaming knife with her other.

The disdain from the crowd switched to anger and fear that played across their faces. The cat hissed at her again and urged her to follow.

Charles and Catherine stepped out. "You need to go," Charles said. "You don't belong here."

Catherine's eyes roamed over her with contempt. "So gauche. Chucky, what did you ever see in her?"

Charles' eyebrows furrowed. "I don't know, but new money is better than none at all." He turned and kissed Catherine with passion.

Bix stepped in front of them and wrapped a noose around Faye's neck. He threw the other end up the enormous tree that sprouted where his piano had been. With the strange smile still pasted on his face, he stated with a midwestern drawl, "We have our own kind of justice here."

She tensed, then pleaded, "No. Wait. Please! What did I do?"

"Pull!" Bix called out.

Faye choked and wriggled against the rope that pulled her higher and higher.

A blanket lifted from her face.

Chaska knelt and wiped her brow with a cloth. "Stop struggling," the girl shouted in competition with the howling wind. "You have fever. We're taking you for help."

The whittling man reached underneath and lifted her.

"This is Dooly," Chaska introduced.

Dooly offered her a closed-mouth smile and readjusted her with his strong brown arms. The wind whipped hard against Faye's face, striking with tiny bullets of sandy grit. Her body ached to the marrow of her bones. She turned her face and hid against Dooly's shirt.

Chaska yelled, "We ain't gonna make it to town in this. I know a place. Follow me."

Chapter 17

The dining room was too fancy and made him nervous. Rudy always worried about his manners and that his cloth napkin would slip off his lap.

Grandpa Hahn was telling him the importance of being a self-made man. He'd heard the story more times than he could count, how Grandpa's folks had been among the first German settlers in western Kansas. They'd braved Indians, bandits, and all kinds of other trouble. Had built a sod structure on the plains where the ranch house stood today. Grandpa said his kin came from hearty stock—whatever that meant—and they'd earned everything they had through good, hard work. But he was also widely known for his tall tales. Ma had once said that Grandma Hahn was no poor German but came from a wealthy Italian family. Rudy wasn't sure who to believe.

Head tucked in prayer, he peeked at the heaped bowls on the center table. His mouth watered from the combined aromas of seared meats, freshly baked loaves of bread, and thick gravies. Well, wherever Grandma was from—she sure as heck knew how to cook.

After grace, she retied her checkered apron and served over his shoulder, piling more and more food onto his plate. He made sure the dumb napkin was still on his lap.

Grandpa put down his pipe and thumbed his suspenders. "Are the rest of us to eat, Mother? Or just watch the boy?"

She sighed. "Look how thin he is. Not right—the two of them alone with no woman to tend them."

"Flo, don't fuss the boy." Grandpa tilted his bald head toward his son. "He's the same size Wilbert was at that age. Perfectly healthy."

Uncle Will patted his blue work shirt over his round stomach. "See what you have to look forward to?"

Rudy smiled. He couldn't imagine being as big as Uncle Will or as strong as Pa. But he hoped to be someday.

Grandma served everyone's plates and then took a seat. "I think someone should talk to Jake about allowing Elsa or myself to clean and cook for them, especially once wheat harvest comes 'round the bend."

Aunt Elsa shook her head. "Jake doesn't want us there, Momma. He's made that very clear. We should respect his wishes."

"Never seen two young people so suited for each other." Grandma Hahn kept on. "Although sometimes a woman needs to give a little nudge. Let a fella know she's sweet on him."

This caught Rudy's attention. Did she like Pa?

Her cheeks blushed red as a beet, and she tossed down her fork. "My sister runs off with my beau, so I should go after Jake. Is that what you're saying?"

Grandma folded her arms over her apron stomach. "I don't think going to the picture show and a few kicks and twirls around the barn dance floor made Garron Schmidt your beau." She tsked. "So, if the opportunity presents itself, yes. Jake is a good man. Ten times the man Garron was. Sarah did you a favor."

"Sarah never thinks of anyone but herself," Elsa snapped, then looked at Rudy. "Sorry, Bug."

He shrugged and continued eating. Grownup talk sure was confusing.

Uncle Will cleared his throat. "Word is Jake purchased Hi-Bred corn seeds for his next crop."

Rudy swallowed and nodded. "He read they need less water to grow."

"Is he reading that Doyle and Son Journal again?" Grandpa slapped the table and guffawed. "They are Irish, for God's sake. What do they know about farming? They need to go back to their own country and learn to grow a proper potato."

What was wrong with the Irish potatoes? Rudy set himself to take another bite of mash.

Uncle Wilbert frowned. "That famine was because of blight, a fungus that started here in America."

Fungus? *Yuck*. Rudy turned his spoon and plopped the mashed potatoes back onto his plate. He munched buttered bread to rid the taste.

Grandpa pointed his way. "The Indians worked the soil of the plains way longer than the Micks. They took the best seeds from their crops and replanted them the next year. Mark my words, boy—the spring rains will come, and Jake will have wasted good money on useless magic beans when he should have bought a cow—the cow being a tractor. It will double his growth with half the work."

Jack and the Beanstalk. Pa had read that to him when he was little.

Uncle Will scoffed. "Jake wouldn't borrow money from Bern Schmidt to buy a tractor if his life depended on it. Unless, of course, it was to run over Schmidt's son."

Rudy silently chuckled at that. The Schmidts were bad people. Someone needed to run them out of town. He pictured himself riding a horse next to Buffalo Bill as the banker ran for his life.

A tutting sound brought him out of his imagination.

Scowling, Grandpa shook his finger at Uncle Will. "That same lack of ambition and bullheadedness cost him his wife in the first place and now leaves her care on me again."

Rudy wondered what that meant. Aunt Elsa halted her spoon of corn halfway to her mouth. Everyone else stopped eating and stared at Grandpa Hahn.

Grandma's fingers tapped over her throat. "You heard from Sarah?"

"She wrote." He nodded. "Things are mighty grim. Garron Schmidt done run off and left her. She was living by her wits on the New Orleans streets. I had to send her money." His grandfather sighed as his eyes met Rudy's. "May as well know now, my boy. Your mom is coming home."

"Oh, *thank* the Lord," Grandma Hahn cried. "My baby. My dear, sweet girl is returning to me."

Rudy was unsure how he felt about the news, how Pa would. He looked over at Aunt Elsa.

She seemed close to tears. Pouting, she tossed her napkin over her plate and ran from the room.

✌

He froze in place, startled by a loud banging outside the barn. Betsy heard it, too. She shifted her weight, her hooves stamping the ground.

"It's okay, girl." Rudy patted her tan, furred side. "Just the stupid duster." He was soothing himself as much as the cow and resumed milking.

He hated to admit that he got scared being home alone. Pa warned him against borrowing his friend's *Ghost Stories* magazines and reading creepy tales of werewolves, vampires, and the giant made by Frankenstein; a monster brought back from the dead. Said it was all make-believe nonsense. Rudy wasn't so sure.

Something pounded harder on the barn door.

He went to it and pressed on the latch to make sure it would hold. With a shaky voice, he called out, "Who's there?"

"Open up."

He bit his bottom lip. His dad wasn't due back until tomorrow evening but might have turned back in the dust storm. "Pa? That you?"

The pounding on the door increased in urgency. "Open the damn door."

He released the wood bolt and the doors swung out. He protected his eyes from the sandy grit that blew in and squinted up at a giant hooded figure. A woman lay draped across its massive arms. She looked dead.

Rudy screamed and stumbled back.

The monster strode inside. It placed the woman on a bed of hay, raised back up to its full height, and began to unwrap the dirty material that hid its face.

Rudy ran for a pitchfork. He raised his weapon and yelled, "Whaddaya doin' with that girl, monster?"

A dog barked and entered the barn. Chaska and Niya followed.

Rudy moved to save them. "Stay behind me. Frankenstein's demon is here." He braced himself, fearing the first sight of mismatched slaughterhouse and graveyard parts on the creature's face.

The monster turned away. "Beware, farm boy. You make me angry." The creature roared and swiftly faced him with meaty outstretched arms.

Rudy sucked in a hard breath, but then his widened eyes returned to normal.

The monster was just a man.

Chaska hooted and bent over with glee. "You shoulda seen your face. Dooly really had you goin.' That was great."

Lips twisting in anger, Rudy dropped the pitchfork and balled his fists. "That was really stupid. Yer darn lucky I didn't have a gun."

They looked sorry. Chaska helped him close the barn doors.

Rudy relit the lamp and held it up. "Is she dead?"

Faye blinked awake and stared up at a white blur. Slowly her vision cleared on a goat sporting what looked to be an Amish beard. It stood over her and chewed a piece of straw. She attempted to push it aside but was so weak it may as well have been a ten-ton boulder. The goat continued its chew.

If she'd ever felt this miserable, she could not recall it. Beyond the chills, her whole body hurt, and her stomach clawed with a gnawing hunger.

The animal finally moved on its own accord. She looked beyond its twitching tail to see her friends seated on haystacks and talking with a new boy. She angled her ear their way, trying to hear them.

"My pa went out of town, but I don't know fer sure how long he'll be gone. And I already have some bad news to tell him, something I can't figure out the words to say."

"He won't travel by wagon through this dust." Chaska dug through her belongings and held out something in the palm of her hand. "You know what this is?"

The boy shook his head.

"It's an arrowhead. A sharpened stone my people used to hunt with. It's yours to keep if you help us this last time."

He reached out and turned it, studying the object with interest.

Faye slowly sat up. A clammy wave of dizziness swept over her. She cleared her throat to draw attention. "Please. I can't go on just yet."

He chewed his lower lip and looked reluctant, but his eyes softened at her.

Chaska bartered with the boy for food and to allow Faye to clean herself. She was grateful beyond words for his generosity.

Dooly carried her to the house. It looked welcoming despite its roof missing half of its shingles, dirt coating the windows, and the flaked white paint clapboards. But due to his size, she feared Dooly's heavy steps would bring the whole back porch down.

The farm boy readied a bath. He heated water on the stove and prattled on like children were prone to do. Faye politely listened, but her headache and bodily weariness made concentration impossible.

Dooly brought in her case and placed it in the bathing room off the kitchen.

She caught his arm before he could return to the barn. "Thank you, Mister Dooly."

He nodded in the direction of her wound. "I think it's gone bad. Be sure to clean it, even if it hurts."

After he left, she yanked shut the flimsy curtain that served as their door. She braced herself against the washbowl counter and waited for another wave of dizziness to pass. The mirror's reflection made her gasp. She ran her fingers through her limp, lackluster locks and brushed off her dirt-powdered face. Bloodshot eyes blinked back at her. She looked as if she'd been through Hell and back. Time to fix that. She dug through her case and uniformly placed her toiletries on a shelf along the cast-iron tub.

A bath. How heavenly. She eased into the thick steam and sharply inhaled between her teeth when the heated water lapped over her cut. The room spun. She held the sides of the tub until the motion subsided. She wouldn't have understood if someone had told her weeks ago a mere bath would feel this luxurious. How much most take for granted the everyday necessities of normal life. She washed her face and hair and added scented lavender oil to the bubble bath. Bone-tired, she leaned her head back and closed her eyes. A bit of rest would help her feel like her old self and ready to return to her old life.

The wind howled and drowned out the wagon's creaking approach. As soon as Rudy stepped outside to return to the house, his dad jumped down from the wagon and stretched, his shirt billowing from the wind.

"Unhitch and care for them," Pa yelled. "I'll be back to help unload."

Rudy panicked. "Where yuh going?"

"Got a whole desert in my eyes." His dad strode toward the house.

Rudy groaned. There was nothing he could do. He guided the mules into the barn then untied the cloths that shielded their eyes. He called out to Chaska, who peeked out from the tack room.

"Is that him?"

"Yep. My pa's back early. He went inside. What do I do?"

"He may not see her. Don't borrow trouble until trouble is due." Chaska's face said something else. That Rudy's goose was cooked.

"B-but what if he does? How do I explain this? Allowing a stranger in to take a bath."

Chaska seemed to think hard on the matter. "Just tell him she was lost. That you gave her shelter until the weather cleared. She's hurt. She's pretty. Men can't resist that."

Rudy shook his head. "You don't know my pa."

The curtain divider wisped to the side.

Faye snapped open her eyes. At that moment, a tall man lumbered into the small bathing room. He bumped against the washstand and rubbed his crusted eyes, sending bits of dirt flying from his coated skin.

Her mind scrambled, but she forced herself to calm down.

He had sun-weathered skin, dark hair three inches longer than the respectable style, and his jaw boasted three days of whiskery growth. His gruff appearance, size, and mannerisms put her on edge.

But she could see enough of a resemblance to the young boy to figure out this must be his father.

From how the poor kid worried about this man finding her in his home, he didn't sound like father-of-the-year. Was he dangerous? Did the boy fear him?

Adrenaline spiked through her veins. She wasn't a scrapper, nor could she envision herself fleeing through the countryside soaking wet without clothes.

She looked down. His dirty boot stamped marks on the bloomers she'd left on the floor. Her cheeks warmed at the thought of him seeing them. Then panic set in as that same boot moved closer to her open case. It stopped just shy of the handle.

He unbuttoned and threw off his shirt.

She wrinkled her nose as his musky smell overpowered her bath perfume. There was no way out of this. He would discover her shortly. All he had to do was open his eyes and look in the mirror or turn around. She ever so slowly guided the bubbles from the edge of the tub to cover her breasts.

And if he did? Then what could she do? Scream for help? Surely, Dooly was close by. They were close to the same size. Her friend would give Paul Bunyan here a run for his money.

The man poured water from a pitcher into a large bowl. His back and arm muscles flexed as he lathered up his hands with soap and circle-rubbed the suds over his cheeks. He bent over and splashed the water violently to rinse them away. Suds. Rinse. Repeat. He must have thick skin to put up with such a polishing.

Suddenly, he reached out and patted the rack for a towel. There wasn't one there. The only one she'd found hung directly above her head.

Her breath caught in her throat as he turned and felt for it, his hand coming within inches of her several times.

She slid down until her chin touched the water.

His searching fingers found her only source for cover. He whisked it away and patted his face dry. At any moment, he would open his eyes and discover her naked in his bathing tub. She scooped more clustered bubbles to cover her middle parts.

But then he tossed the towel over his shoulder and took a few steps toward the flimsy curtain, mumbling something unintelligible to himself.

Faye released the breath she'd been holding and relaxed, sending a ripple of water sloshing the side of the tub.

The man glanced over his shoulder and did a double take. His expression flitted from surprise to embarrassment.

She blinked.

"Who—who the hell are you?"

"I'm..." She stammered, unsure what to say. "I uh—"

"How did you get in here?" He jerked back a step, his complexion turning scarlet.

"Well, um..."

The man's face grew stony, and his fists balled up at his sides. She swallowed a squeak. Was he the type of man who would hit a woman?

"Speak up, for god's sake," he yelled. "Are you dim?"

She flinched. "No. Goodness, I'm trying to answer your questions." A dull pain throbbed under her forehead. She rubbed her temples. "Please stop shouting."

"Don't tell me how to speak in *my* own house, dammit."

"Then calm down and lower your voice."

"Are you alone?"

"I'm—"

"Who else broke in here?"

"I didn't break in. Your son..."

His gaze bore into hers. "My son? Did you threaten my boy?"

"I would never—"

"If you harmed him in any way, I swear..."

Faye heaved a heavy sigh and crossed her arms protectively over her breasts. She glared at him, barely holding on to her last remaining shreds of patience. "In my opinion, you could learn a thing or two from him."

He narrowed his eyes. "Are you a whore?"

"Excuse me?"

"A hoboess—the kind that gets her kicks spreading diseases to unsuspecting men for things."

Rude. "How dare you!" That he thought her capable of such a thing bothered her. Why should she care whether this oversized cretin mistook her for a woman of ill repute? Unless he planned to force himself on her. She shuddered.

He spoke to himself. "Gonna take my whole supply of lye to clean that tub. To get rid of the lice." He scratched his head. "I guess I could mix in some rodent killer and Scheele's Green arsenic."

That upset her more than him thinking her sullied. Her temper warmed from a simmer to a froth. "I don't have bugs!"

"Don't give me the innocent doe eyes. I'll not be taken in by your feminine wiles."

"You think I'm trying to seduce you?" She'd laugh if the situation wasn't so dire.

He lifted a brow. "From what I can see, you've got a nice package for your unsavory character. But I'm not interested."

"Rest assured, I don't want anything from you, especially that." She couldn't wait to get away from him. "So, if you are quite finished browbeating me, sir, will you please allow me to get dressed?"

He yanked the drape shut behind him and stomped away.

"Rudolph!" his dad roared from a distance.

Rudy jolted as if struck by lightning. "See?" He swallowed hard. "He never calls me by my given name. He's mad. Really mad."

Chaska looked at him with pity. "Just remember what I told you. You'll be fine."

He dawdled, dragging his feet on his way to the house like a convict headed to the gallows. He softly latched the door closed behind him and forced himself to look up.

Pa paced back and forth with flared nostrils. He speared a finger. "What did I tell you to do if a stranger approached when I'm not here?"

Rudy looked down and toe-turned his shoe on the kitchen floor. "Point the rifle and warn 'em to go away."

"And if they don't?" His dad stopped in front of him, huffing. "Huh?"

"Shoot 'em." He peered up and tried to remember what Chaska told him to say. "Buh—but she's lost—and hurt—and pretty."

Pa's brows shot up toward his hairline. "What the hell do you think this is? A bathhouse for beggars and thieves? Huh? Should I offer her a cup of tea now?" He raked his fingers through his hair. "You don't understand. Railway tramps are dangerous regardless of how nice they look or pretend to be. They will slit your throat for a loaf of bread without thinking twice about it."

"But she ain't like that." Why did his dad always think the worst of strangers?

"Oh? A man of the world, are you?"

Faye pulled open the curtain and slowly put one foot in front of the other. Her wet hair dripped down the back of her day dress, and her head felt like it would split in two. The room spun, but she intended to fix this misunderstanding for the boy's sake.

"Please. Stop. Yelling. I'm hardly a threat." She swallowed against building nausea. "Quit picking on your son. You should be proud. He went above and beyond the rules of hospitality. After all, good manners are about helping people. Without them, there'd be anarchy."

"Get out." The man looked at her like she'd grown an extra head. "Get out of my house. Wherever you were going"—his voice boomed—"*Keep going.*"

His roar rang between her ears. She rubbed her upper neck. The movement caused a sharp pain to bolt down her side. She tightened her lips and breathed through the agony until it passed. The room spun faster, and the ringing in her ears increased in volume. She could practically feel her blood coursing through her veins to her thumping heart. Her focus and ability to concentrate diminished. She stumbled to the side.

"Are you drunk?" The man gave her an incredulous look, seemingly appalled.

Unable to hold back her temper a second longer, she glared at the obnoxious man. "No. I'm injured. You, you, *you,* sir, are a brute, a bully, and—"

"Get out!"

The room tilted in her vision. There were now three men, whereas a moment ago, there had been only one. She grasped the middle oaf's shirt and slid down the front of him.

Chapter 18

Rudy stood at the threshold of his room. Inside, his dad leaned against the wall with a scowl on his face.

Doc Adams tended the woman. He reached into his bag. "Someone made a crude attempt to stitch up the cut, from the looks of it, caused by a blade of a knife or sharp object. Curious." He looked toward Rudy in the hallway. "Do you know who attacked this lil' lady?"

Rudy rubbed the back of his neck. They'd just said she was ill, not how she got sick. What a pickle.

Pa stared hard his way. "Speak up, boy."

He drew his shoulders up and shrugged. "Um, they—she didn't say."

His dad's eyes narrowed at him.

"You need to wash the wound with soap and warm water three times a day, pat it gently dry, and put this cream on it." Doc held out the jar to Pa.

He crossed his arms. "She's not staying here."

Doc put the jar on the dresser. "I drained and restitched the wound, but she won't be able to go anywhere until it heals and to heal, she needs care. Clean your hands before you change the bandage." He placed an aspirin block next to the jar. "When she awakes, give her some of this for the pain."

Pa shook his head. "She can't stay here. Please, Hank. I'm begging you. Take her with you."

Doc went to a bowl, washed his hands, and dried them with a cloth. "Jostling her about in the back of a wagon will reopen the wound." Heavy lines creased his forehead as he raised his bushy white eyebrows. "And how would it look? Me, an old bachelor, taking in a young girl to tend."

Pa spread his arms. "Better than a man and a boy way out here."

"At least you have your son to chaperone."

"I'm not going anywhere near her." Pa moved closer to the door.

"Don't worry, Jake. She'll be out of your hair in no time." Doc patted his shoulder. "Come. Show me which mule is having the problem."

Rudy backed down the hall.

His dad pushed out of the bedroom and glared down at him. He looked mad enough to kill two pigs with one hand. "Get to tending, Florence Nightingale. She's your responsibility now. I want her gone—yesterday. You hear?"

Rudy nodded. He listened as his dad and Doc Adams clomped down the stairs. Then, he tiptoed into his room and peered down at the woman. She looked so small and fragile. His responsibility. Well, he'd show them. He was going to be the best healer that he could be.

He tried to remember what his dad did when he was sick. He leaned over and palmed her forehead. It was hot, and her hairline was damp with sweat. He wiped his hand on his pant leg and formed a plan.

In the downstairs bathing room, he opened the medicine cabinet, picked up a bottle of camphor oil, and read the label. "Relieves hysteria." Whatever that was. "Food poisoning, insect bites, and coughing fits." He placed it on the counter, picked up a ridged bottle of tincture of iodine, and studied it. His dad dabbed this on whenever they got cuts and stings. Rudy added it to a basket on the floor along with sulfur tablets, the camphor oil, cough wafers, and Foley's pain relief for colic and bowel complaints. After wetting a washcloth, he returned to his room with the basket, folded the cloth, and carefully placed it on her forehead. Then he propped next to her on his bed, prepared to keep vigil all night if need be.

The agony in Faye's head would bring a strong man to his knees. She fluttered her eyes open and focused on a dresser with a blue floral-patterned pitcher on top. A turn of her head seared a sharp pang down the side of her neck to her shoulder.

A boy leaned over and replaced the cloth on her forehead with a fresh, warm one.

"What happened?" she whispered. "Where am I?"

He scooted onto the bed and patted her arm. "It's okay. Yer friends went to yer camp. Chaska promised he'd be back to check on you. Doc Adams says yer really sick, but he thinks you'll live."

Her memories returned in a flash. This was the farm boy with the terrible father. "Doc Adams?"

"Our veterinarian. He's the best around."

"Oh my." What kind of doctor treated humans and pigs? But she didn't want to offend, so she said, "That's reassuring."

The farm boy nodded. "When Clarabelle had a breech birth, he saved her and her calf. I helped. That's why he put me in charge of you and yer mending." He showed her his basket of medicine. "Gonna have you up and feeling better in no time."

She managed a slight smile. "What's your name again?"

"Rudy. I'm named after an actor in the picture shows. Rudolph Valentino. My ma said he was real handsome." He blushed adorably.

Faye shivered and pulled the blanket up higher. "I'm Fuh—Faye," she said through chattering teeth. "Why is it s-s-so cold in here?"

"It's not. Yer wound's tainted." He hopped off the bed and left the room. A door creaked. He returned carrying a frayed, patched quilt, covered her, and tucked it under at her shoulders and feet.

Her stomach growled.

"Hungry?"

She nodded.

He set off, she assumed to make her something. When he returned, he fluffed up her pillows and helped her sit up.

"I cooked oats. I like mine with milk and honey, so I made 'em both that way. Hope you like it."

Faye thanked him when he handed her the bowl and spoon. He had changed clothes to brown plaid trousers, a tan sweater vest over a long-sleeved shirt, and his hair was slicked back. She was about to remark how dapper he looked, but she thought it might embarrass him to draw attention to his efforts. She lifted the spoon to her mouth and tasted the oatmeal. "This is good."

Rudy nodded. "I do most of our cooking. Not as good as my gran yet, but she says I'm gettin' there. Do you cook good?"

She got in a few bites before answering, having never been this hungry before. "Not very. I wish I'd learned when I was your age."

He set his empty bowl aside, opened a package, cut off a piece, and then filled a glass from the pitcher. "Here. Take this."

She swallowed the aspirin and drank the whole glass of water. It soothed her throat and almost made her feel human. She would never take it for granted again.

The boy partially unwrapped a dish towel and handed it to her. "What's this?"

"Boiled onions. Place it on yer neck. It's supposed to absorb the sickness. Old German cure for all that ails you, at least, that's what my grandpa says."

She crinkled her nose at the pungent smell, but at this point, she'd do anything to feel better.

He pulled a bottle from his basket. "Are you suffering from cough, insect bites, or hysteria?"

Faye blinked and slowly turned her head.

He opened a small yellow box instead and handed her two tablets.

She looked at them suspiciously. "What are these?"

"Sulfur and cream of tartar. Treats boils, helps yer healing, and"—he read aloud from the package—"is nature's beauty mineral for clear skin and soft, glossy hair. You chew 'em. Don't be chicken. Ain't gonna taste too bad."

She popped them in her mouth and slowly chewed. They had a slightly bitter fruit taste. Not bad, but not good either.

He then opened a blue bottle. The label had a skull with crossbones.

CAUTION: POISON.

Alarmed, Faye asked, "What's *that?*"

"Tincture of iodine. You don't drink it. It goes on yer wound." He looked hesitant. "Do you want me to change yer bandage?"

"I think I can manage." She started to sit up straighter but cringed back in pain. "In a little while. I just need to rest a bit more."

When Faye reopened her eyes, the room was dark. She rolled to the side of the bed and dangled her legs while she mustered her strength. Her whole body shook under her weight when she got to her feet.

She glanced down. Rudy slept on the floor at the base of the bed on a rolled blanket and pillow. Careful not to step on him, she tiptoed out to search for a bathroom.

An oil lamp's soft golden glow lit the hallway. She borrowed it and saw that the first door led to a closet. The other opened to another bedroom. She held up the lantern, relieved that Rudy's father wasn't present. Large rustic furniture filled the space with minimal décor. No luck here, either. Whoever planned the design of the house obviously wasn't a professional. Resigned to take the stairs, she made her way down at a snail's pace while holding the railing.

Rudy's dad read a book in the sitting room. He looked at her and frowned.

Head swimming, she wobbled at the bottom of the stairs. "If you'd point me toward your facilities, I'll stay out of your way."

"Facilities?"

Must she really spell it out? "A toilet, please."

He tossed the book down. "The outhouse is out back."

Another house? She let go of the handrail and teetered toward a sturdy chair. Her forehead dewed from the exertion. Had she ever been this weak before? She felt like a day-old kitten.

After an exaggerated exhale, Rudy's father stood, took the lantern from her, and offered his arm.

"I don't want to be a bother."

His expression indicated that she was worse than that. She latched onto him, and he helped her down the back stoop to the yard. Her bare feet recoiled from the cold, hard ground. Each slow step pounded at her wound.

Rudy's dad held the lantern toward a crude structure. A gardener's shed of some sort, smaller than a closet.

"Why have we stopped?"

He opened the door. She wrinkled her nose from the smell.

"Hurry up. I don't have all night." He handed her the lamp.

She took a deep breath and then closed the door behind her. A swarm of flies greeted with an *a capella* chorus. Faye batted them away and hissed valuable air through her teeth. She hurried and reached to get the toilet paper ready. A stack of magazines and catalogs was all that could be found. She tore off a page featuring farm women's winter clothing. They looked the same as a man's.

"You okay?"

"Fine," she said with a grumble as she situated her clothes. Eager for fresh air, she thrust the door open and stumbled out.

Rudy's father caught her before she fell and took back the lantern. He had an earthy scent with a hint of something sweeter. Much better than the smell she'd just experienced.

"What were you reading?"

He helped her to the house.

She didn't think he would answer, but he finally said, "War and Peace."

"Oh, Tolstoy." That he had tackled a literary work of substance surprised her. She'd figured him more suited for the pulps. "I preferred Anna Karenina. Have you read it?"

Again, he took his time answering. "No."

Once inside, the muscles of his arms tightened under her hand. He pulled away.

The back of her neck prickled with the awareness of his presence as she climbed the stairs to the second floor. "This world of ours is only a speck of mildew sprung up on a tiny planet, yet we think we can have something great. They are all but grains of sand."

He mumbled something indistinctly.

"That's Tolstoy. You should read Karenina next. It is one of my favorites."

"Don't need you to tell me what to read."

"I didn't mean to offend."

He followed her into the bedroom and looked down at his son.

Faye sat on the bed and whispered, "He's a good boy."

He nodded. "Don't take advantage of his kind nature," his soft tone not diminishing his underlying threat. "You will regret it if you do. I'll make sure of it."

He bent down, rose back up with his son in his arms, and left the room without sparing her a second glance.

His threat bewildered her. Couldn't he see she was a good person? What had happened to him that made him so leery and suspicious of other people?

Day by day, Faye felt her strength return. She watched from the bedroom window as Jake and another man worked in the fields. He'd probably be too tired to take her to town today. She'd ask him tomorrow. It was frustrating to be dependent on someone who didn't like you. And she hadn't heard from Chaska. Perhaps the kids already moved on, figuring she couldn't pay.

Rudy entered the room, cradling books in his arms, and dropped them onto the bed. "Do you mind if I do my schoolwork in here?"

"Not at all. I could use the company." She sat on the edge of the bed and picked up a book. "What are you working on?"

"Arithmetic, science, writing, and story readers."

"Which one is your favorite?"

"Reading—unless it's boring. Then it would be my science workbook." Rudy glanced over at her. "Do you know how to read?"

"Of course. I graduated a couple of years ago. I loved school."

He bit his lip and then asked her shyly, "Were you a slow learner?"

Faye picked up the reading book. "No. Why do you ask that?"

Rudy shrugged. "I don't know anyone who went to school for that long."

"Really?" She leafed through the book. "It's common where I'm from. I received honors in literature, was in charge of our yearly school banquet, and ran relay for our field day competitions. I was the fastest girl in my school."

"I'm pretty fast, too. When you get better, I'll race you." He paused, clearly in thought, then said, "You must be kinda smart. We need a teacher so my school can reopen. My pa tries to help me, but it ain't the same. I miss my friends. Do you want to be our new teacher?"

His eyes pleaded, and she didn't have the heart to deny him outright. She would be on her way to Colorado soon enough, and he would forget all about her. "Is that what you want to be when you grow up? A teacher? Or a farmer like your dad?"

He reached under his bed and brought up a stack of dime novels and magazines. He pulled one out and showed her the picture on its cover, illustrating a cartoonish woman tied up and a man in a white hat there to save the day. The front cover read: DETECTIVE TRUE CRIME STORIES OF ACTION, A SAM CALLOWAY MYSTERY.

"I wanna be a detective." He pointed at the man and woman. "Sam Calloway and Finny Fairweather solve crimes that have the police stymied." He picked up a dime novel. "But maybe I will be a soldier, cowboy, or Wild West showman like Buffalo Bill. You can be my Annie Oakley." He looked at her questioningly. "Can you shoot a gun? Annie could shoot real good."

Faye shook her head.

"Oh, well. You'd need to practice. I'll show you how when you feel better."

She decided to nip these expectations in the bud before he became too attached. "Do you have any extra paper so I can write to my family and friends to tell them I'm okay and will see them soon?"

"Sure." He picked up a different dime novel and pointed. "Look. Buffalo Bill is chasing Wyoming bank bandits. He throws his knife at Trevor Jenks from twenty feet away." He grabbed his chest, swirled, and fell to the floor.

She peered down at him. "Rudy, you know I can't stay here, right?"

He stood and brushed off his trousers. "Pa'll let you. He just needs to get to know you better, like I do. He'll come 'round."

She sighed. "I like you. I truly do, but I don't belong here."

"Don't *say* that." He frowned and ran from the room.

Sweet kid, but she wanted to leave just as badly as his father wanted her gone. The boy's reaction, though, troubled her.

The following day, Rudy acted as if nothing had happened between them. Faye was still curious about why he had reacted so.

It was clear outside, so she invited him to sit on the front porch swing. She'd subtly work in her questions to avoid upsetting him again.

He read aloud from his grammar story textbook. "Now it says to make my own story. Here are some suggestions—Mister Rabbit goes to town. Missus Squirrel plans a dinner party for her friends. Mister 'Possum goes to the county fair."

"Hmm," Faye mused. "Back home, I could plan a squirrel party in my sleep, so let's do the fair one."

Rudy stood and cleared his throat. "I'll start. Mister 'Possum rode his tractor to the county fair."

"He was grand marshal and led the opening parade." She asked, "Did your parents ever take you to one?"

"Nope."

She startled when Jake and his field hand stomped up the porch steps. She knew from Rudy that the other man's name was Brody, a half-American Indian. Handsome, his skin had a deep bronze glow over a muscular frame without an ounce of fat to spare. His black hair lay long and straight, the same length to his shoulders like he'd escaped off the pages of a Wild West novel.

The boy wouldn't open up to her with his father here. As they poured themselves glasses of the lemonade Rudy had made for her, she went back to the play. "Mister 'Possum rides a Ferris wheel high up in the sky."

They sat, and Jake took off his hat and fanned himself. He didn't bother to introduce his friend to her. Typical.

"Good one," Rudy said. "Mister 'Possum ate the most peach pies in the pie-eating contest."

She laughed. "That's a mouthful."

Jake looked over at Rudy. "Which book is this from?"

"Reading. We are making up a story about what Mister 'Possum does at the fair."

Jake turned in her direction and lowered his brows. "He needs help with arithmetic. Not silly stories that have no benefit."

She tightened her lips. Clearly, rugged good looks did not ensure an agreeable personality. "Encouraging imagination is not a waste of time. It warms up his brain for harder tasks."

The fieldworker laughed. He brazenly winked at her and said with a grin, "Mister 'Possum watches the dancing girls kick up their frilly dresses while the Hutch band plays."

Rudy snickered.

Jake kicked underneath Brody's chair.

Faye looked out at the fields. If she couldn't get answers from the boy, go to the probable source of his angst. "What are you growing out there?"

Jake continued fanning himself, rested his eyes, and leaned his head against the rocker. "Winter wheat mostly. We also have a family garden behind the barn."

"But why are the plants that bluish-green color? I thought wheat was tan."

Brody replied, "Hard to say how this crop will turn out. Dry is one thing, but we've been in a serious drought."

"Why's it called winter?" Faye asked. "That seems odd."

"The seeds go in late in the fall, germinate, then stay dormant until the ground thaws."

"Germinate?" She didn't know this word.

Brody looked about to explain further when Jake interrupted. He propped up his work boots on a stool and cracked an eye. "Planning on farming?" he snapped.

She shot him a look. "Doesn't seem that difficult, really. All you do is poke a seed in the ground and watch it grow."

Jake teetered back and almost tipped. He recovered his balance. "Farmers are the hardest and most honorable workers you'll ever meet."

She guessed she'd hit a nerve. Good.

He went on, "They are the backbone of this whole country. But what would you know of it? Have you ever earned anything through real hard work? Received without stealing or scamming some man to get it for you?"

She'd had enough of his cheap shots at her character. "Women work as hard as men. We just don't get paid for it."

"Most women I've known have no problem getting what they want with little effort."

"Ha! I'd like to see you manage a formal dinner for the mayor and twenty guests."

Jake hooted. "Darlin', the only way you've entertained a politician is in a back alley with a cheap bottle of wine."

He still thought her a lady of the night? She clenched her teeth and was about to let him have it when Rudy intervened.

He cleared his throat. "What do you want to be? If you could be anything?"

Faye relaxed back against the swing. She would not let the ogre get under her skin. She smiled. "When I was a girl, I assumed I would become a wife and mother." Which was true. She thought her world would revolve around her family's wishes and entertaining to boost their status and support her husband's ambitions, giving up her own achievements. "I would like to open another dress shop. One that sells affordable dresses, hats, and gloves. Someday, design my own."

Jake frowned. "I'm sure you will sucker some poor man into financing it. There's one born every minute." He tapped his foot under Brody's chair again. "Break's over."

Faye borrowed one of her grandmother's withering stares. "I will make it on my own, dirt digger, without help from any man. I've learned the hard way not to rely on any of you, regardless of your social standing—or lack of."

Brody motioned toward the stairs. "After you, Mister Dirt Digger."

Jake mocked in falsetto, "I don't need help from a man." He slapped Brody's offered hand with his fan.

She glared at their backs as they playfully pushed each other on their way to the barn. "How you are his son is beyond me. You must take after your mother."

Rudy's face fell. "I'm nothing like my ma. She left us and done run off with a no-account sluggard."

Faye cringed. She figured his mother was out of town visiting or had tragically passed away. Not that his mother had abandoned him. She could understand why a woman would leave his hard-headed father—even feel slightly sorry for her. But Rudy? How could his mother leave him behind?

Oh, fudge. She deflated back against the swing. "That's why you were mad at what I said yesterday."

Rudy blushed.

She set the book aside and clasped his hand. "A part of growing up is realizing that our parents are people and people have flaws. Some more than others, like your Neanderthal father, but no one is perfect."

"My pa hasn't always been this way. He ain't been the same since my ma left. He wanted to make her happy, but the more he tried, the more she complained. She said he didn't make enough money, so he took more jobs. Then she complained that he wasn't home enough." Rudy scratched his head. "Last Christmas, I used my egg money to buy Leatrice Lawson a hair ribbon. She said she didn't like the color and threw it on the ground. Why are girls so hard to please?"

"Perhaps girls and boys don't think about things the same way."

Rudy gasped, and his eyes widened. "Are yer brains different?"

He looked so appalled that she couldn't hold back a laugh. "No, that's not what I mean. Sometimes, a girl will do the opposite of what she should or wants to do. I would bet my last dollar that Leatrice likes you a great deal. She's probably shy, and your kind gesture frightened her."

Rudy worked that like he was trying to solve a complex math problem, but then his mouth formed into an oh like he just solved a boy's biggest quandary.

Chapter 19

MR. FEDORA HAT MAN.

He was trying to kill her again. A hand touched her shoulder. Faye swung her fist with all her strength.

"Son of a bitch. What the hell's the matter with you?"

She warily glanced around the room, then peered up at Jake, who stood over her with his hand covering half his face.

He rubbed a soon-to-be fresh black eye. "You were shrieking like a trapped fox."

"Sorry. I had a dream."

"Pretty bad one by the sound of it. I think they heard you in town."

His sleeveless white undershirt accentuated his broad shoulders and muscular arms, and his draw-stringed pajama pants were sloppily tied. He must have come straight from bed.

"When my boy has a nightmare, he recounts it out loud so it doesn't return."

Did she want to talk about it? She did. Not with him, but as they say, beggars and borrowers can't be choosers.

She nodded. He awkwardly sat on the side of the bed, steepling his fingers between his knees.

Once she started talking, she couldn't stop. She told him about her father's murder, but she couldn't tell if he believed her or not. While she explained, he leaned forward with his eyes cast down. When she spoke of Charles calling off their engagement, he raised one brow and an emotion flickered by so fast she barely caught it. But she could tell she had his attention when she came to the train attack by the man with the scar. His flint eyes looked beyond her with the intensity of a coming storm. Lips pressed tight; they looked almost white in the lamplight. He flexed his hand with the occasional crack of knuckles and seemed so upset that she stopped the story at the part where she'd fallen off the train.

He stood and took a deep breath. "I'll take you to the sheriff's office in town tomorrow."

"But..."

"Try to get some sleep." He shut the door behind him.

Faye blinked at the ceiling and swallowed past the thickness in her throat. She didn't know what she'd expected. That maybe he could help her figure out what to do, or that she'd feel better? But tomorrow, he planned to unload her on some Podunk town sheriff and make her someone else's problem. *Well, good riddance to you too, big dumb oaf.*

The screeching wind pounded on the bedroom wall. The window vibrated and rattled.

With her first step, something stuck to the bottom of her foot. *Sand?*

She tipped her tongue across her bottom lip, encountering tiny grains. Her back teeth crunched on the grit.

What fresh hell is this? She threw on her robe, lit a lantern, and poured water into a bowl on the dresser. Holding the light up to the mirror, she gasped at her reflection. A layer of silt coated her face, and specks of dirt peppered her hair. After bristling them out with her hairbrush and washing her face, she hard brushed the inside of her whole mouth and rinsed several times to get rid of the grit.

She eased down the stairs to find answers.

Jake and Rudy were in the kitchen, wetting towels and old rags in the sink.

She held up the lamp and gasped. Layers of dirt were rippled across the kitchen floor. Dusty earth coated every surface. "It's *everywhere.*" Faye limped toward them, her toes scrunching in the substance. "What happened?"

Jake wrung out cloths and handed them to her. "A roller. The worst we've seen yet."

A roller must mean a dust storm. She mentally filed the new word in her new vocabulary. "But how did it get inside?"

"The door blew in." He handed her more damp rags. "Shove these along the windowsills and between the sashes."

The wind whistled between the tiniest cracks, bringing with it more sand grains. On the other side, soil coated the window glass. It looked like someone had thrown dark paint on it. She stuffed the rags in smaller apertures. Rudy pushed large towels under the doors. Jake tied a bandana around his face, careful of the bruise around his eye. He brought another for her. The back of her throat tickled. She had a sneezing fit that sounded like a choir of mice supported by a tiny horn. Jake handed her a cloth for her face and took the other to Rudy.

They made breakfast. Unable to open the back door to get to the icebox, Jake opened a can of beans and poured it into a pot. Rudy sliced the bread. Father and son worked with ease in a familiar routine. While the food heated, Faye set the table.

"How long will this last?" She stared at the door. It sounded like it might break free of its hinges at any moment.

Jake spooned the beans into three bowls and served them. "Not long, but it takes a bit for the dust that got kicked up to settle. We won't be going to town anytime soon." He blew on his spoon and took a bite.

Faye suddenly thought of her friends who might be out there with nothing but that tiny shelter. "What would happen if someone was caught in the storm?"

Jake poked around his beans. "Out in it long enough without protection, I imagine you could lose your sight. Can't see but what's right in front of you and breathing is like sucking air through a straw. Get off track, and you could lose your way, or worse, suffocate and die. You never want to be caught out here unawares."

Her eyes teared up. She tried not to picture what Chaska and Niya might be going through.

Jake stopped eating. "You don't need to worry. We are perfectly safe in here."

Faye sniffled and took a sip of water. She told him a little about the children who had saved her and bartered with him to help around the farm if he took her to them.

When she finished, Jake stood up and stretched. "They sound like smart kids who would find shelter. I'm sure they're fine." He picked up the bowls and piled them in the sink. "Once it clears, we can go check on them if it would make you feel better."

Shocked he agreed to her offer, she tried not to feel bad about not telling him she didn't know where the camp was. She'd deal with that when the time came.

He added, "I'm sure they'll be happy to join up with you and eager to be on the way."

So that was it. He wasn't being nice. He was just impatient to be rid of her.

Jake rinsed off the dishes and then suggested they play a game to pass the time. He set up a table in the sitting room and dealt a deck of Old Maid picture cards.

Faye set down a match of Bo Peep looking for her sheep. Rudy picked a card from her hand and passed.

"How far is the camp from here?" Jake asked as he set down a pair.

She picked a card from him of Mrs. Flirt, her legs crossed demurely. "Not far." She held out her cards to Rudy.

The boy picked a Buffalo Bill card from her hand. "Yes," he said with glee, placing the pair on the table.

She picked a card after Jake's turn and laid down a pair of Susie Sweets. "Has your family farmed here long?"

Jake shook his head. "I grew up in Kansas City. My old man still lives there."

"Oh? How did you end up way out here?"

"This was my Uncle Ray's place. I moved in with him when I was fourteen to help him around the farm."

"Quite the change from city life."

"I'm better suited for it. Ray taught me a lot about farming. Sadly, we lost him a few years later from a leg wound that turned bad. He was a good and giving man."

Her turn again. Faye tried to read his face for her next pick. "How old were you then?"

"I was sixteen and newly married. I thought I knew everything about running the farm and starting a family." He said to Rudy, "It wasn't long after you came that I realized I didn't know as much as I thought I did."

Faye was surprised he'd married so young but didn't comment. His wife was most likely a touchy subject. She picked the Old Maid card from Jake's hand.

He gave her a smirk.

Ignoring the slight, she held her remaining cards for Rudy to choose. After the final round, she ended up the Old Maid—no doubt, she figured, a sign of her rejiggered future.

After the wind died that afternoon, Faye braided her hair, put on a day dress and her broken shoes, and headed down the stairs.

Jake looked up from his farmer's magazine. "You need something sturdier than that." He left the room and returned with clothes in his arms and boots dangling from his fingers. "Just 'cause the storm passed don't mean the way going will be easy. Put these on."

She entered the bathing room and changed into the overalls over a long-sleeved shirt. The garments fit a little loose, and she wondered if they belonged to his wife or him when he was younger.

When she returned to the sitting room, Jake reached up on the coat rack, plopped a hat on her head, and handed her a new bandana. "In case the wind kicks back up."

He tied it loosely around her neck. She stayed still, eye level with his flannelled chest and breathed in his earthy scent.

"There you go."

She glanced in a mirror and giggled at her reflection. Like the infamous Pearl Hart, she looked ready to rob a wayward stagecoach.

After tugging on the boots, she joined Jake and Rudy while they surveyed the damage outside. It was like walking through a hazy, powdery fog on a gloomy, sunless day. The farmhouse was worse than before; the bared wood stripped down to but a few streaks of white paint. The windows were caked solid. Unmoving waves of dirt peaked at the fence. Only the top of the poles let it be known it was there.

When they reached the fields, Jake bent down and unburdened a damaged wheat plant. "Confound it."

Most of the crop looked in sad shape except for a small patch protected by the trees' windbreak.

Faye tipped back her hat. Who knew wind could be so destructive?

Jake grabbed a handful of dried earth and threw it. He uttered a few choice bad words that ended with, "I'm cursed."

He strode to the family garden behind the barn. It had fared better than the wheat, but not by much. The cows, mules, and goats had been fine in the barn, but two chickens had been buried alive in the coop.

Despite the devastation around them, Jake readied the wagon. Her climb up it pulled at her wound, reminding her to still move with caution. After a wordless signal from his father, Rudy turned away and set off to do his chores.

"Yaw!"

The mules and wagon wheels moved forward and kicked up billows of dust.

At the first divide in the road, Jake asked, "Which way?"

Fearing he would not go if she admitted not knowing, she pointed to the path that looked the easiest to travel.

The fields they passed were like a wasteland, vegetation smothered under brown mounds, littered with broken tree branches and scattered tumbleweeds. A dead deer sprawled stiff on the side of a ditch. A little farther along, another one blocked the path. Jake got down and pulled it off the road. Faye looked away, an ache in her chest. Such beautiful creatures. Such a terrible end. Worry for the children twisted the insides of her stomach.

Everywhere she gazed lay desolation. It was as if the whole land had turned into desert, like a picture show she'd seen once about a sheik, played by Valentino, who'd kidnapped a British socialite and dragged her across the desert to his palace tent in the Sahara. But Jake was not Valentino. She was not Agnes Ayres. And she may not know where she was going, but no luxurious palace was waiting for her at the end of this road. Of that, she was certain.

Jake climbed back up onto the wagon, took the reins, and clicked his tongue.

She tightened her bandana more snuggly over her nose. "Do you ever go back to the city? See your dad?"

"No," he said without hesitation. He was quiet for so long that she thought that was the end of it, but he said more. "My old man doesn't keep with the best company. His brother was right to bring me here so I wouldn't be tempted to follow in my father's line of work."

"What does he do for a living?"

Jake squinted his eyes as he stared ahead. "This and that. Most of it illegal. *Whoa!*" He called for the team to stop and jumped down. "Stay here," he ordered her.

An automobile in the ditch was turned on its side. Jake circled it and then tried to open the door facing the sky. It seemed jammed.

"Hello? Anyone in there?" Jake wiped at the driver's side window with his sleeve. He paused and then climbed the small hill and searched the back of the wagon.

"Is someone trapped?" She half-rose.

"I thought I heard a sound. Stay put." He took out a long piece of metal from his tools, slid down the incline to the auto, and used the device to pry open the door. He spoke in low tones to someone inside and helped an older man through the opening.

"Anyone else in there, McKay?" Jake asked.

The man shook his head no. Mr. McKay had a large gash on his head and problems standing alone.

Jake walked him to the wagon and helped him up. "Did you get caught in the storm?"

McKay nodded. "My Meggie must be scared out of her wits. I didn't think I'd ever see her again. Thank you, lad. You're a godsend."

Jake motioned toward Faye. "I wouldn't have ventured out in this without prodding."

McKay smiled and thanked her. "They have a way of making you do what you don't want to," he said to Jake with a gleam in his eye. "But what would we do without them?"

Jake mumbled something she could not catch as he climbed onto the bench. He called out to the mules, and they were on their way again. Pulling the reins, he took a right at the next crossing.

A short while later, they passed by more damaged crops, more broken trees, and more of the ever-blowing tumbleweeds. The wagon bounced along a rutted path, ending at a small house in desperate need of repair. A gaunt woman and a frisky barking dog burst from the porch.

"Ethan?" the woman called out. She strode to the end of the wagon and placed her hands on her hips. "Ethan McKay, where have you been? I've half a mind to..." The woman stopped and gasped. "You're *hurt*."

Ethan sat up. "Just a scratch, my love. Nothing so bad that your tender hands cannot heal."

Jake climbed over the seat and helped the old man down.

Mrs. McKay hugged them and peered up at Faye. "Thank you for bringing him home to me."

Faye smiled, the warmth of a blush building underneath her bandana.

Jake shouldered Ethan to the house and returned a short while later, his arm muscles taut from carrying a box laden with food supplies. He was so different from the men back home. The way he moved fascinated her in its efficiency and purpose. He was a man who knew what he wanted, and his body had adapted to the pursuit. Unsettled by the thought, she forced herself to turn away.

"They insisted," he said as he loaded the wagon. "Nice folks. You'll not find people like this in a city."

"I don't know about that. I think there are good and bad people everywhere." She thought about the woman who'd stabbed her and shuddered. She had not told Jake how she got hurt and decided not to disillusion him about his perfect country life.

He climbed on the bench, clicked his tongue, and guided the mules back the way they came.

After a few turns down unfamiliar roads, she was about to come clean and admit she was lost. But then something caught her eye, and she yelled at him to stop. A twisted tree with white bark leaned on the side of the road.

"There." She pointed toward it. "The camp is down there. I don't remember seeing any roads that went to it, so you wait here."

Jake caught her arm and plopped her back down on the seat. "If you think I'll let you wander in there yourself, you've got a loose peg somewhere. This road isn't traveled much. I'll tie the team and cover the back. Just give me a minute."

She tapped her foot and crossed and uncrossed her legs, praying all the while, *please let them be okay.*

Jake finally finished and reached up to help her down. She barely touched him when he withdrew his arm.

"I forgot," he said and stepped aside. "You don't need help from a man."

Chin high, she wriggled down on her own, grimacing when her feet hit the ground. The pain that shot up from her old leg injury prodded caution. She stepped lightly, but with no set path, thorns tugged at her arms and legs. The brush basin merged into a dried gully. She came close to falling. Jake's arm intercepted and steadied her despite what he'd said. This time, he didn't tease her.

"There." She pointed at a place where Chaska's rabbit trap had been.

She saw the horrid truth when they reached the camp: it was buried and destroyed. Her eyes filled with tears. "Chaska?" she called out. "*Niya?* Dooly? Is anybody here?" She went over to where Maria's shelter would be and started to dig with her hands and move debris.

Jake stopped her. "Don't," he said gently. "They must've moved on."

A dog barked in the distance. Faye staggered toward it and slid down a graveled slope, landing hard on her side. A stinging pain stole her breath.

Jake carefully made his way down. "Are you hurt?"

She shook her head even though it felt like her wound had re-opened. After a moment, she managed to say, "I'm okay."

The dog barked again. Closer.

"Please help me up." She grabbed his hand, and he helped her through the brush to a small clearing near a rocky outcrop. There she saw the wolfdog.

"Chaska?"

This time she received an answer.

"Over here."

Faye let go of Jake, limped to Chaska, and embraced her, even though the girl squeezed her in her still-tender parts. Wincing, she reluctantly pulled away.

Eyes glazed over; Chaska stared at her with bewilderment. "You came. You came back for us."

"Of course," she said softly. "Where did everybody go?"

Tears escaped down the girl's cheeks. Chaska's jaw protruded, and her bottom lip shook. "They're gone. I heard them screamin' when it hit, but I needed to get Niya somewhere safe, and I'd seen this place on my hunting trips. I got her out just as the walls blew in and ran with her here. I t-tried to go back for Maria and Felipe, but the wind was strong, and I couldn't see nothin' in the roller. When I got back, everyone was gone except Felipe. He was half buried already, his mouth and nose filled with dirt, Maria's serape gripped in his hand." Chaska's voice shook. "It's my fault he's dead. I should have gone back for them."

Faye pulled her close, stroked her back, and spoke soothingly. "There was nothing you could have done."

Niya hugged both their legs.

Faye pushed the little girl's hair back from her grimy face. "You okay?"

Niya coughed, then gave her a serious look.

"Let's clean you up and find you something to eat. That sound good to you?"

Niya nodded.

Faye squared off with Jake, communicating with eyes and body: they would be taking them along, and he dared not deny her this.

Jake took a deep breath and glanced up at the sky. He walked over and gently lifted Niya into his arms.

S'unka growled and barked.

"Better come get this dog," Jake said, staring it down. "It bites me, it'll be the last thing it'll do."

Chaska grabbed her dog and said something to it in her language. The girl picked up her meager belongings and led them back to the camp. Jake took the lead the rest of the way to the wagon and grabbed a shovel from the back.

Faye asked, "What are you doing?"

"Felipe," was all he said.

Chaska and Niya huddled together in the back of the wagon. Faye gave them water as they waited for Jake.

Chaska took a healthy sip and then held the cup to Niya's lips. "I thought we were goners. Thanks for saving us."

"I'm sorry we couldn't get here sooner. Do you think anyone else needs help? We could search—"

"I have. There's nobody."

"If Maria survived, won't she return to look for Felipe?"

Chaska stared down at her hands. "I hope she doesn't. Best for her to believe he's out there somewhere safe, livin' a better life."

She wished she could help, but words escaped her. Instead, she sat quietly, hoping her presence would assure the girl that this particular nightmare was over.

After a while, Jake climbed the hill.

S'unka growled and snapped his teeth.

"I should make you walk the whole way," he said to the dog. He threw the shovel in the back. "It would improve your mood."

Seemingly unphased, S'unka jumped in the wagon and curled next to Niya.

As Jake gathered the reins, Faye patted his arm and said, "If that's true, I hope you're wearing comfortable boots."

Chapter 20

As Rudy rummaged through his old clothes for something that might fit Chaska and Niya, Jake readied the kids a bath.

While Chaska bathed Niya, Faye washed up with a damp cloth at the cabinet and removed the soiled wrap covering her injury. The edges of her wound had separated and bled, the surrounding skin appearing swollen and reddened. She applied ointment, rebandaged, and then carefully pulled a loose housedress over her head.

Her clothes needed a good scrubbing and to dry overnight. Tomorrow, Jake promised to take her and the girls to town. Finally, she would be able to contact her friends and family and let them know she was alive and somewhat well.

She ran a brush through her tangled hair. The bristles hung up on a knot. She worked it out the same way as her current dilemma—with patience and focus, a few strands at a time. Perhaps her aunt would send her money for a train ticket to resume her journey, with some left to give Chaska so the two girls could move on to someplace better. For the first time since being forced into this godforsaken part of the country, she no longer felt fear in the pit of her stomach. Everything would be better once she reached Colorado. There, she could take back control and set into motion the plans to return home and find her father's killers.

Chaska looked up from shampooing Niya's hair. "You keep starin' hard in that mirror; it'll crack and bring you bad luck."

"I don't see how things could get much worse."

Chaska grunted. "Oh, believe me, it can." She leaned Niya back to rinse her hair. After a whistled inhalation of breath, the little girl immediately splashed upright, coughing uncontrollably.

Niya slapped Chaska's hand away from patting her back. "Nah—no, Kimi."

"Sorry." Chaska carefully tilted Niya's head and sluiced it free of suds, then held up a towel. "Out you go. My turn."

Faye dried Niya and dressed her in Rudy's old clothes. She asked Chaska, "What does Kimi mean?"

"It's my real name, short for Kimimela. It means butterfly."

"That's pretty."

"My mama said when she gave birth to me that the Ancestors landed one on her stomach. It meant that I'd have a colorful but wanderin' life, always changin'and I would fly free from the cocoon too soon."

"Prophetic. Does Chaska have a meaning?"

"Somethin' like the firstborn son, I believe. I borrowed it from a friend, an older boy who taught me how to hunt." Her face reddened.

Faye figured he was the girl's first crush. She wouldn't tease her about it. A girl's first love belonged to her heart alone. She reached out with her brush to untangle Niya's hair.

"*Noo.*" Niya blocked her with her tiny hand and skirted a few feet away. Another round of deep coughing followed.

Faye finished brushing her own hair and brought out bottles of lotion and powder from her case. She made a show of smelling each before applying the products to her face and skin.

Niya tiptoed closer. She reached for a bottle. "Me."

Faye held up her brush in one hand and the lotion bottle in her other. "Let me get out your tangles. Then you may smell nice, too. I'll be gentle."

Niya crossed her arms and scrunched up her face.

Chaska leaned back in the tub and held her hand out to Faye. "I want to know what it's like to smell like a girl."

Niya pushed at Faye. "No. Me." She moved closer and turned. Faye gathered a few strands and carefully began the monumental task.

Chaska smiled and slipped beneath the suds.

Jake was quiet throughout dinner, but Rudy made up for him. The boy chatted nonstop, asking Chaska question after question about their life on the road. Faye figured he'd be disappointed when he found out Chaska was actually a girl. But that was a problem for another day.

Niya kept her head down and slowly ate her soup. Between the occasional spoonsful, she rubbed at her eyes and nose and hacked a cough.

Jake side-eyed the child. "Tomorrow, we'll stop at Doc's on our way to town."

Faye nodded. The little girl's flushed cheeks and glassy eyes revealed she wasn't well. Chaska observed her sister with a sense of unease.

After dinner, Faye took Jake aside. "That cough—do you think we should send for help now?"

"I think she can wait until morning. The boy should sleep in the barn tonight."

"The boy is a girl."

Jake raised a brow.

"And should be close by in case Niya needs her," she added.

Jake reached into a closet and tossed her a blanket. "Guess it's you then. I've only got the two beds." He stretched his arms and yawned.

Faye bit her lip but kept her tongue. He was sheltering them, and that was all that mattered. She bid him a good sleep and went to help the girls get ready for the night. After declaring the bed too soft, Chaska took to the floor and stretched out on a blanket.

Faye tossed her a pillow and then tucked Niya beside herself. She reached to lower the lamplight.

The little girl pulled away, taking most of the blanket, and wriggled to the base of the bed. "Night-night story, Kimi."

Chaska groaned. "Not tonight. Go to sleep."

Niya crawled back and put her small hand on top of Faye's. Her bottom lip protruded. "Story."

She tried to think of one, but her mind was exhausted from the day. "I can't remember any."

Chaska spoke from the floor. "Just make somethin' up. She ain't gonna last 'til the end. Never does."

"Okay, then. Let's see, um..." Faye brushed Niya's hair back with her fingers. "There once was a city mouse."

Niya tapped a finger on Faye's lips. "Name?"

She thought for a second. "Um, her name was Pip."

Chaska blew a razz sound. "That's a dumb name for a mouse."

"It's a swell name." She frowned at the foot of the bed as Chaska peered over her toes. "Do you want to tell this story, or shall I continue?"

Chaska covered her hand over her mouth.

Faye settled back onto her pillow. "Now Pip lived in the walls of a big house named Willow Wood."

Chaska scooted up on top of the bed. "Why'd the stupid house have a name?"

"Grand estates sometimes are named."

"No shit?"

Faye gave a look of censure and continued. "Pip loved Willow Wood. It was where she would someday raise her family and where she'd live out her gray-mouse-haired years."

Niya yawned.

"Pip had many friends and entertained all the big-name mice and fat cats, which was her family duty."

Chaska scoffed. "Her job was to talk to people and eat good food? Are you serious?"

"It is more difficult than it sounds."

The girl rolled her eyes. "Uh, huh. If'n you say so. All that yummy food musta made Pip mighty plump and tasty lookin.' Do the fat cats end up eatin' her?"

Niya's eyelids drooped. Her lips parted and closed with tiny puffs of breath blown.

Faye peered up at the dirt-stained ceiling. Would the cats find her in Colorado? One had found her on the train. She shivered. Niya's mouth went slack. She draped the blanket over the little girl and said goodnight to Chaska.

"But how's it end?"

She shrugged and whispered, "I'll let you know when I know."

Chaska muttered something, then followed her wall shadow to the floor.

Faye shut off the remaining light from the lamp and plumped her pillow. She finished the story in her head. At least this night, Pip would have her happy ending.

Teetering the cliff's edge of sleep, an acrid scent of smoke teased her nostrils. Unable to relax until she was certain the house wasn't on fire, she crept to the window and peered down.

Jake sat before a small campfire, the soft light fighting shadows over his face. She was too far away to discern his mood, but his motions were succinct with sips from a bottle and tosses of something into the fire.

Curious, she put on her robe and padded down the stairs. Sprawled on the front porch, S'unka raised his head. Somewhere out in the night, a whistle-happy whippoorwill competed with chirping crickets and a lonely howl.

By the time she reached where Jake had been, he was gone, the fire tamped down to burning coals. A glowing line encroached over a brown envelope where two crumpled twenty-dollar bills were set ablaze.

Chapter 21

The following morning, Faye woke with a start. Niya wheezed through every breath. The sheets were damp.

She pressed her hand on the girl's cheek. *Fever.*

Her little body shook with tremors in a fitful sleep. Faye slid off the bed and shook Chaska awake. "Niya's worse. I'm going to send Jake for the doctor."

Chaska climbed into bed, cuddled her sister, and cooed soothing words.

Faye limped down the hallway and barged into Jake's room.

He lay sprawled across the mattress in a deep sleep. Rudy snored softly on his side of the bed.

She leaned over Jake and poked at his arm.

Eyes shut, he hauled her down and drew her against his body. His legs pressed against her backside, and his heavy arm weighted her against the mattress. He exhaled a contented sigh.

Good grief. She attempted to crawl out from under him, but he was too heavy. She back-kicked his leg instead.

He snorted awake. For a moment, he gave her a glazed look. Then, the realization seemed to hit him. He grimaced and pushed her off the bed. "What are you doing?"

"Niya is worse this morning." She lifted herself from the floor. "I think you should bring the doctor here."

He waved her away and lowered the blanket from his bare chest.

She couldn't keep herself from staring at his boulder-like shoulders, dark-haired chest, and sculpted stomach. A hard-working man's body that looked so different from the softer male forms she'd seen at the country club swimming pool.

He gestured toward the door. "After I get dressed."

"Oh. Right." Warmth crept up her face. She closed the door behind her and pressed her cheeks. She couldn't be attracted to a gruff, dirt-loving farmer, probably not right in the head. Who but a crazy person would use money to kindle a fire?

☙

While Rudy and Jake went to fetch Doc Adams, Faye headed out to the chicken coop to get eggs for breakfast. The flock of chickens huddled in one corner of the pen, a few resting in their nesting boxes. She peered through the wire. Perched high, a red-headed rooster cocked its head to the side and blinked in her direction. Just below him were three brown eggs in an unguarded nest. She needed those eggs.

She watched the rooster, considering. It stared back with a one-eyed challenge.

Faye gathered her courage, opened the wire door, and stepped inside. The hens on the ground clucked softly and moved out of her way. The rooster jerked his head into a new position and looked down at her.

Avoiding his beady stare, Faye moved toward the egg boxes. She reached for them while gently cooing, "Good birds. Nice birds. I just want the gifts you left behind, and then I'll get out of your way."

The rooster rose to its full height, flapped his wings, and crowed.

Uh-oh. She froze in place and lowered her head submissively. "Okay, okay, no need to be upset. I agree. This was a bad idea. I'll go." She turned her back on the rooster and unlatched the handle on the door. The back of her neck sparked a warning.

With a slapping flap flap flap of its wings, the rooster flew down along her back. Its claws attempted to hook in.

She screamed and flapped her arms, swatting him away.

The rooster thumped the ground in a skid, recovered, and defiantly glared her way. The hens' repetitive clucking and chatter grew into a symphony of noise.

Stay calm. She hiked up her dress, prepared to escape.

The rooster then attacked with its spurs. She fought it off. Blood welled on her leg and arm. Shouting, she kicked its breast and unleashed a list of curses at it and its mother hen.

She shoved open the wired door and tried to run, pain streaking up her leg. The rooster followed, close on her heels.

The demon bird chased her in circles around a tree. Suddenly it stopped, shuffled sideways, and cocked its head to the side.

She gripped the tree bark, huffing, ready to sprint in the opposite direction it chose to move.

S'unka ran toward them.

The door to the farmhouse banged shut. Chaska clapped her hands. "No. Bad dog."

S'unka skidded to a halt.

"What're you doin'?" Chaska asked.

Arm out, Faye warned, "That bird has gone mad."

Chaska strolled over and tossed down a torn piece of bread.

The rooster gobbled it up.

The girl batted her lashes. "Like me, he probably doesn't appreciate his morning being disturbed by a shriekin' white woman. Who would?" She flashed a lopsided grin, knelt to pet the rooster, and offered it another piece of bread in the flat of her hand. The bird took it and then pecked at something invisible on the ground.

"Now I know why they call you fowl." Faye speared her finger at the rooster.

Chaska laughed, then clicked her tongue and said, "Tuk, tuk, tuk." She walked with the bird, side by side, to the pen.

Faye let go of the tree but refused to move until it was safe.

With the aid of her dog, Chaska corralled the escaped hens back into the pen. She returned with eggs cradled in her arms. "You have to let him know who's in charge. It has a brain the size of a marble. Don't be outwitted by somethin' that eats its own shit. Feed a male species, and he'll follow you anywhere."

That sparked an idea.

Humming softly, Faye cracked and whisked the eggs in a bowl. Would she have accommodated a group of strangers pleading at Willow Woods' front door? Most likely not.

She searched through their cabinets for items needed for the recipe. They were fairly bare, reminding her once again of Jake's generosity, even though he seemed reluctant to give it.

The ingredients needed for the pie crust looked easy enough. Flour, salt, water, and lard. She found the latter underneath the kitchen sink. After rolling out the dough, she placed it and crimped the edges along the decorative pie plate she'd seen in the pantry. Lining the bottom with cheese slices, she added the eggs and sprinkled them with a red powder found on the spice shelf. *Pretty.*

Killing several matches while failing to ignite the coal in the oven, she tore out pages from Jake's farmer magazine, rolled them up, and lighted the ends. Pleased with her ingenuity, she placed the pie and closed the oven door on her accomplishment.

When Jake and Rudy returned, Faye called them to breakfast while Doc Adams tended to Niya.

Admittedly, the dish she'd made was not as grand as what she'd had at the country club, but she awaited their appreciation as they spooned her creation.

Chaska took a small bite with the appetite of a debutante attending her first formal. She dipped her spoon and then turned it to the side. The eggs dripped back onto her plate. "What do you call this again?"

Faye raised her chin. "Cheese quiche. It's French."

Rudy pushed his food around with his fork. He eyed his dad. Jake gave a minimal nod toward Rudy's plate. The boy sighed and then took another small bite.

Jake tasted the food on his own plate and winced. He drank half a glass of water and cleared his throat. "We're not used to fancy food." He dug a little deeper with his butter knife. "What's this on the bottom?"

"A crust—mostly lard and flour."

"Where did you find lard?"

"From the container under the sink."

Jake scraped his tongue with his napkin and gulped the rest of his water. "That's not lard." He picked up their dishes, scraped the food into the garbage, and frowned at the ripped-up magazine. "I was still reading that."

Faye's bottom lip quivered. Could she not do anything right? How would she survive alone when she couldn't collect eggs, identify lard, or properly light a stupid fire? She pushed back her chair, dabbed her eyes with her napkin, and ran to the front porch.

Chaska joined her soon after. "What's wrong?"

She tried to choke down her emotions, but like everything else, she failed miserably. A sob broke loose from deep inside as she burst into tears. "Go away."

Chaska went to the swing and sat next to her. Her tone uncertain, the girl asked, "Is this about the food?"

Faye shook her head and then nodded. "No, well, it's not just that." She took a deep breath and let it out. "I don't belong here and don't know what to do. I don't know who I am anymore." She let go a heavy sigh. "I tried, but I'm incapable of doing anything right."

"Yeah, I feel like that sometimes, too."

"You do?"

Chaska nodded. "Sure. But then I pick myself up by my suspenders, dust myself off, and try again. Someone once said, if you want somethin' you ain't ever had, you gotta do what you ain't done. It also helps to remind yourself about the good things you already have."

Faye blew her nose into the napkin. What could the girl mean? She was worse off in every way. Homeless, penniless, and burdened with a sick little sister. "What's good for you?"

Chaska stared up at the porch ceiling. "A roof over our heads. Makin' you mad and Niya smile. A bubblin' pot of rabbit stew." Her stomach growled. "Gosh, I'm hungry."

Faye sobbed a laugh. "I guess there's more to cooking than just throwing a bunch of ingredients together." S'unka trotted up the porch with a bone and dropped it by her feet. She patted his head. "Thanks," she said, directing it more at Chaska than the dog. "To make amends, do you think Jake will let me help with dinner?"

The girl's eyes widened in mock horror. "I honestly hope not."

Chapter 22

Doc Adams diagnosed Niya with dust sickness. He gave Chaska a list of home cures to make her sister more comfortable.

Faye rode with Jake to town to pick up items on the list, get animal feed, and mail her letters. On the way, he spoke only a few words to her and only when prodded.

He pulled the wagon to a halt in front of the general store, hopped down, and tied the team to a post.

Three men seated on a bench outside a barbershop sat up straighter. "Hey there, Jake. You get a new mule?" They were staring at her.

"Just a loaner," Jake said and chuckled.

The old men burst into laughter.

Were they making fun of her? She narrowed her eyes at them and then wriggled down from the wagon.

"Nice rump on that hinny," one of the old cronies called out.

They broke into laughter again. Not acknowledging their rudeness, she headed toward the post office with her spine straight and nose in the air.

A postal worker in a nickel-gray shirt and a numbered eagle-badged postal hat attended a woman wearing a very wrinkled and faded house dress.

"Postmaster Nelson, now you know I'm not one to complain, but this is now the third month my *Woman's Home Companion* magazine has not arrived." The woman counted on her fingers with emphasis on the last number. "I want it reported that someone who works for the United States Postal Service is either a half-wit dunderhead or a bad egg brazenly committing a crime."

The postal worker gave the woman a standard professional smile. "Missus Patterson, I looked into your complaint from last month and wrote to the source. Their accounting department claims your subscription ended last January, and you must send them a dollar twenty for the service to resume."

The woman pounded the counter hard enough to knock loose a Strowger telephone's earpiece from its cradle. "That's outrageous! I want a complaint form, young man, and I want it now." She waggled her finger at him. "I was going to leave your name out of this, but now..." She jerked the paper from his hand and stomped out the door.

The postmaster grimaced and then addressed Faye. "Hello. How may I help you?"

Worried that he wouldn't help her following the irrational customer, she laid on her womanly charm. Straightening her shoulders, she beamed a bright smile. "I have a dilemma. You see—I need to send a telegram to my aunt requesting that she wire me money. I also need stamps but cannot pay until the money arrives. What should I do?"

Postmaster Nelson rubbed his chin. "My, that is a pickle. Do you have a record of birth document stating who you are?"

Faye shook her head.

"Hmm." He studied her as though assessing her character and trustworthiness. "Do you know any good members of the community who would witness for you?"

She doubted Jake would make his list of upstanding citizens, but he was her only hope. "Jake Boyd?"

Postmaster Nelson smiled. "Yes, certainly. Jake's word is very good."

"He gave me a ride to town. I'll be right back." She exited the post office and glanced left and right. The men on the bench were still there. Didn't they have anything better to do? Jake was nowhere in sight. She went over to them and enquired where he may be.

"He went to talk to the sheriff," said one old man. His face bore an uncanny resemblance to a sad potato.

"No," a man with a long white beard insisted. "I saw him go into the bank."

"Yer both wrong," said the youngest of the bunch. He looked to be around ninety. "He's gettin' supplies at the general store. Saw him go in there five minutes ago."

Apropos of nothing, the potato face man said, "Warm one today."

"Mhmm," his friend replied. "Dry and dusty."

They all nodded.

Fanning himself, the younger man said, "After a roller, I came home to find my wife cheatin' with another man on my kitchen floor."

The bearded one asked, "What'd you do?"

"What yuh think? I poured him and me some of my best moonshine and handed the missus a broom."

The men burst into laughter.

Horrible old geezers.

"Aw-*ee*-aw," sounded behind her as she turned.

She ignored their immature geriatric fun and headed toward a large barn structure. Its sign read WILSON'S GENERAL STORE. A bell tinkled her entry, and the smell of cinnamon and freshly brewed coffee warmly greeted. The inside had a quaint country décor: clothing, fabric, gardening supplies, groceries, and more packed the space.

She found Jake by the toys. With a ridged brow and focus, he stared down at a doll with red yarned hair in one hand and a teddy bear in his other. He gave a slight hop when she spoke from behind.

"Are you almost done here? I need a favor."

He put back the items and squinted an eye. "What kind?"

"Nothing big. I need you to assure the postmaster I'll make good on my bill."

He raised a brow in question. "Will you?"

"Of course." She batted her eyelashes.

"You got something in your eye?"

So much for that. Big, dumb oaf.

After attesting for her at the post office, Jake took her to see the sheriff. The brick jail was small inside, having two cinderblock cells, each with a single cot.

Only one held a prisoner, a large man coated with dirt. He looked up. The whittling man, Dooly.

Happy he'd survived the storm, Faye dashed forward. Dooly's eyes widened. He shook his head. For some reason, he didn't want it known that they knew each other. She gave him a confused look but remained quiet.

At his desk, the sheriff adjusted his western shirt, removed his cowboy hat, and rubbed his badge with his handkerchief. He moved around some items on his cluttered desk, set aside a pencil and paper for notes, and directed the conversation at Jake. "I phoned the station in Philadelphia as you asked and informed them of the situation. They are sending a detective out to question Miss..."

"Harmon," Faye injected, annoyed that he was talking to Jake when she was the one who had experienced the assault.

He barely glanced her way and rubbed his hand over the horseshoe-shaped bald spot on his head. "To question Miss Harmon in three weeks." The bit of color in his lips practically disappeared with a broad grin. "A *real* detective. Mighty exciting news. They won't believe this one at the barber. Me—assisting a big-city gumshoe."

Faye struggled not to roll her eyes. He'd most certainly be the envy of Podunk.

The front door banged open. A man rushed in carrying a wooden baseball bat and shook it at the sheriff. "He's at it again. If you ain't gonna do something, I promise you I will."

The sheriff grunted and stood. "Don't go anywhere," he said to Jake. He grabbed up his hat and tipped it at Faye. "Law and order await." He followed the other man out the front door.

"Unbelievable," she muttered and walked over to the cell.

Dooly looked up from the cot.

"Why didn't you want the sheriff to know we're acquainted?"

He rubbed a hand down his dirt-caked face. "It'll make things worse for me if he does." He gave Jake a nervous, sideways glance. "I begged people in town to help the camp. But they all said no, and the sheriff threw me in here for disturbing the peace."

Jake spoke behind her. "They've wanted to clear out those camps for a good while now. They were never going to listen to you."

Dooly wrapped his large arms around himself. "But there are women there—and children. They need help."

"Were." Faye clenched her hands. "Chaska and Niya were the only ones left. Everyone else fled the storm." She left out what had happened to Felipe, not wanting to upset the man further. She turned to Jake. "The sheriff obviously won't listen to anything I have to say." She gestured toward Dooly. "When I was ill, he carried me to your farm. I owe him my life. You'll have to be the one to get him out."

Jake stared at Dooly as if sizing him up. He nodded. "You won't like what I'll have to say." He took her aside, then added, "But if it's going to work, you'll need to hold your tongue and trust me."

She was about to ask him what he intended to do when the door opened. The sheriff's peacock walk indicated he'd accomplished his task.

"Dylan O'Shea and Ross Lee were at each other's throats again." He laughed. "You should've seen what Ross Lee—"

"Sheriff," Jake interrupted. "That man there. What'd he do?"

"Well..." The sheriff rubbed his weak chin. "That'll be for the judge to decide in a few weeks when he makes his judicial rounds."

"I only ask because I need extra help on my farm, and a man that size could do the work of two. I'll compensate you, of course. And you won't have to feed him. That's a good deal for both of us."

The sheriff seemed to chew on that idea. He glanced at the cell, then at Jake, and back at Dooly. "You'll watch him? Tie him up at night so he won't run away? I don't got no one else for the judge to try this month and I already sent word for him."

"I will do what needs to be done."

The sheriff nodded his approval. "Sure, Jake, sure. But don't rough him up too much. I need him presentable for court." He jingled his keys and opened the cell door.

Faye made a face at the sheriff behind his back. Her large friend softly chuckled.

Dooly told his story on the way back to the farm.

While he came from a family of Kansas homesteaders, he'd left and found work in an orchard, where he met his wife in California.

Turned on the wagon's bench, Faye smiled.

"The work wasn't that hard, and we got enough food to keep our bellies quiet. But my wife, see, is the most beautiful woman that God permitted to be put on earth. I saw how the other workers, and even the bosses, followed her with their eyes. I'd hoped I was wrong—where I come from, the small town of Nicodemus, Kansas, people were good to each other. Neighbors helped neighbors. A man was judged by his character and worth, not the color of his skin." Sadness clouded his face.

"One night, after a fine dinner my wife had worked on for half the day, I went outside to have a smoke." He rubbed his hand over his face, flaking off more caked dirt. "Men jumped on top of me. I don't know how many—four maybe—but one shoved a dirty rag in my mouth, and another hit the back of my head. They put me in a train car between cartons of fruit. When it stopped in Colorado, the bulls that checked the cars untied me and forced me off. I've been walking back to Nicodemus ever since."

"That's *awful*," Faye exclaimed. "Your poor wife must be sick with worry."

Jake glanced behind. "Will you return to her?"

Dooly sighed. "I will, but what will I find when I get back? Will my wife still be there? Will the men who did this?"

Jake called out to the mules and brought the wagon to a halt. He turned on the bench and regarded Dooly. "Careful how you settle the score. You don't want to make things worse."

Dooly nodded. "Thoughts of what I'd do to them kept me company for many nights. If my wife is unharmed, I won't risk the chain gang and lose her again. We'll move on and start somewhere new. I'll be better. Wiser."

Jake reached into his pocket and pulled out a few dollar bills. "You best get started. Not much, but this should get you to Nicodemus at least."

Dooly's eyes widened. "You're letting me go?"

"We Kansas farmers stick together. Best of luck getting home to your folks."

Dooly hopped down and shook Jake's hand. He rounded the wagon and looked up at Faye. "I hope you find your way, too. No more scrapping with crazy women with knives."

Despite his size and strength, he had a gentle and kind soul. She didn't know how far his hometown was but knew he wouldn't dally returning to his wife. A pang of envy reared. Would anyone ever love her that much?

"I promise." She reached down for his large hands and squeezed them. "I owe you my life. Maybe someday I can return the favor."

"You already have." He walked away, spread his arms out, and smiled up at the sky.

While Jake unloaded the feed sacks in the barn, Faye went inside to check on Niya. Chaska was speaking aloud even though Niya slept.

The girl looked up as Faye entered. "Her fever's down, but she's been in a bear of a mood. Didn't eat much today."

Niya's chest rose and fell with rapid breaths. She coughed in her sleep, a wet cough too robust to come from someone so young. Faye felt her forehead and sat on the bed. She told Chaska about Dooly and the trip to town.

Chaska snorted. "I wish I coulda been there, but then I'd be behind bars, havin' to listen to that ferret of a sheriff." She paused in thought. "Won't Jake get in trouble for lettin' Dooly go?"

"I guess he'll cross that bridge when he gets there. He was different today. Helpful. Almost enjoyable to be around."

Chaska lifted a brow.

Faye rolled her eyes. "Not *that* enjoyable."

The girl chuckled. "I see the way he stares at you when he knows you can't see him."

She frowned. "I'm only saying he acted more like a human being than a gloomy grump."

Rudy called up the stairs to come for dinner.

Faye bent down and picked up a book. "*Our Mutual Friend* by Charles Dickens. Where did you get this?"

"Jake's room. The bottom of his closet is stacked full of them. I was hopin' you'd read it to us. Might make Niya feel better."

She nodded, placed the book on the dresser, then leaned in and tucked a blanket around Niya. "Best not let Jake know you went through his things. We don't want to be kicked out before we're ready."

"Maybe he won't make us leave if you're nice to him."

The girl's words tugged at her heart. It never dawned on her that they would want to make this their home. She sighed. Another task to add to her list before moving on to Colorado.

Chapter 23

The following day, Jake and Brody went to a neighbor's place to help fix a threshing machine shared by the farmers for harvesting.

True to her word, Faye helped Rudy with his chores. She wasn't stepping another foot inside the chicken coop, so he put her to work tending the garden. The problem was that with the drought, the plants were not much bigger than the stuff she was supposed to pull. The look of horror on Rudy's face was the first clue she'd done something wrong. The second was how quickly he replanted half of her work. He then set her to hauling water for the animals and moving the wood he'd chopped to the wood box. A form of penance, she figured.

She leaned on the fence he was fixing. "How much more needs to be done?"

Rudy laughed. "We just got started. You can quit if you want."

"No, I promised to help. But do you have something a little less physical? My arms feel like they're about to fall off."

"Washing needs hung. Trash needs to be gathered and burned."

After hanging the clothes twice—he had to show her the proper way—he handed her a box of matches.

"In that burn barrel over there goes the stuff that don't decay into compost, the pile I showed you by the garden."

Faye brought out the kitchen waste basket and was about to dump it into the barrel when the corner of a brown envelope caught her eye. She dug past the newspapers, onion skins, eggshells, chicken bones, and meat scraps. A gag flexed her throat, but she managed to keep her breakfast.

Addressed to Jake, the return location was Kansas City. Inside, a stack of money. No note, but they were wrapped with a rubber band and a piece of paper with the number twenty written on it.

Faye counted the bills. They tripled more than twenty dollars. A small fortune for a poor farmer. Was he mentally ill? Mad as a March hare, as her grandmother would say. But it was the end of April. And this definitely wasn't Wonderland. Curious, she searched for Rudy and found him in the barn.

"You ever milk a cow?" he asked.

Perhaps if she tried it, she could get him talking. "Sure. There's a cow on every corner in the city of Philadelphia."

"That'd be a no, huh? City folk wit." He moved a stool and bucket next to the animal's side. "Sit here and hold the bucket between yer legs."

After she sat, he set a pail of soapy water beside her. Faye rapidly blinked up at the cow. "How do I keep her from kicking me?"

"If yer calm, she ain't gonna move that much. Wash and dry yer hands and then wash and pat dry the udder."

"Which part is the udder?"

Rudy tossed her a cloth and pointed. "That big ole sack of milk. You sure you want to do this?"

"I can do it. Me and—what's its name again?"

"Her name is Betsy."

Faye washed and dried her hands and then cleaned underneath the cow. The large creature looked back at her and swayed its body. "Whoa, girl." Faye patted its side. "Be patient with me."

A loud squeak came from the cow's back end.

"Well, that wasn't very ladylike." Faye covered her nose.

Rudy chuckled. "Yer lucky she didn't burp. That's way worse."

"Now what do I do?"

"Put yer fingers and thumb there and pull down."

Faye yanked on two teats. The cow mooed and shot her another look.

"Gently," Rudy said, taking hold of her fingers and showing her the way. Warm milk spurted into the bucket.

If only her friends back home could see her now. Willa Cather's Antonia brought to life. Would they be shocked or get a good laugh? Probably both.

"Your dad certainly depends on you and makes you do a lot of work. Do you ever wish for something more? A different way of life?"

Rudy seemed to give that thought. "I like the knowin' of it. The day-to-day of it, but sometimes, while doing my chores, I let my mind wander."

"To where?"

"Places I might go when I get big. Things I might do."

"My father used to take me with him on business trips. Does Jake take you places? Kansas City to see family?"

Rudy shook his head. "Ain't been farther than Garden City, and there, only twice. Never met Pa's family. He talks a lot about his uncle, but I don't remember him."

"Your dad is fairly eccentric for a farmer."

"What that mean?"

"Behaves funny sometimes."

Rudy smiled. "Yep. In the springtime, he chases deer. Not to hunt but fer the fun of it. He says to shed his soft winter body."

If this was Jake's softer body, what did it look like in midsummer? She shooed the thought from her mind. "I meant he seems kind of whimsical."

"When he was my age, he said he was crazy about the circus. Even thought about joining up with 'em and traveling the world. I guess that's where I get the hankering from."

"What was it about the circus that captured his fascination?"

"His ma'd run off, just like mine. Grandpa Boyd told him she left to join with the Ringlings."

Faye contemplated that. No wonder Jake seemed reluctant to trust her, first abandoned by his mother and then reliving that pain through his son's eyes. She was gaining a better understanding of his behavior, but that still didn't explain why he burned perfectly good currency. "I've always wanted to see the World's Fair. Chicago is hosting it this summer. They are going to have exhibits about science and production in the future. You mentioned science was one of your favorite subjects in school."

Rudy's face lit up. "That sounds super swell. I'd like to see that fer myself."

"Maybe your dad will take you if you ask."

His happy glow dimmed. "He'll just say what he always does. That we ain't got the money."

Faye stopped milking the cow and reached under the bib of her overalls. She opened the envelope and showed Rudy the stack of bills. His expression didn't change.

"You shoulda left 'em where you found 'em."

He knew. Faye couldn't hide her exasperation. "To be burned? Why?"

"It's bad money."

What the heck did that mean? "I don't understand."

"Bad men my grandpa works fer take it from hard-working, decent folks to protect 'em from other bad men. Pa said he won't benefit from other's misfortune."

"But why not give it away to someone in need?"

"He said that's just as bad. Robbing Peter to pay Paul. Or Paul to pay Peter. Something like that."

The stool tilted underneath as the cow stamped to the side. Faye saved the bucket from tipping but splashed milk onto her overalls. Her other hand landed in a sloppy pile of manure.

"Fudge." She flung off as much of the muck as possible and then dipped her hand into the pail of soapy water. The towel she'd used was wet, so she asked Rudy, "Can you get me something to dry with?"

He scooped up the pile of so-called bad bills and offered them. Obviously, the apple didn't fall far from the tree. She headed to the house to clean herself up.

Thump.

Faye stepped from the tub and grabbed a towel.

Thump, thump, thump.

What now? She grabbed her robe from a hook, slid it on, and investigated. After opening the front door, she nudged the screen.

A pretty blonde woman wearing a floral dress was set to knock again. She stepped back as if surprised and clasped the braided straw hat on her head. Her gaze wandered over Faye's face and then down. The woman frowned.

Self-consciously pulling in the top of the robe, Faye asked, "May I help you?"

The woman's cheeks flushed red. "I brought a package for Jake." She tucked it under her arm.

"He's not home, but I'll make sure he gets it." Faye reached out.

The woman looked through the screen as if she doubted her word. "Did he say when he'd be back?"

Who was this woman to Jake? She seemed overly familiar with him. It never occurred to her that he might be seeing someone. A jealous vine of thorns prickled underneath her skin, but she refused to let it take root. "He's away for the day."

"Is Rudy here?"

The woman's eyes were the same soft blue as Rudy's. She had the same cute button nose. Family? *Shoot.*

Wanting to repair the wrong impression she'd made, Faye put on a pleasant smile. "Rudy's out back. They kindly allowed us to stop and rest before resuming our journey." She didn't explain who the 'us' pertained to, figuring if the woman thought she was married, all the better. "My name's Faye." She held out her hand.

The woman's face visibly relaxed. She accepted the shake. "Oh, nice to meet you. I'm Elsa. Rudy's aunt."

"Have a seat, and I'll tell him you're here."

Elsa settled on the porch swing.

Faye ran upstairs, yanked on a dress, and hopped into her boots. She hurried out of the backdoor, found Rudy by the burn barrel, and told him his aunt had arrived.

He tossed the remaining trash into the fire and, almost as an afterthought, added the envelope from Kansas City. Faye's stomach twitched as the flames consumed her ticket away.

Rudy lifted the empty basket and headed toward the house. "She never comes here anymore. Must be something real important."

She was curious about what that was. So she could eavesdrop, she offered to bring them refreshments.

Rudy hugged his aunt.

He relieved her of the package. It came from Kansas City. Elsa said she was in the post office when the parcel arrived. The postal worker undoubtedly gossiped about the strange woman Jake was with the day before. They were probably the talk of the town by now. All it took was three bored old men on a bench to get the ball rolling.

She handed Elsa a glass of lemonade.

The woman took a dainty sip. "I figured it must be important and brought it straight out."

Faye slowly poured Rudy a drink. Did the package contain more money? Could she open it without Jake knowing? She could be on her way tomorrow to Colorado and surprise her aunt. It wasn't stealing, after all, if they were just going to burn it.

"Your ma's back," Elsa said softly.

Faye fumbled with the glass and spilled some of Rudy's lemonade. He grabbed it before it toppled and pursed his lips.

Sorry, she mouthed.

Elsa continued, "I've not given her the time of day, but the rest of the family acts like nothing happened. Mama dotes on her as if every day is Sarah's birthday. I don't know how much more I can take. I thought about asking Jake if I could hide here for a while. At least until I can find someone else to stay with."

Rudy shook his head. "Ain't told him."

"Whyever not?"

"I'm not ready yet. I ain't figured out the doggone darn words to say."

"Better to come from you than Jake running into her unawares on the street. Don't you think?"

He set his glass on the porch floor. His face bloomed pinkish red, and he stood with his hands on his hips. "Then you tell him. Why it got to be me?" He huffed and stomped into the house, letting the screen slam.

Elsa's gaze lingered on the door, her face a myriad of thoughts and confusion. She then seemed to remember Faye's presence and composed herself.

Faye stole the seat Rudy had abandoned. "You and your sister don't get along?"

"We used to, but something changed in her after she married. She was desperate to leave here. To go to a big city. For Jake to provide her with a different way of life, one of excitement and adventure." She took a sip. "Sarah's complaints were unending, mostly about money. She claimed Jake had no plan for their future. She blames him for ruining their marriage."

"But she'd abandoned them."

Elsa held the glass against her forehead. "My family has a lot of influence in these parts. Jake needs to know she's back. I think she's plotting to take Rudy away from him."

That would kill Jake. Anyone with two eyes could tell how much he cared about his son.

Elsa frowned. "Sarah has a way about her. She has always sought men's attention and wields her beauty like a weapon. Plays men like a violinist, fine-tuning her repertoire. Even my beloved Garron."

"Is Garron your boyfriend?"

"Until Sarah saw him as her way out. Jake, Rudy, and I were fishing at Miller's Pond. Sarah stayed behind because she detested the smell of fish. When we returned, Sarah was kissing Garron by my tree swing, and..." Elsa's eyes teared up. "Garron had her wrapped in his arms, kissing her with a passion that he had never shown me." She dabbed the corner of an eye with a sleeve. "Jake's anger exploded, not from jealousy with Sarah, but outrage for me. Sarah just stood there with a stupid grin on her face as Jake and Garron fought. But I..." She swallowed the last bit of liquid in her glass. "I was going to forgive Garron. I loved him that much. All for naught. Sarah packed her bags the day after and ran off with him."

What a terrible betrayal to endure. Faye's heart went out to the woman. What Charles had done to her was wrong, but what Sarah did as a sister seemed worse. She patted the back of Elsa's hand.

"Be forewarned." Elsa stood and handed Faye her glass. "If you see my sister, be sure to keep a tight hold on your man."

Faye sat on the porch swing, buried in her thoughts and the new revelations that Elsa had shared. S'unka lay curled by her feet. Jake joined her on the porch after his bath, tossed something in her lap, and then plopped down on the rocker.

S'unka growled low.

Faye looked down at her shoes and their repaired heels. "You fixed them?"

He leaned back. "I figured you'd need them when you leave."

She turned a shoe. It must have taken days to carve the heels and paint them. "You do good work. Thank you."

He gave a half-hearted shrug and swung his feet onto the railing, his denim overalls cuffed over his bare feet. His damp cotton shirt clung to his sculpted muscles as he shifted.

Faye blinked away. She remembered the package and reached underneath the swing. "This came for you today." There was no way to open it that wasn't noticeable, so she would figure out how to get the money before they destroyed it.

After reading the return address, he grunted and set it back down.

"Aren't you going to open it? It could be important."

"It'll keep." His eyes half open, he asked, "How's the girl?"

"Niya's fever broke, but the infection is deep in her chest. Doc Adams suggested we give her warmed milk with honey."

Jake closed his eyes the rest of the way. His fingers pressed the bridge of his nose. "Did he say how long until she's out of the woods?"

He sure seemed eager to be rid of them. This and his non-reaction to the package agitated her. She decided to poke the bear. "No, but Elsa said that dust sickness is common around here, and most recover from it."

He made a sound in the back of his throat. "Where did you see Elsa?"

"She came by this afternoon to drop off your parcel." Faye smiled. "She's nice. It was good to speak with another woman my own age."

A side of his jaw ticked. "What did you talk about?"

Faye gave a flippant wave of her hand. "Oh, this and that. Girl talk, mostly. You know..."

Jake shook his head. "No, I don't know."

She didn't elaborate, enjoying his discomfort. Instead, she reached under the swing and ruffled S'unka's fur.

"Did she discuss her sister?" When Faye said nothing, he answered himself. "Of course she did."

"You mean, Sarah? Your wife?"

"Ex-wife," he said, his reply curt.

S'unka raised his head and growled again. Jake gave the dog a look that would cause a lesser animal to cower.

"She didn't sound like much of a wife to me. Or much of a mother to Rudy."

"We were too young to know what we were getting into." He picked up his package and stood. "It was just as much my fault as Sarah's that things went south. Elsa needs to move on and accept it."

She wondered if he would still feel the same way if he knew Sarah was back in town. She imagined not, but it was not her place to inform him.

Jake strolled away to open his mail in private. Disappointed, she opened the screen door and headed upstairs to change clothes for dinner.

Chaska held a book from Shakespeare. The girl pretended to read to Niya, making up a story that would turn the famous playwright in his grave.

Preoccupied, Niya cuddled a rag doll in one arm and a teddy bear in her other.

Faye's heart warmed. She recognized them as the toys Jake had been looking at in town. "Who do you have there?"

Niya held out the rag doll to her. "Nese." And then she held out the bear. "Mato."

Faye sat on the edge of the bed. Niya offered her the bear. Its golden-brown mohair felt soft to the touch. Black boot-button eyes, a black stitched nose, and the smiling mouth on its face would cheer the grumpiest patient. "Hello, Mato," Faye said. Then pretended to speak for the bear. "Hello."

Niya giggled and reached for it. The little girl looked so much better.

Chaska closed the book. "Jake's spoiling her. Me too—he said we could read his books."

Faye glanced over the titles to decide which to read for them tonight.

Chaska nodded toward Niya. "Now that she's feeling better, I told him I can help more around the farm. Do you think he'll let us stay a bit?"

"I don't know. If not, once I can pay you, you'll have money to move on if you wish."

Chaska's shoulders drooped. "We like it here. I don't think we'll be allowed to stay if you don't." Her words sped up with a plea. "It ain't like you got anyone waitin' for you in Colorado except an old aunt you hardly know." She paused and added softly, "We'd be a family."

The girl looked so hopeful that Faye wanted to say yes. But she couldn't embrace the fate that had pushed her off a train into this godforsaken dust bowl. A woman had to plan and build, even scheme to get ahead in this world. And once she returns to polite society, that's what she aims to do. "I believe you have a better chance if I go. Jake barely tolerates me."

But Faye couldn't build that plan with Chaska and Niya tugging on her heart. She needed to make sure they'd be all right, and for that, they needed Jake. Trilling sounds through the screen door told her he was on the porch.

She dried her hands with a dishtowel and looked out.

He stopped playing the mouth harp. "Sorry. I'm out of practice."

"It sounded good. A little sad, but good." She opened the screen door. "Mind if I join you?"

He shook his head.

She sat next to him and placed the dishtowel on her lap. "May I see it?"

He gave it a light toss. The harmonica had been well used. She put it to her lips and blew a warbled note. "Yours?"

"No, it belonged to Patrick Healy. Everyone called him Harp; he played this thing so damn much. We were friends as kids in Kansas City." He pulled at a ring on his finger, seemingly unable to get it off. "Also willed to me from my good buddy, Harp. What a pal. I'd be tempted to kill him myself if he weren't dead." He sounded more dejected than angry and tried to pull the ring off again.

"Hold on." Faye went to the bathing room and returned with a bottle of her lotion. Kneeling before him, she rubbed the lubricant on his finger above and below the ring, then successfully twisted it off.

He flexed his hand and gave a thin laugh. "Thanks. I was afraid I'd have to cut my finger off."

"That's a bit extreme."

"Better than stuck wearing that thing. I don't know why I tried it on."

She turned the ring, studying it. Sterling silver signet, rather plain, but for the letters KEA engraved. The hint of a memory niggled at the back of her mind. "What do these letters stand for?"

"The first letter is for the city, the E and A for Entrepreneurs Association, a joke really, considering most of the members are dim-witted thugs. The silver is for middle management, gold the higher-ups. Mobsters. Well-connected, dangerous men always looking for a leg up on their competition."

Like being splashed with frigid water, Faye remembered where she'd seen it. Hiding underneath her father's bed. The flashlight on the floor illuminating the ring as the man tied his shoe. Black and white oxfords speckled red on the tip. The rings were too alike to be a coincidence. "The man who tried to kill me. He wore a ring like that, but the initials were PEA instead of KEA."

Jake groaned.

"I don't understand. Why did they go after my father? He wasn't a mobster." She would have known. Wouldn't she? "The money you burned—"

"How'd you know about that?"

"—came from the Mob?"

He nodded and took a bundled stack from his pocket. This one had a paper with the number three on it. "I started receiving them a month ago—incentive to take Harp's place in the organization. My old man set up a meeting in Kansas City with his boss three days from now, and I have until then to figure a way out of this."

"Why didn't you just send the money back?"

"I wish it were that easy. You don't say no to these guys. But I need to find a way. Not just for me but for my son. I won't have him dragged into that life."

She'd misjudged him. He was doing the right thing. She handed him back the ring. "I'm going with you."

He shook his head. "Hell, no."

She fixed her eyes on his. "These people may know who killed my father and who is after me. I'm going."

He let out a snort. "And you think they'll tell you? That simple." He snapped his fingers. "Just like that."

She frowned at him. "No, but I have three days to think of a reason they will."

Chapter 24

Rudy jammed the tip of the shovel into the manure, filled the blade, and then flung the muck into a wheelbarrow. His dad came into the barn and called out his name, but he refused to answer. Instead, he attacked the manure pile for another scoop.

Pa entered the stall and quietly observed. After a time, he remarked, "You're going to hurt your back doing it that way. Slow and steady wins the race. Jerk and thrust stuck in bed past dusk."

Stop talking. Just go away. Rudy increased his movements, huffing breaths.

Pa crossed his arms. "I just came in to say goodbye. We shouldn't be gone long—a week tops. Be sure to mind Brody. Help Chaska keep house." He shoved his hands into his pockets and cleared his throat. "Faye's asking about you. Aren't you going to see us off?"

Rudy threw the shovel down. "Why you taking her instead of me?" He scrunched his nose and forehead. "Are you two sweethearts or something now?"

"I told you—she has her own business to take care of—problems that don't concern us."

"She's my friend. And yer gonna ruin it, just like you ruin everything else."

Pa flinched. He leaned against the stall and said softly, "She's not your mother. We can't keep her."

"You couldn't keep Ma either." He picked up the shovel and continued his chores.

Pa hung his head. He left the stall but turned back. "Is there anything you want me to tell your grandpa?"

Rudy stabbed and lifted another full shovel. "Never met him, so what would I say?"

The sound of his dad's footsteps faded away from the barn. Rudy paused from his work and wiped his forehead with his shirt sleeve. He regretted what he said but hated that his dad was keeping stuff from him. His ma had been sneaky about things, so look how that turned out. He ran a hand over his stomach and pulled a face. Not telling Pa she was back was a mistake he'd fix once his dad returned. Because he knew better than anyone—family secrets always ended with pain.

Jake had borrowed a neighbor's Studebaker for the drive to Kansas City. It looked a little worse for wear. Faye wondered if it would reach there and back. Its door squeaked and hung low on hinges as she loaded her travel case.

Jake emerged from the barn, a frown on his face. Rudy wasn't with him. Faye sighed. The boy had seemed upset at breakfast and barely spoke. He was probably feeling left behind again. She'd decided not to intervene between father and son. She was lucky Jake was letting her tag along and couldn't risk him changing his mind. She'd find a way to make it up to Rudy when they returned.

Brody stepped off the porch with Niya happily perched on his shoulders. She gripped his hair with both fists and urged him on with her heels. Chaska followed, carrying a basket with food and drinks.

"I made your favorite," she said to Jake. "Smashed baked beans on buttered bread."

Jake ruffled the top of Chaska's hair. The simple act made the girl's face beam with joy. She set the things on the front seat floorboard and hugged Faye.

The girl asked, "You coming back?"

Faye squeezed her. "I'll try." She turned away and waved at Brody and Niya. She shouldn't make promises she might not be able to keep. Who knows what lay ahead, where this trip might take her?

Jake gave a final troubled glance toward the barn.

Brody patted him on the shoulder. "Don't worry. I'll keep him busy. Do what needs to be done and hurry home."

Jake clasped his friend's arm. "I'm grateful. Should be but a few days."

Faye settled in the car and struggled to close the heavy passenger door as Jake closed his side. The automobile whined a cranky start, and a plume of smoke coughed from the exhaust with a loud bang.

She cracked her window as they set off. The annoying whistle of air was better than the exhaust fumes and burnt cotton candy smell that soon permeated the interior.

The vibrating dash made a loud rattle. Jake shouted over it. "Better than walking."

Not by much, she wanted to say.

He settled into a long silence but seemed to grow increasingly restless, his movements varying from rubbing his neck, jaw, and leg to excessive gestures as he drove the automobile. He struck the dashboard, making the rattle even worse.

Between his driving, the bumpy road, and the smells, she grew increasingly queasy. Perhaps coaxing him to open up about his feelings would help. "You'd better talk about it before you beat what's left of this jalopy into pieces."

He grimaced. "It's just...my old man...he just..." Jake clenched the steering wheel and blew out a breath. "Sorry. It's complicated."

Faye ran her hand over the car's dash. She gave it a healthy thunk to no avail. "We have a long drive, so there's time."

Jake spoke about his childhood. His father, Gus Boyd, worked for a man everyone referred to as Boss Tom. Gus ran Boss Tom's gambling hall, cat house, and saloons.

His voice grew louder as they hit another bumpy road. "Gus took me to work with him to further my education. My buddy Harp and I ran their errands. Boss Tom provided bicycles for us to get around town. Mine was a real beaut—a Mead Ranger—red and black frame, fastback seat, and coaster brakes that stopped on a dime. She really hauled. Harp and I would play cards to win her before deliveries, but I always won. She was my first love. Not to be shared."

While he spoke about his bicycle, his agitation was replaced with a boyish look that made Faye smile.

He tapped the speedometer and dropped his speed. "Boss Tom had his hands on more dough than Holsum Bread bakers. He controlled judges and the police, kept them underpaid so they'd take bribes and leave his booze and gambling places alone. Gave the north side, 'Little Italy,' to the Sicilians. Prohibition was a gold mine for the Italians. They were the only group bootlegging alcohol. Boss Tom gave them free hand to do the grunt work because he received the largest cut without lifting a finger. Favors were traded regularly to everyone in good standing with him and his brothers."

She cranked up her window, the noise hurting her head more than the fumes. "He helps people?"

Jake nodded. "He did, but that was the secret to his rise in power. He used the common man, pretended to be just like them, so he could buy their loyalty and own their votes."

"If he was a politician, he can't be all that bad. Maybe he's more reasonable than you remember. If you explain that you have a different way of life now and don't want to come back, perhaps he'll agree."

"I don't have the luxury of deciding the direction of my life. Every seaman eventually seeks a peaceful port, just as most in the life of crime eventually seek a way out. But in the old timers' view, I haven't put in time. I haven't paid the devil his due." He shifted the gears and glanced over at her crossed legs.

She contemplated his words but, at the same time, was distracted by his attention. He reached down next to her calf, causing her breath to catch as her nerve endings streamed tiny sparks in anticipation of his touch.

Instead, he picked up his thermos bottle. "Can you open this?"

Oh. She opened the lid with more power than needed and sloshed the water into the tin cup. She crossed her legs the other way, aware of her disappointment and troubled by her reaction. She returned to their conversation. "Did anyone ever try to remove Boss Tom from power?"

Jake nodded. "Once that I know of for sure. It was mid-afternoon on a sunny summer day. I parked my bike outside Tom's club called The Little Bitsy. That was where Harp and I picked up the packages to deliver. Boss Tom had a meeting with his top men. I heard the cars screech to a stop out front before the gunfire and dropped to the ground as the front windows shattered. The only one standing was Boss Tom's accountant, Two Cents, named because he counted the money, but more so because he had an opinion on everything and was always putting in his two cents' worth."

The rattling in the dash quieted. Jake lowered his voice. "I remember thinking I should close my eyes and be afraid. But the dance the accountant did to avoid the bullets kept him on his feet long enough to fascinate me. In fact, I remember being more upset about the destruction of my Mead Ranger than the brutal murder of my dad's associate. Soon after the funeral, my uncle insisted I live with him. I guess he saw something in me that troubled him." Jake grew quiet.

Faye stared out the window. What kind of people would put a young boy in such danger? What kind of man was Jake's father to allow that? What if something like that happened to Rudy? No. She couldn't let that happen. She had to find a way to help Jake out of this and still get the information she needed.

Rockhill Gardens looked more like an upscale neighborhood one would find in England, not the American Midwest.

Faye glanced over at Jake. He drove at a snail's pace, his jaw tight as he squinted at the house numbers. He stopped in front of a brick and timber pseudo-Tudor and looked down at the address written on a piece of paper.

"This can't be right," he said.

"Only one way to find out." Faye opened her door and stood, eager to stretch her legs.

Jake took his time joining her on the sidewalk. He stared at the house and shook his head. "This isn't right. Gus wouldn't live here." An expression of doubt and something else flitted over his face.

Faye took his arm and coaxed him past the perfectly pruned shrubbery to an arched, ornate wooden door. She knocked.

A pretty woman with short red hair answered, drying her manicured hands with a dishcloth. "Hello." She stared up at Jake and then batted her eyelashes. "You must be Jake. I'd know that Boyd handsome face anywhere." She pulled him in for a hug.

Jake's eyes widened. He didn't return her greeting.

The woman didn't appear to notice his discomfort. She smiled at Faye. "I'm Nora. You must be Sarah. Come in. We were just finishing dinner. Your dad's been so looking forward to seeing you."

Faye was about to correct her and give her real name, but Jake grabbed and squeezed her hand, slightly shaking his head.

She mouthed, *Why not?*

Later, he mouthed back and nudged her into an entryway.

Figuring her questions would keep, she went along with it. A pretty Tiffany lamp on a small table caught her eye, as did the framed family photos. Jake didn't appear in any of them.

Arched doorways framed the hallway. She glanced left at a cozy-looking sitting room with a large stone fireplace as she followed Jake and Nora down the hallway. The savory scent of cooked meat and onions grew stronger.

A newspaper blocked the face of a man seated at an elegant dining table. A boy about Niya's age ate pot roast. His face resembled Rudy's, but his hair was tinged red.

"Darling. They're here."

The man lowered his paper. He looked like an older version of Jake but had a stately, refined build. Streaks of gray blended with his dark hair. Handsome for a man around fifty. This was his father. Most definitely.

"Well, hello there." He came over and clamped Jake's shoulders. "My, how you've grown. Must be all that fresh air." He gripped down Jake's arms. "A strapping young lad. Wouldn't you say, wife?"

Nora nodded. "Very strapping." She picked up her husband's plates. "Jake, Sarah, may I get you something to eat? Such a long car ride. Gus drove us to Denver once. I thought we'd never make it. Those long stretches of nothing but flat grassy plains for view."

"No, thank you," they answered in unison.

"Some coffee, then." Nora picked up her son's finished plate. "Schoolwork, Rabbie, then get ready for bed." She went into the next room.

The boy picked up his toy plane, "Brrrd" it around the grown-ups, and clomped up the stairs.

Jake's dad turned his attention to her and pulled her in for a hug. "You're just as pretty as Jake said." He kissed her cheek. "My home is your home. Where's my grandson?"

Jake crossed his arms over his chest. "You're unbelievable. A selfish, thoughtless bastard. A wife? Another son, Gus? Really?"

His father took a slight step back and rubbed his jaw. "Yes, I have a new family. Why not? A grown man isn't meant to be alone."

Jake narrowed his eyes. "Because it worked out so goddamn well the first time." He sneered in a low voice. "With my mother? With me? Now you involve more innocents?"

Jake hadn't mentioned his mother to her. What had Rudy said? That Gus told Jake his mother joined the circus? By the anger on his face and hurt tone of voice, this was still an open wound that hadn't healed.

Gus threw up his hands. "Please, let's not argue. That was ages ago. Things are different now. Go out on the street and ask anyone whose city this is. They will all answer the same thing—Tom's town—because he owns it and everyone in it. No one would dare cross him."

Jake raised a brow. "What about Chiappetta?"

"*Pshaw*. Lucky Leo? He's more a politician than a gangster these days. Like I said, you've been gone a long time."

Nora brought four steaming mugs of coffee on a tray and set them on the table. "I made up the guest room, so just let me know what else you may need."

Faye cast a look at Jake.

He turned to Nora. "You shouldn't have troubled yourself. We planned on getting a motel room."

Rooms. Motel rooms. Faye corrected him in thought.

Nora waved him off. "Nonsense. You're family. I won't take no for an answer. Cream and sugar?"

"Black." Jake shrugged at Faye.

She forced a smile. "One cube, please."

The conversation lightened. After coffee, they played cards. She nervously watched the clock as the hour ticked and the sky grew dark.

She'd never shared a bed with a man. What if she snored? What if she drooled in her sleep? What if he tried to kiss her? Her heart skipped a beat at the thought. *Get a grip.*

The room could best be described as cozy. Faye stared at the bed.

How will we fit?

Her notion that Jake could sleep on the floor went out the window. The bed and dresser left little room for anything else.

Nora poked her head inside. "A little snug, but the bed is comfortable. The bath is across the way. Sleep tight." A moment later, a door shut at the end of the hall.

Jake stood beside her at the foot of the bed. "This hasn't exactly gone as I planned."

Pfft. "Understatement. Why didn't you tell them I'm not your wife?"

"Keep your voice down." He rubbed the back of his neck. "It saves us from figuring out who to say you are. That maybe if he saw us happily married and content, my old man would talk Boss Tom out of forcing us to move back."

"But won't they find it fishy—me asking questions about the Philadelphia Mob when I'm supposed to be from Kansas?"

Jake shook his head. "No, because you won't be talking to anyone, not even their wives. You don't know these people. They'd sell you out faster than a wildcat hits the ground running. We'd be worse off than we are now."

She didn't like it, but there was no sense arguing with him. With discretion, she'd make her own inquiries. Finding her father's killers and those pursuing her must be her main priority. "Fine. You know best, but what do we do about this?" She waved her hand over the bed.

"We can make do for one night. It'd hardly look like we're a happy couple if they find me sleeping in the hallway. You want the bath first?"

She breathed in and exhaled slowly. One night. She could do one night. She picked up her case and crossed the hall.

The bathroom appeared to be rarely used. Modern in design, it was cheerful with vibrant colors of sea-foam green, dark pink, and cream tiles. The toilet, tub, and pedestal sink were a lighter pink. Pretty.

She opened her case and retrieved her toothbrush, paste, and soap, not wanting to unwrap the rose soap provided. After washing up, she untied the fancy ribbon on the folded towel. Refreshed and feeling a bit better, she slipped on a peach chiffon and lace night-gown. Light and flowy, she loved the way it draped her form. She dug further into her case. No robe.

"Oh, crackers."

She couldn't go out there like this. She checked her case for some-thing else and noticed a tear in its interior lining. The glint of some-thing metal showed within. She made the hole bigger with her finger, worked it out, and turned the small key in the light. Engraved on the flat part was etched A N BANK with the number 227 beneath. American National.

Why did her father have a hidden key belonging to his competi-tor? Penn's voice entered her mind: *"I'm following a paper trail that I hope will prove his innocence. Did he ever mention anything to you about moving money? Or did you find any keys that did not match a lock?"*

Her feet tingled with the urge to run to Philadelphia and find what it unlocked. She placed the key back in its hole and latched her case. Her gaze swept the bathroom and landed on the towel she had used. She wrapped it over her bare shoulders and opened the door.

Jake was waiting for his turn. She bumped into his chest and lost her grip on the towel.

He glanced down at her and jerked his head back up. A muscle twitched in his cheek. "What the hell are you wearing?"

Her face instantly heated. "Keep your voice down," she bit back and reached for the towel. This was all his fault. She would not let him belittle her. "This," she said and swept her hand across the bed-room door, "is your doing, Bucko. Not mine. I'll wear what I damn well please." She closed the door soundlessly, not wanting to disturb the household from its sleep. Slipping between the iron bed and the wall, she yanked loose the sheet and the green, blue, and gray floral bedspread, the same pattern that papered the walls. Once situated, she stared at the bottom of an embroidered curtain over a small window.

Why did he get under her skin so? *Why do I give a fig what he thinks?*

She would not let him cost her a moment's sleep. She flicked off the lamp, plunging the room into darkness. Laying on her left side, she hugged the pillow.

A few minutes later, the door opened. The hallway light beamed Jake's shadow on the wall and then disappeared as the door clicked shut. The bed moved with a bump.

He cursed low under his breath.

She smiled and hoped his shin hurt.

The mattress dipped; the iron bed groaned.

He exhaled a sigh. "I'm sorry. I didn't mean to hurt your feelings."

"You didn't." The reply came out more curtly than she intended. "Goodnight."

The bed squeaked more.

She gripped the edge of the mattress to keep from rolling back to him, but the bed barely fit them both, and she couldn't hold on and sleep at the same time. She let go and slid into him. He reeked of rose soap.

"You smell like my great-aunt Polly." She waved a hand over her face.

"Hush. Go to sleep." He settled on his back.

Her nightgown offered little protection from the hairs on his arm. Trying to ignore the itch, she readjusted to find a better position.

"Great Gatsby," he said through his teeth. "Will you please stop wiggling like that?"

She turned over and the top of her breast bumped underneath his chin.

Jake swore an oath.

Embarrassed, Faye thanked the heavens for the darkness so he couldn't see her blush. She quickly plopped over and offered him her back again.

The movement rolled Jake to his side. Like a great wall, his body hovered over and behind her, his warm breath tingling the back of her neck. Goosebumps freckled her skin. She snuggled her face against her pillow. The more she concentrated on not moving, the more her body rebelled. A phantom itch on her back hopped to her side, leg, and then thigh. She finally gave in and scratched at it.

Jake exclaimed, "For Pete's sake! Lay still." He jammed his pillow between their waists.

Faye bit her lip. "Who is Pete?"

"Huh?"

"You said 'for Pete's sake.' Why not Tom, Dick, or Harry's sake? Why Pete?"

"Saint Peter, who wants very much for me to sleep, and for you to pray quietly."

She liked the weight of him against her back and snuggled deeper into her pillow. "Honest to Pete, for the love of Pete." She tittered. "Why happy as a clam? Why would clams be happy?"

"I don't know. Never seen one."

"Skin of your teeth. That makes no sense at all."

Jake groaned and rolled over. For a while, she listened as his breath evened out. A low-timbering snore reverberated in his throat.

This wasn't how she'd thought sharing a bed with a man would be. Indeed, if she ever did marry, she'd insist on separate beds. *Heavens to Betsy.*

Chapter 25

Faye dressed and made her way downstairs. Nora was cooking break-fast.

"May I be of help?" She stood at the counter beside a carton of eggs.

Nora turned and offered a pleasant smile. "Aren't you dear. No, you're the guest."

Jake probably told her not to let me near the stove.

Nora gestured at a seat at the kitchen table. "I'll pour you some coffee and us girls will chat a bit. Get to know each other."

Faye took a deep breath. Little did she know she'd have to under-study the role of Jake's ex-wife and Rudy's mother. She hoped she got the story straight.

"One cube? Is that right?" Nora brought over two cups of steam-ing coffee.

"Yes, please." She stirred to dissolve the sugar faster. "Where's Jake?"

"He went with his father to meet Boss Tom this morning."

How could he leave without her? He knew how important it was for her to be there. Not wanting Nora to know how upset she was, she composed her tone. "Did he say how long he'd be gone?"

Nora took a sip. "Jake said you might be disappointed, but wom-en aren't permitted at their meetings, so we thought you'd be more comfortable here. But you'll get your chance to meet his new em-ployer tonight. Boss Tom is throwing a dinner party in Jake's honor. A welcome back to the fold soirée."

She scuffed her chair closer. This party didn't sound good for Jake, but excellent for her. Tonight would be her only chance to get the names of the upper-ring-wearing members of the Philadelphia Mob. To possibly find those responsible for her father's death and the identity of Mr. Fedora Hat Man. Her heart sank. To do that, she'd need to be at her best. To look her best. "I'm afraid I didn't bring anything suitable to wear."

Nora smiled. "Well, it just happens that I am friends with Ellen O'Connell, owner of the best garment company in the Midwest. I'll give her a call and see if she can loan you something and fit us into her busy schedule."

Faye had heard that name before. Then it dawned on her. "You know ELOC? I adore her designs and collections. I've worn them back in—" She almost said Philadelphia but caught herself. "I remember reading about her in the newspaper. Something that happened last year…"

"Oh my, yes. It was all anyone talked about. I'm not one to gossip, but you should know before we meet with her. Ellen and her chauffeur were abducted and held for ransom last Thanksgiving. For almost two full days. The brutes demanded seventy-five thousand dollars for their release."

A fortune, even for a woman of means. Faye nodded. "Yes, I remember. It made national news. There was something about her lawyer finding her."

"Don Deed. He lived next door to Ellen and her husband at the time. The note said not to involve the police, so her husband asked Deed to contact his connections, mainly Lucky Leo Chiappetta. Deed and Lucky Leo's men stormed the house where Ellen had been held. And now she and Deed are to marry. It is all so very romantic."

"But I thought she *was* married?"

"Oh, yes. Another terrible tragedy. Her husband had an unfortunate accident soon after Ellen was found. And the poor dear was just finding out she was pregnant then. How much misfortune can a woman bear? But her business is thriving, and she's happier than I've seen her in years."

And she's living my dream. Faye hoped to make a positive connection, talk fashion with her, and pick the woman's brain about her business success.

❧

The gate surrounding Ellen O'Connell's mansion looked as secure as Fort Knox.

Who could blame her? Faye couldn't imagine how terrified the woman must have been, held against her will, not knowing if she'd live or die.

The mansion seemed well maintained but a century old—a Victorian Gothic design of red brick with large stone-lined windows. Nora opened the front vestibule doors that led to another door inside a small entry chamber. There, she rang the bell and adjusted her floppy hat and floral print dress.

Several locks clicked on the other side, and then the door opened. The butler ushered them into a beautiful sitting room fit for a Victorian queen.

Nora introduced her to Mrs. O'Connell, soon to be Mrs. Deed, and another woman named Lucy Chiappetta.

Mrs. O'Connell appeared to be only a few years older than her and didn't seem as intimidating as Faye had anticipated. She was stunning and stylish from head to toe with a pageboy haircut, a rose print sundress made of chiffon, and burgundy leather high heels. Her hands settled on her belly, some halfway through her pregnancy.

Mrs. Chiappetta was also fashionably dressed if one was attending a funeral. Her black and gray hair was pulled tight with strict precision. The woman looked her up and down as if appraising her worth. "Who are you, girl?" she asked brusquely.

Caught off-guard, Faye almost blurted her real name.

Mrs. O'Connell interceded on her behalf. "Lucy, this is Jake Boyd's wife, Sarah. I told you; they are farmers from western Kansas."

Lucy harrumphed and stared at her with shrewd eyes. "If this is a farmer's wife, then I'm Italy's Donna Rachele Mussolini."

Faye gave a nervous laugh, joined by Nora, who looked unsure why she was laughing. "It is a pleasure to meet you. Thank you, Missus O'Connell, for loaning me a dress for tonight."

"Call me Ellen. Turn, please."

She slowly circled.

Ellen sighed. "You have a lovely figure. Soon I won't be able to lace my own shoes. But pregnancy has some things in its favor—like eating whatever you want." She held up her hand. "Face me again and set your shoulders back."

"Head up, girl," Lucy Chiappetta scolded. "Don't slouch."

Faye mentally patted herself on the back for her country-girl performance.

"A dinner party, you say?" Ellen tapped a finger to her lips. "Is your husband going white or black tie?"

Lucy snickered. "He's probably wearing overalls and a straw hat."

Faye pressed her lips. In truth, the same image had crossed her mind, and though she had made fun of Jake out of anger, she disliked Lucy putting him down and felt inclined to defend him. "I believe he packed black tie," she lied.

Ellen clapped her hands together. "I know just the thing. I'm bigger boned than you, so I'll have to take it in. Come with me."

Faye followed, relieved to get away from Mrs. Chiappetta's prying eyes.

❧

Rose-colored lipstick filled her lips. Faye rubbed them together and blotted them with a tissue. In the mirror's reflection, she pulled loose a few tendrils to soften her upswept hair. Stepping back, she surveyed herself from the waist up, lightly running her fingers over the forest green velvet and beaded bodice. Sheer sleeves wisped her shoulders. The long, flowing skirt of the dress swished as she turned her hips. "Eat your heart out, Kate Hepburn."

She carefully moved down the steps in Ellen's high-heeled sandals to the Boyd's sitting room. The men stood.

Nora gushed forward. She looked pretty in a colorful silk floral. "Oh, Ellen was right. It's perfect. You look so beautiful, my dear."

Faye's cheeks warmed. "Thank you." She looked past Nora at Jake.

Staring, Jake took a step back, lifted his chin, and ran a finger under his collar. At some point today, he'd received a haircut and shave. Tapered on the sides, he'd left his dark hair longer on top in tousled waves. New clothes, too. He wore a dark dinner suit with a white starched shirt and bow tie.

Faye's breath hitched in her throat. Tingling heat spread down her neck and across her chest. She forced herself to look away from him and smiled at Nora instead.

"Shall we go?" Gus asked.

Nora shook her head. "I have the perfect necklace to go with that dress." Her heels clicked up the stairs.

Gus sighed, plopped back down in his chair, and picked up a newspaper.

Jake came over to her. The heady mix of citrus and spice from his cologne tickled her nose. He cleared his throat. "We need to go over a few things."

Really? Not a—Gee, you look swell. Just straight back to business. Faye frowned. "I know my role."

"Look, I know I'm asking a lot, but I need you to trust me."

She did but didn't agree he knew how to get answers in a social setting better than she did. "Keep the conversations light and blend in with the wallpaper. That sum it up?"

He nodded.

Nora clicked back down the stairs. "Here we are. Jake, will you do the honors?" Nora handed him a delicate emerald necklace.

Faye beamed. "Oh, Nora, it's beautiful. Thank you." She turned her back to Jake. His warm hands brushed over and settled against her skin as he worked the clasp.

The tiny hairs on the back of her neck stood at attention. She adjusted the gleaming gem in place above her cleavage and turned back with the whoosh of her skirt. "How does it look?"

Jake stared down at her with an odd expression. "Green," he said and then abruptly strode out the front door.

Chapter 26

Boss Tom's security put Ellen O'Connell's to shame. Surrounded by a high spiked fence, the grounds were illuminated with spotlights bright enough to land Lindbergh's Spirit of St. Louis.

Faye gave Jake a sidelong glance. He seemed calm, staring out the window. She wiped her hands on her dress and worked to slow her racing heartbeats. The unknown bothered her more than anything else.

Jake's father stopped his luxury Cadillac at the gate and rolled down his window. A group of men with intimidating guns immediately surrounded the car.

A man beamed his flashlight at Jake's dad. "Evening, Mister Boyd."

Gus held up a hand over his eyes. "Evening, Duff. Nice night for a party."

The light briefly shone on Nora. "Indeed. Who do you have back here?" He switched the light to Jake and held it on him.

Gus introduced them. "My son and his wife."

The light scanned over the back seat and then beamed on Faye. She closed her eyes, uncomfortable with the bright intrusion. Jake took her hand and squeezed.

"Clear," the man shouted.

Faye opened her eyes as Jake took back his hand. She mourned its reassuring loss.

The gates cranked open. Gus drove up a long driveway that ended at a French Provincial three-storied mansion. He stopped and tossed his keys to a man in charge of parking cars. Fifteen automobiles lined the outer drive.

Faye took a deep breath. So much for a small dinner party. Jake opened her door and acted like the gentleman he hadn't been on the farm. She tightly held his arm along the walkway that curved around an illuminated fountain and led to a grand veranda.

Two men in white suits opened the huge wooden double doors.

Jake's hand on her back escorted her in, his touch comforting.

To Faye, the foyer looked like an entry to heaven. It was all white, from its marble flooring to its cathedral ceiling and a staircase that curved out of sight. The place smelled of soap with a hint of lilacs. Under a dramatic crystal chandelier, a marble statue of a life-sized angel posed with its wings spread. Large paintings depicting scenes from the Bible lined the walls.

It was so ludicrous to see this décor in a gangster's house that she struggled to keep a straight face and quell a hearty laugh. The tightness in her shoulders eased.

The man in the white suit said, "Guests are in the ballroom."

Jake's father thanked him. But instead of going where they were instructed, Gus took them on a tour of the main first-floor rooms.

Each one grander than the previous, he guided them to a music room, a library, a woman's study, a place to play billiards and other games, three parlors, and a fabulous indoor swimming pool surrounded by indoor plants.

Jake's scowl deepened with every room.

Faye couldn't blame him. Boss Tom was obviously a man who bought whatever he wanted. She wondered how badly he wanted Jake. Her worry returned. How does one negotiate with a man who already has everything?

Gus opened a pair of French doors, revealing a balcony with a sculpted balustrade. The night's breeze carried the pleasant fragrance from a garden as pretty as a painting. Beyond the trees, a manicured hedge maze was wrapped in tiny white twinkling lights. Water sprayed up from a large fountain.

It was all so elegant and romantic. Faye wished she could just relax and enjoy the evening. But that wasn't why she was here. She had to figure out how to get Boss Tom alone and get the information she needed.

"There you are, Gus." A heavyset man in a white dinner suit and matching Bollman hat strolled the balcony toward them.

Jake's dad shook his hand. "I was just showing my kids how the other half lives."

The man smiled. "More like one-fourth nowadays." He glanced over at Jake, then set his eyes on Faye. "Is this the little wife you mentioned?" He slapped Jake's dad on the back and burst into a hearty laugh. "We should have searched the countryside for a farm gal instead of marrying city broads. Right, Gus?"

She cringed, unable to imagine being married to such a man.

Gus chuckled nervously. Nora didn't react at all.

Faye stood still as the man's gaze roamed over her, then his plump lips pressed against her wrist with a kiss. His chubby fingers glided along her arm to her shoulder and squeezed as though inspecting her for ripeness like fresh fruit.

Her nerve endings squirmed under each touch, but she steadied herself.

He finally let go. Jake mercifully tucked her against his side. "Boss Tom, this is my wife, Sarah."

She couldn't conceal her shudder from Jake, but she hoped she'd managed to hide it from this chauvinistic headman. She forced a slight smile. "Pleasure to meet you."

Boss Tom gave another jowly chuckle, but his mirth didn't reach his beady eyes. "The pleasure is all mine, my dear. Did your husband tell you the good news?"

Jake stiffened beside her. "Not yet."

"Well, allow me. Jake's agreed to help with certain problems I'm having in Philadelphia. I hope you're ready to leave the cows behind and take on the big city."

Jake did it. He had somehow finagled their way back to her home. She nodded yes, a million questions running through her mind. But they would have to wait.

Boss Tom led the way to the dining room.

Six centerpieces of fresh red roses were prominently placed on the table where candles flamed on silver candelabras. A quick count of seats told Faye it was set for twenty-two.

Chaska's voice entered her mind. *Her job was to talk to people and eat good food? Are you serious?*

Faye could now see things from the girl's perspective. Such opulence flaunted while so many now went hungry. And she had once been a part of that lifestyle, not giving the slightest thought to those who went to bed with empty bellies and without a roof over their head. Of those who lost so much because of her father's greed. She needed to fix past wrongs, and once she returned to Pennsylvania, she would do just that.

Jake pulled out a plush red chair, scooted her in, and positioned himself between her and Boss Tom's oversized host chair. Gus and Nora were situated across. Other guests trickled in from the ballroom.

She recognized a few: a silent film actress whose name she couldn't recall, a horn player from Paul Whiteman's orchestra, the renowned surrealist artist Mavor, and Lucy Chiappetta. The older gentleman who accompanied Lucy pulled a chair out for her next to Faye.

Lucy introduced her escort with a bouncy Italian dialect. "My husband, Leonardo Chiappetta."

Lucky Leo wasn't what Faye expected. Shorter than Lucy by half a foot, he was skinny, bald, and feeble looking. Hardly the imposing figure Jake had made him out to be.

He gave her fingers a weak, minimal shake and took his seat.

Lucy unfolded a cloth serviette and smoothed it on her lap. "I heard the news about your husband's new position in Philadelphia. Congratulations. I have connections there who will help you adjust if you wish."

Goodness. Word spread faster here than in Jake's small town. "That's very kind of you."

"Have you been there before?"

Boss Tom saved her from answering, dinging the side of his glass with a spoon. "Welcome old friends and new friends to our humble home. For those unfamiliar with your evening's hostess, may I introduce you to my new wife, Candace."

Guests clapped as a heavily made-up bleached blonde entered in a red satin bejeweled gown with a feathered shoulder piece.

Lucy leaned to the side and whispered, "Candace, my eye. Her name is Candy. She was a dancer at his dance hall."

Faye choked on her wine but quickly recovered.

A server ladled the soup over her shoulder and sprinkled the top with chopped chives. The creamy puree smelled delicious.

"What is this?" she asked Jake.

"Potato and leeks. From the old country. Ireland."

"Are you Irish?"

"No, Scottish, but he overlooks that in our case." He turned his attention back to Boss Tom.

According to her British grandmother, being Irish and Scottish was the same thing. That Boss Tom would fault Jake and his dad because of their heritage seemed wrong.

The next serving was a pâté of fatty goose liver, an odd choice after the soup. After that, a baked fish with a buttery cream sauce. Rich following rich, with France in the middle. A poorly chosen menu. It upset her stomach.

Lucy Chiappetta's gloved hand pressed her own. "A proper lady doesn't finish her plate." She set her entrée aside. "*Capisci?*"

She attempted to look grateful for the older woman's guidance.

Lucy patted her arm. "See that man down there with the boutonnière?"

Faye gazed at the far end of the table.

"That's Don Deed, Ellen's fiancé. I will introduce you after dinner."

Having finished speaking to someone she couldn't see, Deed leaned back in his seat and revealed a woman beside him.

Faye's heart leapt into her throat. *Oh, my God. Jennifer.*

The woman dated her father's partner, Penn. One of many past girlfriends from five or six years ago.

Faye snapped back in her chair. Her head bumped the server's arm as he gathered her plate, but his quick reflexes saved her from being covered in fish sauce.

Lucy gave her a look of censure.

She tried to force her hand to stop trembling. What were the chances someone she knew would be here? Slim. Very slim. She glanced over at Boss Tom. Maybe his offering Jake a job in Philadelphia was not due to Jake's negotiations or luck. *Maybe the old fox knows who I really am.*

☙

Faye excused herself right after dessert and hid in the guest powder room.

How was she to avoid Jennifer all night? She took a deep breath to calm herself. Perhaps the woman wouldn't recognize her. After all, they'd only spoken a few times, years ago.

Jake. She needed to discover what was said in this afternoon's meeting with Boss Tom.

She opened the door and bumped into Jennifer.

Crackers. Faye quickly turned her head.

"Pip?" Jennifer squeaked. "Pip Harmon? What on earth are you doing here?"

Ugh. Not good. Faye pulled her into the bathroom and closed the door. "Hi, Jenny. I'm, um—here with my husband. He has business with Boss Tom." Best to keep it simple.

Jennifer gave out that ear-piercing squeal that had doomed her relationship with Penn. She accented her excitement with a few hops. "Me too! I'm married. Going on four years now." She held up and waggled her ring finger, which displayed a large rock.

Faye hid her ringless finger behind her back. "It's lovely. Listen, I don't go by my old name. It's Sarah Boyd now. I've made a new start, and I prefer people here are not privy to my past. Could you do me that favor? As a friend?" She wasn't friends with the woman but needed to be sweet as cake and lay the icing on thick. "Penn still mentions your name as the love that got away. His biggest regret."

Jennifer twisted the ring on her finger. The twinkle in her eyes faded. "Oh, I had no idea. He stopped calling, so I just assumed..." Sadness clouded her face. She looked down at her ring finger, this time with despair. The woman looked like she wanted to rip it off and dart back to Philadelphia.

Maybe she'd gone too far. Faye tried to pull it back. "But he had to move on, as you have. He's engaged to be married." At this rate, her lies were accumulating, and they were sure to trip her up if she wasn't careful.

Jennifer's eyes teared.

Faye hugged the woman. "There now. He's hardly worth spilling tears. Tell me about your husband."

Jennifer sniffled. "I drove all this way to surprise him, but he's barely spoken with me tonight. He's angry. Doesn't like me involved in his business."

"Are you still in Philadelphia?"

The woman nodded. "But lately, my husband spends most of his time here. He claims it's for work, but I fear he's seeing someone else. A woman senses these things—you know?"

"I suppose." She hadn't a clue, being that Charles was her only steady boyfriend. Did he cheat on her with Catherine while they dated?

Jennifer brought her attention back. "Would you mind if I introduced you? See for yourself if he's acting strangely. Perhaps this is all in my head..."

It was a small request, but she worried Jennifer would slip up and reveal her real name. If what the woman said was true, at least she hadn't been found out by Boss Tom. It was just a coincidence she and Jennifer had run into one another.

"I'd like to meet your husband, but first, I must find mine." She shut the bathroom door behind her and hurried down the hallway.

Stupid Penn. Of course, she'd run into someone he'd slept with halfway across the country at a religious gangster's estate. He'd probably bedded half the single women in the Commonwealth. This night couldn't get any worse.

Lost in this labyrinth maze of hallways, she spotted Lucy Chiappetta having a low-toned conversation with Don Deed.

She quietly backed up to retreat the way she'd come.

Lucy called out, "Missus Boyd. Come meet Ellen's fiancé, Mister Deed."

Drat. Faye pasted on a smile.

Debonair and well-attired in his black waistcoat, wing-collared starched white shirt, and a fresh boutonnière, Deed made an impressive figure. He took her hand and kissed it.

"Your husband's a lucky man."

Odd. Deed had a South Street Philly accent.

"Thank you. As are you. Ellen is an amazing woman. Are you originally from Philadelphia?"

"Why, yes. How did you know?"

Shoot. How *would* she know, being from Kansas? "Lucky guess. You sound eastern...um, easternly." *Quit babbling.* "Like, uh... like a Dutch Yankee." She rolled her eyes at herself.

A thin smile lined the corners of Lucy's eyes.

Whether it was the woman's disingenuous manner, her overall unpleasantness, or the power of female intuition, something about Lucy Chiappetta made her skin crawl.

"There you are, darling." Jennifer walked toward them down the hallway.

She was looking straight at Deed. His eyes narrowed and he mumbled something under his breath.

"I see you found my husband on your own," she said to Faye.

Husband? But Deed was engaged to Ellen. She glanced at Lucy. The woman tapped a finger over her lips—a warning to keep quiet. The menacing look that followed sent a chill down her spine. She needed to do damage control before Jennifer blurted out her secret.

"We met in the powder room." Faye held Jennifer's stare, willing the woman to understand their story. "Your wife kindly offered to show me around Philadelphia."

Deed formed a tight smile. "We must have you and your husband over to dinner sometime."

His tone implied that was the last thing he wished to do.

"Speaking of husbands, I need to find mine." She took Jennifer's hand and squeezed it. "It was so nice to meet you. I'm sure we'll be the best of friends."

The kind of friend that would piece her back together once the woman fell apart. Poor Jennifer.

Faye found Jake in the billiards room with his father. He set up his shot. She cleared her throat behind him. He missed the ball entirely.

She whispered in his ear, "We need to talk."

He handed his stick to his dad. "My wife wants to walk the grounds."

Once outside and out of earshot, she stopped alongside a patch of blooming daffodils under a tree decorated with twinkling lights.

Jake crossed his arms. "This something that'll wait until we're away from here?"

"No, it cannot." She told him about her run-in with Jennifer and Deed, the bigamist. "I feel bad. Do you think I should somehow warn her? She's already suspicious he's having an affair."

His face hardened. "I told you not to pry with these people. Do you have any idea what they'd do to you if they discovered who you really are?" His jumpiness was infectious.

"Don't you find it odd that Boss Tom would place you in Philadelphia?"

He rubbed his chin. "I'd asked him about his connections there before he suggested we go."

Was he saying this was her fault? That he was being dragged back into his old life because he did her a favor? "If you remember correctly, I wanted to get information from him myself."

"Keep your voice down." He pulled her closer. "Boss Tom is watching us."

Faye turned her head and peered up at the balcony.

Jake guided her chin back to his chest. "Don't look, listen. He questioned me tonight, noticing no affection in our marriage. He needs to know I have my wife in line and that you won't be a problem for the organization."

"Why is that his business?" She resented the idea that Boss Tom would probe into the private affairs of her fake marriage. The irony of it all did not escape her.

Jake spoke softly into her hair. "Because he needs to know everyone who works for him is completely loyal, including their families. Harp wasn't the only one killed. His wife was with him. Gus told me that Harp and his wife had problems. That she'd talked to one of Boss Tom's political enemies. They were both taken out."

She shivered.

Jake rubbed over her arms. "Turns out a banker in Philadelphia moved most of the bank's cash and gold to an unknown location. Not a hundred thousand, publicized by the press, but closer to a *million*." He took a deep breath. "Every snake in the crime world is slithering out from rocks. Boss Tom expects me to beat them to it and figure out where it all went."

An overwhelming sensation of dread draped over her. They must think her father was responsible. Could he be? Or was this just a rumor gone horribly wrong? "Even if it's true. I don't know where it is."

"They won't believe you." He glimpsed toward the balcony. "He's still there." Jake lowered his head. His warm breath tingled her ear as he said, "Sorry about this."

He grabbed her firmly by the waist and lifted her to the points of her shoes. Sweeping her in close, he claimed her lips with a firm kiss.

Robbed of breath and what she was about to say, her words came out like a muffled hum. There was nothing passionate about the kiss. This was all for show. To prove he had control over her to satisfy his prurient employer. It bothered her beyond measure.

She nipped his bottom lip.

He flinched and drew back. "I'm trying to keep you safe."

"No, you're being his puppet. Doing what he wants like everyone else around him does." She huffed. "Well, I don't have strings."

Jake smashed her against him and dipped her into a deep kiss. His lips more pliable now, his tongue invaded, exploring her mouth, then coiled with her own.

Taken off-guard, she clutched his shoulders. He tasted like full-bodied wine, rich and intense and satisfying. Pleasure coursed through her veins as her body came alive with feeling. Goosebumps rose behind his calloused touch on her skin. She closed her eyes.

His kiss turned hungry. Carnal.

She melted against him like hot wax, no longer able to firmly support her own weight.

He brought her up, parted her legs, and straddled her over his thigh.

Slowly, he moved beneath her—friction building heat against her most sensitive parts.

His leg muscles twitched, and he began to quake.

Something like a small heartbeat thrummed inside below her navel.

She wanted more.

His hand skimmed over her bodice, settled on her velvet-covered chest, and stroked her breast through the fabric.

Tingles danced over her skin. Her chest felt heavy with a dull ache.

He moaned low, left her mouth, and feathered his lips down her neck.

Heat spread down that side like a current of electricity, sparking here and there under her skin.

She pressed closer to prolong the feeling. Her body wanted more.

His arms surrounding her started to shake.

A door near the balcony slammed shut.

Jake stopped moving and slowed his breathing. Unwelcome cooler air invaded her skin as he drew back and gently set her on her feet.

"He's gone," he said, his voice thick and husky. He bent over and stared at the ground, his hands on his knees.

Faye opened her mouth to respond but was unable to form a word. Her lips, tender and swollen, still felt the lingering imprint from his kiss. Her head felt stuffed with cotton, her emotions so jumbled she wasn't sure what to feel.

He straightened up and reached for her, but she stepped back.

"Don't." She warded him off with her hand, afraid if he touched her, she'd shatter.

A flush crept up his neck to his ears. "Faye, I'm sorry. I got carried away and..."

"Sarah." Saying the woman's name choked her throat. "If we're going to play the part, we should follow through with your whole stupid plan."

"I'm trying to protect you."

Were all men so sure of themselves in their heroic beliefs?

"I don't recall asking you to." She picked up Nora's loaned purse. "Just go. Your staged scene worked." She wiped off the bottom of the small handbag and tried to tamp down her body's residual responses and emotions.

He rubbed his hand over his face. "We should go—"

"I need to be alone." The hedge maze beckoned. Privacy to shield herself until she could get herself together.

"That's not a good idea."

"I'm not asking. Don't follow me." She walked to the entrance and hid behind the tall hedge. There, she drew in a shaky breath and slowly let it out.

She chose to go right on the pebbled path and ran her hand along the bushes to guide her, the moon half-hidden behind a dark cloud.

I'm not in love with him. She turned left.

Big oaf.

He had seemed just as affected by the kiss as she had. Maybe more so. She hadn't imagined that.

A kick of gravel stopped her short. She squinted down the path and saw the dark shape of a man turn the corner.

"I don't want to talk." She crossed her arms.

He moved closer. Not as tall as Jake. Not as big in build. The shape of a hat on his head. Jake didn't wear a hat to the party.

"Who's there?"

He didn't answer her. The back of her neck prickled a warning.

"What do you want?"

He picked up speed. She turned and ran, arms out, crashing against the side of one hedge and then another. She lost track of direction. Tiny cuts on her hands stung. Nora's purse slipped from under her arm.

She heard him, just as he probably heard her. He was close.

She turned left, then another left, and tripped over something on the path. She fell on top of it just as the moon brightened.

Jennifer. Her eyes were half open, and her shocked facial expression was frozen into place. A trickle of blood had run from the corner of her mouth down her cheek. Her skin felt cool to the touch.

The man's steps on the gravel slowed.

Scrape. Crunch. Scrape. Crunch.

Then he stopped.

Faye clamped her hand over her mouth, her body paralyzed and sprawled over her new friend's corpse. The man chasing her was probably the murderer. She willed her hand to move and clutched a pebble. Throwing it high, it plinked the ground on a different row.

Crunch—crunch—crunch—crunch.

She shuddered and rolled off Jennifer. The man moved away.

Chapter 27

Faye stayed huddled in the maze until her leg cramped. In the distance, Jake called out for Sarah. It upset her more than it should have. Every time she heard his ex-wife's name, it grated on her last nerve. She stood and stretched the kinks from her muscles. It had been a while since she heard the man chasing her skulking around. And now people were searching for her. If he had half a brain, he would have abandoned the chase.

She picked up her pace, glancing around corners, eager to get out. At a turn, she bumped hard into a man. A scream built in her throat until moonlight shone on Mr. Deed.

"Goodness." Faye held her hand to her chest. "You startled me."

A hard object poked her side. A gun.

Deed placed a hat on his head. "Move." He poked her again with the barrel. "Quietly."

Her mind swirled. She balanced the odds of his shooting her if she screamed. Not good, considering he had probably just killed his wife.

Her heart palpitated. "Why are you doing this?"

He didn't respond, shoving her to a gap in the maze that appeared to be the back of Boss Tom's property.

Jennifer. Did she mistakenly let slip who she was?

"You're making a big mistake. My husband is practically family to Boss Tom."

"I don't care who you are, and I'm not concerned in the least about Boss Tom or your farmer. Keep moving."

She slowed her steps to stall, but the urge to flee was strong. Images of what could happen flashed through her mind—she could lunge at him and possibly wrench the gun away. Plead. Or bargain and offer him money. The thought emboldened her. "My father-in-law is wealthy. He'll pay you good money if you release me unharmed," she claimed with false bravado.

He nudged her toward a black car with its engine running. "You assume this is a cash transaction. Believe me, Gus doesn't have what I want."

Faye stopped walking and turned. Exasperated, she asked, "Then why are you doing this?"

She didn't think he'd answer, but after a long silence, he said, "For Ellen."

He was covering his tracks, getting rid of anyone who saw him as he truly was—everyone who might cost him the woman he loves.

Jake's worried voice yelled in the distance.

Faye readied herself, splayed her hands, and lunged at Deed.

He hit the side of her face. A sharp pain bolted down her neck, her vision blurred, and an unpleasant ringing sounded in her ears. He dragged her the rest of the way to the car.

"*Grazie*. I'll take her from here," Lucky Leo said. He tied her wrists behind her back.

Deed walked toward the maze. Probably to retrieve Jennifer's body before it's discovered. She lost sight of him when Chiappetta tied a cloth over her eyes. He lowered her head and then pushed her inside the automobile.

Would Jake figure out what happened to her? Or would he think she'd run off like the first Sarah? Maybe he would be relieved she was gone. Tears dampened the cloth tied along her cheeks.

A foul stench coated the room. Faye wrinkled her nose. It smelled like a pack of wet dogs eating rotten eggs.

She winced and rubbed at her freed wrists, the marks still visible from the ties. No matter which direction she turned, she couldn't find a comfortable spot on the grimy cot in the dank cellar. The dim light from a hanging bulb was no match for the shadows that lurked in every corner. Large wooden barrels cast ghoulish silhouettes on walls splotched with mold. Something irritated her throat. The culprit was most likely the many shelves of dust-laden wine and liquor bottles that filled the creepy space.

She sneezed a *choo* and then briskly rubbed her arms to warm her raised goose flesh. Her hands felt like ice.

Why had Chiappetta helped Deed? What obligated him to take her hostage?

Deed said it was because of Ellen. How had Chiappetta known the location Ellen had been taken? How did he know—unless—he was the one who took her?

Her scalp prickled.

Nora's voice entered her thoughts. 'Deed saved her—Deed was madly in love with her—Ellen's husband died right after her rescue. A tragedy.'

She pushed herself up from the old cot and stood with a slight stumble. Why didn't anyone else put this together? But maybe they did. Jake had said that Boss Tom had the police in his pocket. The Chiappettas probably had a few loyal to them, also.

They had presumedly abducted Ellen for ransom money.

Would the Chiappettas demand money for her release? She shuddered. Probably not. She knew too much. Something terrible was about to happen. She needed to get out of there.

Faye went back to the door. *Think, damn it, think.*

A picture show she'd seen a long time ago had an actress who used a hairpin to escape a locked room. She reached up and extracted a few from her disheveled coiffure. If she remembered correctly, the woman had inserted the doubled metal prongs into a keyhole and moved them back and forth.

Steadying herself, she bent down, squinted one eye, and poked the hairpin inside the keyhole.

Footsteps sounded on the other side of the door.

Faye quickly grabbed a bottle from a shelf and jerked upright.

Plan B: Whack him over the head—just desserts for the rough treatment he'd given her.

Lucy Chiappetta kneed the door open. She held a tray in one hand. In the other was a gun.

Faye set the bottle back on the shelf.

Lucy smirked. "I didn't take you for a woman of violence."

"I didn't take you for a criminal. My mistake."

"I'm a businesswoman. To be a criminal, one must first be caught committing a crime. I assure you, I'm not that careless." Lucy set the tea tray on the cot and wrinkled her nose. "I'll bring you something to clean with. A way to spend your time. But don't be unnecessarily concerned about the accommodation. You won't be with us long."

Her last words hung in the air. Lucy didn't seem worried about being identified and charged with kidnapping.

Feeling faint, Faye sat on the cot. "I'm the daughter-in-law of Boss Tom's right-hand man. Do you truly believe they will not investigate my disappearance?"

Lucy smirked. "You are not the first Missus Boyd I've made disappear. And in all that time, not a peep at my front door."

Who? Jake's mom?

"Oh?" Lucy tapped a bony finger over her thin lips. "He never told you about his mother? You being his wife?" She said the last word with skepticism.

"It is difficult for him to speak of her."

"Why would that be? That was twenty years ago. Jake was just a little boy." Lucy cat-smiled, then went on, "Like you, his mother was a petite, beautiful brunette. Also, like you, she wasn't very wise, always sticking her nose where it didn't belong."

Faye stared at the gun that was now pointed away from her and calculated her chances of reaching it before being shot.

"My husband had a roaming eye back then. Kept me busy scaring off one immoral floozy after another. But he'd been captivated by Sugar, even after she married Gus and gave birth to Jake."

Faye inched to the edge of the cot and planted her feet.

Lucy continued, "Leo doesn't have the stomach nor the brains for this business. It's always been up to me to keep our organization relevant. To show Boss Tom we're still in the game."

"I guess that includes kidnapping family of the men who work for him? For what purpose? What could you possibly gain?" Was this about money or power?

Lucy set the gun on top of a wine barrel. "Since our family came here, we've been completely loyal to Boss Tom. Paid him for doing nothing while we supplied every drop of liquor, ale, and wine that crossed his city's border."

Faye eyed the gun and clutched the cot's edge, hoping her legs would support her when the time was right.

"Those pious temperance prudes didn't keep alcohol out of the reach of their sons and husbands. It was as easy as offering a tit to a babe, and they adored me for it. The milkweed white men called me Mama Lucy, and my beautiful Italian boys named me *Madre che Provvede*, a mother who provides."

Faye rose another inch, ready to strike.

"But like every good thing, it must come to an end. Ever since Congress passed the proposed Amendment that would repeal Prohibition, Boss Tom got it into his head to break our deal. He's planning on his own distribution ring and bringing in a bunch of Irish Paddy Nobodies to work it. Giving me no choice but to retaliate."

Faye leaped for the gun.

Lucy snatched it up and pointed it at Faye's forehead. She scolded, "I'm not finished."

Faye crouched low and held up her hand as a barrier.

"Where was I? Oh, yes. Boss Tom's betrayal. He has forced us into battle, and as any good general knows, it takes money to win a war. I have business associates in Philadelphia who are very anxious to have you back. You, Pip Harmon, are worth your weight in gold."

The Mob. Lucy was going to sell her like a prized cow. *Think, damn it, think.*

Lucy headed toward the door.

Faye panicked. "Ellen O'Connell. You kidnap people for profit. But she's your friend..."

Lucy stopped and tilted her head. "*Infatti*. That plan went sideways, so I had to think of another way. I knew Deed was in love with her. He paid a healthy ransom, and in exchange, we made her husband disappear."

Faye's throat constricted. If Lucy and Leo had no qualms about taking a friend hostage for money and murdering her husband, what would become of her? The Philadelphia Mafia seemed to want her alive, but would the Chiappettas kill her if she tried to escape? Chalk it up to a loss? Did this ever end well for the victim? Ellen seemed happy, sure, but Faye doubted the woman realized snakes surrounded her. And Jake's mother, Sugar. What had become of her?

"What did you do to Jake's mom?" Faye asked with a tremor in her voice. "Kidnap her, too, and sell her to the highest bidder?"

Lucy moved over to a wine barrel and looked down with a hint of a smile. "I didn't send her away. I needed to keep her close." She drummed her long fingernails on the oak cask's lid. "A reminder of what happens when someone crosses me. Beautiful Sugar. She's been marinating here a long time."

Faye gasped and pressed her hand over her mouth.

She'd been right about not trusting Lucy, but the woman was worse than she could have ever imagined. Truly wicked. "How could you? *Why?*" Her mouth watered an early warning, and then she bent over a cask barrel and heaved up last night's dinner. Wiping her mouth with the back of her shaking hand, Faye backed away to the farthest wall, crumpled to the floor, and hugged herself. This woman was profoundly evil.

The joy her fear brought to Lucy was evident. The woman's voice sounded almost jovial. "I'm so pleased to be the one to introduce you. Try anything, and you will join her fate. I have a nice *Riserva Red* that will have your name on it."

She opened the door, the small handgun dangling on her bony finger. "Your tea is getting cold."

Faye trembled as the lock clicked the finality of her fate.

An hour passed. Maybe more.

Faye worked up her courage and stood. Her legs shook, but she leaned against the wall and forced them to support her. With no more tears to give, she scolded herself, "You can crack later."

Giving Sugar's coffin barrel a wide berth, she picked up a hairpin and took the long way to the door.

The pin scraped just outside the keyhole as she repeatedly tried to connect it to the release inside the lock. Frustrated, she grasped her wrist and forced the pin in, moving it side to side and up and down.

Nothing happened.

She pulled loose another hairpin and cascaded her hair around her shoulders. Biting her lip, she put the two pins together and turned them like a key.

Something clicked, and then the door cracked open. Not taking the time to congratulate herself, she rushed out and climbed the narrow stairs.

Her pulse thrummed throughout her body.

A long hallway showed lights on in several rooms. The house was eerily silent.

Staying in the shadows, step by slow step, she willed her feet to move.

A floorboard creaked beneath her.

Faye froze in place. Every hair on her arms and head prickled, her ears alert to the slightest sound.

After a moment, she moved again and peeked into a dark space. She stepped on a linoleum floor and squinted in the dark. A pungent smell of cooked onions and tomatoes lingered in the room. *Kitchen.*

With her hands out front, she moved by touch along a wall, her knee bumping a sharp edge. She stifled a cry, gritted her teeth, and inhaled sharply through her nose.

Footfall down the steps from the second story sent her into a panic. She frantically felt around, her touch landing on a handle. Rushing into a small closet, Faye closed the door behind her as the kitchen light beamed on. She crouched down and glanced around the pantry for a weapon. Food cans, cooking oil, a sack of flour. They would have to do. Through the slats of the door, she watched Lucy move around the kitchen.

The woman made up a plate of food.

Please don't be for me.

Lucy placed a fork on the plate, then shook her head and tossed it into the sink.

Definitely for me.

The light shut off and plunged Faye into darkness again. Lucy's footsteps sounded on the stairs to the basement.

Faye darted out of the pantry and hurried to the kitchen door.

"*Leo*," Lucy shouted below. "She's *gone.*"

Faye turned the knob and thanked all that was holy that it wasn't locked. Latching it closed behind her, she then sprinted across the yard.

Faye clung to the dark of back alleyways, ducking behind structures and cars every time an automobile or person passed. She leaned against a brick wall and breathed deeply, in and out, to slow the rush of her thumping heart. Her hands still trembled like a withered leaf.

Mind racing the way it was, she had no idea how far she had run or even what part of the city she was in. Knocking on one of the doors and asking for help in the run-down neighborhood didn't seem the best idea. But who could she trust?

A police car cruised down the road at a snail's pace. Faye crouched behind a garbage can in the alley and watched it pass. She couldn't trust the police. They could be in Lucy's pocket. No, she had to find a way back to Jake. He was the only person she could trust—if that offer in Philadelphia, the "promotion," hadn't changed him.

She figured a taxicab was her best bet. Maybe she could talk the driver into collecting the fare when she reached a safe place. But wouldn't Lucy have thought of that?

Faye shivered at the thought of being returned to that foul woman.

Could she trust any stranger at this point? No. Better to be wary than careless and rash.

She crept to the end of the alley and uneasily glanced at the street. A dive saloon down the road had the only activity this time of night. She headed the opposite way, staying close to the buildings on the sidewalk.

A strong industrial smell coated this side of the city. A faint whoosh of a river and the blaring sound of a boat horn sounded.

Headlights beamed from an automobile down the street.

Faye rushed to hide under an awning of a closed grocer. The car approached, lighting the space across from her. A wooden booth with the sign PUBLIC TELEPHONE above made her heart leap. After the vehicle ventured past, she slid open the accordion-style door and snatched up the receiver. A dial tone buzzed in her ear. A plastic direction card attached to the phone instructed the caller to dial zero for the switchboard operator.

She circled the dial and sat on the bench.

A woman's voice on the other end said, "Name of exchange and number, please. Then insert coin."

"I don't know the number."

"Is there a directory book provided?"

She stood and glanced around the booth. On a shelf was a large book connected to the wall. "I found it." She tilted the directory toward the streetlight and searched down the B page. G. Boyd's number was listed. She rattled off the information to the operator.

"Insert coin, please."

Faye stuck her finger in the coin return. *Empty.*

She held the receiver in one hand and frantically swept the floor with her other. Under the bench, she felt a small coin.

Mentally thanking the stranger, she inserted the nickel into the slot. A ting chimed. After one ring, a harried voice answered, "Hello."

"Jake?" Her voice shook, and her eyes watered again.

A heavy exhale was followed by, "I've been worried sick. Where are you?"

Her lip trembled. "I don't know for sure. Somewhere near a river. I'm calling from a phone booth at Wilson's Grocer."

"Stay put. I'll be right there."

"*Jake.*" She panicked, thinking he'd hung up.

"I'm here."

She let her tears fall. "Be careful. Deed and the Chiappettas kidnapped me. They might be watching the house."

He was quiet for a moment, and then she heard a deep guttural sound on the line. "Don't move." He hung up.

Faye placed the receiver back and rubbed her arms. She'd felt better while speaking to him, but now she was overwhelmed by helplessness. The half-hour that followed were the longest minutes of her whole life.

Headlights shone on the road as the Studebaker screeched to a stop. Faye rushed to open the passenger side and leapt onto the seat. She barely shut the door before they were speeding down the route.

"Are you all right?" His gaze swept over her.

She gave a slight nod.

He pounded his fist against the car door. "What the hell were you thinking?"

The car veered a hard left.

Faye braced her feet against the floorboard and splayed her hands over the dash. "Slow down, or you'll get us both killed."

His knuckles whitened as his hand clenched around the metal lever. The gears grated as he shifted. "Oh, now you worry about danger? You ran off—"

"—I was taken."

"Before that." His cheeks flushed. "After the kiss."

"Are you somehow implying this is my fault?"

"I've been out of my head since you disappeared. Banging off the walls wanting to search for you, but not knowing where to look." His right eye twitched.

And he never would have found her. Just like his father never found Sugar.

His voice quieted. "I thought you ran off without even saying goodbye."

Not sure what to say, she stammered what was to be the beginning of an apology.

A bright light beamed behind them.

Jake stared hard in the rearview mirror. "Get down!" He grabbed her, pushed her head onto his lap, and ducked over.

Boom! Crash! A loud gunshot blasted and shattered the rear window.

Faye screamed.

Jake jerked his head up and yelled, "Hold on." He swerved the car to the right.

Tires squealed, followed by the smell of burning rubber. The automobile accelerated faster and faster, and it began to vibrate, shake, and rattle.

She glanced up at Jake. His face tight with concentration and tendons standing out on his neck, he downshifted and took another turn.

Bullets pelted the top of the passenger seat. Its stuffing swirled and fell like snow. Jake's arm came down over her like an iron bar. His foot switched to the brake, sending the motorcar into a skid as he downshifted and cut the wheel.

The vehicle tipped as if it would flip over, then hit hard upright, jarring her shoulder.

It continued on.

The grating and pitched hums of the gears, ascending and descending.

The thrum of the wind, whooshing.

The sliding shards of glass tinkling.

"Son of a bitch," Jake said through his teeth.

Faye peeked over the dash. A traffic light ahead turned red, and another car headed for the intersection. They'd never make it.

Jake turned the wheel and veered onto an empty parking lot. The car swerved and bucked as Jake braked hard. Then, the vehicle stalled.

A horn blared, and then a loud crash reverberated. The car that had chased them smashed into the one Jake had avoided. After a moment, a man stumbled out from the driver's side and shouted as he headed toward the gangsters' car.

Faye's heart leaped into her throat. *No. Don't. Run.*

Doors opened, and four men got out and fired their weapons. Bullets ripped through the innocent man's chest.

Jake tried to restart the Studebaker. The engine cranked but wouldn't catch hold. He cursed a word that made her blush. The men with guns moved in their direction.

"Jake," Faye's voice trembled.

Brows furrowed, he continued trying and pumped the gas pedal. The men were almost upon them.

"Jake!"

He glanced out the window. "I know. I see."

A man lifted his gun and pointed it at Jake.

He gunned the gas, and the car lurched forward over a curb. Gunshots rang out.

Faye curled into a ball. She wondered if the man had a family, which made her think of Rudy, Chaska, and Niya. Tears ran down her cheek.

Soon, a light shone over the car.

A man yelled, "Open it up."

The clanging of a gate sounded, and then they were moving again at a slower pace.

Boss Tom's. She wondered why Jake came here instead of his father's house. He stopped the car and shut it off.

She couldn't stop shaking. Jake rubbed her arm and smoothed her hair. When she composed herself, he helped her out. Two men in white suits approached.

"We have two cases in the back," Jake said. "Careful of the glass."

One man did his bidding as the other guided them to a suite with a sitting room, a bedroom, and a bath.

Jake helped her onto the bed and went into the bathroom.

Exhausted, Faye wrapped the blanket around herself and closed her eyes. The surprised look on the man's face when he was shot scrolled through her mind like a silent film. The rattle of her teeth echoed the gunfire.

After their bags arrived, Jake took hers into the bathroom. He came back and coaxed her up. "I ran you a bath. Come on. You'll sleep better."

She clutched his arm. "Please don't leave."

"I'll ask a servant to bring a pot of tea—unless you want something stronger."

She nodded and entered the powder room. Leaning against the door, she cringed at her reflection in the wall mirror. Wild eyes stared back. Her cloud of tousled hair looked like Medusa styled it. Her ashen skin like she'd come back from death. She'd be a real hit at a Hooverville ball. Hands uncooperative, she attempted to undo the gown's buttons. It would need cleaning before being returned. She hoped Boss Tom's wife would help with that.

The image in the mirror mocked her. She could have died less than an hour ago, yet an innocent man paid with his life. Did he have a wife? Children waiting eagerly to greet him at home? But now, she was worried about a stupid dress. This was all her fault. She should have listened to Jake's warnings about these people. Should have stayed on the farm until her aunt sent money and then disappeared from the lives of everyone she cared about.

Finally undressed, she eased into the tub, the warm water working on her frayed nerves and tense muscles. This liquid cocoon got her blood moving and pinked up her skin. But deep inside, an aching coldness settled into her bones. She stared at the tiled wall, fighting back horrible thoughts and visions.

Once the bath water cooled, she forced her legs to stand. After drying off, putting on her nightgown, and brushing her hair free of tangles, she joined Jake in the seating room.

A warm fire crackled in the hearth. Jake sat in a butterfly wing-back chair and sipped an amber liquid from a snifter. He appeared deep in thought.

Faye poured herself a cup of tea and added a splash of brandy to it. "Why did you bring us here?"

"Gus suggested it when I told him what was going on. He brought his family, also. Said it was the safest place he could think of."

"But is it safe? Truly?"

Jake rubbed a hand over his face. "I don't know." He seemed tired; the adrenaline from the automobile chase drained from his system.

She told him what Lucy had told her about going to war against Boss Tom.

He stared hard at the fire. A muscle twitched in his jaw. "That complicates matters."

"Should we try to go? Give some excuse?"

"No." Jake shook his head. "We'll leave tomorrow. Running out now would look suspicious, and the car needs repairing." He stood and walked to the door.

Her pulse sped up. "Where are you going?" Surely, he wasn't going to leave her alone.

He locked the door and placed a Victorian-looking chair in front of it. "Nowhere. I'll sleep in here. You should go to bed."

There wasn't a chair in the room that looked comfortable enough to sit on, let alone sleep on. And he needed his rest to be alert tomorrow. "Don't be ridiculous." She set down her cup. "That bed is twice as big as the one we shared last night. And I...I sure would feel safer with you next to me. I'll lay still. You won't even know I'm there."

His expression implied otherwise.

Chapter 28

Tires squealed. The air filled with the smell of burning rubber. The Studebaker tipped and rolled. Jake smashed against the steering wheel as the top of Faye's head hit the roof, bringing instant pain. The car landed upside down. Jake groaned, blood running in a stream down his face. Outside, footsteps approached.

"Jake!" she shouted, shaking him. "We need to go. They're coming!"

He blinked at her with a look of confusion. The driver's door wrenched open.

Lucy's voice came from above. "Missus Boyd. Come out, or your husband will pay with his life."

She attempted to open the passenger door, but it was stuck.

"Last chance," Lucy chided.

"Wait! I can't get it to open. Don't shoot!"

Bullets punched through Jake's chest.

The room was dark except for the light from the moon. It took a moment for Faye's eyes to adjust and to recall where she was.

A strong arm wrapped around her waist and pulled her in. Jake.

He was alive. *Safe.*

Warmth radiated from him. She relaxed and molded into the rigid contours of his body. Sleepy puffs of breath on the nape of her neck tickled her skin.

"Bad dream?" he asked, his voice drowsy.

She rolled over and rested her head in the crook of the arm that propped his head. The nightmare had shaken her to the core. She'd come so close to losing Jake tonight and her own life before she could live it fully. To love someone fully.

She couldn't find the words to tell him about his mother, but she planned on informing his father before they left. Gus deserved to know what had become of his first wife. Lucy Chiappetta's luck at escaping justice was about to run out.

"Will I need to come back and testify against the Chiappettas?" she asked.

"I doubt there'll be that kind of trial, in a courthouse, that is."

"Oh." A shiver ran over her skin.

He pulled her in closer. "Boss Tom requested a private meeting with you in the morning. You need to be careful what you say. Like the reason you were kidnapped."

"I don't want to be alone with that man."

"You won't. I'm not allowed to be there, but I insisted my old man be. Gus may not've been the best father, but he wouldn't let anything bad happen to his family."

Tell that to Sugar. "But I'm not his family," she said instead.

He gently rubbed over her shoulder. "No, but he doesn't know that, and even if he did, he knows you're important to me. That's good enough."

Her heart skipped a beat. *Am I important to him?* This was the closest he'd come to saying he had feelings for her. Warmth spread down to her toes.

She found herself staring at his form, outlined by the moon's ethereal glow.

He spoke with a halting rasp. "You should go back to sleep."

"In what way am I important?"

She wasn't sure he'd answer, but he eventually said, "You are a woman alone in my care."

Not exactly the romantic prose she wished to hear, but most men were not good at sharing their emotions. Beyond hunger, anger, or tiredness, he was very closed off. "Is that all?"

"Are you fishing for compliments?"

"I didn't think you liked me very much."

The corner of his mouth twitched. "Not at first, no, but you grew on me."

"Like wildflowers in springtime?"

He chuckled. "More like thistles and thorns."

She mock-slapped his arm. "You make me sound like an acquired taste...like spinach."

"I like spinach," he whispered.

This seemed the best he could do. Faye glided her hand up his sleeveless undershirt and rested her palm on his chest.

His heart thumped at a steady pace underneath. The silence turned awkward. Getting him to kiss her was like squeezing wine from a turnip.

She took the initiative and leaned in.

His lips moved beneath her own. Ever so slowly, halting and bittersweet, pleasant yet almost painful in ambiguity.

Had she misunderstood his affection? Was she making a fool of herself? She pulled away, but he brought her back. Tipping up her chin, he captured her mouth. Deepening the kiss, his hand dipped below her waist, caressing her backside. His fragrance wafted, earthy with a bit of spice, a scent uniquely his own. She explored lower.

He drew in a sharp breath and gripped her roaming hand. A sultry moan escaped the back of his throat and tingled her spine. "We shouldn't be doing this."

"Just a bit more."

"Any longer," his voice broke, "I won't be able to stop."

Unsure what he meant by that, curiosity about how men functioned perplexed her.

Jake throated another sound, wrapped a finger around the strap of her nightgown, and moved it off her shoulder. The palm of his hand brought heat and fit perfectly over her breast. He grazed his thumb over her nipple, causing electric zaps to ripple across her chest.

His kisses came rapid and soft, yet she craved something more.

She intertwined her leg with his, pulled him closer, and explored his hidden valleys. His reactions to her touch captivated her.

His tongue circled hers and plunged deep.

Faye strained against him, stretching to prolong the pulses streaming through her body.

His lips feathered down the side of her neck and traced along her collarbone. He kissed her nipple, then his mouth enclosed it in a warm, wet embrace, gently sucking.

Her body burst alive with more feeling. Pleasure branched out. Senses inflamed to another level. It was as if a thousand tiny sparks ignited underneath her skin. As though her flesh depended on him to reach the height building inside. A whimper escaped her lips.

Bathed gray in moonlight, Jake rose, worked her nightgown over her head, and lowered her satin bloomers. She could sense his eyes penetrating the shadows that hid part of her body from his sight.

"My God, you're beautiful."

Those words warmed her blood more than anything he'd done to her body thus far.

He yanked his undershirt over his head and tossed it. Fumbling with the tie on his pajama pants, he kicked them off and nudged her legs wider apart.

The weight from him added pleasure. His hard erection poked her swollen, wet heat, seeking entrance. He entered her with a thrust.

A sharp pain ripped inside. Faye bit her lip to keep from crying out.

Jake rushed out a ragged breath and abruptly stilled. "Oh, hell, kid. I'm sorry. I—I didn't know." An expression mirroring her pain crossed his face.

Was it over?

Jake flopped next to her and covered his face with his arm.

For the most part, it had been enjoyable, except for the last. Did it hurt like that every time? Her married friends had occasionally spoken about such intimacies but not in detail. Now she wished she'd asked more questions, unsure what the big whoopee do was all about.

The silence of the room lay as heavy as thick fog. The slow creep of time spanned until he spoke again. "You should've told me."

She closed her eyes. "I didn't think it pertinent at the moment."

"If that means 'important,' then you're dead wrong."

She sighed. "I fail to understand why you are upset. I needed comfort, and you provided it." Why did men make everything about themselves?

"Comfort?" He huffed. "Darlin,' that was way more than just consoling you for a horrible night."

"I'm corrected then."

He wouldn't let it go. "I—" He cleared his throat. "We...this can't go anywhere. I'm not who you think I am."

"Oh?" The soreness she'd felt was evaporating. "Then, tell me. Who are you?"

"I'm not a good man."

What the heck did that mean? Did she do something wrong? Was he disappointed with their lovemaking and now searching for a reason to back away from her? "So, you're—what? A bad one?"

"I've done terrible things."

To his wife? Was that the real reason Sarah had left him? Was there more to the story that he hadn't let on? She didn't want to hear this but, at the same time, knew she must. "Did you hurt Sarah?"

He brought his arm down from his face. "What? No! It happened before I came to the farm."

She exhaled a breath she hadn't realized she'd been holding. "When you were a kid?" What could possibly be so terrible back then? "You were a boy. Boys do mischievous things—"

"—I killed a man."

What she'd been about to say went out the window and got sucked up to the sky. "By accident?"

He shook his head.

"I see." But she didn't.

He shifted and rolled on his side away from her. "Go to sleep."

She hugged her pillow. The gap between them had become a canyon.

Jake wished he could take back his confession. He gazed fondly at her sleeping figure to capture the memory. She would leave him once they returned to the farm. He couldn't blame her. But she deserved an explanation. He searched his mind for the words.

Gus had been sent on a mission: to fetch Rory, Boss Tom's youngest brother. After the attack and Two Cents was killed, the men were out for blood. They took out some members of a local street gang they were sure was responsible. Rory had gotten into a fight with another card player at the Trap Room and had been three sheets to the wind. Although it was dark outside, Rory noticed a DeSoto going the opposite way that he swore belonged to the head of the gang.

He pounded the dash until Gus relented, turned the car around, and followed.

'Hang back,' Rory slurred. 'Don't want them onto us.'

The DeSoto drove to the railroad district, crossed the tracks, and turned down a dirt path to a dead end.

Gus turned off the headlights and crept his car to a stop nearby. 'Listen, Rory. I don't think this is a good idea. I got my kid in the back seat, and I'm not packing. We'll get them another time when we're better prepared.'

Rory looked over from the front seat. 'How old are you, Jake?'

'Fourteen.'

'Practically a man.' Rory checked his Colt handgun.

Gus said, 'Stay close to me, son.'

Rory advanced toward the DeSoto with cautious steps. The windows were fogged. He jerked open the driver's side door and aimed his gun. 'Out. Don't try nothing, or I'll shoot you where you is.'

A kid, maybe seventeen, stepped out. Following him, a girl about the same age. She looked disheveled, unsteady on her feet, trembling and sobbing.

'You know who I am?' Rory asked.

The young man took a defensive stance to protect his date. 'Yes, sir.'

'What's your name?'

'Ellis.'

'Well, Ellis, my boy, does your pop know you're out with his ride?'

The youth shook his head and appeared weary of the situation he'd found himself in.

'A shame, that,' Rory said. 'Take them out.'

The Colt shoved into hand was weighty. Cool to the touch. The girl's sobs grew hysterical. She wetted her skirt and over her shoes. Ellis talked low to himself or prayed. The boy reached into his trousers and pulled something from his pocket.

Ellis waved a pocket knife. 'I don't want to hurt anyone. Just let me and Susie go, and I promise we won't tell anyone.'

'How many ways stupid do you think I am?' Rory sneered. He turned. 'What the hell you waiting for, Jake? I gave an order.'

'I—I can't.'

'You raising some kinda pansy, Gus?'

Gus stepped forward. 'They're just kids, Rory. We don't have no beef with them.'

Rory attempted to take back the gun. 'If you're son ain't man enough...'

A loud *bang* followed the click of the Colt. The gun now warm in hand.

Rory roared with outrage. 'Goddamn, you, Jake. You shot me!' Blood seeped through his fingers. 'You're dead. You hear me? Tommy will flay your skin off and butcher you like a pig.' He held his gut and crumpled to the ground.

Ellis grabbed Susie and pushed her into the DeSoto. He gunned the gas and sprayed dirt. The car bounced over Rory.

They'd buried him there and never again spoke of it. Never told another living soul what had happened that night. Rory had never been found. But he knew—Boss Tom would never stop searching for his younger brother. And those responsible.

Chapter 29

Come morning, Faye sat in Boss Tom's study, fiddling with a loose thread on the chair upholstery. The wood-paneled walls seemed to be moving, soon to enclose her in a life-sized mahogany box.

Boss Tom sat behind a no-nonsense desk in a big, masculine chair. He took his time finishing whatever work he deemed essential enough to make her wait. Jake's father reclined next to her, relaxed, his eyes closed.

Faye crossed and uncrossed her legs and then bounced her knee. She wanted to get this over with. To be on the road with Jake and never return to this godawful place.

Why is it so silent in here? If the quiet-as-a-tomb torture was meant to intimidate and unsettle her, it was working.

Thump. Boss Tom closed the thick ledger and stared at her with his beady, ever-assessing eyes. "My apologies for keeping you waiting." He didn't look sorry at all. "I'll come straight to the point. A man doesn't get to be where I am without being cautious about the men he surrounds himself with."

Gus nodded in agreement.

Boss Tom stood and rounded the desk. He leaned back against it and crossed his arms. "I knew Jake's wife had left him long before I set up the meeting which brought him here. I also have a photograph of them together. Your appearance couldn't be more different. So, the question is—who are you? And why are you pretending to be someone you're not?"

Faye clasped her hands together and tried to keep from fidgeting. She wished Jake was here. But he wasn't, and this was her decision to make. She decided it best to come clean and take her chances. "My name is Faye Harmon. I'm from Haverford, Pennsylvania."

Boss Tom smiled like he already knew this. *A test.*

Gus's mouth gaped open. He obviously hadn't known. So much for being kept in the loop. Boss Tom kept his secrets close.

Faye spoke to Gus, "I believe the Philadelphia Mob knows who murdered my father and is attempting to kill me as well. We didn't mean to deceive you. Jake was just trying to protect me."

Boss Tom nodded like he knew that, too. He picked up a card from his desk and handed it to her. The inscription read DARTON STREET DANCE HALL, the address of a seedy part of downtown Philadelphia that everyone called 'The Tenderloin.'

She flipped it over and glanced at the back. It was blank. "What's this?"

Boss Tom moved back to his desk chair. It squeaked as he plopped down. "I believe I know who ordered your father's death, but before I help you with your situation, I need two favors in return."

Faye's stomach told her this wasn't a good idea. She frowned. "What do you need from me?"

Boss Tom tapped a fleshy finger on his desk. "First, I need you to talk Jake into selling his farm. He seems to think this is a temporary position, but I need someone in Philadelphia I can trust."

Without fully thinking, she said, "I can't do that."

Gus placed his hand in warning on top of her own.

Boss Tom furrowed his forehead and narrowed his beady eyes at her. "No? I don't think you understand—"

"I'm sorry." Faye realized she'd overstepped a line. "But I won't be the reason he's obligated back into your, er...organization. He—" She figured she was all in now. "He wants a different way of life."

Boss Tom's mouth twitched. Jake's dad pressed firmer on her hand.

Faye's speech sped up, stumbling over her words. "Mainly because of his son, Rudy, a sweet boy. You see, he's not cut out for city life and would be so lost and confused. And the girls—oh, my goodness. Where would Chaska hunt? And Niya barely speaks English. Not to mention their dog—he's part wild, as are they."

Boss Tom and Gus stared at her like she'd grown a second head. This wasn't going well.

"I cannot endanger them just to get what I want." She turned to Gus. "I know you think you can protect your son and Rudy, but the

Chiappettas are horrible people, and no matter how hard we try, we can't always save the ones we love."

Gus patted her wrist. "Don't worry your pretty head about my family. I've been at this game a long time. Lucky Leo works for us and would never have the guts to go against the boss here." He tilted his head toward Tom.

"But, um, you don't understand—"

"I know this must be difficult for you to take in." Gus's eyes softened. "This life isn't for everyone, but I can tell you and my son care about each other."

"Lucky Leo isn't the threat," Faye said with frustration. "Lucy is. She kidnapped your first wife and killed her, and I almost—"

Gus kicked his chair back. "*What?*"

"Sugar is in a wine barrel in their cellar." She didn't mean to blurt it out that way, but his expression frightened her.

Gus's lips curled over his bared teeth as he searched for something to hit. He found the wall, over and over. Faye had never seen anyone so angry.

"I knew they had something to do with Sugar's disappearance," he shouted. "You talked me out of it. We need to settle this *now*."

Boss Tom pinched the bridge of his nose and tapped his pinky on his cheek. "Agreed. It appears we've more problems in our backyard than we thought. You have my permission to deal with this unfortunate new development as you see fit."

Gus threw open the door and stomped from the room.

Boss Tom glanced back her way as if he had forgotten she was there. He cleared his throat. "My home is your home. Please tell Jake I need to speak with him at once." He waved a hand toward the door, dismissing her.

Probably a mistake, she reminded him about the second favor. "Um...you mentioned there were two," she said with trepidation.

"Right." Boss Tom smirked and stared at her legs. "How are you at dancing?"

Faye hoped she'd done the right thing, hoped Jake would see it that way, and that she hadn't made things worse for him. She found him in the billiards room shooting balls by himself.

He dropped the stick on the table. "How'd it go?"

She inhaled a deep breath and let it out slowly. "Boss Tom knew who I was, has known since we arrived here. He wants you to let go of the farm and go to Philadelphia. Permanently. He said he needed someone he could trust."

Jake ran his hand over his face. "I guess I always knew this day might come. I'll sell the farm to the bank, take whatever I can to set us up a new life somewhere else. Texas, maybe. Try my hand at growing cotton."

Faye wished she could think of another way. "That sounds like a good plan. I do hope you'll take Niya and Chaska with you. They are great kids, and they adore you."

Jake cocked his head at her. "I already planned on taking them with me...with us. I thought that went without saying after last night." He led her to a chair and knelt beside her. He took a blue string from his pocket and tied it in a bow on her finger. "I don't know when I'll be able to afford a ring, but I give you my promise to take care of and protect you."

"Are you proposing because of what we did last night?"

He answered her with a slight nod. "In part, yes. Because it is the right thing to do."

'*The right thing to do*' repeated over and again in her head. Not the words that would have counted: that he loved her and didn't want to live without her.

Jake placed his hand on her knee. "You could be with child. That's a responsibility I don't take lightly. I won't have a kid of mine born out of wedlock."

Faye stared out a window at the landscaped grounds. In truth, last night happened partly because of what she'd gone through and her strong feelings and attraction to him. A baby never factored into her thoughts. Now that he'd mentioned it, the possibility took the forefront position in her mind. She gazed down at the string around her finger. "I'm not ignorant. I know how babies are made." Her friends had told her about their lovemaking experiences but nothing about what came after. Jane had said that a girl couldn't become pregnant her first time. But Jane had been a virgin herself, so maybe that wasn't entirely true.

Jake squeezed her knee and stood.

Faye remembered her errand. "Boss Tom needs to speak with you in his study. It sounded important." Would Boss Tom tell him about Sugar? Would Jake's vow of loyalty be as worthless as this string if he found out she'd kept his mother's death from him?

Jake stalked into the bedroom suite.

His face tight, he threw their cases on the bed. "Pack up. We're leaving." He went into the bathroom and slammed the door.

Was he upset with her? Faye tossed the *Ladies Home Journal* she'd been skimming into the magazine rack and went to the dresser. She'd only unpacked a few things, so it didn't take her long to repack.

Jake emerged from the bathroom a few minutes later with a damp towel around his waist and water beading across his chest and broad shoulders.

Her gaze followed his jerky movements. With caution, she asked, "Where are we going?"

"Home. We need to swing by Boss Tom's auto repair shop and pick up the Studebaker first." He chose the clothes he'd wear and latched the case. Without another word, he went into the bathroom and closed the door.

Faye sat on the edge of the bed they'd shared last night. She ran her hand over the sheet and visualized him there. Would he forgive her for not telling him about his mother? Or was the real reason they were returning to his farm because he couldn't wait to get rid of her?

Jake stayed silent during the ride to the auto shop. He parked his dad's Cadillac in the parking lot.

"I need to run in Gus's keys." He tilted his head toward a large brick office building. "Stay here. I won't be long." He slammed the door, sprinted across the street, and entered through the front.

Faye worried her hands and stared out the window. He'd been so distant since meeting with Boss Tom. There wasn't anything she could do now if the horse had left the barn. He either would forgive her or continue to be upset all the way home. Regardless, she hoped he hurried, eager to put distance between her and this corrupt city to which she'd never return.

An automobile screeched to a stop in front of the office building, joined by three more. Men with long guns emerged and rushed through the main door.

Faye's breath hitched in her throat. She pushed the passenger door open and got out as gunfire sounded inside the building. A glass window shattered on the third floor.

She ran toward the auto shop to get help. A car in an alley blocked her path. The doors opened. Lucy, Lucky Leo Chiappetta, and two armed men exited. Lucy locked eyes with her. The men raised their guns.

Lucy's thin smile broadened. "Nice of you to join us, Miss Harmon, Missus Boyd, or whoever the hell you claim to be today. You've caused me a significant number of problems. It is appropriate that you see what your foolishness has brought."

Lucky Leo stared up at the building. A flash of light flickered in a window. "There's the signal. All clear."

Lucy's thug grabbed Faye's arm and forced her to cross the street. Tears blurred the building where Jake had met his end.

Lucy patted the back of her shoulder. "Your selfishness killed him, you know. None of this had to happen if you hadn't run off."

A sob escaped Faye's throat. Lucy strolled in first through the office building's door. A security guard lay sprawled in a pool of blood on the floor.

Faye turned away. Lucy was right. Who else had died because of her choices? She shouldn't have involved Jake and his family. Everyone would have been better off without her.

Lucy picked up a framed photograph from the desk. "This man

had a beautiful young wife and child. So much to live for. Because of you, she is now a widow." She placed it back and headed toward the stairs. "I told my men to keep Boss Tom alive long enough for me to speak with him. I wish him to know how much I respect him before taking over his city and life."

When they reached the stairway door that led to the third floor, Faye struggled against the man holding her. Better to be killed now than to see Jake's dead body. It was futile, though. The man too strong, and Lucy was enjoying herself too much to offer a quick and merciful death.

The large office took up the whole floor. Wooden file cabinets lined a room cluttered with desks, typewriters, and metal chairs. The scent of gunpowder filled the air and bloody spots spattered the floor. No one was in sight, and no sound, save the wall clock tick ticking away the seconds.

Lucy turned in a circle. She narrowed her eyes and frowned. "Marco? Donte?" She glanced over at her husband. "Something isn't right."

Cracking noises sounded, then *thunk thunk*. The man next to Faye jerked back. His mouth fell open as he stared down at his groin. Blood gushed from his lower abdomen and upper thigh. He crumbled as a *pop pop* dropped the other thug with a chest shot and one to his forehead.

Lucky Leo ran for the door.

"I wouldn't do that." Gus stepped out and aimed the pistol at Leo's back.

Leo froze in place and held his arms up.

Lucy dove for a handgun on the floor. Another shot rang out, skidding it out of her reach.

Faye squeezed her eyes shut. When she reopened them, Boss Tom was standing over Lucy.

"It's over, you old crone," he said with a wooden expression. He handed his gun to Jake. "Finish her."

Faye swayed on her feet. Tears welled from the relief of Jake's resurrection and worry for the horrible circumstance he now found himself. She rubbed her thumb over the blue string around her finger.

Lucy crawled onto her knees. "Thomas, this isn't what you think. We were coming to save you."

Boss Tom seemed to be enjoying this. "Are those the words you choose to be your last?"

"It's the truth." Lucy's chin trembled. "We heard about someone sending men to take you out. I'm so relieved they failed."

Boss Tom shook his head. "Don't warn me through wolf's teeth about the lions circling."

"Jake, my boy," Lucy pleaded. "Remember when I gave you sweet treats? Cold drinks on the hot days when you made your deliveries?" Her tone changed from sweet to sour. "I was always good to you."

"Out of guilt for killing my mother."

Lucy's eyes widened. "Is that what she told you?" She gestured Faye's way. "That girl is **a** deceiving, no-good common thief, like her father."

Were they buying Lucy's act? From the looks on their faces, not a one.

"Do it," Boss Tom ordered Jake. "Before the police show."

Standing rigid and frowning at the gun, Jake glanced at her sidelong.

Was it Boss Tom who had ordered him to kill a man when he'd been just a boy? Was he about to make another detrimental decision that would haunt him forever? The tension in the room warred on her nerves.

"No," Jake finally said, "I can't." He handed Boss Tom the gun.

"Your son's grown weak, Gus." Boss Tom didn't attempt to hide his anger. "It'll be up to you to toughen him up again."

Gus aimed his gun at Lucy with a stare that could freeze flaming coal. "Go home and get your affairs in order," he said to Jake, not taking his eyes off Lucy.

"Don't do this. It won't bring my mother back."

"I need to do it for me," Gus said. "You best leave."

Jake grabbed Faye's hand and hurried her past Lucky Leo, who was curled over and frantically sobbing. Sirens sounded closer.

Once they were out of the building, two gunshots rang out.

❧

Jake stopped to fuel the car.

Faye walked on wobbly legs to the side of the station and leaned against the building, her body weak, her skin cold and clammy. Was she now an unwitting accomplice to double murder?

Jake came to her and handed over a paper cup of water. "They were bad people. They don't deserve your tears."

"I can't get it out of my head. They were alive this morning, breathing human beings, and now they're dead."

His eyes locked onto her own. "Because of the things they did. My mother wasn't the only one they'd killed. Many more poor souls had crossed the Chiappettas the wrong way."

"Did you know Boss Tom was going to kill them?"

"I knew there would be no talking Gus out of his revenge. And Boss Tom couldn't have Lucy or Leo striking a deal with his enemies. So, yeah, I knew it would happen this way."

How could they think so little of taking a human life? Boss Tom to maintain his power and wealth and feed his oversized ego. Gus, out of anger, seeking vengeance. Deed, purchasing murder for a love who had belonged to another.

How much of their humanity was lost with each life taken?

No one seemed consumed by guilt but Jake. But was that enough for her? Should she stay with someone capable of murder? Did she ever really know him at all?

Chapter 30

Pink clouds hovered over the sunset as the coming evening began its rhythmic hum. Seated on the porch swing, Faye read her letter from her aunt. Her possessions had arrived safely in Colorado. The elderly sisters she had traveled with on the train delivered her handbag and stayed with her aunt until word came that Faye was safe. That was kind of them.

Her wired money now available in town; she had the means to leave but wasn't free to go her own way. The final deal she'd made with Boss Tom would get her the information needed and free Jake from working for the organization.

There was also a catch. She couldn't tell Jake she'd return to Philadelphia, pose as a dancer, and spy on the dance hall's owner. A man named King. Oh, and find a way to steal his financial ledger, for what end, she wasn't sure.

One thing certain. It was about to storm, and now, she was smack dab in the middle of it—without shelter or even an umbrella.

Niya's giggle filtered through the open window as Jake read to the children in the sitting room. Chaska leaned her head on his shoulder, Niya was stretched across his lap, and Rudy turned the pages. Even S'unka had somehow managed to wiggle his way inside. The dog's big head rested atop Jake's crossed ankles.

They looked like a real family. One she didn't belong with. She swallowed past the thickness in her throat. They would be better off without her, but just the thought of leaving them twisted her insides.

The next day, Faye found a cabinet sewing machine while dusting. Despite being an older style, it still worked. Buried behind were fabric rolls uncut. The clothes she'd brought with her now looked a bit worse for wear, and Chaska and Niya could also use something not so boyish. Thrilled to find everything she'd need to make several new dresses; she sought out Jake to ask his permission.

In the barn brushing down a mule, he shrugged when asked to use the sewing machine and fabric. "They were a wedding gift from Sarah's mother. She never bothered to learn, so use what you wish. Not like we'll have room to take most of this stuff with us."

Faye flinched. It was time to tell him that they were parting ways. "I heard from my aunt."

"Good news?"

"My possessions arrived at her home. She wired my money to Union. Will you take me to retrieve it?"

He nodded and busied himself sorting nails into glass jars. "We can meet with the banker while in town. Bankers, bullies, and bosses. All roads lead to Rome," he mumbled.

"Pardon?"

"In the end, the big guy wins."

"Not always. Don't worry. I speak banker."

"It'll be good for you to be there and keep me from killing him."

Faye knew what he said was in jest, but knowing he had killed someone, the flippant remark bothered her. Now the hard part. Her mind raced to find the right words.

Jake stopped what he was doing. "Something wrong?"

"N-no," she stuttered. "It's my aunt, you see. She's unwell." A lie, but she needed a reasonable excuse for leaving. "I need to help them. She and her husband never had children of their own."

Jake nodded. "We can stop there. Take the long way to Texas."

She hadn't expected him to offer that. This was becoming more difficult than she'd imagined. It would be so much easier if she didn't care about him. But even though she did, she wasn't about to marry a man who would only take vows out of obligation. Not to mention— an ex-hitman for Boss Tom.

"My monthly arrived. I'm not pregnant."

An emotion flitted across his handsome face and his hands sped up the sorting task. It took a long moment for him to reply. "I see."

He cleared his throat. "What a relief. Huh?" He didn't look relieved. He seemed disappointed.

She stopped herself from telling him everything, that she was going for their own good. That he wouldn't have to constantly watch over his shoulder because she'd found a way out for him. As long as she stole what Boss Tom wanted, Jake and the children would then be free.

After washing, drying, and cutting the soft fabric, Faye busied herself at the old treadle sewing machine. It felt good to do something familiar. To know where the sweet spot on the foot pedals balanced best to drive the band wheel. Her attention focused as she guided the fabric under the threaded needle, removing pins before it penetrated. Like a purring cat well petted, the whir from the black machine brought her a sense of peace. And even though it only allowed a single straight stitch, it was fun to use and kept her mind from wandering to unpleasantness. She glanced up to find Jake staring at her.

"Am I disturbing your reading?" she asked.

He set the *Grass and Grains* newspaper aside. "Not at all. You're good at that."

"Thank you. Hopefully, I'll do well enough to support myself."

His slow smile returned to a flat line.

Chaska let the screen door bang shut behind her. "Got a minute?"

"Sure." Faye held up the dress she'd been working on for Chaska. Not too frilly, but an attractive design. She placed it against the girl's shoulders and studied the fit.

"What's that?" Chaska tilted her head down and frowned.

"A dress, silly. For you."

Chaska jerked back as if the material burned her skin. "I don't wear dresses."

Faye sighed. "You'll need one in Texas for school and church."

The girl vehemently shook her head and glared over at Jake. "I don't like school, and I don't like church."

Jake shrugged and returned to his reading.

Faye carefully folded the dress and set aside her work. "Up to you. I'll also make you new trousers and shirts."

"That I'll wear." Chaska patted Faye's back. "C'mon. I got somethin' to show you."

She followed the girl to the backyard. There, Brody and Niya sat on the ground. Brody placed a long blade of grass between his thumbs, pursed his lips, and blew against his cupped hand. A low-pitched whistle grew gradually higher and louder.

Niya squealed with delight and clapped. "Do again!"

"Fascinating," Faye said to Chaska and turned to return to her sewing.

"That's not it." Chaska hooked her arm. "It's about what happened to you in Kansas City. I'm thinkin' you should learn how to protect yourself."

"Not necessary. I'm never going back there." She slid her arm from Chaska's elbow.

"That isn't the only place you'll have trouble, you know. And just 'cause you're smaller than someone doesn't mean you're without might. You just got to be quicker and smarter than them." The girl ordered Brody, "Come at me."

Brody stood and dusted himself off. "This ain't a game girls should play, and I got work to do."

Chaska grabbed his arm and flipped him over. Brody landed with an "oof" and wheezed out a ragged breath. Eyes wide, he groaned and rubbed his lower back. Chaska smiled down at him. Niya giggled.

Chaska helped Brody to his feet and said, "A while back, we met up with a China man named Chen. He was a small railroad worker bein' picked on by men twice his size. Chen took down all three of them on his own. He showed me some tricks on how to deal with troublemakers." Chaska once again used Brody. "Grab his arm like this and pull him toward you. Throws off his steadiness. Turn, using your hip against him, bend, and flip."

Brody pulled away. "If I know it's coming, it won't work."

Chaska nodded. "That's when you hit their side with your elbow, strike their nose with a rock, and kick'em behind the knee or between the legs."

"Whoa!" Brody stumbled back.

Chaska stopped short of kicking him in the testicles, yet Brody's face still paled.

"I don't think I can do that," Faye said.

Chaska frowned. "You're smaller and weaker. It's him or you."

They spent the afternoon with Chaska showing how to get the advantage over an attacker. Faye was surprised at how quickly she caught on. Felt more empowered after. Poor Brody called his workday to an early end, claiming body aches and injured dignity.

The following Friday, Jake took Faye to town. The old men were seated once again on their bench.

"Jake," one yelled. "That gal ain't handcuffed you to the alter yet? Made you an honest man?"

The others chuckled.

"Mind your potatoes, you old wisecrackers." Jake jumped down from the wagon and half-circled around. He offered his hand.

She shot the geezers a look of satisfaction as Jake swung her down. The old men seemed disappointed their fun with her was over.

After acquiring the postmaster's slip, Faye went to the bank with Jake.

He stopped outside the entrance door, took a deep breath, and then let it out. "I can't promise this will go well, but I'll try to keep my temper." He opened the chiming door and followed her in.

A teller greeted them. "Mister Boyd." He bowed his head toward her. "Ma'am. How may I be of service?"

Jake shook the man's hand. "We're here to meet with Schmidt. He in?"

The teller's mouth dropped open. "Um, I will ask if he is available. May I inquire about the reason for your visit?"

Jake seemed to have problems forming the words.

Faye placed her hand on his arm. "Mister Boyd is considering selling his farm."

"Oh. My. Certainly. Please have a seat." The plump man shuffled to a back office and closed the door.

Jake ran a hand through his hair. "Maybe this is a bad idea."

Before she could answer, an older man appeared at the office door. "Mister Boyd, I will see you."

The teller skirted back to his cage.

Faye remembered the slip in her hand and handed it to him through the bars. "I need to cash this."

The man squinted at it. "Nine hundred dollars? I must confirm the authorization first and get Mister Schmidt's permission. Can you come back before closing?"

Faye glanced up at Jake. He stared at Schmidt's open door with dread on his face. His mind somewhere else, she tugged his sleeve.

"The teller asked if we'll come back later." She added for understanding, "For my money."

He nodded absently and headed toward Schmidt's office, his pace of a man slogging through a swamp instead of striding across the bank's gleaming tiled floor.

Faye followed.

An American flag took up one wall of the banker's office, and pictures of him with President Hoover and other well-known politicians lined another. A framed photograph of a homely woman with a pinched expression was set in an honorary position on his desk.

"Have a seat." Mr. Schmidt looked to be in his sixties with a trim form in a pinstriped suit.

Jake pulled out her chair and cleared his throat. "I'm thinking about selling my farm." His voice wavered, but he went on. "I was wondering what you'd give me for it."

Schmidt quirked a brow. "Interesting. May I ask why?"

Jake narrowed his eyes. "A change of scenery."

The banker glanced over at Faye like he was trying to deduce the real reason. He licked his lips. "Did you bring the paperwork needed?"

Jake pulled the folded pages from his pocket. Schmidt reached across the desk and had to loosen the documents from Jake's grip. He unfolded his spectacles and perched them on his nose. As Schmidt studied the figures, Jake tapped a finger on the armrest of a chair. Faye rubbed his forearm to calm him.

The banker looked up, his expression all business. "Seems like you had a bad last year." He studied the page again. "Sold only one hundred and ten bushels of wheat and fifty bushels of corn. How do I know that grounds not spent?"

Jake's arm twitched beneath her hand. "You know damn well we've been in drought. I brought in twice that amount two years ago."

Schmidt sniffed. "That was then." His lips turned down. "You led the farmers in a revolt against me at the Thompson's auction. Why should I help you now?"

Jake shot up from the chair. "This was a waste of time."

Schmidt held up a hand. "Calm down, son. It was a reasonable question, but water under the bridge. Sit. Please."

Jake glanced at Faye. She tilted her head toward the chair. He plopped back down and exhaled.

Schmidt rubbed his smoothly shaved chin. "Many farmers want help. Selling for pennies on the dollar. But considering the unfortunate incident between your wife and my son, I'm willing to give you eight hundred dollars for it."

Jake coughed and gripped the sides of the chair. "That's five dollars an acre and *nothing* for the house and barn."

Feigning apathy, Schmidt stated, "Times are hard right now. That is the best I can do."

By the looks of his expensive suit and furniture, Faye doubted his sincerity. Jake had no choice but to sell, and this weasel of a man was his only chance to do so in a timely manner. She smiled at the banker. "We thought twelve hundred would be a fair price—"

"You thought wrong," Schmidt said, barely acknowledging her presence.

"He will include the livestock, furniture, and farm equipment. Twelve hundred is a steal."

The banker ignored her and said to Jake, "Eight hundred is my final offer. Think it over, but the deal expires by seven o'clock tonight. Now, if you'll excuse me." He rose when Faye stood and opened the door.

Jake looked like he'd been punched in the stomach. Once outside, he leaned against a brick wall.

Faye placed her hand on his shoulder. "I'm sorry I couldn't help."

"There was nothing you could do." He shook his head. "Schmidt knows I wouldn't come to him unless desperate."

As they walked down Main Street, music filtered from a barn structure. Through a gap in the open doors, men practiced on musical instruments. A sign on the barn read, THE JUG BAND THIS FRIDAY NIGHT.

Jake took her hand, then wrapped his arm around her waist and drew her close.

His lips found hers with a deep kiss.

He swayed her to the music, and she wished they could stay in this moment forever, without worries about what was to come or where they belonged.

But there was not to be a 'them.'

Jake looked up and stiffened.

Faye followed his line of vision.

The townsfolk stared at them. One of them looked like his sister-in-law, Elsa.

Dressed in the frilly blue and white polka-dotted dress she'd created, Faye grabbed a shawl before making her way downstairs.

Chaska looked up from the game she played with Rudy and Niya and wolf-whistled through her fingers. The kids stared her way. Jake's gray gaze lifted from the magazine he'd been reading, grazed slowly down her, and settled on her face.

Chaska grinned. "Hubba, hubba. Where you going?"

Faye's cheeks warmed. "To the bank in town."

Jake stood and wrapped the shawl around her shoulders. "And a dance. Don't stay up late." He offered Faye his arm.

Surprised by his offer, the warmth on her cheeks spread over her face. Why not celebrate what would be their last night together? They both needed some fun.

In good spirits on the way to town, Jake was talkative about their future. He also included Chaska and Niya in his plans, which comforted her. But guilt also gnawed at her for putting off telling him about her intention to go her separate way. Then again, they both needed a night without dramatics.

He reined in the mules to a halt beside the bank and helped her down.

The teller smiled when they entered. "I have everything ready for you, Miss Harmon. Mister Schmidt is waiting for you in his office, Mister Boyd."

Faye glanced around at the customers seated with worried faces. The men were most likely farmers with weathered skin and stoic expressions. The women seemed anxious as they attempted to keep their children quiet and entertained.

Jake nodded a greeting at a man, then said to the teller, "We can wait. They were here first—"

"Mister Schmidt told me to send you in as soon as you arrive."

Before entering the office, Jake shook hands with the men waiting and said something she couldn't hear.

After the teller finished counting money onto her hand, a loud thud sounded inside Schmidt's office. Faye stuffed the bills into her pocket and rushed to the open door.

Jake had his hands wrapped around the banker's throat.

Schmidt's eyes were wide with fear. He mouthed for help.

Behind Faye, the teller gasped.

"Jake." She rounded the desk and tapped on Jake's arm. "*Jake.* You're hurting him. Let him go."

The banker's complexion turned rouge-red.

Jake stared at her with confusion etched on his face and then seemed to come back to himself. He removed his hands from Schmidt's neck. The banker gasped for breath.

Jake shook the deed to the farm. "We had an agreement, dammit, and you will *abide* by your word."

Schmidt wheezed to the teller, "Get the money." He inhaled and exhaled more deep breaths.

Jake scribbled his name on the paperwork and threw down the pen. He followed the teller to the front.

Faye borrowed one of her grandmother's withering stares. "You give bankers a bad name." She slammed the door behind her and went to Jake. "Are you okay?"

He nodded, but his hands still shook. The nervous teller counted out the eight hundred in bills. Jake snatched it up.

The waiting farmers stood and patted his back on his way out.

It took three steps to his one to keep up outside the bank. Band music blared out the dance barn's door. She caught hold of his arm. "Hold up. What the hell happened in there?"

He stopped his stride. "Schmidt tried to go back on our deal, offering half of what he said he would."

"I'm so sorry you had to give up your farm. I know how hard that must have been for you."

His pained expression tore at her heart.

He stared hard at the bank's door. "But now I made things worse for the farmers in there. Schmidt will take his bad mood out on them. Because of me, they'll lose everything."

She hadn't thought of that. It was so unfair for one man to have that much power over other's lives. Celebrating their good fortune seemed wrong now. "Maybe we should head home..."

He kissed the back of her hand. "Damage done. I'll figure out some way to help them."

Jake hid their money in a slit under the wagon's bench seat, then strolled with her toward the barn.

The whole town seemed to be there. Jake wrapped his arms around her waist and maneuvered her around sweet-smelling hay bales, wheelbarrows with potted flowers, and candle-lit open jars. Quilts nailed to the walls made the barn feel homey. On the sawdust-strewn floor, dancers formed squares, four couples in each. The men wore colorful bandanas around their necks, brightening their worn flannel shirts. The women's flowing dresses were mainly faded prints, accented with beribboned hair. The dancers moved in unison to a peppy beat. A man on stage rhythmically sang out the dance steps to the music played on fiddle, banjo, slap drum, and even an old jug.

Jake scooped a paper cup into the punch bowl and handed it to her. He chose from platters of cookies supplied on a checkered gingham-clothed table.

A handsome man came up behind him and slapped him on the back. "I wouldn't have entered the horseshoe toss competition if I knew you were coming." The man looked Faye's way and tipped his cowboy hat.

Jake shook his hand. "I'm just here for the music."

The man light-heartedly punched him on the arm. "I'll bet. Who's this here?"

Jake introduced them. "Getz, Faye. Faye, Getz."

Getz took her hand and kissed the back of it. "Mind if I borrow her for a round?"

Faye looked up at Jake in question.

Jake chuckled. "He's asking you to dance."

She shook her head at the man. "Oh, no, thank you. I don't know this type of dance."

The floor cleared as the caller instructed more dancers to take the floor.

Jake took her cup away and handed it and a half-eaten cookie to Getz. He grabbed Faye's hand and led her into a square with three other couples. "You'll know soon enough. Just follow my lead."

The music started up again. Faye watched what the other couples did and mimicked their steps. The dance moves were fun. She especially liked it when the caller called her home to return to Jake's strong arms.

When was the last time she'd had this much fun? The music sped up. It was like flying free. She laughed as Jake held on and spun her over the floor.

Face flushed, he joined her laugh. It took years off his face. When the song ended, he quickly led her to a dark corner at the back of the barn. His lips claimed her own and kissed her long and with passion. Her heart pumped harder than the dance caused, and she clutched his red flannel shirt, not wanting to let him go.

A cough interrupted them from behind.

Faye turned and locked eyes with a man so out of place here that she didn't recognize him at first. Her mouth fell open. "Penn? What are you doing here?"

Penn glared at Jake. "I was worried about you. Now I see I had good cause."

Jake stiffened in her arms. He seemed to be sizing up Penn.

Faye pulled away and smoothed her dress. "I'm fine. How did you find me?"

"The letter you sent me was stamped from here. I've been asking these people about you all day, but they weren't very helpful."

Jake crossed his arms. "We don't trust strangers."

The way they stared each other down made her nervous. She smiled at Penn. "Silly, there was no reason for you to come all this way."

"Isn't there? I'm not so sure. When I read your letter, I realized I made a mistake letting you go off on your own."

He'd told her to go. *Men.* Would she ever understand them?

"I'm here to take you home," Penn concluded.

Jake's nostrils flared. He looked like he wanted to punch Penn.

Faye needed to lower the tension. "Jake saved my life."

"And this is what he expects as a reward?" Penn narrowed his eyes. "Taking advantage of an innocent young woman?"

Jake took a step forward, his fist clenched.

Faye pressed her hands on his chest. She looked back at Penn. "Who I choose to be with is none of your concern."

The music from the dance grew louder.

Penn shouted over it, "Can we go somewhere and talk? Somewhere quieter, without...him."

She willed Jake to understand. "He's my friend and came all this way."

The crease between Jake's eyebrows deepened as his lips tightened. He stormed away.

Faye sighed. She went with Penn outside the barn. "I appreciate your coming to check on me, but I'm fine. Really."

"You need to come home."

She lifted her chin. "I can do so on my own. In my own time."

Penn glanced around, then said with exasperation, "You have nothing in common with these people. With—with *him*. You should be around your own kind. Your father would expect that from you."

She firmed her stance, hands on her hips. "I'm done living my life to satisfy others, happy being free to choose my own path. I regret if I caused you concern and that you've wasted your time, but I'm not the same girl you once knew."

He pulled her into an embrace and kissed her words away.

Caught off guard, she was slow to stop him.

Penn suddenly jerked back.

Jake yanked him up by the collar and then punched his face.

Penn fell flat on his back and winced.

Jake shouted, "Get up!"

"Stop it!" She pulled on Jake's arm with as much success as a ragdoll. "What are you doing?"

"Did you want him to maul you?" He scrunched his face. "Huh?"

"No, of course not, but I can handle myself."

"Not what it looked like to me."

"I wish people would stop saying that. I'm perfectly capable of—"

Penn started to stand. Jake moved forward.

"No, no, no." She stood between them. "Do not hit him again."

Jake frowned down at her. "I see. Maybe you liked what he did. Maybe I've just been a distraction until you could return to him. Is that it?"

"Of course not. You're acting like a possessive, jealous, immature bully."

He turned and stalked away.

"*Jake.*"

"Let him go cool off." Penn stood and dusted himself off.

Faye groaned.

"You're in love with him," Penn stated. "I'm sorry. I didn't know."

She sighed. "He's perplexing at times, but I do love him." The words flowed easily from her lips, and hearing them spoken aloud, even to the wrong man, stunned her.

"I didn't come here to make things harder on you. I was genuinely worried and couldn't get our last kiss out of my head. I see now that I'm too late."

His words, which once would have meant everything to her, fell flat. "I appreciate your coming all this way, but I can manage my own life." She stared into the dark that had swallowed Jake. "I need to go after him. I shouldn't have said what I did."

Penn nervously glanced around and then held out his hand. "Still friends?"

"Of course." She sandwiched his hand between her own. "I've known you my whole life. A little misunderstanding isn't going to end that."

Penn chuckled. "Go on. Smooth the beast's temper before he comes at me again."

Faye hurried back into the barn and scanned for Jake. She didn't see him but caught sight of his friend Getz. She went over and tapped his shoulder. "Have you seen Jake?"

He turned and pushed the brim of his hat up. "Did he leave you without escort, darlin'?"

"We had a bit of a fight."

Getz laughed. "That sounds like Jake. Come with me. I'll help you find him."

Faye felt a little nervous, leaving the crowd with someone she barely knew. But he was Jake's friend. He led her around the barn and then to a horse stable. Jake stood before a stall, knuckle massaging a horse between its eyes.

"There yuh go." Getz lifted the cowboy hat and gave her a mock bow. "Go easy on the man. That big heart matches his size, and he wounds easily."

Faye thanked him and walked down a ramp into the stable.

Jake glanced over. He patted the horse, then met her halfway. "I lost my head."

"Penn shouldn't have kissed me. I swear to you that I didn't encourage him."

"When I saw you in his arms...I can't explain it."

Faye stood on tiptoe and kissed him with all the meaning words couldn't say. Being wrapped in his arms was like being covered with a soft blanket—comforting and firmly rooted—like coming home. He pulled her closer and kissed her.

A different type of volley burst through her defenses.

She wanted him, but it wasn't fair to him to string him along. She withdrew. "We should get home."

"We don't have a home. The bank owns it."

A wrong choice of words. She couldn't add to his misery of the day. She'd tell him tomorrow that, though she had feelings for him, she must go.

When they headed toward the barn, she noticed Penn was still at the dance. He leaned over a pretty blonde. It certainly hadn't taken him long to get over her rejection. Jake abruptly stopped and stared. Faye glanced from his hardened expression to the woman and back to him again. She was the one who had stared at them earlier, kissing outside the bank. Then, it dawned on her who the woman must be. Rudy's mom. The real Sarah.

Bees on a bonnet. The woman's timing couldn't be worse.

"Jake." Sarah smiled. "Aren't you going to say hello? Welcome back your wife?"

Penn looked confused. Jake's jaw twitched.

Sarah posed seductively. "Didn't you miss me, Jake?" She practically purred with a breathy, "I missed you."

Inside, Faye felt something she couldn't describe. Inadequate? Jealousy? Sarah wasn't just beautiful. She was voluptuous in all the right places. Every man's dream of what a woman should be. Penn had obviously fallen quickly under her spell. But what about Jake? She glanced his way.

His stare ran cold. "Didn't notice you were gone."

Sarah pursed her lips then said, "We both know that's not true."

Jake grasped Faye's hand.

Sarah's sweet mask stripped to her genuine self. "I heard you took in a stray kitten." She focused her attention on Faye. "I see you cleaned her up to make her presentable." Sarah narrowed her eyes at Faye's new dress.

Did she recognize the fabric?

Jake's grip tightened. "We were just leaving. Need to get home to the kids."

Sarah glared at that. "No one will accept her in this town. There's been talk."

"I can guess who started those rumors," Jake said low.

Sarah splayed her hand across the low-cut neckline of her bawdy dress. "Me? Are you accusing me of misdeeds while you shack up with this flossy whore under the roof you share with our son?"

Ouch. Faye bit her bottom lip to keep her tongue.

Penn moved forward. "Hear, now, no call for that."

Sarah gave Penn a scathing look, then looked back at Jake. "Guess it musta got awfully lonely up there on your high horse. Hmm, Jake?" She moved closer and speared a finger at him. "I'm taking my son back."

Faye pulled at him to keep walking.

Jake planted his feet. "You'll have to go through me. Better bring an army." The muscles and veins in his neck strained against his skin.

"He deserves to be with his real mother."

"You abandoned him. Hurt him more than you'll ever know."

Sarah slapped his cheek. "Your heart abandoned me a long time ago." She went to strike him again, but Jake caught her wrist.

Drawn to the commotion, a few men exited the barn.

Sarah twisted like Jake was hurting her. The sheriff rushed forward. Jake let Sarah go.

"I told you about his temper," Sarah whimpered and rubbed her hand. "Aren't you going to arrest him this time?"

Faye started to quiver as anger built up inside. "She hit him."

The other men backed the sheriff. "The banker also lodged a complaint." The sheriff moved forward and cuffed Jake's wrists. "Sorry 'bout this. But the judge will sort it out. I'll need to collect the prisoner working your farm, too."

"I let him go," Jake said defiantly.

The hole he found himself in had just gotten deeper.

"But you gave me your word..."

"I said I'd do what was best, which I did."

The sheriff pushed him to move. Sarah smirked at Faye.

How could that woman be so vindictive?

She wanted to curse at Sarah, but that would make things worse. She begged the sheriff instead. "Please, I witnessed everything. Let me explain—"

"Save it for the judge," the sheriff said as he and the other men urged Jake along.

Jake grimaced. He jerked them to a halt and looked back at her. "My fault. I was upset about Schmidt taking advantage, so I poked Sarah's nest."

The men pushed at him.

He turned his neck her way. "Find Getz. He'll see you home."

Faye watched them until they disappeared into the dark.

"I'll take that dance now," Sarah said to Penn.

The woman's voice made something snap inside. Without thinking, Faye lunged at Sarah, but a strong arm wrapped around her waist and drew her back.

Fighting against Penn's restraint, she struggled to break free.

"Whoa, there, Tiger. Let it go."

Sarah laughed and entered the barn.

Faye craned her neck to look up at him. With an indignant gasp, she asked, "Are you smiling?"

He chuckled a "No."

He was smiling. She glared up at him.

"I'm sorry. I haven't seen this side of you. Feisty."

She blew out a breath to ease her trembling temper. "That woman deserves much worse than what I could give her."

He tilted his head in thought. "I never had women get in a cat brawl for me," he joked.

She play-punched his arm. "I shouldn't have."

"This isn't your fight," he said in a serious tone. "I have a room in town. We can be on the next train out of here tomorrow."

She shook her head. "Not yet." But every day she'd put off telling Jake and the kids goodbye seemed to make it even harder to do so.

Chapter 31

With Jake in jail awaiting his turn to appear before the judge, he tasked Faye with picking up supplies for their journey to Texas.

Rudy hitched the mules and took her and Chaska to town. Niya was happy to stay behind and shadow her buddy, Brody.

Faye wondered if Rudy would be sad about leaving the only home he'd ever known, but the boy chatted excitedly about the adventure. Impressed by his ability to handle the team, the way went without incident, and in no time, he brought the mules to a halt behind the general store.

To make the tasks more manageable, they divided the list. Faye studied hers as a familiar voice called out her name. The sheriff strolled her way.

Chaska mumbled under her breath and turned her head.

"Miss Harmon. I was gonna come fetch you. That big-city detective's here to take your statement." The sheriff squinted at Chaska.

Faye distracted him and steered him toward the jail. Edgar Elmsworth stood as she entered. Behind bars, Jake sat up on the cot.

The smile she sent his way quickly faded when Elmsworth blocked her view of the cell. "Detective," she greeted with a flat tone. She'd been less than impressed with how he'd handled the break-in and murder investigation at Willow Wood.

Elmsworth gestured for her to take a seat.

"Any progress yet in discovering my father's killers?" she asked.

He jutted his chin. "That case has been dropped."

Faye tensed. "What? Why?"

"There's no evidence or indication anyone other than your father took his life. I drew the short straw in my department to be sent on this wild goose chase and appreciate it if you keep things brief."

She shot out of the chair, her face heated. "Other than one of the thugs trying to kill me, too. How do you explain that?"

He stood, moved closer to intimidate, and glared down at her. "Lady, I don't appreciate my time being wasted. You may get your kicks like this, but I promise you, the next canard fairy tale that comes from your mouth, I'll throw your sweet patootie behind bars so fast your head will spin."

More than anything, she wanted to slap the superior dominance off his face. He wouldn't have dared to speak to her in such a manner in her old life. If she were a man. Did he treat all women like this? She glanced at the ring on his finger. Poor Mrs. Elmsworth.

She looked toward the sheriff for assistance. His eyes widened, and he quickly turned away. *Spineless.*

Elmsworth's grin claimed a smug win. "Do us both a favor, girly. Find a husband to take care of you and manage your affairs."

She glanced over at Jake. He gave a slight shake of his head.

Faye bit her tongue. Every fiber of her body wanted to put Elmsworth in his place, but she had no misgivings that he'd enforce his threat. And she needed to be in good standing to witness for Jake before the judge.

She answered Elmsworth's brief, trivial questions, certain that he disbelieved her every word.

After he callously dismissed her and left the jail with the sheriff, she visited with Jake and then went to finish her errands.

Something about today had her on edge like a storm was brewing she couldn't see. Chalking it up to Elmsworth's atrocious behavior toward her and anxious to be on her way, she finished her tasks in good time.

With her arms filled and her head down to check that she hadn't missed anything on her list, she bumped into someone.

"Pardon me..." her words suspended as she stared at a pair of Oxford shoes speckled red on the tips. Her vision slowly scanned up at him. A barrel of a handgun shown above his trousers' waistband.

Mr. Fedora Hat Man gave her a menacing grin.

A gasp escaped her throat.

He gripped her shoulders, digging in his fingertips.

She dropped everything, the pain spreading down her arms. Voice high-pitched, she asked, "What do you want from me?"

He narrowed his good eye, a patch covering his other. He didn't answer her.

Faye's mind raced with options. She felt the weight of her experiences: just six months ago, she never would have believed a man with a vendetta would shoot innocent men, women, and children, but now, she knew better.

Down the aisle, a brood of kids followed behind an exhausted-looking woman. A little boy begged for something on an upper shelf and, when denied, reached for it himself. A loud crash followed as the jar shattered on the floor. A cacophony of cries erupted from his siblings as the frazzled woman tried to keep them from stepping on glass.

Momentarily distracted, Mr. Fedora Hat Man lessened his grip.

Faye's urge to flee surged.

Chaska's instructions sounded in her head. *Pull him toward you. Throws off his steadiness.* Faye grabbed his upper arms and took a few quick steps back. It worked and upset his balance. She broke free of him.

Hit him in the side with your elbow, strike his nose with a rock, and kick 'im between the legs.

She did the latter first, figuring that would bring the most pain. She kneed his crotch and then palmed a can of peas from a shelf and smashed his nose with it.

He cried out, his hands guarding his lower region as blood ran freely from his nostrils.

Faye pushed him against the shelves and rushed to find Rudy and Chaska.

The girl was examining a pocketknife. "Can I have this?"

"We need to go. Where's Rudy?"

Chaska motioned to a corner of the store. Faye pulled the girl to move, glimpsing the aisles first to make sure they were clear. Rudy had a basketful of things from his list.

"We need to go. *Now.*"

Whether it was the urgency of her tone or the fear that probably showed on her face, the boy didn't question her.

Once outside, Faye allowed herself to breathe.

"What's wrong?" Chaska asked, her forehead scrunched.

"Stop. Thief!" a worker from the store yelled.

Faye looked down at Chaska's hand. Grasped in it was the pocketknife.

They were drawing attention.

Mr. Fedora Hat Man exited the door.

Faye panicked. "Run!"

"Rudy," a woman called out.

Faye glanced back. Sarah stood in front of the store with her hands on her hips.

Mr. Fedora descended the steps.

"Son, *wait*," Sarah called out.

Whether or not he had heard his mother didn't show. They hurried to where the mules were tied. Rudy made quick work with the ropes, jumped up beside her, and hollered, "Yaw!"

Faye turned on the bench, but a cloud of dust blocked her view.

Seated behind her, Chaska coughed between saying, "You want to tell me what in tarnation is going on?"

"The man who tried to kill me was in the store."

"How'd he find you?"

"I don't know."

Rudy clicked his tongue and turned the team south. He poked Faye's arm. "Look."

The western sky was enveloped in a haze. In the distance, what looked like a solid dark wall went all the way up to dull orange clouds.

Rudy urged the mules faster, though they traveled at one speed—a trot. "It's gonna be a bad one. We need to beat it home."

Faye glanced at Chaska. The girl's face filled with worry.

"Brody won't let anything happen to Niya. He'll keep her safe."

Chaska nodded, but her eyes stayed glued on the menace gathering strength on the horizon.

Faye wished she was on her way to Colorado and Jake and the kids to Texas. Because one thing was certain: they'd all stayed a day too late.

❧

Faye held on as Rudy brought the team to a halt in front of the barn. Chaska jumped off the wagon and ran to her sister. Brody helped Rudy get the animals into the barn.

In the barn's tack room, Faye dug through a box that was packed and ready for Texas. She took the book, *The Keeper of the Bees* by Gene Stratton-Porter, she'd been reading from her suitcase and tossed it on top of the sheets and towels to bring inside. It was going to be a long night.

"It's almost here!" Rudy shouted over the screeching wind.

With her arms laden, Faye hurried out. Rudy and Brody struggled to latch the barn doors closed. Inside, the animals sounded in pandemonium.

The wind whipped her hair over her face. She readjusted her burden. Objects flew close, and grit pelted her skin as she struggled toward the house. Her book slid underneath her arm and fell, pages flapping. She stooped to pick it up, but a firm grip pulled at her.

"Leave it," Brody yelled, pushing her and Rudy up the porch. Visibility was fading fast.

The dark wall began to engulf the farm. An automobile pulled into the yard as Brody opened the kitchen door.

Jake? Faye squinted through the swirling dirt and held her hand to shield her face.

A loud crack sounded over the wind. Wooden splinters flew.

Brody thrust her inside the house.

Rudy hit hard on his hands, his palms smarting. He rolled out of the way as bullets thunked like marbles against the open kitchen door.

Several hit Brody. He jerked, stumbled to the side, but finally slammed the door shut. Groaning, he collapsed to the floor, blood seeping through his fingers. Faye grabbed kitchen towels and crept to Brody.

Rudy squirmed at the sight as his eyes tried to deny what they saw.

Brody cried out, "Who the heck is that?"

Faye's face turned pale. She looked like she might throw up. "They must have followed us back. It's me they're after. Oh, Brody." She hovered near him, seeming unsure what to do.

Niya went to Brody and embraced his neck, pressing her rag doll against his chest.

He kissed the top of her head. "Where are the guns?" he asked Rudy while tightening a towel around his leg.

Rudy eyed the door, expecting it to be crashed open at any moment. A quiver rippled inside his stomach. This was his fault. He should've been more careful and aware on their way home. "In the barn."

Brody grimaced. "Shit. Help me up. We need them."

Rudy squared his shoulders. "I'll go. You'll never make it with yer leg like that."

"No," Faye and Brody said at the same time.

It irked him that they didn't believe he could do it.

Brody's face now showed his pain. "No one goes out there. You hear? Think, boy. There must be something in here we can use."

What was needed was out that door, but he'd try it their way first. "I'll check the basement." He picked up the lantern and opened the cellar door. The storm was full upon them, the wind hissing like a monster snake hidden in the dark. With courage he didn't feel, he held up the light and descended.

Chaska followed. "Whoa. Where do we start?"

Pa had a collection of broken things down here, dust-covered and scattered with no order to it. Rudy sneezed, lifted the lamp higher, and scanned the area. He handed Chaska the bottom of a snapped-in-two pitchfork, a rust-laden shovel, and a hay sickle. Propped against a wall was Old Bertha, a Winchester shotgun once owned by his great uncle.

Rudy hefted it and searched for a box of shells. He found a few loose ones and scooped them up. He and Chaska lugged everything of use up the stairs.

Brody squinted at the gun. "That the only one we got?"

Rudy nodded. "Doubt it still shoots."

His friend seemed to be struggling to keep his eyes open. Sweat dripped down Brody's nose and off his chin. The pile of towels next to him was drenched with his blood. Rudy took him the gun and then handed over the shells.

Brody loaded it.

Another round of shots pelted the outer house. Rudy crouched low again, disgusted with their meager weapons. "We're bringing sticks and rocks to a gunfight."

"You use what you got."

Crash. The quiet of the sitting room was shattered as a window broke. Outside, a man appeared, his hair and forehead covered with dirt, a grimy bandana across his nose and mouth.

He stuck the serious end of the gun through, knocking a lit lantern from a small table.

Suddenly, a growling blur of fur jumped on the man and clamped its jaws on his arm. The man screamed as the dog attacked. The barrel disappeared, and a loud boom erupted, followed by the dog's high-pitched whine of pain.

Chaska shouted S'unka's name. The only answer was the howling wind as a whirling mass of dirt blew past the shards of glass left hanging.

Whoosh. A fire leaped to life around the broken window. Flames quickly climbed the curtains, consuming everything in its path. Ghost-like tendrils of white smoke drifted up and coiled along the ceiling.

Rudy ran to the sink and filled a pot with water. Faye and Chaska grabbed a pillow and blanket off a rocking chair and frantically beat at the fires. Orange and yellow tongues of flames licked the wall and caught hold of the furniture.

Rudy tossed the water on the curtains as a bullet zipped by. He retreated to the kitchen, Faye and Chaska close behind. Shame burrowed in. Buffalo Bill never got scared of being shot by a villain.

"Kid," Brody shouted and motioned for Rudy to come to him.

Fighting back the tears, he obeyed.

Brody grabbed his arm with a hard grip. "Wet towels for your faces. Go out the cellar's bulkhead doors. I'll hold them off here."

Rudy shook his head and whimpered. "No. We all go together."

"I'm not going to make it. Will only slow you down."

"If Pa was here, he'd make you."

"He put me in charge."

"But—"

"The fire's spreading! Where we go?" Chaska yelled.

Brody shouted, "Get everyone out."

Rudy's bottom lip quivered. He gathered up the clean towels and then wet them in the sink.

Niya cried, "Mato," and ran up the stairs to save her bear.

"No!" Chaska headed after her. "Git back here."

Faye followed.

Rudy crouched next to Brody and pleaded with him. "Please get up. I can't do this."

"Be strong for them."

Black, ominous smoke expanded inside the sitting room. The fire snapped and popped, fueled by the gusting wind.

"Tell your pa he owes me. He'll know what I'm talking about. Tell him I expect payment in our next life." He hacked a cough and then motioned. "Go."

Sobbing, Rudy grasped Brody tight. He tried to mask the fear of failure that swelled inside. To prove he was brave and no longer a boy.

Brody pushed him away. "Hurry."

Shaking, Rudy ran up the stairs.

The upstairs hallway smelled like a dead cat trapped in a chimney. He held his breath and crawled along the warm floorboards. The above timbers groaned, raining parts of the ceiling on him. He pushed open his bedroom door, then headed into the thick gray wall of smoke.

Heavy smoke filled the upper floor, making it impossible for Faye to see what was right in front of her.

"Chaska?"

The only answer came from something creaking, the crash of falling debris, and the constant hiss and screams of the wind. Then fierce flames forged the outer wall, casting an eerie orange glow in the room. Fear seized her like never before. Sweat ran down her face, stinging her eyes. The taste of bitter ash coated her tongue, and it felt like her lungs were melting, and some invisible force around her throat was trying to choke her. It was growing hotter and hotter by the moment.

Leaving Jake's room, she saw Rudy entering his own.

"Rudy—" she cried out, doubling over with a rack of coughs.

The smoke shifted. She caught a glimpse of Niya and reached for her. The frightened little girl shied away, burying her face into the toy bear.

"N-Niya." She tried to coax her up.

The roar of the fire grew deafening as the flames raged. Heat blistered skin. She couldn't wait for Niya's compliance any longer. Grasping the girl's arm with force, she yanked up. Niya didn't make it easy on her. Struggling at first, then dead weight. Faye stumbled with her into the hallway.

Just as they made it out of the bedroom, the ceiling creaked a death rattle.

A form moved inside the room. Chaska's face appeared, her body following into the hallway. She reached for Niya, coughing uncontrollably.

"Where's Rudy?" Faye asked.

Chaska gazed up with a glazed look.

An inner wall inside the bedroom burst ablaze. The light helped her to spot Rudy, who was curled on his side, not moving.

Faye took a deep breath and rushed in. She gripped his shoulders and dragged him out. He wasn't breathing.

"No, no, no." She rolled him on his side and patted his back. "Come on, kid. Don't give up."

Chaska shook his arm. "Wake up!"

Rudy gasped a breath, then coughed.

Thank you, God. Faye helped him up, squeezed him tight, then shouted, "Go!"

They clambered down the stairs, the air becoming less breathable by the second. Faye barely touched the metal railing and jerked her hand away from the blistering heat. The first floor looked like the bowels of Hell, the fire surging, unable to quench its thirst for dry kindling.

Her blood pulsing as hot as the air she breathed, she trembled as she took in the devastation. Rudy stumbled to the kitchen sink to rewet the towels.

Faye went to Brody.

"Get *out*." He grimaced in pain but balanced the shotgun on his thigh aimed at the door. "What're you waitin' for?"

"You!" She tried to force him up, but he refused to budge.

Black smoke billowed into the room.

Niya cried out and tried to break free of Chaska to go to Brody. Chaska forced her down the stairs.

Tears streamed down Faye's cheeks. She locked eyes with the man.

"Go," he mouthed with a stern expression.

She frantically shook her head. "I can't leave you. Please."

"Rudy," Brody shouted.

A loud creak sounded, the ceiling crashing down in the sitting room. The boy grabbed and pulled at her arm.

A sob scorched her throat, the heat of the room unbearable.

Rudy forced her down the stairs.

She stopped at the bottom and turned. She'd drag Brody out the kitchen door if need be.

Boom. The earsplitting sound of the shotgun halted her steps and tore at her heart. Was that Brody ending his pain or a threat coming after them? She didn't know, but she knew he was gone.

Rudy worked the latch on the cellar's doors. Chaska flung them open.

"Stay together," Rudy shouted and helped them up the slide stairs.

Faye wrapped a towel around her head. The projectile-filled wind felt like it could flay skin. The house creaked and groaned, then gave a giant crash as a large section caved in and threw sparks, carried high by the wind.

Frightened and sobbing, as a group, they battled their way into the storm.

Alone, knocked down by a powerful punch of a grit-pelting gust, Faye curled into a ball and wrapped the encrusted towel around her head. Worry filled her mind, but also hope. She prayed that the kids had found shelter and safety.

The last glimpse of Brody haunted. Guilt gnawed at her stomach. She should have moved on sooner and not put them all in danger.

The screeching winds taunted, punishing and chafing her skin. Her breaths became heavy; her lungs felt lined with clay.

Jake. She pictured his crooked smile and that same smile on her daughter's face—a child who would never be born—her dear Rose Petal. There was so much yet to live for, but her body was losing the fight. Chaska, Rudy, and Niya's faces flashed before her.

I love you all. Please know that.

"I'm so sorry," she mumbled over and over until she could no longer give the words life.

ও

Someone lifted her.

Clutched close to a chest, Faye tried to open her eyes, but they remained crusted shut. She gasped a whistling breath as pain tore through her head and rippled down her chest.

Jake's voice sieved past the clog in her ears. "I...lost you...want... will never..." His words came in choppy bits and sounded somewhere distant rather than so close that his breath tickled her ear.

He carried her a long way, setting her down now and then when she had a coughing fit.

Did the kids make it to safety? Was she now blind? She wanted to ask Jake but couldn't speak. When she tried, it came out as gibberish, all distorted vowels.

After a while, the acrid smell of smoke penetrated her nose.

He set her down and pressed something against her lips. "Drink... make you...er."

She took in the liquid, but the obstruction in her throat swelled. Someone pounded on her back. She heaved up something rank from her stomach. The pounding lessened to a gentle pat. Something wet splashed over her eyes and trickled down her face. A soft cloth gently wiped her eyelids, forehead, and nose and then moved to her lower face.

She slowly managed to open her eyes. A blur of shadowy forms filled her vision, and then Jake's worried facial features cleared. Flanked by him were three sweet, dirt-encrusted faces and a filthy dog.

Faye croaked out a husky sound of relief. They'd survived the night. They'd survived the Mob's gunfire, the smoke and fire, and the suffocating dust storm. She gazed over at the smoldering embers that used to be their home. *Brody.*

Chapter 32

Covered with grime and clinging soot, Faye and the kids helped pack Jake's new automobile. The fire had mercifully missed the barn, sparing their belongings packed for the move and the animals promised to Jake's father-in-law. They would stay at the Hahns' for the night, and Jake and Hahn would move the livestock in the morning.

Faye didn't want to go there. She'd already resolved to convince Jake and the children they'd be better off without her. She needed to run somewhere far, someplace where she wouldn't be the cause of hurt and destruction to those she loved.

Her voice needed to rest the night, though. She struggled to swallow past the thickness in her throat that still stung and punctuated a stab with each hoarse word.

At least Elsa would be there. Faye liked her, but the thought of seeing Sarah again made her stomach tighten.

One night, she resigned. *I can endure one night for the children's sake.*

Jake drove along the drive of the Hahns' vast ranch, slowly making the way through the cluttered maze of debris. The storm had hit here also and uprooted trees and exposed their serpentine bases, battered structures, and tattered and toppled fences.

Faye ran a hand through her dirty hair. This wasn't how she wanted to meet Jake's in-laws. To have Sarah see her in this state. She leaned against the window and twisted the blue string on her finger. It would never become a ring, but she'd cherish it more than any gold circle or topped diamond.

Jake stopped the Ford in front of the house. He pulled her into a hug and stroked her back. "It'll be okay. Back in a jiff."

Niya murmured to her doll in the back seat, and S'unka panted heavily. Benumbed and bewildered, the older kids were also at a loss for words.

Faye eyed Sarah's childhood home and wondered how the woman could want more when she's had so much: a nice place to grow up, a good husband, and a wonderful son.

A heavy weight filled her chest at the thought of leaving them. She pressed her hand over her hollowed heart. At least she was departing for a good reason—because she loved them too much. But would they see it that way? Or, in their eyes, would she be no better than Sarah? She couldn't bear for them to think of her that way.

A few minutes later, Jake emerged with Elsa and a woman who looked like Elsa and Sarah. Mrs. Hahn.

The older woman squinted at the window, past Faye, and on to the back seat. She rushed to open Rudy's door and pulled him into her arms.

Faye caught a glimpse in the rearview mirror of Chaska's reaction—the girl's expression filled with longing at the maternal display. Chaska and Niya had missed out on so much. Faye hoped Jake would fill that void in their lives since she couldn't. Give them security and love.

Rudy let his grandmother fawn over him. S'unka leaped out from the back seat and trotted off to explore.

Elsa waved at Faye.

Cued to get out of the car, Faye opened her door and ushered out the girls. If there was ever a more ragtag group of pitiful waifs, she couldn't imagine. The look on Elsa's face said it all.

"Oh, you poor dears." Elsa didn't seem sure where to put her hands, hovering without touching them. "Let's get you cleaned up and more comfortable."

Faye smiled at her with sincere appreciation.

The storm had coated the outside of the house with muck, but the inside was lovely. More importantly, they had indoor plumbing and *two* bathrooms with large porcelain clawfoot tubs.

Faye was also thankful Sarah wasn't home. With any luck, Jake's ex-wife would stay away the day.

༄

Sarah came home as the grownups were taking their seats for dinner. Having eaten earlier, the children and Rudy's uncle played outside.

Faye steeled herself for unpleasantness.

Sarah's eyes widened on Jake and then narrowed at Faye. "I didn't realize we had company." She scuffed a chair back, smoothed her pink afternoon dress, and shifted the chair forward. "Who invited the gypsy?"

Mrs. Hahn served her a plate. "Don't be uncouth, dear."

Faye took a bite of onion potatoes, finding it best to ignore the jibe. Jake picked up her glass and refilled it with water. She nodded a quick thank you.

Sarah's upper lip twitched. "Your friend wasn't very nice to me at the dance. A real hoity-toity snoot, that one. Not that I cared. I prefer my men more rugged." She glanced Jake's way.

He ignored her and addressed Sarah's mother. "I forgot what a good cook you are, Mother Hahn. This beef cuts like butter." His fork speared a healthy bite of meat, potato, and carrot.

Mrs. Hahn blushed.

"Where have you been all day, Sarah?" Mr. Hahn asked, slicing a piece from a loaf of bread. "Your son needed you."

Sarah elbowed the table and propped her head with a fist. "He seems to have a new mother now."

"Nonsense, dear," Mrs. Hahn censured. "Your son will always need you. Your father meant to say that they had the most terrible scare last night."

"Oh?" Sarah looked down at her plate. "What happened?"

"Their farmhouse burned to the ground. The storm blew a heavy tree branch and broke a window." Mrs. Hahn turned Jake's way. "And overturned a lantern?"

Jake nodded.

Sarah stared at him, then said, "If our son had been here where he belongs, he would have been perfectly safe."

Jake's expression darkened.

Sarah shifted her attention back to Faye. "Word in town says you spoke to a detective and claimed someone tried to kill you.

What made you run yesterday like the devil himself was chasing you?"

Faye tensed. She could sense the Hahns' probing eyes. The detective or the sheriff let the cat out of the bag. Unprofessional to the utmost for their line of work. She would mail complaints about both to higher authorities once situated someplace else.

Sarah leaned back in her chair and smiled as if savoring Faye's discomfort.

Jake intervened. "Not your concern."

"My *son* is," she fired back. "And the people you choose to have around him."

Faye hated to admit it, even to herself, but Sarah was right. She had put Rudy, Chaska, and Niya in danger. And Brody, while trying to save them, had paid the ultimate price.

Jake spoke low and slow to Sarah, emphasizing each word. "You. Walked. Out."

"*She* put our son in danger."

Jake's face hardened.

Sarah responded with a throaty hmm.

Mrs. Hahn's fingers flitted over her throat. "Who's ready for dessert?"

Clearing his throat, Mr. Hahn drew attention. "Is any of that true?"

Jake took a deep breath. "I'm handling it."

Sarah's father frowned. "Son, I'm not wanting to pry my nose into your business, but I'm concerned. What thoughts have you given on where you'll live next? You are more than welcome to build here, and I think it best the boy stays with his mother, but I need to know what's really going on before I invite a stranger into our midst."

Even though he was right, it still hurt to be labeled an outcast aloud. But before Jake said something he might regret, she needed to tell him she was leaving. She tapped his leg. "We need to talk. Take a walk?"

Jake nodded.

Faye offered Sarah's mother gratitude. "Thank you, Missus Hahn. Dinner was wonderful."

The woman smiled. Sarah's brows lowered.

Once outside, Jake wrapped his hand around her own. They strolled casually along the fence line. "Sorry 'bout that."

Faye sighed. "Sarah is the least of my worries."

He sidestepped a broken post. "I don't want you to worry about anything. I'll handle the Hahns. In a few days, we'll leave our problems in the rearview mirror and begin our new life."

She pulled away and placed her hands into her pockets. "I'm not going with you." She didn't mean to blurt it out that way and regretted her choice of words. The hurt expression on his face broke her heart.

She stammered out, "I put you and the children in d-danger. Because of me, Brody's d-dead." Her last word ended with a sob.

Jake's face relaxed. He brought her into a hug. "None of which is your doing. Brody sacrificed himself—"

"If I'd left when I should have, he'd be alive, you'd have your farm, and the kids wouldn't be distressed. Penn was right. I need to go back. Fix this mess my father caused before someone else gets hurt."

"Leave that for the police to solve."

"The detective said they've dropped the case. They don't believe me or even believe my father was murdered. I need to find proof. I need to go home." Her breath hitched. Tears flowed.

He tightened his arms around her. "Okay, but I'm going with you."

"What? No. What about the children?" She shook her head. "It's too dangerous."

"Unlike Sarah, the Hahns are good people. They'll watch them until we know it's safe to return."

"But then you'll be forced to work for Boss Tom."

"Like you, I need to face my demons." He kissed her forehead and wiped a tear from her cheek. "You're right. Running isn't the answer."

She wasn't sure what to say to deter him, but all thought went from her head as he pulled her closer and kissed her, not with passion this time but with promise.

ॐ

Faye readied Niya for sleep in Sarah's bed. Chaska took to the floor.

Elsa rubbed in a face cream as she sat on her bed. "Do you have a nightly beauty ritual, Faye?" The scent of cinnamon wafted from the jar.

"I did until I came here," Faye replied, trying to get one of Jake's undershirts over Niya's head.

The girl was uncooperative and refused to raise her arms to help. She ducked away.

Faye attempted to sound stern. "A proper young lady does not sleep au naturel."

Niya crossed her arms and frowned. Faye couldn't blame the little girl for being upset. They were all taking the loss of Brody hard. Rolling the edges of the shirt up to the collar, she tried again to secure the child's night dress.

"No." Niya threw her bear at Faye. It hit her waist and dropped to the floor.

She sighed and patiently reached down to retrieve the toy. Something sparkly under Sarah's bed caught her eye. She picked it up and studied it. A rose-gold watch with a heart where the three should be. The Valentine's gift from Charles. She frowned, held it up, and asked the children, "Have you been going through my things?"

They shook their heads.

Elsa had moved on to applying a complexion mask. "Sarah was wearing it this morning. Said a suitor gave it to her, that he reminded her of a pirate, with an eyepatch and a scar."

Faye's blood ran cold. The watch had been in her travel bag before the storm. How did it come to be in Sarah's possession? Faye knelt and looked under the bed again. The spine of the book she'd dropped last night, *The Keeper of the Bees*, partially showed underneath a dirty sweater. Faye lifted the garment and breathed in. It reeked of smoke.

Dear God.

Elsa fanned her mask to dry. "Something wrong?"

Faye wasn't going to accuse Sarah without being sure. She held up the sweater. "Does this belong to Sarah?"

"No, that's mine. Sarah is always borrowing my things without asking."

"Where is Sarah sleeping tonight?"

"Mama banished her to a cot in the workers' quarters for being rude to guests." She hopped off the bed, motioned to follow to the window, and pointed at a structure below.

Faye gripped the sweater and marched outside. She found Sarah sitting before a flaring campfire, drinking wine from the bottle.

"Something else of mine you wish to covet?" Sarah glided her hand over her wool wrap. "My only blanket?"

Faye tossed the garment at her. "You were there last night."

"Where?"

"You showed them where the farm was."

Sarah threw the sweater on the ground. "That doesn't even belong to me. Perhaps it is my sister you should be speaking with?"

A sudden coldness hit Faye at her core. She shook not from a chill but with anger. "How could you? Knowing your son was there. How could you put him—put us in such danger?"

"You're insane."

Faye bent, snatched up the sweater, and started to walk away.

"Where are you going?"

"To show what I've found to Jake and your parents. See who they believe."

"Wait."

Faye turned.

"Please don't tell my parents. They'll throw me out, and I have nowhere else to go." Sarah's forehead wrinkled. "I wasn't aware..." She rolled her neck side to side. "I mean, I didn't know they'd attack like that. They told me no one would be hurt. That they just wanted to take you back to Philadelphia."

"And you believed them?"

Quiet for a moment, Sarah ran her hand down her face. "What did you expect me to do? Once it started, I hid in the barn. They had guns. I was scared. Then when the house caught fire…" She stopped talking and stared at the fire pit.

Faye collapsed in the chair next to Sarah. "Why did you want them to take me?"

"Because I thought if you were gone, I might have a chance at coming back. Fixing what I did wrong." She looked off somewhere distant. "I'd known Brody most my life."

Faye released a deep breath. She hadn't imagined having anything in common with this woman, let alone grief for a brave man gone too soon. She studied Sarah's tear-stained face for sincerity. "Are you still in love with Jake?"

Sarah nodded.

So, they also had that in common. "I'm leaving. You probably will never see me again, but I need your word that you'll treat Rudy and the girls well while they are here. As compensation, I'll keep your secret about last night."

Sarah's level gaze served as a handshake.

Rudy pulled away from his dad's hug. Left behind again, and this time with *her*. He ran down the dusty path, slowed once out of the women folk's sight, and rubbed the tears from his face. Big boys don't cry like babies.

The sun beat down on his back, comforting and soothing. Giving him more warmth than his mother ever had. How long would she stick around this time? Not that he cared. He'd done this long without her and could do so again. But Pa?

He leaned on a pole of the fence and watched the cattle graze. His grandfather had lost half the herd in the storm. The stench still clung to Rudy's clothes from helping dig the holes and piling dirt on top of cow after cow. Burying money, Grandpa had said, fretting about paying bills to come, about being saddled with more mouths to feed.

Too dangerous, Pa had claimed as the reason he couldn't go. *Won't be gone long*, he'd promised. *Get to spend time with your mother.*

Rudy picked up a stick and flung it toward the cattle. Even they paid him no mind. "Stupid walkin' meat."

Footsteps sounded on the ground behind him.

"Move over," Ma said with a smile and propped her boot on the lowest string of barbed wire. She put her arm over his shoulder. "Taking your anger out on the cows?"

Rudy shrugged.

"We don't need your dad to have fun." She hopped over the fence, carefully stepped around the cow patties, and petted Daisy. "Ever ride one?"

Rudy nodded. "When I was little." But she knew that. Was the one who had held on to him as it had moved beneath.

"Remember that do you?" She climbed atop the red and white Hereford and straddled over it. She looked ridiculous sitting on top in her long skirt, lace blouse, and cowgirl boots. "Come on." She urged it to move. The cow began an easy gait.

He was too old for this. Just wanted to be left alone. What was the sudden interest in him now when she couldn't give two licks about him for months? Except for giving him those whatchamacallits—soupenears? A stupid, decorated cup and spoon, and a plastic toy alligator from New Orleans.

Still, he found himself leaping the fence, pulling himself up the friendliest-looking milker, and following behind the woman who was sure to break his heart again.

That night, Grandma Hahn tucked him in. She'd made sure Chaska, Niya, and he got their baths, brushed their teeth, and combed their hair. Chaska made a bed on the floor. After Grandma tucked Niya in, the girl slid out of bed and latched onto Grandma's arm.

"Oh, baby girl. What's wrong?" Grandma bent down and hugged her.

Niya whimpered.

"She wants to sleep in your bed," Chaska explained from the floor. "Faye spoiled her."

Grandma said goodnight and murmured gentle words as she guided Niya toward her room. Rudy wondered what Grandpa Hahn would say about their visitor, but he had no doubt Grandma would win her way.

"She's nice," Chaska said. "Are all grandmothers that way?"

"I think she's special." Rudy turned on his side and hugged his pillow. "She can silk corn and snap green beans faster than anyone I know, and her pies are the best in the county—ask anyone. And she can be funny. Sometimes she has me rolling on the floor with laughter."

Chaska sighed. "Yeah. She's got a way of makin' you feel important. Praises everythin' you do. Would miss you and be sad if you weren't 'round."

"Yep. When she loves somebody, it's with her whole heart."

Chaska was quiet for a moment and then said softly, "I wish I had a Grandma Hahn."

Rudy knew how lucky he was, but his grandmother had lots of love to give. "You do," he promised Chaska.

Chapter 33

Boss Tom's company provided a small yet quaint apartment on the south side of downtown Philadelphia. It had all the necessities: furniture, kitchenware, linens, and towels, and it was close to Jake's work and had a bus stop right out front.

After hours of tossing and turning the first night, Faye got out of bed and padded to the kitchen. Quiet as could be, she put the kettle on for a cup of chamomile tea. Though not thrilled to be indebted to Boss Tom, having a free place to stay was too good to pass up. Tomorrow she'd begin her search into the seedy underworld of organized crime. She didn't tell Jake about her deal with Boss Tom, how she'd promised to work undercover at his competitor's dance club to free Jake from his obligation to the company. He would try to talk her out of it, perhaps forbid her outright. She was through with people telling her what to do, even if their hearts were in the right place.

The kettle whistled. She reached to remove it from the flame.

Rubbing his eyes, Jake entered the kitchen wearing blue boxers. "First night in a strange place. Can't sleep?"

Distracted by his bare chest, she grasped the metal part of the kettle's handle, jerked her fingers away, and cradled her hand. "Shoot, shoot, shoot." The circle dance performed did little to ease the sting.

Jake turned off the burner. "Here. Let me see." He ran cold water from the faucet over the burn, then blew on it.

The pain pulsing in her hand didn't overshadow the warmth from his touch. He gently wrapped over the burn with a wet dishtowel.

"Better?"

She nodded.

"Must feel strange to be back home," he said.

"In some ways. It doesn't quite feel like home anymore. Does that make sense?"

He poured the hot water into a teapot and steeped the floral leaves. "I felt the same way in Kansas City. What do they say? You can't go home again?"

"Perhaps. Maybe Haverford will bring it back." She adjusted her robe, pulling it in tighter. "Seeing my old friends."

He almost dropped one of the teacups. Grumbling under his breath, he balanced them and the teapot. "I think you should be careful who you let know you're back. The Mob has a long reach."

She added honey to her tea and took a cautious sip. "Are you nervous about your first day tomorrow?"

"Doesn't sound like much to it. Supervising concrete pouring over a parking lot. Unless there's a body buried underneath."

Surely a joke, but yet, she flinched.

"You trust me to keep you safe here, don't you?"

"I do."

"You seem different since Kansas City."

"I think it's best not to overcomplicate matters."

Jake shifted in his chair and drew a deep breath. "I know what's been bothering you. I'm ready to tell you if you want to hear it."

Faye nodded. He wouldn't meet her eyes, so she stayed silent, giving him time to get his thoughts together.

"I wasn't candid about why I moved in with my uncle. After the attack and Two Cents was killed, Boss Tom's men were out for blood. They took out some members of a local street gang they were sure was responsible." Jake cleared his throat, his knuckles white as he gripped his cup. "Gus was sent to get Rory, Boss Tom's youngest brother, who'd gotten into a fight with another card player at the Trap Room. Rory was three sheets to the wind, and it was turning dark outside, but he recognized a DeSoto going the opposite way."

His gaze grew distant as he told her the story. At times, he seemed to will her to understand. Faye couldn't hide her reactions or anger at those who put a fourteen-year-old boy in that situation. Her opinion of his father plummeted.

"Ellis grabbed Susie and pushed her into the DeSoto. Dirt sprayed as he gunned the gas. When the car ran over Rory, Gus and me jumped out of the way." Jake studied his hands. "We buried Rory there. He was never found, but Boss Tom never stopped searching for his brother." He grimaced. "I don't know if me shooting him was justified, but it happened. Right or wrong, I've had to live with that bruise on my soul."

It hurt to see the pain in his expression. "You had no choice." She reached across the table and clasped his hand.

"I guess that's why I took to farming. Bringing things to life."

She'd had no right to judge him before learning the whole story, but the more she knew, the scarier their world was becoming.

The following morning, Faye examined the newfangled toaster and pried it open. After placing a piece of bread, she closed one side of it and turned the knob on the side to the right. While setting the table, she hummed softly until a thin stream of smoke caught her attention as it wafted across the room.

"Shoot." She hurried to the toaster, fiddled with the latch, jerking her fingers away. "Ouch!"

Jake came into the kitchen. He sprung the side open on the toaster and juggled the half-black toast to the trash. He turned her hand and checked the burn. "Keep this up and you won't have any fingertips left."

Faye winced more from the rebuke than the pain.

He caressed the back of her hand. "Sorry, bad joke. You'll figure it out eventually." He downed his juice. "But maybe we should eat out tonight." He kissed her on the cheek and left for his first day at Boss Tom's concrete company.

Faye washed the dishes, tidied up the kitchen, then entered the bedroom. The domestic chores of making their beds, unpacking their clothes, and organizing everything in their new temporary home brought her a sense of peace. She checked her case one last time for anything she may have missed when the glint of metal showed from a gap in the lining. She made the hole bigger with her finger and worked it out, turning the key in the light. Engraved on the flat part was etched A N BANK with 227 beneath. American National. Her father's competitor.

She could finally see what this key unlocked. She recalled Penn asking, *'Did he, by chance, ever mention anything to you about moving money? Or did you find any keys that did not match a lock?'*

The A N Bank would close before Jake got off work. She didn't want to go alone, so she picked up the handset and dialed Penn.

The American National Bank manager led Faye and Penn to where the lockboxes were stored.

"Insert your key and turn it to the right," the manager instructed. He stayed in the hallway.

Faye searched for the box number. Penn started on the opposite side. They met in the middle.

"Here," Penn said, the eagerness in his voice thinly veiled.

Faye couldn't hide her excitement either. Her pulse quickened as she turned the key and withdrew the metal box. With fumbling hands, she opened it. They both stared down.

"What the hell?" Penn said.

Faye recognized the handmade gifts she'd given her parents. They were worthless things, but her father thought them special enough to keep them safe. A few prized pieces of her mother's jewelry lay scattered at the bottom. She picked up an elementary math test with a circled red A grade and a smiley face. Her father had helped her learn to write numbers. His handwriting reminded her of his words, but the ink was new compared to the faded writing long ago. Puzzling.

His face flushed, Penn pounded the table. "What kind of game is he playing?"

Even though her friend was upset, Faye's heart warmed. She cradled the jewelry pieces in her hand, images of her mother wearing them flooding her mind.

"This was a complete waste of time," Penn said, turning to go.

Faye studied one of her mother's necklaces closer. Something was different. "Wait." She unhooked a key looped on the gold strand and held it to the light. "There's another key. A larger one."

Penn came over to look. "A vault key." A smile broadened on his face. "A vault key! You clever bastard, Marshall." He called out for the bank manager.

Faye emptied the contents from the lockbox into her purse. When she found Penn and the manager, they stood before an enclosed strongroom.

Penn hit the wall with the side of his fist. "It takes a combination."

The bank manager turned to Faye and said, "Every vault has a six-numbered sequence specifically chosen by the depositor."

"But he's dead," Penn yelled. "I keep telling you this. So your bank is obligated to open it for the beneficiary."

The manager narrowed his eyes. "Only if the name is listed. Which hers is not."

Penn's face reddened, and the veins in his neck strained against his skin.

A bank employee called the manager away on urgent business.

"If you'll excuse me," he said to Faye.

Penn turned the dial on the vault clockwise and counterclockwise, trying different combinations on the lock. After a while, he sunk to the floor, his expression crestfallen.

Faye slid down next to him. "Don't despair. What have you tried so far?"

"The bank's opening date, your parent's anniversary, his birthday—"

She stood and turned the big black dial with bold white numbers. "My mother's birthday?"

"Don't you think I tried that?"

Her curiosity was killing her. She rotated the dial to the numbers of her birthdate. Nothing happened.

Penn cradled his head in his hands.

Six numbers. Not a date. When she was little, the silly rhyming chant her father used to teach her how to draw numbers came to mind. She dug into her handbag for the old math test, the oddest thing saved in the lockbox. Six words were written in her father's hand.

The first was Heaven. Faye could hear her father's singsong voice, *Across the sky and down from heaven.* Seven. The next word tree. *Around a tree, around a tree* makes three. Stick—*a straight line really quick*—the number one. Loopyline—nine. Railroad. *Around and back on a railroad track—*the number two. Li'l Ducks. Five. Her hand shook, but she forced herself to go slower and lined each number with the center spot. Something clicked, and the door popped open a crack. She pulled it wider. The interior glistened. Faye sucked in a deep breath.

Penn stumbled up from the floor. His expression filled with awe as he gazed into the room.

Gold bullion bars and coins gleamed inside the vault. Jewelry, family heirlooms, and paintings stacked the shelves.

"You did it!" Penn pulled her into his embrace. His heartbeat thumped with excitement, matching her racing pulse.

She bent down and opened boxes filled with stacks of cash. Another box held her father's personal, business, and bank papers. On top, an enclosed envelope with Mr. Simmons' name and a word in big letters—URGENT. She slipped it into her handbag.

Penn tugged her sleeve. "We need to go. If anyone else sees this—you are in so much trouble."

"Whatever for?"

Penn shook his head. "Are there no radios in Kansas? Owning more than five gold ounces is now illegal, punishable by ten years in prison and thousands in fines. There is enough here to put you away for life."

"I didn't know about that"—she waved her hand—"or anything about this."

"You're his daughter. They will never believe you. Whether intentional or not, he made it look like he stole from our bank to provide for you, then took his life because of guilt."

"But the people need their money returned..."

Penn nodded. "And we will. I just need time to keep us from being implicated in your father's scheme." He pushed the safe door shut, reset it, and handed her the key. He gripped her upper arms. "Promise me. Don't say a word until I figure this out, not to your lawyer or your"—he made a face—"boyfriend."

She agreed though she didn't like keeping more secrets from Jake.

The bank manager cut them off from the front entrance. "Did you retrieve everything you need?"

Faye tried to keep her voice light. "Yes. Thank you for your assistance."

"My pleasure." He opened the door for her.

She attempted a carefree walk and held her breath until she was out of the manager's sight. It was now undeniable. Her father was a thief. And she was the daughter of a mobster.

Chapter 34

Faye boarded a train to Haverford, anticipating seeing Abigail and her other friends who had worked at her father's house. She was looking forward to catching up but also wanted their insight. Household employees usually knew more about the family they worked for than the family themselves.

When she gazed at the new Willow Wood, she was taken aback by the massive change. The château's facade had an art nouveau design. The front outer stone third level had a red mural center stage, and trim around the windows and doors painted an ostentatious gold. Trees that had once stood tall and proud were now gone, their roots hidden underneath weeds and other ground covers. Etched flower and vine motifs at the entrance took the place of the actual rose gardens, now buried under decorative white rocks and tacky yard ornaments. A stone boy urinated into a cement fountain, and a red-coated lawn jockey held a lantern in greeting to the veranda.

A plaque reading THE KINGDOM was affixed above the stairs. Good heavens. They even changed the name.

"Oh, Willow," Faye whispered, "What have they done to you?"

Fearing what she might say to the new owners, she went to the back of the house instead of knocking on the front door. When no one answered at the delivery entrance, she let herself in. Abigail bustled about the kitchen in a black and white uniform that looked two sizes too small.

"Abby?" Faye said softly.

Abigail's expression shifted from gloomy to elated. "Pip!" She rushed forward and enveloped her in a big hug. "Me heart's own."

"I missed you so." Faye came up for air and laughed. "How have you been?"

"Hanging in by the tippy tips of me fingers. I'm the only one left. The new mistress dismissed all the old staff. She'd do away with me too if she could, but the master loves me cooking." Abigail motioned to the table. "Sit, please. I just popped on the kettle and'll slice us a bit o' apple cake."

Faye's mouth instantly watered. She so missed Abigail's desserts. "You relax and I'll serve." She reached a shelf for the plates.

Abigail smiled. "Are you enjoying your auntie's place? Have you met someone nice?"

Faye stopped in mid-motion, confused. "Didn't you receive my letter?"

"The missus inspects the post first. I fear she most likely threw it away."

The new lady of the house sounded like a real tyrant. "Abby, that's horrible. Why don't you find better employment? Someone who appreciates how wonderful you are."

"Me sister's ill. I can't risk being without pay but can tough it out a wee bit longer."

As they ate and drank, Faye summarized what had happened to her in the last few months, both good and bad, and her friend responded appropriately throughout the story.

"*Sweet* baby Jesus," Abigail exclaimed when Faye finished. "You've been put through the wringer."

"Do you know anything about Daddy's last days? What he was up to?"

Abigail frowned. "I think it best you let it be and move on with your life. Go somewhere where you'll be happy. Things have changed here, and not for the better."

"I can't do that until I know why he did what he did and return the people's money." Faye reached into her handbag, tore off a scrap piece of paper, and asked for a pencil. "This is the telephone number where I'm staying. I'd love for Jake to meet you next time you're in the city."

A service bell chimed. Abigail's eyebrows lowered. "They were supposed to be out for the day." She seemed agitated. "I'm sorry, but I need to get back to work. You'll let yourself out?"

Faye stood and hugged her.

Her friend kissed her cheek and then scrambled away to answer the bidding. Puzzled by Abigail's behavior, she gathered her things.

She needed to use the facilities before the long train ride back to the city. A gasp escaped her throat when she entered the foyer. Modernized, and not in a good way, it was a chaotic mix of bold colors, brass objects, and odd decor that was so overdone she grew slightly disoriented.

Out of curiosity, she peered into the parlor. It, too, was a hodgepodge of Moroccan patterns, Asian ceramics, and decoupage-decorated furniture. A large painting over the hearth featured the subjects responsible for the vulgar makeover. The man appeared stern with an impressive, overgrown handlebar mustache.

She knew the woman. Had sat across from that smug face at many functions. Helen Garvey. Her father's last girlfriend.

"Oh, Daddy," she whispered under her breath. Mulling over this new revelation, Faye headed toward the powder room. A woman rounded the corner. Her pinched expression was as tight as her ringlets of curls. The same face on the painting in the parlor. *Helen.*

"Pip Harmon? Who let you into my home?" Helen asked, her tone like ice.

Faye didn't want to get anyone in trouble or to lose their job, especially Abigail, though she wondered why her friend hadn't warned her about Helen.

She was about to offer a reasonable excuse when Helen yelled, "Maid! Cook!"

Great Scott. The woman still didn't even know their names. Poor Abigail.

Her friend entered the hallway alongside a frazzled-looking maid. Faye gave a slight shake of her head to convey to Abigail to keep quiet.

"I let myself in," Faye admitted. She decided to fall further on the sword. "I accidentally left something of my mother's behind. It's not worth much to anyone else but means a lot to me."

"A thief, just like your father," Helen snarled. "Call the police!" she commanded the maid.

Brows furrowed, Abby stepped forward, hands on her hips. "Ma'am, I can attest for—"

Faye shook her head. "Do you smell something burning?"

Helen dismissed Abigail.

➶

Two police cars roared up the driveway. Edgar Elmsworth emerged from one of them.

Why would they send a detective for a petty crime? Maybe he volunteered to make good on his promise in Union to lock her up if she caused any more trouble.

"Detective," Faye mumbled in greeting.

He barely glanced her way, ascended the stairs, and kissed Helen's hand. "I'm sorry this miscreant gave you a fright. She'll not trouble you anymore."

"Thank you, Elmsworth," Helen said.

It figured they knew each other, but the overfamiliarity they bestowed was concerning.

She said to Helen, "I'll not bother you again, Missus Parvenu." She couldn't resist the barb.

Helen glared. "Why you, you, guttersnipe. Better to be new rich than old money poor in prison. Which is where you're heading."

"Being poor is not a crime; being a garish decorator should be."

Helen shouted words that should not cross a lady's lips. Elmsworth held her back and signaled at his men. They grabbed Faye's arms and ushered her to a car.

She worried her hands. Should she first call Jake or her lawyer, Mr. Simmons? This was bound to be costly either way. Jake was right. Now, others would know she'd returned—possibly even her father's killers.

➶

Faye spent the night in the county jail, along with fellow inmates Vera and Hazel, in for prostitution. The women argued with each other constantly.

The cell was fitted with two barely padded bunk beds and one toilet out in the open, offering no privacy. How long would her bladder hold out? She wasn't using that thing.

A female guard brought their breakfast, lumpy oatmeal with rusty spoons and a tin cup of curdled milk.

Faye grasped the bars as the guard turned to leave. "Excuse me. Might I have a word with Detective Elmsworth?"

"He's not in yet."

"Use of a phone then? To call my lawyer?"

The guard made a face. "Who I look like? Ma Bell? Eat your slop."

"A piece of paper and something to write with?"

"Better not be giving me a hard time if you know what's good for you," the guard warned and then exited.

She plopped back onto the cot, dejected.

Vera said, "I have mail you can reuse. You gonna eat that?"

Faye looked down at her tray of food on the ground. A roach scurried across the spoon. "Be my guest."

Vera snatched it up.

"He's a hard-boiled one, that Elmsworth," Hazel said. "A real wrong number. Put the screws on me and Vera good. Ya follow?"

Faye shook her head.

"He gets tough with women. Enjoys it. Makes him feel like a big man."

She knew the detective was chauvinistic but didn't realize he was dangerous. She needed to get out of here—and quick. Penn contributed to the police fund and schmoozed with the top dogs at the department. If she could get a letter to the chief, that might be her ticket out.

Faye used the remaining oatmeal to reseal the envelope and slid it between the bars. When the guard came back, Vera brought it to her attention. The woman studied the name, then slid it into her pocket.

"Hands to the air, ladies," the guard said as she keyed the lock.

Confused, Faye mimicked her cellmates and raised her arms. It was ridiculous to be treated like a hardened criminal. She'd write another letter to the chief once free from here.

The guard reached and placed Faye's hands behind her back and handcuffed them.

"Where are you taking me?"

"Elmsworth requested your company."

Faye glanced at the envelope tip in the guard's pocket. Her only hope.

Just as she feared, the woman took her to a private room and turned to go.

"Wait, shouldn't you be here when a man questions a female prisoner?" Faye asked.

"I have better things to do than babysit your sorry self. Take a seat." The door locked behind her.

The small windowless room closed in. No sound but the large wall clock ticking away the minutes. She envisioned Jake again. How worried he must be when she hadn't returned last night. Was he searching for her?

The door made a click, and Elmsworth entered the room. He didn't look angry but pompous and self-righteous. "You've found yourself in a pretty pinch, Missy."

"I didn't do anything. Who did I wrong?"

"The nice people who purchased the place you lost due to your father's greed. What made you return?"

"I just wanted to see my old friends."

"Yeah, right. You traveled all the way from Kansas to visit a bunch of servants. That the story you really want to go with?"

"It's the truth," her voice raised. She calmed herself. Best not to provoke him.

"Lady, I don't like having my time wasted. I know you know where your father hid the loot, and I know it is somewhere in that castle or buried on the grounds. If you tell me where it is, the owners promise to drop all charges against you."

So that was it. They'd purchased and torn up the estate, searching for what was in the bank vault. And Elmsworth was now an accomplice. *Think, dammit, think.*

Before she could speak, the detective grabbed her shoulders and lifted her to her feet. Sharp pains traveled down her arms. She gasped as he pushed her up against a wall.

"Where is it?" he shouted.

Tears ran down her face. "I don't know."

He pulled her toward him and then shoved her harder into the wall. Faye clenched her teeth, the back of her head throbbing a dull ache.

"Tell me!" His coffee breath penetrated her nostrils, his fingers digging further into her flesh.

"I don't..." she sobbed. "Please, you're hurting me."

The door to the room flew open. A distinguished man in uniform stood next to Jake.

Relief flooded throughout. She sagged against the wall after the brute released her.

The man barked out Elmsworth's name while Jake barreled forward. He yanked Elmsworth away, twisted him around, and plowed his fist into the detective's face.

Jake drove them back to the apartment in tense silence. He hadn't said a word about how he'd found her nor talked about how close he'd come to being locked away for assaulting an officer of the law. He turned into a parking lot, shut off the car, and flexed his hand, his knuckles still stained with blood. More silence ensued.

The quiet was deafening until he reached out and drew her in. Jake kissed her like he was starving, her lips a gourmet feast. She moved closer, seeking solace.

After a time, his face contorted, pain visible in his eyes. "I thought you were dead," his voice graveled. "That you were at the bottom of a lake somewhere."

"I'm sorry. I should have told you where I was going."

Jake shuddered. "I can't let myself think what he might've done to you if your friend hadn't told me where they took you."

Faye also didn't want to consider the possibilities either. She thanked Heaven and the stars for Abigail.

"I'd have taken you to visit your friends if you'd asked," Jake said.

"I know, but I figured with you starting your new job and all—"

"We're not here for me to line Boss Tom's pockets. I don't want you sleuthing around when we're not sure who we're dealing with."

"I'll stay in the city from now on and blend right in."

"Boss Tom is arriving in town. I'll be working late tomorrow night." His voice quieted. "Please. I won't be able to function if I'm worried about what you are up to."

He wouldn't let it go. But what was the harm of a little Mata Hari spy work in the shadows? "I'll call Jane and spend the weekend at her house. Her family has always been good to me."

Jake nodded his relief and started the automobile again.

When they entered the apartment, he removed his shirt, scooped her up in one swift movement, and carried her to the other room. The material brushed her skin as he slid her dress off and deposited her onto the bed. After removing the rest of his clothes, he crawled beside and kissed her. She moved her palms over his chest, pausing on his toned stomach, tracing the line of hairs down to his navel.

"You make my heart hurt." He braced himself on trembling arms and attended to her breast and then the other with equal fervor. Skimming lower over the sensitive skin beneath her navel, the stubble of a day's chin growth scraped. He pulled down her laced satin bloomers and explored the tender folds between her legs.

Ohh. She arched her back and mewed—the sound so small for the passion screaming inside. Blood sizzled through her veins and liquid lava moved, melting bone. Beyond wanton, her body rippled with desire. She clutched the pillow and clenched her stomach as wave after pleasurable wave danced over. *More.* She needed something more.

She reached under and touched him. His breath hitched.

"*Great Scott,*" he cried out.

Staring into her eyes, he entered her, moving slowly at first, his face a myriad between pleasure and pain.

She adjusted her hips to fit him, wrapping her legs around his waist. He shifted slightly and barely moved as if she were something fragile that might break.

She didn't want to be treated like a porcelain doll. "I'm okay."

His kiss deep and possessive, he touched her body with an urgency that quickly kindled passion. Heat built from the friction, the core of her pulsating with every stroke. Her pulse raced. Quivering, she clenched his arms.

His face glistened, his expressions verbalizing thoughts and feelings without words. A bead of sweat dripped from his forehead and traveled down her breast.

The fire stoked inside as his rhythm quickened. Her whole being seemed to hum as the sensation intensified. She feared her heart would burst from her chest.

His breath quickened as he forged in, his muscles strained, zinging a bolt of heat up her spine. She let out an uncontrollable cry as a volt spread throughout her core.

Jake's body tremored.

Light as a feather, her soul wisped back down to the bed. She dropped her legs, sweet spasms twitching the inside of her thighs.

So that was what the big whoopee do was about.

Content as a housecat curled on a sun-puddled cushion, Faye pulled her knees to her chest. She pictured images of their life together: the wedding kiss, celebrating holidays, sharing a bed with him every night, and growing old together.

I love you. She wasn't sure if she'd thought it or said it aloud.

Jake collapsed on the bed beside her and covered his face with his forearm. And then, once again, there was silence.

Her body still in control, the last impulses triggered throughout.

"You okay?" he asked.

She didn't know how to respond. "Mhm."

He tucked her against him. She melted into his arms.

Chapter 35

Before he'd gone off to work, Jake had cautioned her not to do anything 'harebrained.'

Jane now agreed with him. "This is bat crazy."

"You didn't have to come," Faye answered.

"And let you have all the fun? No way, Pipperoo. So, what's the plan again?"

"I need to find King's office and steal his ledger for Boss Tom. Then, in exchange, Jake will be free, and I'll be told who ordered my father to be killed and why."

"All the while dancing the foxtrot with creepy old men." Jane chuckled. "Of all your ridiculous schemes, this one is the most outlandish to date."

Faye adjusted the tight beaded party dress Jane had lent her. "I shouldn't have let you talk me into this getup."

"You are wearing enough makeup for three women and have more curls than Shirley Temple. An understated dress didn't match," Jane defended her choices.

"I look like a bimbo."

"In less than twenty-four hours, you've trespassed, were accused of pilfering something that doesn't exist, got arrested, and turned me into a taxi dancer. Don't go all righteous on me. This time, you're the bad influence." Jane smirked.

"Hardy-har-har. I guess that makes me Laurel."

"I see myself more like Buster Keaton." Jane smoothed her pink and silver satin gown and offered Faye her arm. "Shall we?"

They entered through the dance club's employee entrance from a back alley.

Down the hallway, an open room on the left contained chairs and a large lighted mirror where a woman sat fixing her lipstick. She wore a subtle gown with a high lace collar, no more provocative than a schoolmarm. Faye grimaced. Jane had been adamant that she knew how dime dancers dressed.

The woman stared at them through the mirror. "I thought there was only one new girl starting tonight."

Faye explained, "I brought my friend. She—"

"Loves to dance," Jane interrupted. "I'll be a great nickel hopper."

The woman frowned. "We don't call ourselves that. We are dance hostesses." Her critical gaze traveled down, then up. She seemed to find them wanting. "Our customers are called patrons. Most are older and widowed. Some are married, footloose globetrotters in town just for the night. Occasionally, we get slummers, wealthy men who are curious and seeking amusement from the low side. But don't you be fooled." She shook her finger. "Don't think for a moment you'll meet your knight in shining armor here."

"Certainly not," Faye said.

The woman's tone went up an octave. "Receiving gifts isn't allowed. No dinners out, drinks, or long drives out to the country. Our matron in charge watches us like a hawk and hears everything, knows everything." She crossed her arms. "In other words—no charity girl work—no offering favors on the side." She motioned to follow her.

Charity girls?

The orchestra's music grew almost deafening. Stairs led down to a large dance hall, sparsely decorated and dimly lit. Faye cast Jane a dirty look. None of the other women were dressed like them. Jane shrugged.

The woman gestured to where other women were standing in line behind a rope. A man strolled by and inspected them as if he were a butcher searching for a cut of prime beef.

"You get in line, and the patrons choose. Mind you, dance the whole song," the woman shouted over the blaring music, "and be sure to get the ticket ahead of time. They are worth a dime each, and we trade them in for cash at the office at the end of the night. Also, any tips you get must be handed in as well. Mister King decides what we get paid."

Faye perked at the mention of King and the office. "Where do we do this?"

"Down in the joint." The woman chinned at the door guarded by a large man in a suit. "He's our barker. If someone gets fresh or rough, you tell him."

Maybe this wasn't the most fantastic idea.

Before they made it to the line, three men hurriedly approached. Jane's hand was yanked away from her grip.

Twirling back, Jane yelled, "Go. I'll find you." She disappeared into the throng.

Faye gasped as a man grabbed her and tunneled onto the dance floor. He shoved a ticket into her hand and jerked her arms, manipulating her movements like a marionette.

"Name's Richard. I own a life insurance business. You're never too young to start preparing for those you love..."

Faye struggled to keep her composure as he rambled on about his career. Bounced off other couples, she finally escaped him into a turn. The band started playing the tune 'I Found a Million Dollar Baby' without, of course, the Boswell Sisters' accompanying vocals. Just as she thought she had found a moment's respite, another ticket made its way into her hand. Her new partner was even worse than the last one, stomping over her toes as he tried to impress her by speaking French. He completely mangled most of the words.

She couldn't take it anymore. "As someone who adores the French and the beauty of the language, on their behalf, I beg you to pick a different geographical region's dialect to slaughter. And while you're at it—this self-improvement for humanity's sake—please purchase a few private dance lessons. I imagine a Quebecer beaver trapper moves with more grace. *Au revoir*, farewell, goodbye."

His mouth hung open. Faye spotted Jane and cut in on her dance partner. The man seemed shocked but complied.

"I'm leading," Jane said, readjusted their hands, and placed her arm around Faye's waist. "Thanks. That last one gave me the itch. His hands were so sweaty I got seasick."

"Mine were no picnic either."

A man reached for Jane. She spun away from him. "And they're so handsy. I don't know how these women stand this night after night. Next man who pinches my backside is getting my right hook."

An idea blossomed. "See the man guarding the door to downstairs?"

Jane nodded.

"I need a distraction so I can get by him."

"I'm always up for a good fracas." Jane grinned. "Be ready." She disappeared into the crowd.

Uh-oh.

Faye worked past dancers to get closer to the door, then made a beeline for an empty chair beside a woman rubbing her foot.

"Mind if I sit?" she asked.

The woman glanced up. "Nope. Free country."

She sat and slipped off her shoe to deter a man looking her way. She mimicked the woman and rubbed her own foot.

The woman gave her dress an odd look. "You don't need to try this hard. You'll attract the wrong kind of man dressed like that."

"Erm—noted. Thanks for the tip."

"I'm Grace."

"Fa—nny. Nice to meet you. You worked here long?"

Grace switched to rubbing her ankle. "Long enough to spot a rookie such as yourself. Why are you here? A young woman like you should have plenty of opportunities. Instead of this night after night, brain in your feet, stockings full of holes, and trumpets tearing at your eardrums."

"I know the owner." She remembered what the card Boss Tom had given her had read. "He said it was easy money. And more fun than work."

Grace shook her head. "Look, kid, do yourself a favor. Get yourself a job as a nice shopgirl. Or a waitress. Better yet, a stenographer with a rich, available boss. You'll be the 'it' girl here for a time, but sooner or later, they'll use you up and throw you out because they found someone younger and prettier to take your spot."

"I'll keep that in mind. Is he here tonight? Mister King?"

Grace chinned toward the door with the large man standing next to it. "He might be downstairs in the joint. Where the real money flows, gambling and liquor, but only the best girls get chosen to work down there—and only if they are in good standing with Deloris."

"Who's Deloris?"

Grace pointed at a blonde bombshell in blue. "She's our matron."

Deloris was talking to someone. As the woman slowly turned, Faye sucked in a hard breath. *Helen.*

What was Helen doing here? "That woman speaking with Deloris looks familiar. What's her name?"

"You mean Helen?"

"How long has she been here?"

"Since the dawn of time. She's married to King."

Stunned, Faye was momentarily speechless. She watched as Deloris and Helen parted ways. The matron entered through the door that led down to the joint. The large man in the suit was still there, standing guard.

Faye was wrapping her mind around this new revelation when a loud commotion broke through her thoughts. Jane slapped her dance partner and then proceeded to scream at him. The barker guarding the entrance to the joint rushed over. This was it. Now or never. She thanked Grace for the advice and made her way to the door. Jane glanced her way, smiled, and then continued her caterwauling.

Entering the smoke-filled basement, Faye stayed near the wall, away from the gambling. Men played at numerous card tables with scantily clad women behind them, cheering them on or serving drinks. A roulette wheel spun, surrounded by eager faces as it plunked a slot, then cheers rose from the lucky winners. Faye made her way to a wooden bar and sat on a stool.

Serious men walked the floor while watching the gamblers. One roughly grabbed a man at a table. "I've warned you about switching the dice," he shouted, dragging the gambler up the stairs.

"What'll you have?"

Faye looked up at the bartender as he cleaned a drinking glass with a bar towel. "A gin and tonic?"

"The safari's drug of choice. Did you know Churchill said that the gin and tonic saved more English soldiers in India than all the doctors in the empire combined?" He flipped the glass in his hand and scooped ice into it.

Good. A chatty bartender was just what she needed. She watched him pour a healthy shot.

"It's the quinine in the tonic water," he said. "Found to be a potent deterrent to malaria-carrying mosquitoes." He held up the bottle so she could read the label. "And this, Sister, ain't no bathtub gin. Comes from London like Churchill himself." He set the drink in front of her. "I haven't seen you around. You one of Deloris's girls?"

"I'm with that man over there." She nodded toward a heavy-set man winning big. "Put this on his bill." Sipping her drink, she noticed a woman's reflection in the mirror. Deloris leaned in.

"Five shots of whiskey, Billy. The good stuff."

Deloris's high-pitched voice was the same as the woman who had broken into Willow Wood. Faye looked down at the woman's shoes. They were the same blue peep-toe heels she'd seen that night.

"Billy taking good care of yuh?" Deloris asked, loading the drinks on a tray.

Faye nodded and managed a weak smile.

"I love your dress. Classy." Deloris balanced the tray on her hand. "You come see me if you ever wanna a job here. I hire mosta the girls." She then headed toward a curtain and disappeared behind it.

Faye turned back to the bartender and asked, "Billy, would you know where I might find the owner, Mister King?"

Billy leaned forward. "Haven't seen him tonight, but nothing stopping you from taking a peek back there." He tilted his head toward where Deloris had just entered.

A red velvet curtain divided the gambling room from the back.

She downed her drink and stood. "Thanks."

Faye inched the drape aside and took a peek beyond. The dimly lit hallway looked neglected with peeled paint and loose wires hanging from the ceiling.

She entered and moved cautiously, searching for King's office. In a room at the end of the hallway, voices filtered out.

"—why is it always me sticking my neck out?" *Deloris.*

"We all have our part to play."

Faye froze in place.

Penn! Why was Penn here? Her mind churned the possibilities. Like her, was he working undercover?

Another man spoke. "You botched your part by letting that slip of a girl get the better of you."

"She's in town now," Penn said. "She trusts me. I'll get the money."

Faye's heart sank. She clamped her hand over her mouth, backed away, and bumped into something solid. Turning slowly, she peered up at a scarred cheek and patched eye. Mr. Fedora Hat Man.

A menacing grin curled his lips.

Her pulse sped up. He was like a bad penny, continuously appearing in her life at the wrong time.

He clenched her hair painfully in his fist and roughly steered her toward the door.

She kicked toward his shin, but he was ready for her and deflected her leg. With a hard push, he thrust her into the room.

Her heels skidded across the floor. Everyone stopped talking and stared. Penn locked eyes, his expression forlorn.

Mr. King smoothed his handlebar mustache. "Miss Harmon. We were just discussing you." He leaned back in his chair behind a desk.

"Why?" she asked in a small voice, more to Penn than King.

Penn didn't answer.

"You have what I want," King said. "The combination and key to the vault. And if you know what's good for you, you'll give them to me."

Faye couldn't take her eyes off Penn. "You were like a son to my father, and I have always looked up to you."

"I didn't mean for anyone to get hurt," he said.

"But people did, Penn." She couldn't hold back a sob. "How could you do this?"

"I didn't have a choice, dammit. But I tried to keep you out of it."

She glanced behind at the scarred man. "Your goon here tried to kill me—twice."

Penn shook his head. "Micky was just trying to get Marshall's case from you."

Faye wasn't buying that for a minute. "The day after I talked with you at the dance, they shot up Jake's house and burned it to the ground. An innocent man died."

Penn didn't respond.

She glared at King. "Your wife was dating my father. So, you were—what? Spying on him?" Things were shifting into place. "The robbery." She stared back at Penn. Her thoughts swirled. "My father didn't rob the bank."

Penn narrowed his eyes. "I borrowed clients' money to invest and increase our profits as your *father* taught me to do. But the market turned, and I lost the Irish Mafia's rainy-day funds. What I siphoned from the bank was a drop in the bucket to how much I still owed them. I needed to stall for time. Somehow Marshall learned about it and moved most of the assets to the other bank's vault."

Her throat went dry. "You had him *killed*?" The room began to spin.

"No! That—that wasn't supposed to happen. King's men—"

"—an unfortunate accident," King said. He didn't look sorry at all. "Now, about that combination..."

She shook her head. "That money belongs to households with families to support. From what I've seen, men in your line of work hardly struggle or do without."

King's face reddened with anger. "I hoped we could do this the easy way, but it seems you need some persuasion. Micky."

Fedora Hat Man grinned. A shiver ran along Faye's spine.

Penn shot out of his chair. "Give me a moment to speak with her alone," he pleaded with King. "We don't need to go there just yet."

King nodded and gestured for Micky and Deloris to follow him out of the room.

Overwhelming rage prevented Faye from feeling any fear. She pushed Penn away.

"I know you're upset—" he started.

"Upset?" Her fury ran so hot she feared she'd explode like a volcano. "There are no words to describe how I'm feeling." She trembled and needed to do something to relieve the pressure building inside. Her hand lashed out, aimed at his lying face.

Penn blocked her attempt. "I'm trying to keep us both alive."

"Don't you dare pretend to be my savior! What you did, has always been about saving your own skin. You don't get to play the goddamn hero."

"Pip, please." He wrapped his arms around her to restrain her. "Just give me a chance to fix this."

She sunk her teeth into his hand.

He yelped and released her, stumbling back and warding her off.

"Are you out of your mind?" she shouted, gripping the desk's corner. "There's no coming back from this—for either of us. You ruined my life and countless others. Because of your choices, Penn, people *died*."

"I'm sorry. Truly. But no one else needs to know."

"*I'll* know, Penn. Do you expect me to just forget about everything? Let you go on with your life as if nothing has changed?" She pounded the desktop. "I can't believe I idolized you. You're a weak, pitiful excuse of a man. Your parents are going to be so ashamed."

His expression turned glacial. "They must never find out."

She realized she'd gone too far. At that moment, he looked like he wanted to kill her himself.

She ran toward the door. Flinging it open, she rushed out and smacked face-first into someone's chest. Mr. Fedora Hat blocked her exit.

Penn yanked her back, shoved her into a chair, and leaned over her. "I'm sorry it has to end this way. I really did all I could to protect you."

She spat in his face.

Penn took out his handkerchief and wiped his cheek. He nodded to the goon. "Get the information out of her your way." He left the room without a backward glance.

Chapter 36

Faye backed away from Micky as he steadily stalked her around the office. Stuck in a cat-and-mouse game, her breath quickened as he continued to inch closer.

Her voice trembled, "How do I know you won't harm me if I tell you?" She skirted around a shabby armchair.

Micky's silent response and intimidating stare made it clear that he didn't intend to spare her any pain.

"I can pay you. Lots more than King." She neared a coat rack, wondering if she could use it as a weapon.

In a flash, his hand shot forward and plucked a bead from Jane's dress.

Faye squeaked and stumbled, then regained her stride. She scanned the items on the nearby desk for something she could use: papers, a pencil, a half-empty cup of coffee, rubber bands, and a ball of string. She snatched a rubber band and flicked it at him, but it bounced harmlessly off his forehead. He kept on. She lifted a small chair and held it between them like a lion trainer.

"Okay, I'll tell you the combination." She rattled off a string of numbers, hoping he would stop and write them down.

He didn't even pause his steps as he continued to circle her around the office.

"I hid the key. Your boss needs that to get in."

He lunged.

She yelped and hurled the chair in his direction.

In a frenzy, she scattered papers on the desk. Her hand landed on a letter opener. She clutched it like a knife.

Micky pulled out a handgun.

Rudy's voice sounded in her memory. *'We're bringing sticks and rocks to a gunfight.'*

A wave of despair washed over her. The letter opener made a pitiful *tink* when it hit the floor. She raised her arms, all hope lost.

He stashed the gun back in his waistband and then grabbed her by the throat. "I've had enough of you." He twisted her hair around his other hand, jerking her head back. "Now, gimme the real numbers."

Struggling for breath, she choked out a "K."

He loosened his grip. She took the opportunity to snatch up the cup and splashed the coffee at his good eye. As he recoiled, she hit him with the cup on the side of his head.

He took her with him as they fell, his hand still tangled in her hair. They landed on the floor with a heavy thump. Something hard pressed against her thigh. She recognized it as the gun and managed to get her hand around the weapon's handle.

"Careful!" he warned and grabbed for her arm.

Bang!

Startled, Faye glanced at his face, which was white as a sheet. She rolled the rest of the way off him and scanned down his torso to his crotch. The pistol's barrel had been pointed up and created a hole in his trousers' material as it exited. She yanked the gun from his waistband and awkwardly stood.

"Where's King's ledger?"

His forehead creased, brows furrowed.

She searched the drawers in the desk, casting the occasional glance in his direction. He eyed the safe behind her, then quickly looked away.

Its door was ajar. Pointing the gun at Micky, she glanced inside. It was filled with documents, cash, and coins. A large book that resembled Boss Tom's ledger was on the bottom shelf.

Micky rubbed his head and glared. "Take that and seal your death warrant. There's nowhere far enough for you to run."

Heavy, the ledger thunked the desk.

She motioned for Micky to sit on the office chair. Slicing strips of the string with the letter opener, she said, "King planned to have me killed no matter what."

Rolling off one of her stockings, she tied it tightly over his mouth. The gun placed in easy reach, she bound his hands and feet to the chair. He pulled against his binds and made a muffled, growling sound.

Her arm muscles stung as she hefted the book into the crook of her arm. She placed the gun in that hand and opened the office door with her free one. The ceiling light flickered and gave off a buzzing sound. With her back to the wall, she crept down the hallway. She needed to find Jane.

A commotion rose in volume on the other side of the curtain.

"It's a raid!" someone yelled.

Faye opened doors, desperate to find a way out. She found Penn instead. Head cradled in his hands, he looked up with tears.

"Thank God you're all right." He rose from the chair and came toward her. "Please, believe me. I didn't mean for things to get so out of hand."

He stopped short when she aimed the gun. His gaze moved from it to the large book embraced under her arm. Recognition flickered. "They'll kill us both if you take that."

"You and I both know they would never let me go. I needed insurance."

Penn wiped his eyes. "Boss Tom sent you."

She nodded.

"He's just as bad as King. Worse, actually."

"Better the devil you know than the one you don't."

A side of his mouth quirked. "Marshall would be proud."

"And still alive if it wasn't for you."

Momentarily distracted by screams and shouts in the casino, she took her eyes off Penn. He rushed forward. Startled, Faye squeezed the trigger. The smell of burnt gunpowder filled the air. A look of shock crossed Penn's face. She'd barely missed his leg.

"You shot at me," he said, his tone incredulous.

"How do I get out of here?"

"You *really* shot at me."

"Penn! Is there a back way out?"

He nodded with a stunned expression on his face.

"Show me." She aimed the gun at him again.

He gave her a wide berth and moved slowly back to the office.

"There's no way out in there," she said. He was probably stalling for time.

"King had one made in case he needed to get out in a hurry." Penn's eyes widened at Micky, who still struggled against his binds. "How did you...?"

Micky mumbled something, most likely unflattering. Penn opened a door she had assumed was a closet. Stairs led up to the street. Penn took a step toward freedom.

"No." Faye motioned with the gun. "I can't trust you."

He hesitantly stepped back into the office. "I'll disappear and never bother you again."

She could still see in him the boy he used to be. Light-hearted moments of their friendship flashed through her memory. She was about to concede when King barreled into the room. He glanced at Micky and Penn and scowled at her. It wasn't until he seemed to notice his ledger under her arm that his rage peaked. Shouting nonsensical words, he pulled a gun and aimed it at her. Faye froze in place. Penn stepped in front of her as the loud pop sounded. His body jerked. A look of peace crossed his face as he turned. A splotch of red widened across his shirt.

"Go," he said and winced as another bullet struck his back.

She ran up the stairs and to the parking lot.

Jane leaned against the car. "Where have you been? I've been worried sick." Her eyes widened. "Is that blood?"

Faye looked down and grew nauseous. Penn's blood spotted her skin and dress. She swallowed to keep her stomach from coming up. "He killed Penn!"

"Who? What was Penn doing here?"

"I think he's dead." She sobbed. "There was nothing I could do."

A window of an automobile shattered. King raced toward them, gun firing.

"Holy Moly!" Jane shouted. She ducked into her father's car.

Faye shot toward King to slow him down. She threw the ledger on the floor and slammed shut the passenger door. "Go—go—go!"

"I'm *trying.*"

The engine took hold, and the tires squealed in reverse. King fired again. The bullet hit somewhere along the panel door.

Jane flinched. "My dad's going to kill me."

"Put it in drive, Jane!"

Her friend jammed the gear shifter into first, and the car jerked forward. After another pop, the rear passenger window shattered into a thousand pieces.

"Oh, *come* on," Jane snarled and gunned the gas. "Great. Just great. How do I explain this?"

Faye released a breath she didn't realize she was holding. She peered out the back as King's image grew smaller and smaller.

Penn's killer. Her stomach churned. Penn needed to pay for what he did—but with his life? And in the end, he'd saved her. She couldn't forgive but allowed herself to grieve him.

Jane slowed the car down when they left the city.

"Pull over," Faye said. She stumbled out of the door and threw up on the ground.

Jane turned off the car and got out. "You want to tell me what the hell happened back there?"

Faye wiped the side of her mouth and leaned against the automobile. She told Jane everything, working out the events in her mind.

The night hummed between them when she finished talking.

"Geeze, Louise," Jane finally said. "I was so worried. When you were gone for so long, I called the police and ratted them out for gambling and serving booze."

"You called in the raid?"

"Never saw one before. That part was fun." She bent and ran her hand over the car door. "What do we do about this?"

"Got a tire iron?"

"I think so." She opened the trunk and handed it over. "What do you plan to..."

Faye swung it as hard as she could over the damaged panel. It felt good to take out her frustration on something.

Jane quirked an eyebrow. "This helped how?"

"We'll tell your dad we were in a fender bender. I'll offer to pay the damages."

"Ah." Jane nodded. "Anywhere else you need to go before I'm grounded for life?"

Chapter 37

Rudy was so mad he could spit. His favorite radio show, Tarzan, aired for only fifteen minutes, and his mom's stupid new friend talked through it the whole time.

"Rudy," Ma said, "Dan asked you a question."

Dan, the dumb dumb, had his arm around her and was sitting much too close to her on the sofa.

"That's okay," Dan said. "I just wondered what happened to Tarzan's real parents."

Rudy stormed over to the bookshelf and hurled the first story in the series at him. Dan the dunce probably didn't know how to read. He definitely didn't know how to catch. The book hit him square in the chest.

"Apologize to Dan this instant, young man," Ma scolded.

The word caught in his throat. "Sorry." He ran out of the house and headed toward the barn.

Chaska was shoveling horse manure into a bucket. Rudy flopped down on a bale of hay and sighed.

"You okay?" Chaska asked.

Rudy spat at the wall, pretending the knot in the wood was the man's face. "Yeah. No. I don't know."

"Dopey Dan gettin' to yuh?"

"I'm most mad at myself fer believing she'd be better this time. Why can't she be happy here?" He cupped his elbow and rested his chin on his hand. "One minute, she's fine, then the next, she's mad about somethin' stupid."

Chaska handed him the shovel. "I think when we grow up, we take the worst part of us and hide it, but it still comes out now and then."

"Whaddayamean?"

"Blamin' others when things go wrong, tellin' lies to get outta trouble, throwin' fits. They may be bigger, but they ain't so different from you and me."

Rudy pondered that. "Wish I was big. I'd kick Dan right in the can."

Chaska chuckled.

Raised voices came from outside the barn. Grandpa Hahn was holding up a pitchfork and shouting at Banker Schmidt.

"Get off my land!"

The banker stepped from behind the sheriff and his muscleman. "It doesn't belong to you anymore."

"The hell it ain't." He pumped his fist in the air. "My parents paid for this ground with blood, sweat, and tears before anyone in these parts even settled here."

Chaska throated a sound.

Grandpa grimaced, then corrected, "Well, one of the first white families."

Schmidt shook his head. "They didn't borrow money from me. You did."

"And until now, I've always paid early. I just need a little more time."

Schmidt crossed his arms. "I'm sick to death of you ranchers and farmers pissing away my money and then expecting charity. I have big plans for this region—a whole city named after me which will bring commerce and growth to the plains."

Grandpa Hahn's face turned beet red. "You damn carpetbagger scoundrel! You'll get my land over my dead body."

Something brown splattered Schmidt's fancy suit. Chaska balled a clump of manure and threw a blob. Rudy reached into the bucket and formed another.

Schmidt wrinkled his nose and blocked Rudy's projectile from hitting his face. "Stop this, Hahn!"

Grandpa laughed and joined in on the attack. Brown blobs pummeled Schmidt and his men as they dodged and weaved out of the way.

Running toward his auto, Schmidt yelled over his shoulder, "You have thirty days to vacate, else it'll be lead bullets flying instead of horseshit."

"You know where I'll be, you scavenger vulture!"

After they drove off, Rudy asked, "Whaddayuh gonna do, Grandpa?"

"Fight, boy. Defend what's ours. That's what we Hahns do—'cause we're made of what?"

"Hearty stock," Rudy answered.

But as they headed back to the house, Grandpa Hahn suddenly gasped. His face turned pale white and scrunched like in pain. He grasped at his chest and stepped right and left, and then fell face-first onto the land he so cherished.

Chapter 38

Rather than handing over King's ledger to Boss Tom, Faye met with her lawyer and Penn's father, Edmond Kinsey. After reviewing the incriminating evidence, she knew she had the upper hand.

"As you can see, this will negatively affect your position at the Federal Reserve," she stated firmly.

Mr. Kinsey squinted. "Are you attempting to blackmail me, young lady?"

"Just a small nudge in the right direction. To help you do the right thing."

Mr. Simmons smirked. "My client's requests are quite reasonable, Kinsey. She won't go to the press or the authorities if you comply with these simple demands." He handed Kinsey the papers.

Kinsey's eyebrows rose as he studied the list. "Small requests?"

"And I want to be there personally for the first five," she added, tilting her head. "Unless you don't have the power..."

"Oh, I do. You've been dealing with small timers until now. Trust me, you do not want a man of my stature as your enemy."

She frowned. "I don't want anyone as an enemy. Hence, the list."

"And then you'll give me the ledger."

"Penn saved my life. In the end, he repented. To honor your son, this is how you can help right his wrongdoings."

He flipped to the last page and skimmed over it. "Problem. This bank isn't in our system. It's privately owned by a"— he glanced back at the page—"Bern Schmidt. Roosevelt just signed the new Banking Act. I'll call for an audit, but I can't make you any guarantees until I know more."

She shifted in her seat. This negotiation was not off to a promising start.

"As for clearing your father's name, that shouldn't be too difficult. We can spread news of his bravery and quick thinking—a hero who risked his life to protect the people's savings and paid the ultimate price in doing so."

Mr. Simmons asked, "Might there be an investigation? By the government?"

"Most likely, but as long as the depositors are compensated and the true criminals are brought to justice, I doubt they'll dig too deep. This ledger has enough evidence to put King, Boss Tom, and many other mobsters behind bars, even after all pages pertaining to my son's unfortunate involvement are removed."

That was a relief. With Boss Tom out of the picture, they could finally start their new life without fear or worry. The question was, would they stay together or go their separate ways?

Faye strode confidently through the police department, clad in her new four-piece ensemble in shades of green. She received admiring looks and one inappropriate whistle as she made her way to Detective Elmsworth's desk.

His face bruised, he scowled at her when she sat down.

"You've got a lot of nerve, Missy. Thanks to you, my head is killing me, and I'm stuck on desk duty until my conduct is reviewed."

"You deserve worse than that," she replied coolly.

He leaned back in his chair and crossed his arms. "You've also got a smart mouth on you for a woman. I can't wait to teach you your proper place and knock some teeth loose from that smile."

Her smile widened. "Your days of abusing women are over, Elmsworth. As well as your career."

"Oh really?" He laughed aloud. "Who's going to stop me? You?"

Faye nodded. "Along with taking bribes, working with King to cover up my father's murder, and numerous other offenses, you'll be going away for a long time."

He scoffed. "You think they'll believe some broke broad whose father was a criminal over an upstanding, seasoned officer of the law? You take the cake."

She signaled towards the chief and his men waiting in the outer hallway.

Elmsworth's mouth fell open as they surrounded him. "What is this, Chief?" he demanded. "I don't know what this fruit tart told you, but she's a known housebreaker, embezzler, and liar."

The chief himself handcuffed Elmsworth. "Come along quietly. No need to make a scene."

"No!" he shouted and struggled against his restraints. "She set me up! She *set* me up!"

"You'll have your day in court," the chief said, handing him over to his men's custody.

"You bitch!" Elmsworth yelled as they forced him into the hallway. "I'll get you for this! You hear me? I will make you sorry you ever met me."

"I've regretted your acquaintance since that first night," she replied calmly.

"Well, that was unpleasant," the chief said.

Faye shrugged. She'd quite enjoyed it.

"This is most unusual. Are you certain you need to be there when we arrest King?"

"I'll stay in the car until he's removed. I want to be there when they serve Helen the eviction papers."

The chief shook his head. "You have a steel spine, young lady, and mighty important high-powered friends."

She was sure Edmond Kinsey had made an outlandishly generous contribution to the police department's fight on crime fund.

Faye stared out the automobile's window at the home her family had lived in for generations. Seated in the boxy black police car while the officers went inside Willow Wood to arrest King, life-changing decisions took form. It was now ending with her. She couldn't afford the upkeep here and also help those she'd grown to care about in Kansas. Some guilt came with her resolution, but between making a new life with Jake and the kids or returning to her old life, the choice was easy—if they still wanted her.

She would telephone her aunt and explain the situation. They'd sell Willow Wood and have no regrets. On the upside, Kansas was a lot closer to Colorado than here, so they'd get to spend more time together and would make new traditions and memories to pass down.

Movement at the side of the house caught her attention. A window on the second story opened. Mr. Fedora Hat Man climbed out and then dropped to the ground. King followed. She ducked low as they sprinted into the garage. Her pulse raced.

King and Micky were most likely armed, and the distance was too far for her to run and warn the officers. With the gate blocked, they weren't driving out of here. That meant a standoff, or they'd try to flee on foot through the woods. Maybe they already had.

If they escaped, she'd never have a moment of peace and would forever be looking over her shoulder. Her future with Jake and the kids would be over before it had begun. She couldn't risk putting them in danger again. She'd have to move far away from everyone she loved, change her name, and pray they never found her. It was beyond unfair.

A crackling sound came from the rear trunk then a male voice said, "Attention squads. Crime in progress at Tenth and Lincoln. Be advised. Suspect may be packing heat."

Could that be them? She opened the driver's door, slid out, and crouched next to the gold star on the side. Bullet holes were puckered in its emblem.

She peeked around the hood of the chief's automobile at the garage but couldn't see any movement within.

Bent over, her shoulder hugged the panel as she made her way to the trunk where a tire was mounted. She took a deep breath and decided to make a run for the front porch.

A few steps out, a *pop* sounded. She gasped and pivoted, then hunkered behind the squad car again.

Not sure if she was the one being shot at, she peeked toward the garage. A bullet pinged the side of the car.

"Shoot, shoot, shoot." She had sighted Micky before curling down to safety.

Drawn by the gunfire, the front door to the house flew open. She motioned to the chief where they were. He pressed his palms down for her to stay put.

Two officers raced out the back and flattened their backs against the garage.

If she could make Micky and King mad enough, that might draw them out. No one else needed to get hurt.

"King," she yelled as loud as she could. "I read your book." She was careful with her wording to keep the chief from knowing about the ledger. "Come out peacefully, and we can make a deal."

More bullets plunked against the car.

The chief signaled his men to hold back.

Faye used the words King had insulted Penn with. "Are you going to let a slip of a girl get the better of you? I hope I didn't hurt your hitman too badly."

The chief looked dumbfounded. She shrugged.

With a roar of rage, Micky charged out of the garage with guns blazing.

Faye crawled and hid behind the rear wheel of the car. She covered her ears with her hands and closed her eyes.

It was probably less than a few seconds but felt like an eternity before the gunfire stopped.

She peeked underneath the automobile. Micky's fedora hat bounced away in the wind. He lay on the ground, unmoving.

King emerged from the garage with his arms raised. "Don't shoot. I give up."

The policemen surged forward and threw him on the ground.

Faye exhaled relief.

The chief came over and offered her a hand up. "You okay?"

She nodded, unable to find her voice yet.

"That was a brave thing you did. Probably saved at least one of my men injury." He then went to get in on the action and led King to a car.

Her legs were shaking, and she purposely avoided looking at Micky, instead focusing on Willow Wood. It no longer felt like home.

Clutching the temporary deed, she marched inside to evict Helen.

The woman certainly made a commotion. "Take your hands off me!" Helen shouted at the police. "Where's Elmsworth? You have no idea who you're dealing with. I'll have your badge." Helen looked Faye's way with a scrunched face. "You! Arrest her at once. Where the hell is Elmsworth?"

Faye held up the deed to the house. "In jail. You may voice your grievances while you visit your husband there."

"No!" She shook loose one officer and reached for a gaudy vase. "My things. My beautiful things."

They dragged her, kicking and screaming, out the door. Abigail and the frazzled maid emerged from the parlor.

"Oh, Pip," Abigail said and hugged her. "Are you all right?"

Faye nodded against Abigail's shoulder. Now she was home. "Long morning. I need a cup of tea, some of your oatmeal cookies, and a long nap."

Abigail moved her at arm's length and searched her face. Her friend's eyes brightened when Faye held up the deed.

"Oh, sweet, sweet Jesus! Praise be!" She drew her in and squeezed again. "Don't just stand there, Mary. Go make up a bed with fresh sheets."

The maid curtsied and then scrambled off to do her chores. Abigail held Faye all the way into the kitchen.

Later that day, Faye picked up two cheesesteak sandwiches from Olivieri's diner for Jake's supper and returned to the small apartment.

Jake greeted her at the door, his expression a mix of relief and concern.

"What's wrong?" she asked.

"Hoover's G-men stormed the building this morning and arrested Boss Tom and some of his men. They questioned me but let me go."

"That's good news." She set the sandwiches on the table and reached for plates. "What did they arrest him for?"

Jake got down two glasses. "Robbery and racketeering." He opened the icebox, and took out a pitcher of tea, and then joined her at the table. "Not paying his taxes. The fed agent in charge said this is just the beginning. They have enough on him already that Tom may never walk free again."

"You're truly free of him."

"Seems so." He looked as if he'd died and gone to heaven. "Where did you get these?" he asked, humming through his chews.

"On the corner of Ninth and Wharton. The sign said they are open all night and day."

Faye smiled, happy that he was pleased. Her stomach was still off from the morning's events. She pushed the other half of her sandwich to him.

His eyes brightened. "You sure?" He snatched it up before she could answer and took a healthy bite.

She laughed. This was so easy, being with him and spending time together. But now that their troubles were over, did he still want her?

"What will you do now?" She kept her tone light.

"I need to return to Union for Alfred's funeral. Schmidt is refusing the family from burying him on their land, saying it doesn't belong to them anymore. I'm sorry I can't stay and help you find your father's killers. They could lose everything..."

She reached across and squeezed his hand. "I understand." Schmidt moved to the top of her to-do list. She would explain to Jake everything that happened someday. When they were out on an open field, somewhere without neighbors to disturb when he blew a gasket.

"What did you and Jane do today?"

"Mm, not much. Gossiped, brushed each other's hair, you know—girl things."

"Nice." He looked forlornly at his last bite of the sandwich before popping it into his mouth.

Chapter 39

Union Junction, Kansas

Faye made her way through the growing crowd and marched into where, up until an hour ago, was Schmidt's bank. Due to orders from the Federal Reserve, his banking license had been revoked, citing his morally bankrupt behavior and breaches of agreements. The Reserve and regulators were preventing him from banking in all states. He was lucky not to have his ass thrown in jail.

Schmidt looked up as she entered the office where he was packing his things.

"I don't know how you managed this," he said with a scowl. "But you haven't stopped me. I will fight this injustice all the way to the highest court."

Humming while pounding a hammer on a nail, she hung a Kansas landscape painting on the office wall. Standing back, she tilted her head to admire it.

Schmidt scoffed. "This region has dried up anyway. You won't make money from these poor chumps."

Faye turned to face him, her arms crossed. She borrowed her grandmother's withering stare. "That's one of the many differences between you and me. I want these farmers to succeed—to be able to support their families, their community, and their town. Instead of sinking their dreams, I plan to anchor them through the storm."

"Naïve girl."

"Like they say, 'Pigs get fat, hogs get slaughtered.' If it were up to me, you'd be trussed with twine and turned over an open spit."

"Being smart isn't a crime."

"But cheating people out of their homes and livelihoods should be."

"No one gets anywhere being nice in business. You'll learn that the hard way." He finished filling the remaining boxes with his things. "Barnes," he yelled, "come pack up my auto."

The teller came in and stood next to Faye.

She softly smiled at her new employee. "No one gets anywhere being nice."

"I've heard him say that." Barnes crossed his arms. "But it goes a long way when asking someone for help."

Schmidt's eyes narrowed. "I see. Mutiny. Well, don't expect to come crawling back to me for a job when this place goes under."

Barnes shook his head. "Wouldn't think of it."

Schmidt exaggerated his burden out the door. Boos and hisses came from the crowd outside.

"Everything prepared?" Faye asked Barnes.

He nodded excitedly. "Yes, Ma'am. Half the county is out there."

Abigail and her sister entered. Abby beamed with pride. "Oh, my. The people chased that banker to his car. Some with pitchforks. Who knew small towns on the Plains were this exciting?"

Faye smiled, happy that her friend had decided to work for her here.

"Three old men on a bench brazenly winked at me," the sister said.

Faye laughed, and then Barnes escorted her to the front of the bank and assisted her up the wagon in the center of the murmuring crowd.

Jake and his in-laws were in front with curious and confused faces—all but Sarah, who had run off again with another man. Rudy didn't seem overly upset about that. He smiled up at her while sitting atop his new bicycle.

Faye cleared her throat to quiet the onlookers. She raised her voice. "I'm sure you good people are wondering what all the hoopla is about." She signaled the men on the roof. They tore off Schmidt's name from the building and threw his sign down. The crowd cheered as the men placed a banner. HARMON AND BOYD BANK.

Jake's eyes widened, and he mouthed, 'How?' to her.

She winked at him and held up her hand. The crowd quieted again.

"Mister Barnes here has all the debts Schmidt acquired from you these many years." She nodded to Chaska to light a burn barrel. "But these accounts are no longer binding."

The shocked faces in the crowd were as silent as a church. It was as if the collective held its breath. Barnes made a show of tossing the pages into the fire.

Faye said, "From henceforth, you will start fresh. Jake Boyd will assist in getting you back on your feet again."

A roaring cheer spread and grew louder. Women hugged their husbands and children, and men rushed forward to pat Jake on the back.

Jake made his way to her and climbed up the wagon. The Jug Band began playing a happy tune.

"How did you manage all this?" he asked in her ear.

"A friend owed me a favor."

"Dang. Pretty good friend. But I don't know anything about banking. How will I help?"

"You know the farmers and the townspeople. Know what they need better than anyone. Mr. Barnes will run the day-to-day." She handed him the deed to the Hahn's ranch. "You'll be busy planting crops and harvesting. I know it's a lot, and we'll be extraordinarily busy, but I think we're up for the task."

"So you decided to stay?" His face lit up.

Faye pointed at a deserted building. "I think with the women in town's help, I can start a garment manufacturing and catalog to sell our wares. Jane said she'd manage the shop in Philadelphia. Through the mail, we can sell all over the country. We owe it to our kids to give them the best lives they can ask for. Don't you think?"

"That I do." He laughed and spun her in a circle.

S'unka barked, drawing attention to the kids and a prim woman with a suitcase.

The woman shouted over the music. "Are you Miss Harmon? Mister Kinsey sent me. I'm Miss Merriweather, the new schoolteacher."

Chaska frowned. She said in a high voice, "I ain't wearin' no dress to school."

Rudy's mouth gaped, and his eyes grew wide. "Yer a girl?"

Jake chuckled. "He's always pestering me for a little brother."

Faye caressed Jake's cheek and jaw. "We'll have to work on that, too."

His eyes softened. "Now, darlin', that's the kind of service I'm up to the task to do."

He embraced her and kissed her with promise, their joy and love for all to see.

THE END

About the author

Lisa Warren loves old movies, real English tea, traveling with her eccentric mom, and torturing her characters from her comfy armchair. Please visit her online at thirstyquillpress.com or follow her on Amazon or other social platforms.